WHEN
WE
BELIEVED
IN
MERMAIDS

PREVIOUS BOOKS BY THIS AUTHOR

The Art of Inheriting Secrets
The Lost Recipe for Happiness
The Secret of Everything
How to Bake a Perfect Life
The Garden of Happy Endings
The All You Can Dream Buffet
No Place Like Home
A Piece of Heaven
The Goddesses of Kitchen Avenue
Lady Luck's Map of Vegas
The Scent of Hours

WHEN WE BELIEVED IN MERMAIDS

BARBARA O'NEAL

LAKE UNION
PUBLISHING

Text copyright © 2019 by Barbara Samuel
All rights reserved.

Published by Lake Union Publishing, Seattle

www.apub.com

Amazon, the Amazon logo, and Lake Union Publishing are trademarks of Amazon.com, Inc., or its affiliates.

ISBN-13: 9781542004527
ISBN-10: 1542004527

Cover design by PEPE nymi

Printed in the United States of America

*For Neal, who holds the center no
matter the storm*

Chapter One

Kit

My sister has been dead for nearly fifteen years when I see her on the TV news.

I'd been working the ER for six hours straight, triaging young humans from a beach party where a fight broke out. Two gunshot wounds, one that nicked a kidney; a broken cheekbone; a broken wrist; and multiple facial wounds of various levels of severity.

And that was just the girls.

By the time we made it through the triage, I'd stitched and soothed the lucky ones. The unlucky ones were sent to surgery or to the wards, and I dived into the break room fridge for a Mountain Dew, my favored way to mainline sugar and caffeine.

A television mounted to the wall broadcasts the news of a disaster somewhere. I stare at it sightlessly as I gulp the sticky-sweet soda. It's night. Flames are erupting in the background. People are running and screaming, while a news anchor with tousled hair and a vintage leather bomber jacket offers the news in properly grave tones.

And there, right over his left shoulder, is my sister.

Josie.

For one long second, she looks at the camera. Long enough that there is no mistaking her. That straight, straight blonde hair, cut now into a sleek bob that just grazes her shoulders, her tilted dark eyes and slashes of cheekbone, that fat Angelina Jolie mouth. Everyone always fussed over her beauty, and it's that combination of dark and light, angles and softness that does it. She's an exact mix of our parents.

Josie.

I feel as if she's looking through the screen, right at me.

And then she's gone, and the disaster keeps going. I stare, open-mouthed, at the empty spot she left, holding the Mountain Dew out in front of me like an offering or a toast.

To you, Josie, my sister.

Then I shake myself. This happens all the time. Anyone who has lost somebody they love has experienced it—the head in the crowd on a busy street, the person at the grocery store who moves just like her. The rush to catch up, so relieved that she is actually still alive . . .

Only to be crushed when the imposter turns around and the face is wrong. The eyes. The lips.

Not Josie.

It must have happened to me a hundred times in the first year, especially because we never found a body. Impossible, given the circumstances. Also impossible that she survived. Not for her the ordinary demise of a fiery car accident or a leap off a bridge, though she threatened those often enough.

No, Josie was vaporized on a European train blown up by terrorists. Gone, gone, gone.

This is why we have funerals. We desperately need to see the truth for ourselves, see that loved one's face, even if it's marred. Otherwise, it's just too hard to believe.

I lift the Mountain Dew all the way to my lips and take a long swallow of the thing we shared, this private reminder of all we were to each other, and tell myself it's just wishful thinking.

When I leave the hospital in the predawn stillness, I'm wound up, both exhausted and wired. If I want to get any sleep at all before my next shift, I have to work off the grimy night.

Stopping by my tiny Santa Cruz house, 1,350 square feet on the edge of an almost-not-great neighborhood, I scramble into my wet suit, feed the worst cat in the world his half can of wet food, and make sure to move my fingers around in his kibble. He purrs his thanks, and I pull his tail gently. "Try not to pee on anything too important, huh?"

Hobo blinks.

I load my board into my Jeep and drive south, not realizing that I'm headed for the cove until I get there. Pulling over into a makeshift space alongside the highway, I park and look down at the water. A few bodies out, not many at dawn. The water is northern Cali cold, fifty-three degrees in early March, but the waves are lined up all the way to the horizon. Perfect.

The trail starts where the sidewalk to the restaurant once was and veers down the steep slope in a zigzag carved out a few feet away from the cliff where there used to be stairs, our own private access to the isolated, hidden cove. The hillside is unstable, with a reputation for being haunted, and all the locals know it. I have the descent to myself. But then, I know the ghosts.

Midway down, I stop and look back up to the spot where our house stood, and the restaurant with its celebrated patio boasting the best view in the world. Both buildings lie in rotting planks and debris scattered down the hill, most of it washed away in storms over the years, the rest blackened by seawater and time.

In my imagination, the buildings stand in spectral beauty, the sprawling Eden with its magnificent patio, and above it our little house. Josie and I shared a room after Dylan came, and neither one of us ever minded. I see the ghosts of all of us when we were happy—my parents madly in love, my sister bright and full of boundless energy, Dylan with his hair pulled back in a leather string, racing us down the stairs so we could build a fire on the beach and make s'mores and sing. He loved singing, and he had a good voice. We always thought he should be a rock star. He said he didn't want anything but Eden, and us, and the cove.

I see myself too, an urchin of seven with too much hair, whirling on the beach, the sky overhead blurring blue and white.

A million years ago.

Our family restaurant was called Eden, both exclusive and permissive, frequented by hippie movie stars and their drug dealers. Our parents were part of that world too—stars in their realm, each wielding power on their own terms, my father the jovial, welcoming chef with his hearty laugh and excessive habits, my mother on his arm, a charming coquette.

Josie and I ran around like puppies, sleeping on the beach of the cove when we got tired, underfoot and ignored. My mother was a great beauty who'd come for dinner with another man and fallen instantly in love with my father, or so the legend says. But if you'd known him, you would know it was entirely likely. My father was a massive personality, a charming, bigger-than-life chef from Italy, though people just said *cook* in those days. Or restaurateur, which was what he really was. My mother loved him to excess, far more than she loved us. His passion for her was intense, and sexual, and possessive, but is that love? I don't know.

I do know that it's hard to be the children of parents who are obsessed with each other.

Josie thrived on drama the way my parents did. She had both my father's enormous personality and my mother's beauty, though in Josie, the combination became something extraordinary. Unique. I can't count the number of times people drew and photographed and painted her, men and women, and how often they fell in love. I always thought she would be a movie star.

Instead, she made of her life a great ruinous drama, just like our parents, with a suitably catastrophic ending.

The cove is still there, of course, even if the stairs are gone. I pull on my booties and weave my heavy hair into a thick braid. Light is spilling peach over the horizon as I paddle around the rocks and out to the line. It's only three others and me. A nasty shark attack a few weeks ago has thinned the ranks of the eager, no matter how badass the waves.

And they are badass. Solid nine feet, with a gorgeous glassy curl that's much rarer than people think. I paddle out and wait my turn, catch the line, and leap to my feet to ride right on the edge. This is the instant I live for, that moment when nothing else is in my head. Nothing can be. It's me and the water and the sky, the sound of the rippling surf. The sound of my breath. The edge of the board slipping along the water, cold over my ankles even in booties. Ice-cold. Perfect balance, shivering, hair slapping my cheek.

For an hour, maybe more, I'm lost in it. Sky and sea and dawn. I dissolve. No me, no body, no time, no history. Just the deck and toes and air and water and suspension—

Until it's not.

The wave rips unexpectedly and so fast, so hard that I'm slammed deep into the water, the washing machine of surging surf pounding my body, my head, the board, which tumbles too close, a dangerous power that could crack my head wide open.

I go limp, holding my breath, letting the water suds me. Resistance will break you. Kill you. The only way to survive is to let go. The world swirls, up and down, around, for endless moments.

I'm going to drown this time. The board yanks on my ankle, surges me another direction. Seaweed winds around my arms, swirls around my neck—

Josie's face swims up in front of me. The way it was fifteen years ago. The way it looked on television overnight.

She's alive.

I don't know how. I know only that it's true.

The ocean spits me up to the surface, and I drag a breath into my oxygen-starved lungs. By the time I make it back to the cove, I am exhausted and fall on my belly onto the sand of the protected space, resting for a minute. All around me are the voices of my childhood. Me and Josie and Dylan. Our dog, Cinder, a black retriever mix, romps around us, wet and smelly and happy. Smoke from the restaurant fires fills the air with a sense of cozy possibility, and I hear faint music, weaving through long-ago laughter.

When I sit up, it all stops, and there is only the wreck of what once was.

One of my earliest memories is of my parents locked in a passionate embrace. I couldn't have been more than three or four. It's unclear where they were, exactly, but I remember my mother pressed up against a wall, her blouse shoved up and my father's hands over her breasts. I saw her skin. They kissed so hungrily that they looked like animals, and I watched in fascination for one second, two, three, until my mother made a sharp noise, and I screamed, "Stop it!"

The memory wafts around my mind as I sit down in my backyard an hour later, hair wet from a shower. I sip a mug of hot, sweet coffee and check the headlines on my iPad. Hobo sits on the table beside me, yellow eyes bright, black tail swishing. He's a feral, seven years old. I found him when he was five or six months, starving, battered, practically dead on my back doorstep. Now he'll go out only if I'm with him, and he's never missed a meal. Absently, I stroke his back as he keeps an eye on the shrubs along the fence. His fur is long and silky, all black. It's remarkable how much company he provides.

The disaster on the news was a nightclub fire in Auckland. Dozens of people were killed, some when the ceiling fell down on the revelers, some when fleeing partiers were trampled. There are no other details. With a rumbling sense of a train coming toward me, I click around the pictures, looking for the newscaster I saw last night. No luck.

I fall back in my chair and sip some more coffee. Bright Santa Cruz sunlight shines through the eucalyptus tree overhead and makes patterns over my thighs, too white because I'm always in the ER or a wet suit.

It's not Josie, I think with my rational mind.

I reach for the keyboard, about to type in another search term— and stop myself. For months after she died, I combed the internet for any possible clue that she could have survived the cataclysmic train crash. The explosion had been so severe that they couldn't identify all the individual remains, and as happens more often than first responders and law enforcement will admit, a lot of it was speculation. Your loved one was there; she has not surfaced. All indications are that she died.

After a year, my twitchy need to search for my sister calmed down, but I couldn't help that catch in my throat when I thought I saw her in a crowd. After two years, I finished my residency at San Francisco General and came home to Santa Cruz, where I took a spot in the ER and bought myself this house not far from the beach, where I could keep an eye on my mother and build an ordinary, quiet life for myself. The only things I'd ever really wanted—peace, calm, predictability. My childhood had been drama enough for one life.

My stomach growls. "C'mon, kid," I say to Hobo, "let's get some breakfast."

The house is a small two-bedroom Spanish style in a neighborhood that crouches on the edges of places you don't want to walk at night, but it's mine, and I can be at the beach in seven minutes on foot. I've updated the old appliances and crappy cupboards and repaired the splendid tile work. I'm thinking maybe pancakes for breakfast when my phone buzzes on the counter.

"Hi, Mom," I say, opening the fridge. Hmm. No eggs. "What's up?"

"Kit," she says. A faint pause, enough to make me lift my head. "Did you happen to see the news about that big nightclub fire in New Zealand?"

My stomach drops, down, down, down all the way through the earth. "What about it?"

"I know it's ridiculous, but I swear I saw your sister in one of the clips."

Holding the phone to my ear, I look out the kitchen window to the waving fronds of eucalyptus, the flowers I planted painstakingly along the fence. My oasis.

If it were anyone but my mother, I'd blow it off, run away, avoid opening this particular door, but she's done the work. Every step of AA, over and over. She's present and real and sad. For her sake, I take a breath and say, "I saw it too."

"Could she really be alive?"

"It's probably not her, Mom. Let's keep our heads, not get our hopes up, okay?" My stomach growls. "Do you have anything to eat? I was at the ER until four, and there isn't a damn thing in this house."

"How strange," she says in her droll way.

"Ha. If you'll make me some eggs, I'll come over and talk about this in person."

"I've got to be to work at two, so make it quick."

"It's not even eleven."

"Mm-hmm."

"I am not putting on makeup," I say, which she always notices. Even now.

"I don't care," she says, but I know she does.

It's walkable, another reason I bought in the area I did, but I drive so she won't fret. I bought her the condo a couple of years back. It's a bit dated, the rooms on the small side, but she has a wide view of the

Pacific from the windows of the front room. The sound of the ocean keeps her calm. It's the thing we share, that hunger, bone-deep, for the ocean. Nothing else will do.

I climb the outside stairs to her second-story condo, looking automatically over the waves to check conditions. It's calm now. No surfers, but lots of kids and families playing along the edges of the softly ruffling water.

My mom comes out to her plant-filled porch when she spies my car. She's wearing crisp cotton capris, yellow, with a white top striped the same sunny color. Her hair—still thick and healthy, blonde and gray making it look streaked—is pulled into an updo like a young mom's. It looks just right, even though her face shows the hard years she's lived, all the sun worshipping she's done. It doesn't matter. She's slim and long-legged and deep-busted, and the startling eyes have lost none of their jeweled brilliance. She's sixty-three, but in the filtered light of her simple upstairs porch, she appears to be about forty.

"You look tired," she says as she waves me inside.

Vigorous plants of many kinds fill the rooms. Orchids are her specialty. She's the only person I know who makes orchids bloom over and over. Give her half a second and she'll enumerate the various genus types—*Cattleya*; *Phalaenopsis*, her favorite; delicate and beautiful *Laelia*, all with their proper Latin names.

"Long night." I smell coffee as I come in and gravitate to the drip pot. I pour coffee into the cup that's waiting, the one she saves for me, a heavy green mug with HAWAII painted across the front. Eggs and chopped peppers await on the counter.

"Sit," she says briskly, and ties an apron around her. "Omelet okay?"

"Better than okay. Thank you."

"Open my laptop," she says, dropping a pat of butter into a heavy cast-iron skillet. "I saved the clip."

I follow orders, and there's the piece I saw the night before. The chaotic scene, the screams and noise. The newscaster in his bomber jacket. The face behind his shoulder, looking right into the camera, for the solid beat of three seconds. *One one thousand, two one thousand, three one thousand.* I watch, then rewind and watch again, counting. Three seconds. If I stop the clip on her face, there's just no mistaking it.

"No one could look that much like her," my mom says, coming to peer over my shoulder. "And have the exact same scar."

I close my eyes, as if that will get rid of this problem. When I open them again, there she is, frozen in time, that uneven scar that runs from her hairline, straight through her eyebrow, and into her temple. It was a miracle she didn't lose her eye.

"No," I say. "You're right."

"You have to go find her, Kit."

"That's ridiculous," I say, even though I've been thinking the same thing. "How would I do that? Millions and millions of people live in Auckland."

"You would be able to find her. You know her."

"You know her too."

She shakes her head, straightening her back stiffly. "You know I don't travel."

I scowl. "You've been sober fifteen years, Mom. You'd be fine."

"No, I can't. You need to do this."

"I can't run away to New Zealand. I have a job, and I can't just leave them in the lurch." I shove my hair off my face. "And what will I do with Hobo?" My heart stings—the job I can navigate, since I haven't had time off in three years. But my cat will pine without me.

"I'll go stay at your house."

I look at her. "Stay there, or go in the morning and night and feed him?"

"I'll move there." She slides the omelet, steamy and beautifully studded with peppers, onto the table. "Come eat."

I stand up. "He'll probably hide the whole time."

"That's all right. He'll know he's not alone. And maybe after a day or two, he'll come sleep with me."

The smell of onions and peppers snares my body, and I dig in to the eggs like a sixteen-year-old boy, my mind flashing up images. Josie bending over me to see if I was awake yet, her long hair tickling my neck when we were little; her exuberant laugh; a flash of her throwing a stick for Cinder to chase. My heart literally aches, not metaphorically—a weight of memory and longing and anger press down hard on it until I have to pause, set down my fork, take a breath.

My mother sits quietly. I think of her voice when she told me Josie was dead. I see that her hand is trembling ever so slightly. As if to cover it, as if this is a normal morning with normal things in it, she lifts her cup to drink. "Did you surf?"

I nod. We both know it's how I process things. How I make peace. How I live with everything.

"Yes. It was gorgeous."

She sits in the second chair of the two at the table. Her gaze is fixed on the ocean. Light catches on her serious mouth, and I suddenly remember her laughing with my father, her lips red and wide, as they spun around in a dance on the patio of Eden. Suzanne sober is a far better creature than Suzanne drunk, but I sometimes miss the exuberance of her in those days.

"I'll go," I say, maybe hoping to see a whisper of that younger woman. And for a single moment a flame leaps in her eyes. She reaches for me, and for once I let her take my hand, squeezing it in a fit of generosity.

"You promise you'll actually live in my house?" I ask.

With her free hand, she draws an X across her heart and raises that same hand in a gesture of an oath. "Promise."

"Okay. I'll get out of here as soon as I can arrange it." A wave of mingled anticipation and terror rolls through my chest, sloshes in my gut. "Holy shit. What if she's really still alive?"

"I guess I'm going to have to kill her," Suzanne says.

Chapter Two

Mari

Fingering the blindfold over my eyes, I ask, "Where are you taking me?"

My husband, Simon, slaps my hand away. "Leave it alone."

"We've been driving forever."

"It's an adventure."

"Are we going to have kinky sex when we arrive?"

"It wasn't previously on the agenda, but now that you've brought it up . . ." He slides a hand up my arm, aiming to wander over my chest, but I swat at him. "I quite fancy the idea of you naked and blindfolded, out in the open."

"Out in the open? In Auckland? Uh, no."

I try to puzzle out clues about our destination. We left the highway a few minutes ago, but I still hear no auditory clues to the neighborhood. Distance traveled might be more of a help if we didn't live all the way in Devonport, a long drive to many other areas of the city. I lift my head to smell the air and catch a whiff of bread. "Ooh, I smell a bakery!"

Simon chuckles. "That should narrow it down."

We ride quietly for a bit. I sip my paper cup of coffee and fret about my daughter, Sarah, who had a breakdown over breakfast, her wild dark hair falling in a cape over her arms as she protested going to school. She would not say why, only that she hated it, that it was awful, that she wanted to be homeschooled like her (strange and prissy) neighborhood friend Nadine. Quite the scene for a seven-year-old who'd previously been the star of her class. "What do you think is going on with Sarah?"

"It's likely a schoolyard spat, but we should go round to the school and talk with them anyway."

"Yes, agreed." Even with her older brother offering to keep an eye on her, she hadn't wanted to go. At age nine, Leo is a mirror image of his father, the same thick, glossy dark hair, ocean-deep eyes, and lanky build. He shows every indication of taking after him athletically as well, swimming like a fish from the age of six months. And like his father, he suffers no dark moods or lack of confidence, unlike Sarah and me.

I can't even imagine a life of such calm and sunniness, though I love it in both of them. "She takes after her mother, I'm sorry to say."

"Were you given to moody spells as a child?"

I laugh. "The understatement of the century." I pat his hand on the seat, knowing where it will be even with the blindfold. "Some would say I still am."

"Not I. You're perfect." He squeezes my hand, and we turn sharply, bumping into what I presume is a drive. The car angles upward for some distance and then stops.

"You can take off the blindfold now," Simon says.

"Thank God." I rip it away, shaking my hair and smoothing a palm down over it.

But the view gives very little away. We're in a tunnel of wild bush made up of tree ferns and vines. An overloaded feijoa tree has dropped hundreds of dark-green fruits to the pavement. "Where the hell are we?"

Simon lifts one heavy, dark brow, a small grin playing over his generous mouth. "Are you ready?"

My heart skitters. "Yes."

He drives forward, and upward, upward, the road rutted and neglected, for another minute or two, and then we suddenly emerge from the heavy growth to a wide circular drive fronting an elegant 1930s house, standing by itself against a backdrop of wild blue sky and sea.

The air leaves my lungs, and practically before Simon halts the car, I'm tumbling out of it, mouth agape.

Sapphire House.

It's a two-story Art Deco mansion overlooking the harbor with its line of islands in the distance. I spin around, and spread out below is the city, glimmering and glinting in the bright morning sunlight. Three of the city's seven volcanoes are visible from here. When I whirl back to look at the house again, my chest squeezes. I've been enchanted by it since I arrived, partly for the tragic story attached to it but mostly because it sits up on this hill, so elegant and aloof. Untouchable, like Veronica Parker, the murdered film star who built the house for herself in the thirties.

"Are we going to see the inside?"

Simon holds up a key.

I capture it and fling my arms around his neck. "You are the most wonderful man!"

His palms land on my butt. "I know." He takes my hand and laces his fingers through mine. "Let's go look."

"Did she die?"

"Last month. You should do the honors." He pauses in front of the door. "Since it is, after all, yours."

My blood goes ice-cold. "What are you talking about?"

He tilts his head back to look at the roofline appraisingly. "I bought it." His chin lowers. "For you."

His eyes are the color of the Pacific on a stormy day, gray and deep. Right this minute, they shine with delight in his surprise and the direct, open love he carries for me. A line of Shakespeare, lodged in my head from one of the only classes I ever attended regularly in high school, runs through my mind: *"Doubt thou the stars are fire, Doubt that the sun doth move, Doubt truth to be a liar, But never doubt I love."*

I fall into him, forehead against his chest, arms around his waist. "God, Simon."

"Hey, now." His hands stroke my hair. "It'll be right."

He smells of laundry detergent and our bed and a faint note of autumn leaves. His body is strong and broad, a bulwark against the marauders of the world. "Thank you."

"There is a slight catch."

I lean back to look up at him. "Yes?"

"Helen, Veronica's sister, had two dogs. Her stipulation was that they came with the house, and there will be a society checking in on them."

I laugh. "I kind of love her for that. What kind of dogs?"

"Not sure. One large, one small, that's what the agent said."

Dogs are no problem. We both love them, and our golden will be so glad to have company.

Simon nudges me. "Come on—let's go in."

Heart pounding, I unlock and open the door.

It swings into a foyer two stories tall, with an airy gallery surrounding it. A skylight pours in great bucketfuls of sunshine on such a bright day. The rooms open out in a circle, and the doors are propped open, offering glimpses of the windows and views. Against the wall of what looks to be the long living room, a row of French doors reveals a staggering view of blue-green sea, sparkling and rolling. Far in the distance, a sailboat bobs by.

But inside is even more astonishing. The paintings, the furnishings, the rugs and appointments are all period, mostly Art Deco with its clean, clear lines. A few Arts and Crafts pieces are mixed in. An exquisite black-and-red lacquered cabinet holds a carved vase filled with dry stems, and next to it sits a round chair that has almost certainly never been perched upon. The rug is red and gold, with stylized vines.

My voice is hushed. "Is the whole house like this? So . . . untouched?"

"I don't know. I haven't been inside."

15

"You bought it sight unseen?"

He takes my hand. "Let's go look around."

It's a magical wander—practically a museum of the world in 1932—the furniture, the bedding, the walls and art. The three bath-rooms are tiled, and one in particular, the master bath, is such a jewel that I have to do a little dance of delight in the middle of the room. I run my fingers over the understated green and blue tiles that cover the walls, the ceiling, an alcove for the bath.

The splendor of the house would be a find even if it were classic Art Deco, but this house was built with a sense of Oceanic pride. The stairs are polished kauri wood, the banister Australian blackwood. A theme of stylized ferns and kiwis weaves through the accents and woodwork and tiles, and as we move through the hallways and rooms, I trail my fingertips over the precise inlays and carvings, wondering who the woodworker was. French doors with stylized cutouts lead from room to room and to a vast patio that looks out to sea.

Only three rooms of the twenty-two have been updated—a bed-room and sitting room at the back of the house, which are an ode to the charmless seventies, and portions of the kitchen, which has a stove and fridge that both look to be about a decade old. The stainless steel appliances clash with the rest of the room, which was designed for a household filled with servants and is suitably vast. The tile work is less spectacular here, but the stove sits in a tiled alcove, and I can see that there might be more buried beneath an unfortunate coat of paint.

Simon and I wander back through the butler's pantry, still stocked with everything from fish knives to soup tureens and china in every possible variation. I open one of the glassed doors and take out a bread-and-butter plate with a dark-blue rim on white china, a pattern of dual lionesses and stylized flowers in gold along the edge. "This is . . . in-credible. It's like a museum." Carefully, I settle it back in place. "Maybe that's what it should be. Maybe it's selfish to want to live here."

"Don't be silly, darling." He tugs me through the narrow room and into the dining room and through one of the French doors in the long line. "Look at that." He flings his hand toward the horizon, as if he's painted the view himself. "Imagine our children growing up with this. Imagine that the house finally has life in it."

The breeze ruffles his hair, and I'm drawn, as always, into his vigorous, optimistic view of the world. "You're right."

"Right." He pats my shoulder and slides his sunglasses down to his tanned face. "I'm going to take a look at the boathouse and leave you to your explorations. We'll have lunch at Marguerite's, shall we?"

"Yes. I'd like that," I say, but I'm already drawn back into the house, anxious to put my hands on everything, touch it, make sure it's real.

As I walk through the rooms now, touching doorjambs and walls and artwork and vases, I listen to the atmosphere for anything ghostly or sad, but the rooms are only quiet. Hushed, almost, as if waiting. Leaving the master bedroom for last, I explore it all, then move silently up the swirling staircase to the room that occupies fully a third of the second floor. French doors open to a balcony that extends the length of the room, and opposite rise ceiling-high closet doors, sleek and varnished, with discreet chevrons inlaid along the edges.

Ghoulishly, I look at the floors, parquet covered with pink and gray rugs. This is where the original owner of the house was found murdered, stabbed to death at the tender age of twenty-eight.

Veronica Parker, a dark-haired and voluptuous beauty, was a New Zealand lass who'd risen to Hollywood stardom in the midtwenties. In 1932, the Olympics were held in Los Angeles, and Veronica was part of the welcoming committee for the athletes of her country, which was how she met Auckland native George Brown, an Olympic swimmer. A tumultuous love affair began. Veronica had already built Sapphire House, but George was married to his high school sweetheart, who refused to give him a divorce.

It was, by all accounts, the undoing of Veronica.

The turbulent romance lasted six years. On April 9, 1938, she was found stabbed to death after a party on the hill. Dozens of suspects were interviewed, but everyone was sure it was George who killed her. His world in tatters, he secluded himself for the last three years of his life. Some said he died of grief. Some of guilt.

I toe the floor, wondering, but I can see no signs of foul play. Of course, it was scoured some eighty years before. Still, I find it intriguing that Veronica's sister lived in the house all this time and never slept here.

Or not. Who would want to sleep where a sibling had been murdered? Why did she live here, alone, for such a long time? Had she been so grief stricken that she could find peace only in this house her sister had built? Or was it simply expedient?

Not expedient. She could have done a hundred other things. Sold the house, made it over into her own tastes. Instead, she lived in those three unassuming rooms, leaving the rest of the house almost exactly as it was when her sister was alive.

Except here.

Rounding the room, I open drawers and find them empty. The closets are bare. Only the desk, sitting in the corner, holds any artifacts. Yellowed paper and desiccated sealing wax fill one drawer. In another, I find a dried-up bottle of ink and a fountain pen.

My fingers curl around the pen, and a shimmer of loss brushes the edges of my throat. The pen is substantial, smoothly inlaid with geometric patterns in green and yellow. Tugging off the lid, I find a carved silver nib.

Time slides away.

I am ten, practicing calligraphy with a dip pen as a storm pounds the windows of the bedroom I share with my sister. Her curly hair falls in her face as she bends over her page, meticulously drawing an L, her favorite letter. It's better than mine. Her calligraphy is always better than mine.

I drop the pen back in the desk drawer and wipe my hands on my thigh.

The house might not be haunted, but I surely am.

Chapter Three
Kit

A couple of days later, I'm boarding a big-bodied Air New Zealand plane, feeling oddly nervous. I haven't traveled a lot, not counting spring break trips to Mexico a few times, so I booked myself a window seat in business class. Since I don't buy anything but surfboards and fountain pens for myself, I also splurged on a juicy Airbnb in a high-rise building in the city center, overlooking the water. That way if the whole trip is a bust, at least I'll have had a little vacation.

Cocooned in the white noise of the engines and the murmuring voices, I find myself falling almost instantly asleep. Inevitably, the dream arrives. It's always the same.

I'm sitting on a rock in the cove with Cinder beside me. I have my arm around him, and he leans against my body. We're staring out to the restless ocean, watching waves that are too big race toward shore and smash against the rocks that are so dangerous. Spray splashes us all over, but we don't move. In the distance, Dylan is riding his surfboard, not even wearing a wet suit but only his yellow-and-red board shorts. I know he shouldn't be out there, but I just watch him. The wave is too big to safely ride, but he does it, skates along the center of the curl with his hands out, his fingers trailing in the water in front of him. He's happy, really happy, and that's why I don't want to warn him that the wave is breaking up.

And then it throws him, and he disappears into the sea. Cinder barks and barks and barks, but Dylan doesn't surface. The water goes still, and there is nothing to see but silvery ocean all the way to the horizon.

I jerk awake, mouth dry, and open the blind to look out at the darkness of endless ocean. The moon is full and shines in a line over the water far, far below. Stars glitter above, softening the harsh darkness of black sky.

A yawning hole pulses in my chest for long moments, but as always, if I am still and focus on something outside of myself, it fades.

The only way I survived the losses that marked my early life was by learning to compartmentalize, despite my mother's advice to get some counseling. I'm fine most of the time. But tonight, with the dream fresh in my mind, memories pour in. Me and Josie stealing into the restaurant in the very early morning to pour out the sugar and substitute salt, thinking it so hilarious until our father lost his temper and spanked us both. The two of us dancing on the Eden patio in my mother's cast-off nightgowns. Playing mermaid on the beach or fairies on the bluffs. Later, all three of us moving like a school of fish, Josie and Dylan and me, swimming in the cove or making a bonfire or practicing calligraphy with fountain pens my mother brought back from some trip she took with my father during one of their happy stints, an interest bolstered by Dylan's passion for all things Chinese. Like so many boys of the era, he'd fallen hard for Kwai Chang Caine in the *Kung Fu* television series.

I adored them both, but my sister was first. Worshipped the very air she breathed. I would have done anything she told me—chased down bandits, built a ladder to the moon. In turn, she brought me sand dollars to examine and Pop-Tarts she stole from the pantry in the house kitchen, and she kept her arms around me all night.

It was Dylan who introduced surfing. He taught us when I was seven and Josie nine. It gave us both a sense of power and relief, a way to escape our crumbling family life and explore the sea—and, of course, it was our bond with Dylan himself.

Josie. Thinking of her in the times before she turned into the later version of herself, the aloof, promiscuous addict, makes me ache with longing. I miss my sister with every molecule of my being.

She changed as an early teen, fighting constantly with our father and rebelling against even the tiniest rule. Not even Dylan could rein her in, though he tried. For all that he acted as an uncle or father figure, he was still only a teenager. She started hanging out with older kids on the beach just north of us. Baby Babe, they called her, Surfer Baby. By then she was even more beautiful, tiny and tanned to a deep mocha, her blonde hair sun-streaked and endless.

Josie, Josie, Josie.

At last I doze again, this time falling into a deep, faraway kind of sleep, and do not awaken until a shaft of light plays on my eyelids.

There below me is New Zealand, blue and sinuous in the vastness of the ocean. Little islands dot it all around, and I'm amazed to see both the Pacific and the Tasman Sea. The Tasman looks bluer.

The plane banks and drops, and now I can see the coves and cliffs lining the coast, and my heart jolts a little. Is Josie down there somewhere, or am I on a ridiculous errand?

I rest my forehead against the glass, unwilling to take my eyes off the view. Light skitters over the waves, and I remember when my sister and I thought there were jewels in the ocean, dancing on top of each swell.

One morning when we were small, my mother woke us, whispering into the tent where we were sleeping, Josie and me curled together with Cinder.

"Girls," she called sweetly, wrapping a hand around my foot, "wake up! I found something!"

The air was thick with fog, but the tide had gone out, leaving ironed-flat sand. My mother led us over the path and into a small cave that was approachable only at low tide. "Look!" she said, pointing.

Inside was what looked like a box. Josie bent over, peering into the dimness. "What is it?"

"I think it might be treasure," Suzanne said. "You should go see."

Josie straightened up, crossing her arms. "I ain't going in there."

"I will." Although Josie was two years older than me, seven to my five, I was always the brave one. Filled with a piercing curiosity and a lack of worry over creepy-crawlies, I stomped into the cave, bending over to keep from bumping my head. Even in the darkness, I could see the glitter in the box, things spilling over the sides like cartoon booty. "Treasure!" I cried, and hauled it out to the beach.

Suzanne knelt. "I see. Do you think it was pirates?"

Digging through the pearls and jeweled rings and bracelets and chocolate coins, I nodded. "Maybe it was mermaids."

She unwound a string of sapphires and dropped them around my neck. "Maybe it was," she said. "Now you're wearing their jewelry."

I adorned her arm with bracelets. Josie pushed rings onto Suzanne's toes. We drank hot chocolate and sat on the beach in our finery, and we were mermaids with our mermaid mother.

The flight attendant snaps me out of my reverie. "Miss, we'll be landing in just a little while."

"Thank you."

I blink, bringing myself back to now, where that very mother is waiting to hear what I find out about the daughter she lost. For the millionth time, I wonder how to fit the good and the bad of Suzanne into one package, but it's impossible. She was the worst mother of all time. She was the best mother of all time.

Below, the city is visible, sprawling across a vast, hilly landscape packed with roofs and streets. With a sudden sense of idiocy, I think this is the very definition of a fool's errand. How in the world will I find a single person in that crowded space? If it's even her.

The whole thing is absurd.

And yet I know it isn't, not really. That was adamantly, absolutely my sister, Josie, on that screen. If she's there, in that city below me, I'm going to find her.

By the time I make it to downtown Auckland, I'm so hideously jet-lagged, it's like some evil spell. I'm aware of hauling my bag into the foyer of a high-rise residential apartment building, appointed with nods to an Art Deco past it never had. My suitcase rolls over the marble floors with a whisper, and a young Maori woman in a uniform greets me and then hands over a key and directs me to the elevators. A pair of well-dressed Asian girls passes me, impossibly perfect, and next to them, I am a giantess at five ten, my curly hair wild from travel. Whatever makeup I left California with disappeared many hours ago. I wish for the protection and credentials of my white coat reminding the world that I'm a doctor.

Pathetic.

When the door swings open, a middle-aged couple emerges, cameras in hand, and a good-looking man holds the door open. I give him a nod. *"De nada,"* he says charmingly. I smile faintly as the doors close and rest my head against the wall until I realize I have to press a button.

Eighteen.

I'm the only person in the elevator and emerge on my floor, find the apartment, and let myself in. For a moment, I'm slightly startled. It's roomy and attractive, with a kitchen to my right, a bathroom to the left, a sitting area with a table and a sofa, and then a bedroom with a balcony looking out to high-rise buildings and a harbor.

But even that doesn't really register. My phone is nearly dead, and I'll have to go find a charger, but right now I shed my clothes, draw the curtains against the sunlight, and fall into bed.

When I climb out of my heavy sleep, I don't immediately know where I am. I'm huddled beneath the covers, curled up against the cold air, but not in my bed.

Slowly, I remember everything. New Zealand. My sister. My mom and poor Hobo. Reaching for my phone, I also remember that I don't have a charger and it's dead, so I am not sure what time it is. Without getting out of bed, I reach for the drapes and yank one side open a little.

And there, spread like a winking fabric made of jewels, is the harbor. What seems to be late-afternoon sunlight slants down in buttery glory, and a sailboat cuts cleanly through the water. A ferry scuds in another direction, and in the distance is a long bridge. Office buildings tower around me. I can see people through the windows, walking briskly down a hall, gathering in a conference room, standing around a table, talking. It's strangely soothing, and I lie where I am for a long while, just watching them.

It's my growling hunger that insists I get up. Stretching the kinks of the flight out, I putter into the kitchen area, where there is a bowl of fruit and a French press with a sachet of coffee. Milk in the fridge—a generous size for the space—and sugar packets on the counter. A bright-red electric kettle waits. I fill it with water, set it to boil, and head into the shower, which is a luxurious thing, all glass, with fragrant bottles of shampoo and soap. The water revives me better than anything else, and when I emerge, I'm ready to tackle whatever needs doing. The French press is fussier than I'd like, but the coffee is fantastic, and I open the curtains fully to enjoy my view as I scarf down two bananas, two apples, and the coffee. It'll hold me over until I can get a real meal.

The main thing is the charger. I attempted to buy one before I left, but there wasn't much time, and the shop had only European, British, and Japanese. At the front desk, I ask a slim young man for directions, and he points me out the back door to the main drag.

Outside, the heat swallows me, a thick, humid envelope. For a moment, I stand just outside the door, suddenly and acutely aware that I'm alone in a city of millions, thousands and thousands of miles from home or anyone I know. I feel a little panicked over the fact that I don't have my phone GPS to guide me around. My brain tosses out all the things that could go wrong—getting killed by forgetting to look the right way when I cross the street, veering into an unfriendly neighborhood, stumbling into the middle of a fight by accident.

Not everything is a disaster waiting to happen, I tell myself. Although, strictly speaking, it is.

But I'm not going to let that control me. I dived into a university miles from home without a moment's thought, and nobody had maps on their phones in those days. Looking around, I get my bearings and find landmarks—a big open square with steps is filled with well-dressed young Asians and sweaty European tourists. I hear Mandarin and Korean, a snippet of German, English in several accents.

The medley settles me, reminds me of San Francisco, where I spent almost a decade between med school and post-grad work. Auckland is like it in other ways too, glittery and surrounded by water, crowded and expensive, highly prized.

Looking over my shoulder as I set out, I see that my building, which seems to be at least partly residential, is quite distinctive with its Art Deco accents. It will be easy enough to pick it out. Still, I make a note of the address and the street I'm walking along.

The man behind the desk directed me to a mall, which leads me through a warren of tiny shops belowground, then spits me out on the busy main drag. Queen Street. Here, overhangs cover the sidewalk, allowing the crowds to bustle along in deep shade, and I'm grateful.

The electronics store is exactly like any other I've ever seen. Full of gadgets and cases and cords. The counters are staffed with young men and one girl. She steps up. "Hello, ma'am," she says—which makes me feel ancient—"how can I help you?" Her accent is not at all Australian, which I'd been expecting, but something else entirely, more pinched and lilting.

"Yes." I pull out my phone. "I need a charger."

"American, are you?"

"Yes, but they said it doesn't matter, right? A New Zealand charger should still work with my American phone."

"No worries." She smiles. Her face is round and milky. "I was just noticing. I'd so love to go to America." She cocks a finger for me to follow her. "Over here."

"Where do you want to go in America?" I ask, being polite.

"New York City," she says. "Have you ever been?"

"Once, for a conference," I say, but it's blurry in my memory. "The only thing I really remember is seeing a painting I'd always loved."

"Here we go." She pulls a package off a rack, holds out her hand for my phone, double-checks them both. "Yes. This is right. Anything else?"

"No." Eyeing the cords, I realize I'll need one for my laptop too and tell her the make and model. We head for the cash register, and I give her my credit card.

"What was the painting?" she asks.

"I'm sorry?"

She gives me back the credit card. "What was the painting you wanted to see in New York?"

I smile, shaking my head, unwilling to admit it was a Pre-Raphaelite mermaid. "Waterhouse—do you know his work?"

"No, sorry." She picks up the bag. "Have a nice visit."

The exchange, really the memory of the painting, makes me think of my sister, though of course she hasn't been far from my mind for even a minute since I saw her on the news. "I'm actually here on a sad errand. Do you happen to know where the nightclub fire was? Someone I knew was there."

"Oh!" Her hand covers her mouth. "I'm so sorry. It's not far; just head down toward the wharf and to your left just before the main street." Her cheeks have gone quite red. "You can't miss it, really. There's a memorial."

I nod. It's as good a place to start as any.

She's right. It's not hard to find. The building sits on a corner. Police tape ropes off access on three sides. Smoke marks climb the building to the roofline, black and grim, and I pause for a moment to steady myself.

Then I walk around the corner and see the memorial, a pile of stuffed animals and candles and flowers, some fresh, some turning brown after a few days. There's a smell in the air I associate with burn patients, scorched fabric and hair and blistered skin. Never good.

I'd done some reading on the fire before I arrived, but nothing particularly set it apart. It wasn't terrorism—not an issue in New Zealand, hard as that is to fathom—just a wretched accident, an overcrowded club, a blocked exit, and a malfunctioning sprinkler system. The perfect storm. It only made the news in the US for its drama.

Disasters are always worse when they involve bunches of young people, and this crowd was very young indeed. I walk slowly past the photos that have been taped and tied and paper-clipped to the fence keeping everyone out. Mostly Asian, not a soul past thirty, their eyes still twinkling with everything ahead and nothing too terrible behind. Now they'll be frozen there forever.

The vast losses thud in my gut. The parents who love them, the friends, the siblings, the shopkeepers who enjoyed their jokes. I think about it all the time in the ER, when it's been more ghastly than usual—idiotic car accidents, domestic violence, and bar fights and shootings. Lives wrecked. Stopped. Nothing to be done about it.

It's been getting to me. I've always hated losing patients, of course, but I loved the rush of saving them, being there at the moment of acute trauma and terror and helping bring them back from the brink, like the girl in the ER the night I saw Josie on the news, a bullet wound to the gut. Her boyfriend carried her in, and his hands were covered with blood from keeping the wound compressed. It saved her.

But it's all the lost ones who haunt me lately. The mother who'd slammed her car into a tree, the boy who'd been attacked by a dog, the sweet, sweet face of the little boy who'd shot himself with his mother's pistol.

I shove their faces away and focus on bearing witness to the collection of photos here in front of me, taking the time to look at each one. The girl with purple streaks in her hair and a crooked front tooth. The diva with red lips and a knowing expression. The boy laughing with a dog.

How many of their families will have the satisfaction of actual identification? A scene like this, with so many victims and physical damage, can be challenging.

The car that took the main blast on the train that supposedly killed Josie was in pieces, melted and evaporated, and so were the humans within. They found her backpack and the remains of one of her travel companions, a guy she'd mentioned once or twice in emails she sent home from the odd internet café, and we knew she'd been traveling with the group.

The phone call came in on my cell when I was on my way home to get some sleep after a grueling thirty-six hours of an obstetrics rotation at SF General, walking up the hill to the apartment I shared with four other residents, none of us home enough for it to matter that it was so crowded. The place was a pit, but none of us cared about that either. Food was all takeout, the environment be damned, and a local coffee shop downstairs in the building provided the caffeine. I'd been dreaming of a long, hot shower and washing my hair, then sleeping for a few hours by myself in the house, since I'd left all my roommates back at the hospital.

The phone rang, and it was my mother, howling. I'd only ever heard that sound one other time, after the earthquake, and it is carved into my bones. "Mom. What is it?"

She told me. Josie was dead. Killed in a terrorist bomb that demolished a train in France a few days before.

The weeks after were a blur. When I wasn't on the phone with my mother or the funeral home or the authorities, I worked. Often I took calls between patient visits, ducking into a storage closet to get some privacy. I was too exhausted and overwhelmed to cry. That came later.

Next to me on the street in Auckland is a young woman, weeping, and I move away to give her privacy, wishing to make her path easier, knowing there is only one way to walk that road: step by bloody step.

I'm suddenly so deeply, vividly angry that my hands shake. I have to stop to take a breath, looking up at the building. "What the hell, Josie?" I say aloud. "How could you do that to us? How *could* you?" Even from my self-centered, surfer-loser sister, it's hard to fathom.

It's appropriate that we're in Auckland, the land of volcanoes, because my middle feels like it's turned to magma, burning hot and impossible to calm.

When I find her, I don't know what I'll do. Hit her? Spit on her? Hug her?

I have no idea.

Chapter Four

Mari

Simon and I arrange to meet Sarah's teacher before class. We drive separately so that we can head out on our own afterward, me to Sapphire House to start taking notes, him to his empire of gyms.

I'm in the best possible mood, thanks to dawn sex with my fit and vigorous husband, which made me so cheerful I whipped up blueberry muffins for breakfast, which even Sarah ate with alacrity, after picking at her food the past few days. I peer at her in the rearview, and she's gazing out the window, her dark hair swept back from her freckled face. She's so unlike me that it's a little strange. You'd think your own child would have some resemblance to you, but she's my father and my sister, all in one.

Perhaps a fitting punishment for my sins, though I try not to dwell on it. Accept the things you cannot change and all that.

What I do know is that Sarah will hate it when the other girls stop growing and she keeps on, just as my sister did. Already she has bigger hands and feet than the other girls and a solidness that is nothing close to fat, but she'll see it that way if we don't stay at it, countering the bullshit that she hears day in, day out.

"Swim club today, sweetheart?"

"Yes," she says, her accent so very New Zealand, *yis*. "I beat Mara yesterday."

Her nemesis. "That's fantastic. You're stronger than she is, by far."

She shrugs, then meets my eyes in the mirror. "You don't have to go to the school, you know."

"I don't have to," I agree mildly. "But you don't seem very happy lately, and your dad and I want to make sure everything is okay."

"My teachers don't know anything." Her tone is not scornful, only matter-of-fact.

The traffic is thick, and I have to pay attention to the road for a few moments. At the next stoplight, I say, "What don't they know?"

Her wide mouth flattens into an expression of resignation. She just shakes her head.

"Sarah, it will be a lot easier to help you if you let me in on what's going on."

She doesn't reply. I pull into the school lot. Simon's Infiniti is not yet here, so I turn off the car, unbuckle my belt, and turn around, sorting through the ten thousand possible responses for the one that will help unlock the secret here. "Are you having trouble with a friend?"

"No."

"I'm not sure why you won't just tell me. You know you can trust me."

"I can trust you, but if I tell you, everything just gets worse, and no one will like me at all."

"What will get worse?"

She shouts, "I don't want to tell you! Don't you understand?"

Reaching through the seats, I wrap my hand around her ankle and just sit there, willing myself to believe her secret is not as dire as mine was when I was just a little older. She's a well-tended, well-observed child. "All right. There's your dad. I'll just pop into the school."

I meet Simon at the door, and he takes my hand. Our unified front.

The teacher is young and pretty, and she blushes when Simon shakes her hand. "Good morning, Ms. Kanawa."

"Good morning, Mr. Edwards. Mrs. Edwards. Sit down, won't you?" She folds her hands on the desk. "How can I help?"

We outline the problem—that Sarah wants to be homeschooled suddenly, and it seems there might be something going on. Ms. Kanawa mulls it over. She says, "You know, I wonder if there might be some bullying. One of the girls is quite the queen bee, you know, and all the other girls listen to her as if she's a royal."

"Is it Emma Reed?" I guess. She's a milk-and-peaches child with ribbons of spun-gold hair and enormous blue eyes—all hiding the instincts of a barracuda.

Ms. Kanawa nods. "She and Sarah have never got on."

"Why's that?" Simon asks.

"They're both"—she pauses, chooses her words carefully—"willful girls. And there is some understanding that they are the children of popular parents."

"Popular?" I echo.

"Well-known. Emma's mother is a broadcaster, of course, on TVNZ, and you, Mr. Edwards, are so visible because of the clubs." He's the spokesman for his own gyms, the genial host inviting everyone to visit and experience the health of good exercise. He also conducts fund-raisers every year for the Auckland Safeswim Initiative, a drive to make sure every child in the city knows how to swim.

"I see." I glance at Simon, who is wearing his unreadable genial expression, but I see his displeasure in the hard line of his mouth.

"Have you observed bullying, Ms. Kanawa?" he asks.

"Some name-calling and the like. The girls in question were reprimanded."

"What names?" I ask.

"Oh, I don't think that's—"

"What names?" I repeat.

She sighs. "They call Sarah Shrek. Because she's so tall."

Simon is still dead silent beside me.

"And"—she slants a glance toward Simon—"Science Nerd."

"That's an insult?"

She lifts a shoulder.

"I'll talk to Emma's mother," I say. "In the meantime, will you let me know if there seems to be more trouble?"

"Of course."

Simon's jaw ripples slightly. "How were the girls reprimanded?"

"Oh, I don't . . . I can't remember."

"I believe you're lying, Ms. Kanawa, and I do not tolerate lying."

She colors and begins to protest. "No, I . . . I mean—"

Simon stands, rising to his considerable six-four height. "I would suggest you make certain that any bullying, of any child, is swiftly punished. It's just not sporting, and it should not be tolerated."

"Yes, yes. Of course you're right." Her cheeks burn magenta.

"And do not lie to me again."

Simon takes my hand as we walk out, and he's walking fast enough that I have trouble keeping up and skip behind him. He finally notices and halts. "Sorry. I just hate bullies."

"I know." I never liked big sporting types before I met him, but this particular thing, his absolute adherence to fairness and honor, set him apart immediately. "I love you for it."

His shoulders ease, and he bends down to touch our noses together. "That's not the only thing."

"Not even a little bit."

"Oh, it's not little."

"No, dear. It surely isn't."

33

After the meeting, I head up to Sapphire House for a walk-through on my own. I want the chance to feel the energy, for lack of a better word, and start to figure out a plan and who I'll need to hire to do the work.

As I drive up the rutted road sheltered by overgrown brush, I'm already making plans for how each room will be used and how to best catalog the fantastic lot of antiques contained within. A feijoa tree scrapes the side of the car, and I wince, thinking of what it's doing to the silver paint. My tires must have smashed some of the fruits on the road, because the thick, sweet scent of them wafts in through my open window. On a whim, I stop the car and get out, fetching a canvas carry bag from the back seat.

I'd never heard of a feijoa before I arrived in New Zealand. They're a small green fruit that looks like a cross between an avocado and a lime on the outside, but inside boasts a fragrant yellow flesh with a texture much like a ripe pear's. The flavor is an acquired taste—sweet and perfumed, a combination of a dozen other things—but to me, they are just simply, sublimely feijoa.

With a sense of glee, I gather dozens of them into the bag, imagining the ways I'll use the pulp. Imagining Simon's face—he is nowhere near as fond of them as I am—I chuckle to myself and tuck the bag gently into the bay of the passenger seat, humming under my breath as I climb the rest of the way up the hill.

As I break out of the cover of the bush and into the sunlight, the view again takes my breath away. The sky and sea and the house itself, perched on the top like a queen overseeing the landscape. Sapphire House is an appropriate name for it—she overlooks all the blue jewels of nature. A shiver runs up my spine, a pleasure that's so rich it's nearly sexual. How is it possible that my life has led me here, to this house, which I will share with my children and their father, a man I still can't quite believe is all he appears to be?

As I stand there, admiring the landscape, a cloud scuds across the sun, throwing the scene into sudden shadow. A chill walks down my spine, as if it is a portent—things have been sunny for a long time in my life. Too long, maybe?

But the cloud swirls away, the sun pours back over the scene, and I shake off my sense of warning.

From the bag of feijoas, I grab a handful of fruits and then pick up my canvas workbag packed with notebooks and pens, measuring tapes, and an iPad. The sun beats down on the top of my head, and I wonder if I need to grab my hat. As a surfer girl from California, I thought I knew all about sun, but it took only one serious sunburn in New Zealand to realize how much more intense it is here. No one who lives here goes out without gallons of sunscreen.

But I'm not going to be outside today, and I leave the white cotton hat on the front seat, then swim through the strangely high humidity toward the front door. It could be a miserable afternoon unless the wind starts blowing. At the moment, it's dead still, and perspiration trickles out of my hair down the back of my neck and along my ears.

Inside, the air is cooler, though I doubt there's any air-conditioning. Even in such a high-end house, it would be very rare. Dropping my bag on the buffet by the door, I head for the long doors in the lounge. They face the sea, and when I open them one by one, at least a little whisper of freshness chases away the faint, distinct scent of mildew. There are no window coverings at all, which feels a little uncomfortable to me, even if it's only ocean out there, but the glasswork is so spectacular, I get it. Between each set of doors is a panel of clear leaded glass, the lead forming chevron patterns. I touch the point of one. Remarkable.

Every room is like that, every detail. I do another walk-through on the main level, looking more carefully at what is actually worth saving and what needs to go. Much of it is faded and weary looking but not as bad as I would have expected. Veronica's sister, Helen, must have had good housekeeping over the years.

On a yellow legal tablet, I note that all the sofas and chairs will have to be reupholstered, if not completely let go. Some styles are uncomfortable for actual human beings, and I'm not interested in living in a museum, so they can go to auction. A pair of chairs tucked into a corner are magnificent, if shabby, mirroring each other with a graduating back that looks like stair steps. Keepers, along with the dining room table, credenzas, and a stunning cabinet radio inlaid with abalone and what appears to be teak. Much of the art is unremarkable reproductions of landscapes and the usual classics, but there are also a number of pieces in a modernist style and distinctively New Zealand landscapes that might be notable. I recognize a seafront view in the style of Colin McCahon, those simplistic shapes, but it's much too early for his work. I wonder if Veronica supported local artists.

As I move through the rooms, scribbling notes, I notice there's actually a lot of art, both paintings and ceramics, some of it tucked into small spaces, like the seascape in shades of green and turquoise that graces the narrow wall above a telephone table. A classic black telephone with a rotary dial sits on the stand, and I pick up the handset curiously. A dial tone buzzes in my ear, and, bemused, I set it back down, resting my hand on the curved shape. I'll have to show the children. I wonder if they'll even know what it is.

For a moment, I'm thirteen, doing dishes in our house, the phone tucked between my ear and my shoulder, the cord swinging behind me every time I move. My mother appears, briskly clacking through the doorway. "Get off the phone and get to work. They're swamped in the dining room."

A little wave of nostalgia washes through me, a longing for that particular day, before all of it fell to pieces. Going down to Eden in my uniform to serve my father's Sicilian dishes the customers all came to eat, swordfish rolls and stuffed artichokes and arancini. Such good food. These days, my dad would be a *Top Chef* contender. Back then, he was still something of a king in his world, the dashing and charismatic center of Eden, the man who knew everyone's name and clapped you on the back and gave the best hugs in the world. Everyone adored him, including me, at least as a child.

For a moment, I'm so lost in the memories that the handset warms beneath my palm, and the predictable kaleidoscope of emotions tumbles through me—longing and regret and shame and love. I miss them all, Dylan and my father, my mother and, most of all, Kit.

I grab my bag from the front door and carry it into the kitchen. It's a calm, efficient place, clearly used very little. From a drawer, I take a sharp knife and a spoon and slice the feijoas in half. Within, each boasts a soft jelly center laced with seeds, a design that to me looks like a medieval cross. A couple of them are overripe, but the others are sweet and cool and delicious, and I slurp them up, getting sticky.

Happy.

I've also packed myself a lunch, the same thing I packed for the children, a bento box with cherry tomatoes and green grapes, rolls of ham and cheese on skewers, a little brownie, and a clementine. They love the boxes and love to take turns coming up with new ideas to fill them. They remind me of the little snacks and skewers I helped my dad prepare for happy hour snacks at Eden, long ago.

Around me, the house is very silent, and I'm aware of the size of it, the vastness. It's a little spooky if I allow it to be. I can imagine Veronica's ghost trapped here, wandering the rooms, seeking her lost lover.

A door slams upstairs, and I practically leap out of my skin.

Get a grip.

If there were ghosts on this earth, I'd have met one by now. God knows I've looked for them often enough. To explain. To put things right.

With a deliberate shift, I pop a tomato in my mouth and lean on the counter, wondering what I'm going to do with this space. It's easily big enough to eat in, and we'll have breakfast here almost certainly, but there isn't as much light as I'd wish and no view at all, just the walls of the kitchen. Would it be worth adding some windows back here? I'll have to get Simon's input.

Opening the back door, I toss the clementine skins and overripe grapes for the birds. They land in a thicket of shrubs along a cracked path that seems to loop only around the house. I try following it, but it ends in a tangle of vines that seems to be both roses and scarlet rātā. A tree fern rises above the mess. There might be rats, I suddenly realize, and wonder if I should have left the damn fruit out there.

Whatever.

Washing my hands, I head back into the main living areas on this floor, a long, wide room that can be divided by pocket doors and rather spectacular mosaic screens. We'll want an entertaining room, and it will be stunning at night, with the doors open to the sea and maybe a piano in the corner. I stand in the middle of the room, hands on my hips, letting the vision come to me. Colors of clear turquoise and orange and silver. The mirrors in this room are fantastic pieces, with stair-stepped geometric flares on the sides, and I'll have them resilvered.

Many of the furnishings and appointments are mediocre. There are a number of knockoffs and facsimiles, which is odd, considering how particular the detailing in the actual house is. I wonder, picking up a bowl that looks to be an authentic green Rookwood with Native American styling, if someone furnished it for Veronica. She was a busy actress, much in demand, and although she started spending more time in New Zealand once she fell in love with George, she still didn't have much time.

Or, one presumes, taste? Although that makes my ears flush a little in shame. Who am I to judge? It's not like I had any training—I taught myself to recognize fine things. Maybe she did too. Maybe she just didn't have time to approve everything.

Now I'm curious about her, and to understand what happened to her, and why, I'm going to need to do a lot more research. All I know at the moment is the top level—the doomed romance, the house, the murder. But what kind of woman was Veronica Parker? Where did she come from? How did she become such a big star?

And what about her lover, George?

It seems important to know all of it, to know Veronica's wishes and dreams. Sapphire House was her home, her vision, her dream of luxury, and now it's mine. It seems a sacred undertaking to honor her. By understanding her, I'll do a better job of restoring the house to the glory it deserves.

My time is running out today, but I can at least explore the study. It's a richly appointed room with a view through long windows to the curve of the harbor. In the distance are rolling blue hills rising out of the water with a scudding of long clouds over the peaks. It would be an excellent office for Simon—aside from the noise. He is very relaxed about most things, but when he works on his accounts or marketing or anything to do with business, he likes—needs—complete silence. He'll want a space upstairs, away from everything. Maybe the sister's suite of rooms.

This will be mine, then. I take in a breath and let it go, absorbing the atmosphere. The cherry-wood desk, the bookshelves, the glass light fixtures with their sleek geometric insets. I don't like the desk sitting in the middle of the room, but that's easily changed.

Remembering my task to discover more about Veronica, I open the drawers of the desk and find them all empty. Not just cleared out but untouched, as if they've never been used. It breaks my heart a little. That might mean the books were also stocked by a decorator. Bookshelves run the entire length of one wall, and on several there's a conspicuous elegance—the books' covers are printed leather, all classics.

Other shelves offer more insight. Aldous Huxley and Pearl Buck, along with the local beloved, Katherine Mansfield. Poetry and Maori culture and history, a lot of intriguing titles I want to explore. I touch them, one at a time, to settle their titles in my memory.

At the end of the third shelf is a collection of books with bright, often tattered covers, and I pull one out to see what it is. A mermaid graces the cover, her hair draped demurely over her shoulder, and I hastily put it back. The next is also a book about mermaids, and I shove it back just as fast but not fast enough.

I was eight and Kit six, and we wanted to be mermaids for Halloween. Nothing else would do, no matter how many times our mother said it was impossible to have a tail and also walk around the neighborhoods of Santa Cruz, where we would go trick-or-treating. She found skirts of turquoise taffeta, painted our faces, and—the crowning touch—carefully painted mermaid scales on our arms and legs.

Years later, Kit and I sat side by side in a tattoo parlor, each of us offering our inner left arm to the artists, who meticulously applied mermaid scales.

I hold out my arm, brush my fingers over that tattoo, still sharp and beautiful after all these years, a testament to the quality of the work. BIG SISTER, it reads over the scales. Hers is LITTLE SISTER, though we laughed about it at the time, since she towered over me by then, nearly six feet to my five three.

No. The pain I keep shoved down deep in a cavern leaks out.

Just no.

More than a decade of practice gives me the tools to quash the memories. I have a million errands to run before the children get out of school, and unlike my own mother, I like being there for them. I wonder if Sarah has fared better today. As I turn to go, I spy a row of Agatha Christie and grin, nabbing one at random. A person can never go wrong with Christie.

The timer on my phone goes off, startling me. I've been here for three hours, lost in the past. I collect my things, making sure to double-check the locks and that I've left no lights on.

On the way out, I change my mind and turn on the light in the study, a beacon in the darkness. A sign that the house is not deserted.

It makes me anxious that everyone knows Helen died and the house is empty. To both my and Simon's surprise, there is no alarm system, a fact that is being rectified next week.

I let myself out into the overwhelming heat of early afternoon. The full weight of sunshine slams the top of my head, and I have to consciously take a deep breath in the wet, wet air. As I lock the door behind me, a wash of dread runs the length of my neck.

Mermaids and fountain pens. Across the screen of my memory, Kit and Dylan sat at the scarred, solid table that occupied one corner of the house kitchen, bent over wide-ruled paper, practicing letters with tails—*g, p, q*. I wrote a line of Zs, capital and small, like Zorro.

A ripple of warning moves through me. I raise my head to look around, feeling my ghosts gather and whisper. My father, my mother, Dylan. My sister.

I thought I could walk away. That I would get used to missing her. I never have.

On the way back down the hill, I wonder what would happen if the truth of my life came out. The thought of all I could lose sucks the air out of my lungs, and I have to turn up the radio and start singing to avoid having a panic attack.

"Get a hold of yourself," I say aloud.

Josie Bianci is dead. I intend for her to stay that way.

Chapter Five

Kit

Leaving the site of the nightclub fire, I look around at the other businesses in the area. It's clearly a popular spot—T-shirt and sandwich shops interspersed with restaurants and hotel entrances. Maybe Josie has been to one of them. Maybe somebody will remember her.

I cross the street and peer into each window I pass, but nothing particularly leaps out. She could have been anywhere, doing anything.

A little aimlessly, I walk up one block and down the next, looking for something, anything, that suggests my sister. But there is pretty much everything—a high-end jewelry store, a boutique selling tiny couture dresses, a two-story bookstore packed to the brim. It makes me feel slightly breathless to imagine asking about Josie in any of them, and I can't make my feet stop.

Until the window of a stationery shop halts me, lures me inside with a display of ink in jeweled-looking bottles. At this point, I have more pens and ink than I could possibly use in three lifetimes, but that's not the point. The store has a display of Krishna inks, small-batch inks in swirling, shimmering colors. I have a weakness for shimmery ink, though I have stopped using it for prescriptions and stick with a Very Serious, fast-drying black for those.

The rest of the time, I lean toward the flashy two-tone inks. I've never seen this brand before, and I stand there playing with the colors for quite some time. A Goldfish Gold is amazing, but I never seem to use orange or yellow inks. One called Sea and Storm attracts me, and the nonshimmery but still gorgeous turquoise called Monsoon Sky. It reminds me of another turquoise ink I had at ten or eleven, during the first crazy wave of passion when Dylan, Josie, and I discovered the art of calligraphy. Which of us started? It's hard to remember now, where and how it began, only that we all fell in love with it, writing mannerly notes, leaving them in elegant handwriting for our parents or each other. Dylan loved Chinese calligraphy, practicing the characters for *crisis* and *love* and *ocean* that he found in a library book.

I carry the ink to the counter, intending to then go look at pens, but my stomach growls, reminding me that all I've had to eat are two bananas and two apples.

I force myself to ask the girl behind the counter, "Have you worked here long?"

"A year or so." She smiles, wrapping my ink in tissue paper.

I'm about to ask if she might remember someone, my sister, that is, with her distinctive scar, but my face goes hot as I consider it. Instead, I simply pay and carry my package out with me, cursing myself as I go.

How will I find her if I never look for her?

My feet carry me back up the hill, and I shop in a grocery store tucked into the basement of another building, picking up a bottle of wine and fresh bread, more fruit and a half dozen eggs, and a chunk of cheese, which all fit into my pack. I don't intend to cook for myself much, since all these restaurants deserve sampling, but it's good to have a few things on hand.

Wandering into a little alleyway, I find a row of eateries with tables and chairs set out in the gathering twilight. An Italian spot catches my eye. "One, please," I say to the host. "May I sit outside?"

"Of course, of course. Right this way."

He settles me between a chubby young couple and a sharply dressed businessman who gets up the minute I sit down, chattering irritably into his phone as he hurries away. The Italian host tsks, shaking his head as he clears the table and wipes it down.

"Everyone is so busy," he says, and his voice reminds me, suddenly and acutely, of my father, whose deep voice was laced with his Italian accent until the day he died. "You want wine?" he asks. "I think you like red wine. Am I right?"

"Yes, as it happens. Bring me something you love."

"My pleasure."

I realize I don't have my phone to keep me company. Weird. It's hard to remember the last time that even happened. Years, probably. Instead, I read every word of the small menu, even though I decided on the gnocchi almost the moment I saw it. Leaning back, I think how much my father would have loved this place, the tidy white tablecloths and flowers in tiny blue vases. I finger the carnation. Real, not fake, and I lift the bottle to inhale the bright, peppery scent.

The man returns with my wine, presenting it with a flourish. He has a thick mustache and twinkling eyes. "See if you like this one."

Dutifully, I swirl and inhale and taste. He's served it properly, in a glass with a wide bowl, and the notes are rich on the nose. On my tongue, it's deep and fruity but without heavy tannins. "Mm," I say. "Yes. Thank you."

He gives me a little bow. A lock of his hair tumbles free and falls in his eyes. "And for dinner?"

"Antipasti," I say, realizing now that I've stopped moving that I'm gut-empty. "And the gnocchi."

"Good, good."

The wine gives me something to occupy my hands, and I lean back, watching the parade of humanity passing before me. A lot of businesspeople who have stopped for a post-work drink, the women in heels, the men in stylish suits. An open-fronted bar is crowded with young professionals eyeing each other. No one seems to smoke.

Tourists too are wandering up and down the alleyway. I can spot them by their comfortable shoes and sunburns and the exhaustion with which they peruse the menus. Again, a tumble of languages and accents and cultures.

The host seats a man next to me at the vacated table. To preserve our privacy, I keep my eyes forward, but I hear him order wine in a Spanish accent.

The waiter brings me my antipasti. It's a generous serving of fresh mozzarella, wet and gleaming; curls of salami and prosciutto; a tumble of olives and fresh tiny tomatoes and flatbread. "Beautiful," I breathe.

I tuck in and am transported to childhood, when one of my afternoon chores was to portion out mozzarella and poke toothpicks into the various charcuterie that was served for happy hour, along with Harvey Wallbangers and White Russians and the endless, endless Long Island Iced Teas, my mother's favorite.

"I don't mean to bother you," the man next to me says. "Are you also a tourist?"

Engaged with a particularly stunning slice of prosciutto, I take a moment to savor it, then wash it down with a tiny sip of wine. I look at him. He's a tall man with thick dark hair and the shadow of an unshaven beard on his jaw. A well-thumbed paperback sits on the table next to him, and I think, *When did I stop carrying books around with me?* "Yes. You too?"

He gives a nod. "Visiting a friend, but he had work to do tonight, so he abandoned me." He lifts his glass. Next to the book is a bottle of wine. "Cheers."

"Cheers." I lift my glass but use my body to tell him I don't really want to engage.

Not that he listens. "I would have gone across the way there, to sample their tapas, but I saw you again and had to stop here instead."

"Again?"

"This morning. You arrived from the airport, I think."

His voice is sonorous, vibrant, a musical instrument. I let myself take another long look at his face. Strong features—Roman nose, almost too aggressive to be attractive, large dark eyes. "Yes," I admit. "But I still don't remember."

He touches his chest, hand over his heart. "You have forgotten me already." He tsks, then tilts his head with a smile. "At the elevator."

The moment pops back into my head. "Oh yeah. The *de nada* guy."

He laughs. The sound is robust, full of life. I sip my wine, assessing. It wouldn't be so terrible to have a roll in the hay. It's been a while.

"My name is Kit," I say.

"Javier."

I pick up the antipasti plate and offer it to him. "The salami is very good."

He gestures toward the seat across from him. "Would you like to join me?"

"No, thank you. If we each stay where we are, we can both watch the street."

"Ah." He helps himself to a mozzarella and a salami and deposits them on his bread plate. "I see your point."

"We might as well be at the same table anyway," I say, indicating the narrow space between our chairs. He's close enough that I can smell his cologne, something vaguely spicy.

"What brings you to New Zealand?" he asks.

A shrug. I'm going to have to come up with a way to answer this question. It's a long way to fly for no reason at all. "It's not like anywhere else, is it?"

"No." He sips his wine, and in profile his face is quite powerful. Beautiful. Maybe he's ticking a few too many of my No Way rules.

We'll see. "How about you?"

His shrug is somehow sad, and that ticks another box. No tortured men. They always want saving, and given my childhood filled with broken people, it's an impulse I have to constantly fight. "My old friend invited me. It seemed time for a change. Perhaps I will move here."

"Really?" I eat some cheese, break some flatbread, offer the plate to him again. "From where?"

"Madrid."

"That's a big change."

He nods, smooths his hands together, palm to palm. "I'm weary of politics."

I snort laugh and have to cover my mouth. "Yeah. It's been a weird few years."

"Decades."

"Yeah."

We watch the people walk by. Couples in love, old marrieds, the happy-hour crowd heading home. My body is soft and quiet for the first time in ages. Maybe I'd needed to get away more than I knew. My hand reaches automatically for the ghost of the phone that isn't there, and I open my palm on the table instead. "What are you reading?"

He holds it up to show me. *One Hundred Years of Solitude.* It's in Spanish, of course. "I've read it many times, but I love to read it again."

I nod. Literary too, which isn't on my No Way list, but it speaks to a great mind, and that is.

"Have you read it?" he asks.

"No." I surprise myself by adding, "My sister was the literary one."

"You don't like to read?"

"I do. I just don't read *important* books. That was her thing—all the great poets and writers and playwrights."

"I see." A little quirk of his lips. "You could not share?"

The wine is loosening me now. "No. I'm the scientific one. She was the creative one."

"Was?"

47

"She died," I say, even if I don't know if that's true anymore.

"I'm sorry."

The waiter brings my gnocchi then, delicately arranged and tossed with parsley and Parmesan. I feel my father sit down across the table and fold his arms. His wrists are hairy beneath his shirtsleeves, the cuff links he always wore. I take a small bite. "Oh, that's very good," I say, and my father nods.

"Good, good," the waiter says.

"Will you bring me another glass of wine?"

"Oh, no, no," Javier protests, his hands illustrating his words, flying into the air. "Allow me to share. I will never drink it all myself."

"Never?" I say.

"Well, perhaps. I'd rather share."

I nod. The waiter smiles, as if it's his doing. "I will be right back with your dinner, sir."

The fragrance of garlic rises from the plate, and I take another bite. "This was one of my father's specialties," I offer, and it's out before I realize I'm going to say it. "Gnocchi with peas and mushrooms. I used to roll them out for him."

"Was he Italian, your father?" He leans over to pour wine into my now empty glass.

"Sicilian."

"Your mother too?"

I glance at him. "You're quite forward."

"Not ordinarily."

"Why now?"

He leans closer, and I see by the glitter in his eye that he's going to say something bold. "Because my heart stopped when I saw you sitting here."

I laugh, pleased by this extravagance.

"You think I am joking," he says. "But I swear it is true."

"I am not the type of woman who stops men's hearts, but thank you."

"You have not met the right men."

I pause, fork hanging from my hand, elbow on the table. Behind him, the sky is nearly dark, and the laughter around us has grown more robust. The shape of his mouth makes my skin rustle, and he has that elusive air that makes me think he will be very good in bed. "Maybe I haven't."

He grins at this, and an outrageous dimple breaks in his cheek. He has to lean back to allow the waiter to deliver his food. It's a steaming plate of prawns and crayfish in risotto. A good eater's choice, as my father would have said. He had no patience with picky eaters, the vegetarians who were already dotting the landscape, the ones who didn't eat fish or beef or particular vegetables. *Eat it as it is*, he would say with a sniff, *or don't eat*. Only Dylan was allowed to be choosy. He hated capers and pickles and olives, avocado with a passion, and would rather have starved than eat egg whites or clams. In some way, he filled my father's desire for a son, and for a long time he doted on Dylan.

Until he didn't.

"Did your father cook for you often?" my companion asks.

"Not for me, exactly. He cooked for his restaurant. We grew up in there, eating whatever the special of the day was."

"That seems like an interesting childhood. Did you like it?"

"Sometimes." It's easy to talk to this stranger, someone who will not remember a month from now what I said. I empty my glass and hold it out to him. He splashes in a heavy measure of wine. "Not always. It could be a little exhausting, and my parents were always wrapped up in that rather than their children." Delicately, I balance a perfectly shaped gnocchi on my fork. "How did you grow up?"

He touches his lips with his napkin. "In the city. My mother taught school, and my father was a . . ." He frowns, his fingers rubbing together as if to pull the word from the air. "A clerk, you know, for the government." His face brightens. "Bureaucrat."

"You only?"

"No, no. Four of us. Three boys and a girl. I am second oldest."

The one who needs attention, like me. Aloud, I say, "The oldest always gets everything."

He inclines his head slightly, disagreeing. "Perhaps. My sister is the oldest, and she is not a demanding sort. She's very quiet, afraid of the world."

It's my turn to be bold; the wine has loosened my inhibitions. We're two strangers on holiday, and I don't have my phone to amuse me. "Why?"

His face shutters, and he looks down. He shakes his head.

"Sorry," I say. "Too far."

"No, no." He reaches across the small space and touches my forearm. "She was kidnapped when she was small, so small that no one knows what happened to her. She was not the same after that."

"Poor baby." A little of the sheen of the night washes away, and I think of Josie.

"Pssht," he says, sweeping it away and grabbing his glass. "Holidays are for forgetting, eh? *Salud.*"

I grin. *"Salud."*

Both of us fall to eating then, and the quiet is easy. The garlic of my dish and the extreme garlic of his perfume the air. A pair of boys walks by, shoulder to shoulder, one Maori, the other white, their legs moving in perfect sync, and a clutch of skinny teenage girls skitters by, hyperaware of themselves, chattering in a language I don't immediately recognize. It's still humid and hot but not as terrible.

For once, I'm happy in my skin, just sitting there eating.

Javier says, "My friend is a musician who is playing at a club not far from here. Would you like to go with me to hear him?"

For a moment, I wonder if it might be better to just go back to my room, get some sleep. "I don't feel dressed for that," I say. "And I have groceries to put away."

"It is only a little way to the apartment. We could go by there first, then to the club."

Which is really what I'd rather do. "All right."

Lightning gathers on the horizon as I walk back to the apartment with Javier. He's agreeably taller than me, with a solidness to his shoulders and thighs that makes me feel small as I walk along beside him, not something that's all that common when you're five ten in stocking feet.

He waits in the lobby while I run upstairs, plug my phone into the new charger with a sense of relief, and change into a sundress, with a thin sweater to go over it. The wall-to-wall mirror in the bathroom reveals a madness of curls from the humidity, not something I can do much about. To counter it, I smear on some lipstick. My mouth is my best feature, a mouth that belongs to my Italian side. The matte red lipstick makes the most of it.

When I exit the elevator, Javier makes a show of admiring me and offers his elbow. I take it, and we wander back out into the thick air.

"Do you travel often?" he asks.

I dodge a trio of girls dressed in their evening best and answer on the other side. "Not much at all, actually. It's hard to get away from my work. You?"

"For me it is the opposite. Too much travel the past few years."

"Work?"

He gives a simple nod, doesn't elaborate. In companionable silence, we walk a few blocks. I take in the glitter of lights against the sky, the glimpse of water through tall buildings, the hint of music behind windows. We detour down a bricked alleyway, and he pauses, looks up. "Here we are."

When he opens the door, a roll of sound and scent spills into the street, alcohol and perfume, voices and laughter and the plucking notes of someone tuning a guitar. I enter and Javier follows, and a lot of people look at us, which makes me self-conscious for a moment, until I realize that they probably look at everyone.

And perhaps too, we make a striking pair, me with my red mouth and wild hair, he with those shoulders.

Few tables are open, and he leads us to one near the back of the room, where a girl in skinny jeans and a peasant blouse meets us to take our orders. "Beer for me," I say, sliding into my seat. "Whatever brown ale you have."

"Same for me," he says. "And a tequila, the best you have, neat." The table is quite tiny, the space allotted forcing us to sit close. His thigh bumps my knee. My shoulder brushes his upper arm. He smells of something elusive and rich, and I try to place it for a moment before I turn my attention to the stage, aware of my heightened senses, his elbow, the thickness of his eyebrows.

"Which one is your friend?"

"All of them, really, but Miguel is the one I'm here to visit. He's the one in the red shirt. The good-looking one."

I smile, because it's true. Miguel has an amiable expression and high cheekbones and very shiny, very black hair. He's the one tuning his instrument, nodding to the accompaniment. "Have you been friends a long time?"

"We met through a mutual friend." His smile is wry. "He's my ex-wife's brother."

The server brings our drinks, and the ale is a very nice shade of toffee where the light shines through. I lean in to smell it. Promising. I raise my glass. "Cheers."

For a single second, he holds the glass aloft, his gaze moving over my hair, my mouth. "To new adventures."

I drink, and it's cold and refreshing and spectacular. With a sigh, I set it back down. "Oh, I do love beer."

He holds up his clear tequila. "I prefer this myself." He smells it, sips it, as if it is wine. "But only in small doses."

I chuckle, as I'm meant to do, but a memory flickers in my mind, a vision of a boy in my ER last year who'd immolated himself in a bonfire as a gesture of love after drinking a bottle of tequila. Not exactly a story for polite company. To shift the image, I ask, "Was it divorce that sent you here?"

"No, no." He waves a hand. "We have been divorced a long time, many years." His dark eyes hold my gaze. "And you? Have you ever married?"

I shake my head, turn the glass one quarter. "It's not really on my list."

He inclines his head, surprised. "Marriage is not?"

"No. My parents gave me an example I never want to emulate." In fact, I can't bear to let people close enough for more than a five-minute relationship, never mind marriage.

"Ah." He sips his tequila, the sip so tiny I wonder that he can even taste it, and I like him for it.

The music starts up with a sudden, thrilling strum of the guitar. The handsome Miguel leans into the microphone, making it difficult to talk. Javier and I settle into our seats, and it is impossible that we don't touch a little. It feels companionable and heightens my awareness as the music fills the air. It's heated, passionate, with songs in Spanish. My body sways, and I remember suddenly a guitarist who used to play on the patio at Eden when I was eight or nine, a slim-hipped man my mother flirted with shamelessly. Josie and I wore our dance gowns, two of my mother's silkier nightgowns, old and worn, that she'd sheared off on the bottoms so we wouldn't trip. We swayed and twirled under the wide, dark sky, our hearts bursting with love and wonder and things we barely knew existed.

Now that I've grown into my hungers, I look at Javier. When he feels my gaze and looks back, I see it in his eyes too, and his hand slides along my thigh, just above my knee. I hold his gaze and let the pleasure of anticipation rise. We're adults. We know the dance. I let my guard down slightly, allowing myself to anticipate kissing that mouth, touching those shoulders without the impediment of fabric, the promise of him—

"And now, we would like to invite my good friend Javier Velez up to the stage to play."

The crowd rustles and starts to clap. Javier squeezes my knee. "I will be back soon. Order another beer if you like."

I nod and watch him weave through the tables. He moves as if he's made of water, easily, smoothly, as if there is only one way to go, through this opening, then that, never pausing.

Onstage, he man-hugs Miguel, then picks up a guitar. It leans against him like a child. His posture relaxes, hands settling against the strings.

A sharp cascade of warning rushes through my overheated system. A swath of blue light cascades over his hair as he bends his head, moves the microphone close, and waits for some internal signal, eyes closed. The room hushes, breath sucked in, waiting.

I wait along with them.

Javier looks out over the crowd, then bends his head suddenly and strums a melancholic chord and, right after, quickly coaxes out a complex waterfall of notes. My arms prickle.

He leans close to the mic and begins to sing in a rich, low voice. It's a ballad, a love song, which is evident even if I don't know the words. His voice caresses each syllable, rumbles and whispers, his fingers on the strings keeping time.

A musician. And not a hobbyist. He has captured the room, captured me.

Sexy.

Tall.

Intelligent.

Wry.

And now a musician.

Javier Velez has made my very, very short No Way in Hell list. Never. Nope. Nada.

While he's still singing, I gather my purse and my sweater and slip out of the club into the night, walking fast to burn off the spell he's cast, the spell I've allowed to snare me.

Out in the night, striding up the hill toward my room, I'm aware of the prickling down my spine, along my palms. I'm disappointed. It's been a while since my last short-term, completely inappropriate partner, a surfer a decade younger than me, wandered off to better waves. Sex is a biological imperative, and all sorts of systems are improved with regular intercourse. Sex for one is fine, and it can burn off a lot of bad energy, but sex for two is way more fun. Skin-to-skin eases the human animal.

I'd been looking forward to that.

People have stopped asking me if I'm going to settle down, find a husband. I'm not interested, though I was, once upon a time. It pains me slightly that I won't have children unless I figure out what I'm going to do fairly quickly—I froze some eggs just after I turned thirty, so there's that backup—but I'm feeling so restless in my life that I need to figure out my plan before I add a baby into the mix.

I don't regret not having a long-term relationship in my life. It's surprisingly easy to find men to be a partner for a while, like Tom, the buff surfer who'd kept me company over most of last summer and into the fall. At some point, as I age and become less sexually appealing, it might be more difficult. I'll cross that bridge when I come to it.

What I won't do is allow myself to have sex with a man who has the potential to genuinely stir my passions. Living through the war that was my parents' marriage, then everything my sister ever did, including getting herself killed, taught me to steer clear of intense liaisons.

Thus my rules, the rules that have kept me safe for my entire adult life, and I'm not going to start breaking them now.

Inside the building, I stab the elevator button irritably and wait, staring up at the numbers.

Damn. He had such promise.

Chapter Six

Mari

After dinner, Sarah helps me with the dishes. Our house is a villa that sits on a rise catty-corner to the harbor, and as I wash glasses and hand them to Sarah, I admire the opalescent pools of light playing over the waves. Across the water is a long bluff, just now starting to twinkle with lights coming on for the evening.

Sarah's hair is pulled back in a braid in an attempt to tame it, but wild curls spring out around her face and stand up along her forehead. A grass stain mars her T-shirt, and even over the sweetness of dish soap, I smell kid sweat and dirt. She has a thousand little experiments going on outside—trying to grow shoots from celery stubs and an avocado seed and onion scraps; bird feeders in three styles; a fancy barometer her grandfather gave her to go with the little weather station he helped her set up. My father-in-law, Richard, a longtime widower, has a passion for sailing, and he loves the natural world as much as Sarah does. Every afternoon, she's out there, tinkering and humming to herself and examining everything from feathers to rocks.

A total geek, just like my sister. In every gesture, all her serious attention to science and detail, her sober measuring of the world.

Tonight, she's been quiet, but I'm forcing myself not to ask about school again. It'll just put her on edge. Maybe tomorrow. For today, I'll just love her up at home, and maybe that will fill some of the empty spots mean girls at school are leaving. "After this, you should take a shower, let me do your hair."

She only nods, her fat lower lip sticking out as she dries a plate.

"Whatcha thinking about?"

She raises her head, blinks. "I want to read a story tonight."

"Like an actual story? Maybe Harry Potter?"

"No." She scowls slightly. "You know I don't like made-up stories."

I do know. And it was the weirdest thing in the world to me, a lifelong, die-hard reader, but as soon as she was old enough to think for herself, she questioned things. If there were fairies in books, why couldn't she see them in real life?

When she was barely two, she started picking up bugs to examine them. She trailed after her grandfather as he went on his nature rounds, pointing out various flora and fauna to her. They hiked all the main trails around the city, then went farther afield. He's teaching her to watch the sky, to read the wind and the waves. They are very close.

Something she will never, ever have with my own family, which is all the more painful because she and Kit would be so enchanted with each other.

"Okay, so what book?"

"A book I got at the library on botany."

I will myself not to smile. "I'd be happy to." I hand her the last saucer to dry. "Maybe *The Little Mermaid* after that?" It's the one story she likes. Not the Disney classic but the older, darker Hans Christian Andersen version.

I read her the latter when she was five, and she went crazy for Ariel. The Disney version is fine, but fairy tales are dark for a reason. Kids know that life isn't all sweetness and light. They *know*. "In the new house I bought, there's a whole shelf of mermaid stories. Maybe we can explore them together."

"Okay. Even though mermaids aren't real."

"You don't believe in them, but I do." I think of Kit and my mother, of a pirate chest full of booty. I think of Dylan, who seemed to come to us out of the sea and took himself back into it.

Why am I thinking of all these things all of a sudden?

"Mum, that's just silly."

I point to my forearm, where mermaid scales shimmer against my skin. "I've always been part mermaid."

She shakes her head. "Tattoos don't make things real."

"I don't know about that."

"I do." She plucks a pair of forks from the drainer. "Dad said we're going to live in that house."

"Yeah. It'll take a while to get it ready, but that is the plan. You can have your own laboratory." I give the word the New Zealand pronunciation, with the emphasis on *bor*. "And there's a greenhouse."

"Really?" Her eyes light up, the way another girl's might over new shoes. "When can we see it?"

"Soon." I pluck the dish towel from her hands. "Go shower."

"Will you wash my hair?"

"Yes." She's only been doing it herself for a couple of months, and the results are uneven. "Yell when you're ready."

As I'm stacking plates back into the cupboard, my phone rings in my back pocket. The screen shows that it's my friend Gweneth. "Hey, what's up? Not canceling on me, are you?" We walk every Monday, Wednesday, and Friday right after the kids go to school. She's a stay-at-home mother with a vibrant mummy blog, so her hours are her own the same way mine are.

"No, but JoAnn can't make it. Do you want to hike Takarunga?"

JoAnn doesn't have as much time as the two of us, so we save more vigorous hikes for when she has to get to work early. We have to coordinate ahead of time because I like having a CamelBak for it, which I otherwise leave at home. "Love it."

In the background, a dog barks furiously, and she says, "See you at seven thirty, then! Cheers."

"Cheers."

As I finish up the kitchen, the dogs come tip-tapping in, the two who were orphaned when Helen died and my rescue, Ty, short for Tyrannosaurus Rex. He was named when Leo was in his dinosaur phase. He's a golden retriever mutt, overjoyed to have friends to play with.

"Outside, kids?" I ask, and they sweep their tails. Paris and Toby are a little lost. Paris is a black German shepherd, too thin, with the saddest eyes I've ever seen. She's a big dog with long, beautiful fur, and I bend down to stroke her as she walks by. She allows it, but I think her heart is heavy. I make a mental note to look up ways to help heal a grieving dog.

The other, Toby, is much smaller, maybe a Shih Tzu or Lhasa mix, in need of grooming but otherwise pretty stable. He's white and brown with cheery black eyes, and to my surprise, Simon has gone gaga over him. Already Toby knows he can jump up into his lap when he's sitting in his big chair.

A ripple of lightning edges along the horizon as I open the door, and I smell rain walking toward us over the water, carrying the scent of ocean and sky. "Better hurry, guys."

I stand in the doorway, breathing it in, the soft gathering twilight and the two-note song of a pair of tuis. A seagull sails on currents overhead. The water undulates in green and opal, with slight edges of purple. A storm is unmistakably moving in, and I look at the barometer in Sarah's little shed, but I don't know how to read the bubbles and weights.

Paris does her business, then comes back over to me, sitting on alert next to my leg. "You're a sweetheart, aren't you?" I rub her long ears, and she allows it, but she's scanning the perimeter in case of invaders. I might really fall for this dog. She reminds me of Cinder, the retriever mix we had when I was a child. It was Cinder who alerted us to the stranger at the door the night Dylan washed up at Eden.

A storm had lashed the windows that night too, and it whipped the ocean into a wild monster that Kit and I watched from our living room window in the little house that perched so precariously on the cliff. On clear days, you could see a hundred miles, at least according to my dad, and all of it was ocean. Ocean that changed minute by minute, ocean that changed color and texture, sound and mood. You could look at the ocean a thousand times a day in exactly the same spot, and it would never appear the same.

But that night, it was wild. Kit and I told stories to each other about shipwrecks. "In the morning, we should go down and see if anything washes up from the ships," I said.

"Booty!" Kit cried, her five-year-old fist punching the air.

Behind us, Cinder jumped up and barked his deep warning bark. My mom came out of the kitchen, wiping her hands. It was a slow night at Eden because of the weather, so we were home for once, although she wasn't cooking—why would she, with my father's stuffed squid to devour? One of the kitchen staff, a girl named Marie, had brought up a bowl of pasta with bread and herby olive oil, and we sat together eating it.

When my mother answered the door, a boy was there, soaked and shivering, his long hair stuck to his neck and forehead. His chambray shirt and jeans clung to him, and his face was bruised and bleeding, as if he'd washed overboard from a wrecked ship, or he was the ghost of a seaman who had drowned and didn't know it.

We read lots of stories like that, Kit and me. I read far above my age and loved reading to her from a battered copy of *The Big Book of Pirates*, filled with tales of shipwrecks and ghosts and mermaids seducing sailors to their deaths. Much of it was over our heads, but it fueled our imaginations for years.

My mother brought him inside and fetched towels and a mug of tea. Kit and I stared, captured by his beauty. He was barely a teenager, though at the time, he lied and said he was fifteen, so his skin still had the dewy sheen of boyhood, stretched over elegantly assembled cheekbones and jaw. His eyes were the color of abalone shell, silver and blue and hints of violet, as if he'd been born in the sea.

I whispered to Kit, "Maybe he's a merman."

My mother was not known for taking in strays, not cats or dogs or people, but she took to Dylan as if he were her own child. She shifted Kit to my bedroom so there was a place for him to sleep and gave him a job in the restaurant washing dishes. "You girls need to be nice to him," she said, tucking us in that night. "He's been through a lot."

"Is he a merman?" Kit asked.

My mother smoothed her brow. "No, sweetheart. He's just a boy."

A boy she took in and nurtured from that moment forward, as if he were a lost cat, with no explanation whatsoever.

Just a boy. For a long moment, standing beneath the lightning-lashed sky over Auckland, I think how small that phrase is. How true and untrue, all at once.

A thudding ache pulses in the center of my chest. What if my mother had called the police to report a runaway? What if he'd been sent to a foster home instead of taking root in our family the way he did?

Instead my mother simply lied to everyone and said he was her nephew from Los Angeles. No one ever questioned her, and in those days, my father let her have her way over almost anything.

The dogs, impatient with my woolgathering, swarm my legs and lick my fingers. I bring them in, then go wash my daughter's hair.

------ ⚭⚭ ------

Later, Simon is watching a movie, some kind of adventure through a jungle with lots of mud and things that bite and cut and a sturdy man leading the way. His favorite thing. He doesn't love to read, but he watches all the sci-fi and adventure movies that exist, and when he runs out, he calls up YouTube videos in the same realm.

I'm sitting next to him with my laptop, a blanket over my legs because it's gone quite cold. He's drinking a ginger beer and popping peanuts into his mouth every so often, while I have a cup of green tea that's probably cold. I only have it as company, really.

I'd been pinning ideas for Sapphire House to Pinterest, and then I found a bunch of recipes for feijoas, and now I'm knuckling down to look up more of Veronica's backstory.

My friend Gwen is enchanted with Veronica and has often regaled me and our friend Nan with stories about the Auckland legend. I've long been intrigued by her rise and tragic end. I feel a tangled connection to her attempt to make herself over, become someone new—and she was successful at doing so.

But like a female Icarus, she was punished for her moxie and died young.

On YouTube, I download the movie that launched Veronica's career. She'd been in Hollywood for several years and played many parts, mostly in the jungle-girl realm. But when sound arrived on the scene, Veronica was cast in the role of a vixen, unapologetically ambitious and beautiful, and the sparks flew between her and her costar. There's a famous kiss and a dress so sheer and clinging that she might as well have been naked.

Watching, I'm shocked at the liberal tone of the script and the saucy, tongue-in-cheek way Veronica played the part. Her body in the famous dress is incendiary—a slipping lacy bodice that gives the illusion of nipples, or is it that it's nipples giving the illusion of lace?—curvy hips, slim arms and waist.

The big surprise is the intelligence of both script and actress, plus the fact that this cheeky vixen actually wins at the end. It's as if someone turned the rule book on its head.

Clicking around, I find more info on the era—very short-lived, called Pre-Code. For a brief five years, between the establishment of the sound movie industry and the 1934 enforcement of the Hays Code, there were no morality guidelines, and moviemakers took full advantage. Dozens of movies were made, often with overtly sexual themes and often with women in roles that acknowledged their sexuality and their ambition.

It startles me that there was so much freedom of story, of power in women's hands, such a long time ago. For the space of a few breaths, I wonder how life would be different for women if those stories had been allowed, embraced. Even celebrated.

Veronica Parker, with her elegant long limbs and sexy voice, had made her name there. In five years, she'd made thirteen movies, nearly three a year, and she'd been paid handsomely for it, $110,000 a year. It sounds like a lot of money for the early thirties, Depression years, and I look up the equivalent to now, roughly $1.5 million a year. Clearly enough to build a beautiful house that she barely had a chance to live in.

Post Code, Veronica was not able to land parts in Hollywood as freely, and a director in New Zealand lured her home with promises of starring in a tragic romance, but the movie was never made. According to Wikipedia, the director, Peter Voos, was involved in dozens of scandals around women. His photo shows a handsome blond man with an arrogant brow. I can't find the reason the movie wasn't made, aside from "creative differences." Veronica found work in smaller parts, always as the vamp or dangerous Other Woman.

Curled in my blanket, I wonder how that felt for her, to rise to such heights and then fall out of favor when she was still so young and had so much to give. Melancholy creeps under my skin, and I close the laptop. "I'm off to bed," I say to Simon, and kiss his head. "Don't stay up too late."

"No, no. I'll be up soon."

I make a mental note to find some more of her movies and watch them. Maybe Gweneth will want to join me. She's going to flat-out faint when she finds out we bought Sapphire House.

Chapter Seven

Kit

Jet lag wakes me at four a.m., and I try for a time to go back to sleep, but it's no use.

The curtains are open. Office buildings stand between my balcony and the harbor, but the water lies in inky blackness between the edge of the downtown area and what seems to be an island on the other side. Little lights sparkle there, quiet middle-of-the-night kind of lights. I lie on my side and imagine my sister in a house out there, fast asleep, the same moon shining on her that is shining on me. I imagine that she gets up to go to the bathroom and stops at the window, drawn by my intense gaze, and looks out toward the central business district and my window, invisible amid all the others. She feels me. She knows I'm here.

When we were quite small, before Dylan arrived, we had our own rooms, but I was five when that ended, and up until I left for college, we shared. First the room that looked out over the ocean, when an open window meant the sound of the waves rocked us to sleep, then in the master bedroom of the apartment in Salinas. It took me a long time to get used to the emptiness of a room that contained only my breathing. One of the things I love about Hobo is that he is company at night, curling up against the crook of my knees or creeping onto my pillow to rest his face against my head, as if we are two cats. I ache for him at those moments, and I wonder where his mother went, what terrible things he endured before I brought him into my house and let him stay.

The thought of my cat makes me check the time. It's nearly eight a.m. in Santa Cruz. My mom will be awake by now. I punch her number as I pad toward the little strip of kitchen by the door and fill the kettle. On the other end, the phone rings so long I think she's not going to pick up. A familiar sense of disappointment and worry fills me; she has let me down and hasn't gone to stay with Hobo after all. I think of my poor cat, who trusts only me and was so battered by the world before I took him in, alone in my house—

At the very last minute, she answers, breathless. "Kit! I'm here!"

"You're there? At my house?"

A slight beat of quiet. She knows I don't trust her. "I'm here, Kit. I was just out in the backyard watering your plants and forgot I left my phone inside."

"Did Hobo come outside with you?"

"Oh, no. He hasn't even come out from under the bed."

My stomach squeezes. I can see his black face so clearly, his tufted toes. "You slept there?"

"Yes. I swear. He is eating and using the litter box when I leave. I think he peed on your tennis shoes, though. You left them by the door."

"He's probably claiming me. Keep your stuff in the closet."

"I am. We're fine, Kitten." The nickname is rare, and sweet enough. "Promise. I've had a cat or two in my life."

"Okay."

"It's only been a couple of days. He'll be fine."

"Just make absolutely sure he doesn't get out. I don't want him to come looking for me."

"I promise," she says in a very reasonable voice, and I realize I'm freaking out a little over a situation I can't control.

Shocking.

I take a breath and let it go. "Okay. I believe you."

"Thanks. Now tell me about everything. What's it like? Is it beautiful?"

I walk back to the sliding door and pull it open, letting in a waft of muggy air, and step out to the concrete balcony eighteen stories above the street. "It's amazing. The water and the hills and these strange trees—it's gorgeous. I'll send you some pictures later today."

"I'd love that." Instead of rushing in with questions or comments, she waits for me to keep talking, a listening trick she learned at AA that would have made my childhood ten thousand times better.

"I visited the nightclub site," I say. "It's hard to imagine what she would have been doing there, honestly. It seems like a club that was frequented by very young Asians, not middle-aged white ladies."

"Oh, she'd hardly be considered middle-aged."

I raise my eyebrows. "*If* she's really still alive, she's almost forty-three. Once you cross the line of forty, I think you have to admit to middle-aged."

She makes a dismissive noise, and I hear her light a cigarette. The cigarettes she thinks I don't know she smokes. "Well, what's the next step?"

"I honestly have no idea."

"Maybe you could take a picture around to the businesses in the area. Ask if anybody knows her."

"That's not a bad idea."

"Crime TV has its uses."

I laugh. "Well, if you come up with more tips, feel free to text. This is not exactly my forte."

"If anyone can find her, you can," she says.

"What if I don't?"

"Then you don't," she says firmly. "All you can do is try."

Across the immense miles, I hear a blue jay cawing in my backyard in California. It reminds me acutely that I am a very, very long way from home with no one but myself to keep me company. The loneliness of being unmoored from my little patch of geography, without the cat and—okay, I admit it—the mother I am used to seeing every day is stinging. "I will do my best," I say. "Please keep trying with Hobo. He needs love."

"I will. I bought him some tuna last night, and he did stick his nose out to get some."

I laugh. "Good idea. Thanks, Mom. I'll call you soon."

I settle cross-legged on the bed with a cup of tea on a tray. The cups in the apartment are tiny, and I will need to buy a mug somewhere today. I saw a Starbucks on my travels, but it seems kind of pathetic to visit a brand I know perfectly well when I'm seven thousand miles from home.

Opening my laptop, I bring up a map of the area around the night-club and scan the names of the shops in the buildings nearby. I'd already seen that it was an area of high tourist volume, with cafés and restaurants of all kinds and shops full of postcards and T-shirts. But off to one side is a shopping area that looks more upscale, the Britomart, and it seems to have a higher grade of restaurants, coffee shops, boutiques, and such things. Would that be Josie's kind of place?

It's hard to even imagine who she'd be now. As emotion—anger and fear and a weird sense of hope—starts to gurgle low in my gut, I don my scientific hat. How do you age a person who actually faked her own death and started fresh in a faraway land? Why did she do it? What has she done with the new life? How might she have spent the past decade and a half?

Sipping my tea, I watch a cleaning crew vacuum a floor full of offices in a building across the way. Ponder the possibilities.

One of the last times I saw Josie, she'd come to visit me in San Francisco. I was in med school, studying day and night, and she blew into town the way she always did, calling me on a pay phone from somewhere near the beach. "Can we get together?"

I close my eyes. It had been at least six or eight months since she'd been in town, but I didn't have time. She would want to party all night and eat everything in my meager kitchen and then go out to get more takeout and she'd expect me to pay, even though I had zero money and mostly ate baked potatoes with whatever crappy leftover veggies I could find on special at the supermarket, or else ramen noodles by the truckload. "I'm on rotations, Josie."

"Just a cup of coffee or something? It's been a while, Kit. I miss you."

"Yeah, me too," I said by rote, but I didn't. I'd missed her fiercely a hundred times in my life, but on those long, lonely days in Salinas after the earthquake, when she dived entirely into her dual addictions of surfing and getting high, I'd finally realized she was never really coming back to me. "I just have a lot of studying to do."

"That's cool. I get it. Med school, dude. I'm so proud of you."

The words plucked a string somewhere deep in my gut, and the reverberation released a thousand memories, all reminding me of the ways I loved her. I took a breath. "I'll meet you somewhere. Where are you?"

"That's okay, sis. Seriously. I get it. If you don't have time, you don't have time. I just wanted to say hi."

"Where are you going after this?"

"Um. Not sure. The waves are great in Baja, but I'm kind of over Mexico. Maybe Oz. A bunch of us have been talking about finding space on a freighter or something."

The more she talked in her raspy, beautiful voice, the more I wanted to hug her. "Look, you know what? I can spare a couple of hours."

"Really? I don't want to interfere with anything."

"You won't. It might be ages before you're back in San Francisco. I'll come to you. Where are you?"

We met at a burger joint not far from Ocean Beach. Some guy with a tangle of blond hair and at least three leather bracelets on his arm dropped her off. Josie tumbled out of the truck looking like a creature from a Charles de Lint novel, an urban sprite or fairy walking amid the mortals. She was deeply, deeply tan from her year-round surfing, her hair impossibly long, cascading over her lean arms and past her waist. She wore an India cotton peasant blouse over jean shorts and sandals, and every male from the age of six to ninety-six stopped to admire her. A backpack, battered but strong, hung from her left shoulder.

When she saw me, she broke into a run, stretching out her arms, and I found myself moving toward her, allowing her to fling her slim, taut body into my arms. We hugged hard. Her hair let loose the scent of a fresh breeze, a scent that made me ache to go surfing, to leave this grind I'd put myself in and run away to the beach with her. "Oh my God," she breathed in my ear, her arms fierce around my neck. "I miss you so damn much."

Tears stung my eyes. By then I had my guard up with her, but within twenty seconds, she swept me into her realm. "Me too," I admitted, and this time it was true. For one minute, two, I held on to her, dizzy with love and no thought, only her lean body against mine, her hair in my face. I stepped back. "You look really good."

"Fresh air," she quipped, then touched my face. "You look tired."

"Med school."

Inside the diner, still in touch with the seventies with its red Naugahyde booths and chrome appointments, we sat by the window and ordered cheeseburgers. "Tell me everything," she said, sipping Cherry Coke through a straw.

"Umm . . ." I floundered, trying to think of something that wasn't a grind of books, rotations, notes. I was third year, on the floor for the first time, and it was both exhilarating and devastatingly exhausting. "I don't know what to say. I'm working hard."

She nodded eagerly, and I noticed how red her eyes were. High, as ever. "Well, what did you do *yesterday?*"

"Yesterday." I took a breath, trying to remember. "I got up at four so I could get to the hospital in time to do early rounds; then we had rounds with our team, which is surgical, so I'm working with surgeons and residents. I scrubbed in for a gall bladder removal and an emergency appendectomy." I paused, feeling sleep, like a hook on a slow-moving train, start to reel me under. I blinked hard. Shook my head. "What else? I met a study group before dinner, then ate, then went home to read for rounds this morning."

Her eyebrows rose. "Dude. Do you ever get to sleep?"

I nodded. "Sometimes?"

"I can't believe you're going to be a doctor. I always brag about you."

"Thanks." They drop off the burgers, and all the salt and fat smells so good, I bend in and breathe it deep. "I'm freaking starving."

"Not much time to eat there either. Do you get to surf?"

"Sometimes. Not a lot, but it's okay. Eventually, this part will be done, and I'll be like everybody else."

She pointed a fry at me. "Except you will be Dr. Bianci."

I grinned. "I do love the sound of that." I arranged the pickles and tomatoes on top of the cheese, then added swirls of mustard. "What about you? Tell me about last week."

She laughed, that low, raspy laugh that made everyone lean in close. "Good one." She took a bite of her burger and nodded as she chewed, as if she were thinking about all the things she could tell me. She held her napkin in her lap primly, and in the action I saw my mother. "I bet you do more in a day than I do in a month." She dabbed her lips politely, making sure they were ketchup- and grease-free. "But actually, last week was bitchin' because we were chasing a hurricane up the coast, from Florida all the way to Long Island."

"Wow." I felt a ripple of envy. "Biggest waves?"

"Montauk. You'd love it there."

"Okay, you got me. I'm jealous."

"Yeah." She grinned that impish, charming, encompassing smile. White teeth but not perfectly straight because she should have had braces and my parents never got around to it. Neither of us saw a dentist until we were in middle school, and only then because Josie had a very bad molar, and Dylan had insisted they get her in to see someone.

"Have you ever considered surfing professionally?" I asked.

She stirred her straw around in her ice, gave me a half-tilted smile. "Nah. I'm not that good."

"Bullshit. You just have to focus, make that the center of everything."

She gave me a slow one-shoulder shrug, her mouth twisting into a wry dismissal. "No fun. I don't have your drive."

I ate my burger for a time, focusing there, on the food that wasn't from a box or bag.

"I'm so proud of you, Kit," Josie said again.

"Thanks."

"How's Mom?"

"Fine. You should go see her."

"Maybe." Another dismissive lift of one shoulder. "I'm not here for long."

Maybe I was jealous; maybe I missed her. Maybe it was a combination of both, but I said, "Are you just going to wander around your whole life?"

She met my gaze. "What would be wrong with that?"

"You need a job, a profession, something you can do to support yourself when—"

"When I'm old and ugly?"

"No." I scowled.

"I don't have your brains, Kit. I was a bad student, and no college is going to let me in, so basically I can suffer along at some pissant community college, or I can do odd jobs and surf and love my life."

"Do you love it?"

A flicker over her eyes before she lowered them. "Of course."

I didn't want to fight. "Good. I'm proud of you too."

"Don't say things you don't mean."

I ducked my head, and it was all nothing but polite until the end. She ate every bite on the plate, right down to the lettuce leaf, then blotted her mouth. Cloudy light fell through the window to her bright hair, the tips of her eyelashes. A part of me was suddenly three, leaning on her as she read aloud to me, and five, tucked into a sleeping bag next to hers under the shelter of a tent. The images made me ache. How much I missed her when she deserted me! How much I still did. I looked away, thought of my immunology test. Facts and figures, facts and figures.

"Do you ever think of what might have happened if Dylan never came?" she asked suddenly. "Or if the earthquake hadn't wrecked the restaurant?"

Her words slammed into a heavily fortified box in my heart. "I try to look forward."

"What if, though? What if Dad was still up there at Eden, cooking, and maybe Mom got her act together and we went home for weekends or holidays and Dad told jokes and—"

"Stop." I closed my eyes, an ache along the bottom of my lungs. "Please. I just can't."

Her face was haunted, adding luminosity to her cheekbones, depth to her dark eyes. "What would have happened to us without him?" She shook her head, turned those tortured eyes on me. "Our parents were horrible, Kit. Why did they neglect us like that?"

"I don't know." My words were hard, erecting a wall against the past. "I have to focus on the present."

Again, she ignored me. "Why couldn't we save Dylan?" When she turned that gaze on me, tears edged her lower lids, never quite spilling. "Don't you miss him?"

I clenched my jaw. Swallowed away my own grief. "Of course I do. All the time." I had to pause, bow my head. "But he wasn't savable. He was already too broken when he showed up."

"Maybe." Her voice broke slightly, going husky. "But what if things happened to make him take that last step? I mean . . ."

"What things, Josie?" I was both impatient and weary. She had gone over this subject a million times when we were teenagers. "He was always going to die young. Nothing pushed him over the edge except his own demons."

She nodded, dashed away a tear that dared fall, and stared out the window. "He was happy for a long time, wasn't he?"

I reach out and take her hand. "Yes. I think he was."

She clutched my hand tight, her head bowed, her hair falling in a curtain around her face. The obscuring mists of my emotion cleared, and I could see her objectively, as if she were a stranger who'd wandered into the ER, a too-thin young woman with dry skin and chapped lips. Dehydrated, I'd note, probably an addict. I wanted, suddenly, to take care of her.

"I miss all of it," I volunteered. "Dad and Dylan and Cinder." My voice grew croaky. "I swear to God, I miss that dog like a limb."

"Best dog ever."

I nodded. "He was." I shook my hair out of my face. "I miss the restaurant. The patio, the cover. Our bedroom." I take a breath. "Sleeping on the beach in our tent. That was the best."

"It was."

She ran a fingertip over the scar on her forehead. "The earthquake wrecked everything."

"I guess." A little burn of impatience edged my spine. "Dylan and Cinder were already gone."

"I know that. Why do you have to be so mean in the middle of something like this?"

"It's not mean. It's just reality." Facts and figures.

"Yeah, well, reality isn't always what you think it is. Sometimes things are more complicated than simple facts."

Like our parents. Like our childhood. Like the earthquake. "You weren't even there that day," I said, a rare moment of furious honesty. "I had to sit there on the edge of the cliff by myself for hours, while I knew Dad was probably dead down there. And all you ever seem to remember is that you got a cut head."

"Oh, Kit!" She grabbed both my hands. "Oh my God, I'm sorry. You're right. That must have been terrible."

I didn't take my hands away, but I closed my eyes so that I didn't have to look at her. "I know it was bad in Santa Cruz too, but—"

She slid out of her side of the booth and into mine, flinging her body around me. "I'm sorry. I'm so selfish sometimes."

The smell of her, the essence of Josie, unlike any other scent in the world, enveloped me, and I was lost in my love for her, my adoration, my fury. The hungry, lonely cells of my body drank it in for long minutes. Then I extracted myself.

"Life is always a mixed bag."

"I guess so."

"But I can't imagine who we'd be without Dylan. Can you?"

I didn't even want to. "It doesn't matter. It is what it is."

It was my turn to look away, out the window, to the promise of the ocean on the blank blue horizon. "I could really use a walk on the beach after this," I offered. "Maybe find some mermaid coins."

"That would be really lucky," she said.

That was the day we impulsively got our tattoos, sitting side by side at a tattoo parlor near Ocean Beach as twilight moved in.

I run my fingers over the tattoo. It's elegantly, delicately drawn, and I've never regretted it, though I've never done anything that impulsive before or since. Maybe I just wanted to be close to her again.

Lucky, I think now, sitting on my bed in Auckland, watching a band of light leak into the horizon. It wasn't like she'd had much, something I'd always been too self-righteous to see.

Josie. So beautiful. So lost. So smart. So doomed.

Who would the woman I saw that day in San Francisco have become? Will I find a party girl, somebody still surfing the world? She's pretty long in the tooth for that now, but I wouldn't put it past her. Or maybe she's found a way to be connected to her passion and work with it, like the women who opened a woman-centered surf shop in Santa Cruz. Or maybe she's just a pothead, smoking her life away.

I sip my tea, which is going cold. It's probably not the latter. At some point, she must have turned herself around or she wouldn't have survived. Her addiction had become so extreme by the last time I saw her that nothing short of a miracle would have saved her.

On the laptop, I bring up the image of her from the news. It's a surprisingly clear shot, and there's nothing dissipated or weary about that face at all. The haircut is expensive, sharp, or maybe just recent. Her face is not bloated, which tends to show up on long-term drinkers, and in fact, she doesn't look a lot older than she did fifteen years ago, which is classic Josie. She's still beautiful. Still lean.

Still herself.

Where am I going to find her?

I walk to the sink, dump the cold tea, fill the kettle again, and lean on the counter while it boils, my arms crossed.

In solving medical puzzles, I've learned to always, always go back to the actual known facts. A patient presents with something mysterious— start there. Stomach pain and rash. What did she eat? What has she been doing the past twenty-four hours? How old is she? Live alone? Eat with friends or family? Take a shower?

So I start where I am with Josie.

No. Scratch that.

Start with a fact: a blonde woman with a scar exactly like my sister's was filmed at the site of a nightclub fire five nights ago.

The kettle clicks off, and I pour boiling water over my tea bag in the tiny cup and wish for a mug that would last a little while before I putter back to the computer on the bed.

What time was the blonde woman filmed? I have to look that up and find the time stamp: ten p.m. New Zealand time, which would have been two a.m. my time. Just about right. I must have caught the news as the first reports were coming in.

Okay, what would have been open on a Friday night at ten p.m. in that area? Pretty much everything, I discover. All the restaurants, all the clubs and bars.

But again, facts. She is a woman of means, judging by the haircut and the expensive sweater. Maybe she had met friends . . . I scroll around the map, looking at possibilities to add to my list. One establishment leaps out at me, an Italian restaurant in Britomart, the upscale shopping area next to the harbor. I send the directions to my phone. I'll go down there and show the photo around. Maybe somebody will have seen her. Even better, maybe they know her. Maybe she's a regular.

But nothing is open until much later. It's just now gone seven, and I'm restless. The building has a pool. I'll head down there, do some laps, and then come back and get ready to go out.

Chapter Eight

Mari

I'm frying eggs from Sarah's hens when the earthquake hits. It starts low, that slight disorientation you get that feels like maybe you turned too fast or lost your footing, and then the sound, the tinkle of glasses in the cupboard. Urgently, I turn off the gas and shout for my family, running for the door to open it and let the dogs out. The birds are hushed as I dash outside.

For a little while, I think I'm going to be okay this time. It's not violent, just a slow, easy tumbler, more of an aftershock than quake.

The kids are still inside. I hear something rattling and the thud of something falling over in the shed, and I think I should go check it out, but I'm plastered to the trunk of the palm tree, my cheek pressed hard into the bark, my arms straining.

I gauge the intensity of it from long experience, not a six but maybe in the high-four, low-five range. Enough to knock things from grocery shelves, tools from the shelves in the shed. I wonder where the epicenter is, who is getting it now. Maybe it's offshore, and the damage will be minimal. There have been some substantial earthquakes in the country since I arrived, the worst being the two back-to-back that nearly destroyed Christchurch, and another just a couple of years ago on the South Island near a little tourist town. Simon mourned Kaikoura, a place he'd visited a lot as a child. I'd never been there, but Simon said the destruction had been very bad indeed. The city is recovering, finally, but it has taken a long time.

Auckland feels the quakes, but they're not centered here—it's always somewhere else. Instead, they cheerfully predict a volcano will someday incinerate the city, but it's the kind of thing you can't believe will ever happen.

Unlike the earthquakes that remind us, over and over, that they can do whatever they want. The earth finally stills, but I'm still clinging to the trunk like a five-year-old.

"Mari!" Simon yells, and I hear him running. His hand, that big solid hand, covers my upper back, but I still don't let go, not until he peels one arm, then the other, off the tree and settles them around his waist. "You'll be right," he says, a peculiarly New Zealand phrase. "No worries."

I smell the sharpness of clean cotton and his skin below. His chest is as solid as a wall, his body the thing that will save me, always. Sarah and Leo are suddenly beside me too, their hands on my arms, my hair. "It's okay, Mummy. You'll be right."

Enfolded in their love, I can take a breath, but they don't rush me. "I'm sorry, you guys. I wish I could get over this. It's so silly."

"No worries, Mum," Leo says.

"We're all afraid of things," Sarah adds.

I snort and look at her over my arm. "Not you."

"Well, not me, but most everybody."

My chuckle eases the rigidness of my body, and I force myself to straighten, to let go of my husband, to kiss my children's heads, one, two. "Thank you. I'm good."

Simon's hand lingers on my upper back. "Get yourself a cup of tea. I'll finish breakfast."

I used to protest, but a counselor finally told me that the more I resisted the emotions of my PTSD, the worse it would get. To overcome it, I have to be present with it. So I head inside and pour a fresh cup of tea. The screen of my memory flashes with images from the earthquake that gave me the scar on my face—the noise, the screams, the blood everywhere from the wound on my head and the wound in my belly. All of it.

I stare into my cup of milky tea. On the surface, my kitchen window is reflected in a white rectangle interrupted by the line of pots along the bottom. I force myself to take slow, even breaths. Same in as out, one-two-three *in*, one-two-three *out*, and slowly my trembling eases. The voices of the children, lilting up and down, smooth the gooseflesh on my arms. I sigh, letting go.

Simon, frying bacon, a bibbed apron around his body, gives me a smile. "Better?"

"Yep. Thanks."

We eat normally, and Simon loads the children in the car and turns to me. His gray eyes are filled with concern as he brushes hair away from my face. He knows I suffered through a massive earthquake, though I lied about which one it was. "Take the day off."

"I'm hiking with Gweneth and then meeting Rose at Sapphire House to make some more notes."

"The walk will be good." His palm cups my cheek. "Go to the CBD and visit the cat café or something."

I give him a grin. "Maybe. I really think I'm all right."

He presses a kiss to my forehead, lingering a second longer than usual, then squeezes my shoulder. "I've got the swim fund-raiser tonight, don't forget. The kids and I will be late."

Our division of labor means I don't have to participate in the swim stuff, which I find stultifying—the long, long hours; the drives to various places; the chitchat with all the other parents. I know women knit and read and whatever, and I do show up for the big meets, but Simon loves it madly, and I don't. In return, I do a much larger share of housework and laundry and shopping, which he loathes.

But I *had* forgotten about the meet tonight, and a little knot sticks in my throat as I lift my hand and wave them off, the three of them in a single car, the only things in the world that really matter to me. Maybe I'll call my friend Nan, see if she wants to meet for dinner in the CBD.

A good plan.

I met Gweneth on the ferry. I was pregnant with Leo, irritable in the summer heat, tired of Christmas in the summer, suddenly longing for family now that I'd be adding to it. I missed my father, weirdly, after so long. I'd found myself imagining how my mother's eyes or sister's mouth might look on a baby, if I would see my family in the hands or laughter of a child. I even grieved the fact that my mother would not be there when the baby was born, but perhaps all women feel that way. Pregnancy made me so emotional, in fact, that it frightened me. I constantly worried about the dire things in the world, what might befall a child I loved so intensely even before it was born.

Simon had gently pointed me toward the city and an exhibit on the Bloomsbury Group, which both eased and stimulated me, just as he'd known it would.

Gweneth sat down next to me on the ferry, a tall, slim woman with a stylish air, and offered me an ice cream. "Hokeypokey," she said. "Can't go wrong."

"As far as I'm concerned, no ice cream goes wrong." I paused. "Except coffee."

"You're American!"

"Canadian, actually."

She narrowed her eyes. "That's what you all say, though, isn't it?"

I laughed and stuck to my made-up story. "I grew up on the west coast of British Columbia. Vancouver Island."

"Hard to take the island out of the women," she said, nodding. "I saw you at the exhibit. Which one is your favorite?"

"Vanessa, completely. That earth mother vibe. I want to go live in her farmhouse. You?"

"Duncan. I'm madly in love with him, of course. I know exactly why Vanessa loved him." She licked her ice cream. "I've been to that farmhouse. You can feel her in every room. I wrote a dissertation on the farmhouse itself, as a design idea."

I fell right under her spell. We talked art and artists, then books and writers, all the way back to our respective homes, hers only four blocks away from mine, and we've been fast friends ever since.

This morning, she's waiting for me in our usual spot, near the water. Her long blonde hair is pulled back in a high ponytail, and she's wearing a tank and NorShore leggings that show off her long, lean figure. "Earthquake this morning—did you feel it?" she asks.

I give a curt nod. No one outside my family knows how badly I react to tremors. "Did you hear where it was centered?"

"Offshore." She gestures at the water sudsing restlessly, splashing hard against the land.

"Good."

"Mm." We set off at a brisk pace, hands swinging. Sometimes we can walk a long way without talking, but today my news is so momentous, I can't wait. "So we bought a new house."

"Already! The last project was only finished last week."

"Right. But Simon heard through the grapevine that Veronica Parker's sister died."

She stops dead, her mouth open. "No."

I raise my eyebrows. "Yes. You are looking at the new owner of Sapphire House."

"You're joking." Her face is both blank and blazing.

"No. It's done. He bought it outright."

"Good God. He's even wealthier than I thought."

I take her upper arm and move her body toward the trail that circles up a mountain on the north head of this finger of land. "His father still owns great gobs of land."

"Oh my God!" she cries. "You know I love her *so much*. You have to take me inside!"

"Of course. I want your help."

"When can we go? Not today. I have tons of work to do. But this weekend?"

"Yes. Absolutely. I told the kids we could go over there too. You can come with us."

"Are you flipping it?"

"No." I pause as we start walking up the hill. The sun is bright and hot on my shoulders. "We're going to live there."

"No, you can't!" Gweneth flings her arms up. "I need you here."

"It'll take a while."

"Oh, but then you'll be way over in Mount Eden, and I'll never see you anymore."

"No. We'll make a date and meet in some fab coffee shop in every neighborhood in Auckland once a month."

She takes a sip of water from her bottle. "All right. And you'll have to have grand parties in that house."

"I will. I promise." We start to climb seriously and focus on our breath while we acclimate.

"Hey, hey, can we bring it down a notch?" I gasp.

"Sorry." She slows. "We should have a welcome party or something."

I take a long gulp from my CamelBak. "That sounds like fun. I'm not sure when we'll fit it in, but we can try."

"I know!" She gives me a wide-eyed glance. "When did everything get so busy? I was never so busy when I worked."

"You didn't have children. Each child takes approximately forty-eight hours per day."

"Ah. That's what it is. No one told me that."

We hike in silence for a while. To our right stretch the harbor and the irregular coastline of the city. To the north is Rangitoto, an uninhabited volcanic island popular with tourists. In the far distance stretches a line of mountains meeting the sea, the whole scene painted in blues—blue water, blue mountains, blue skies. I never thought I would find a place more beautiful than the northern California coast, but this is outrageous. "Amazing. I never get tired of that view."

"That's why I never leave. I wanted to as a girl. Go to Paris and New York and all those places. But I visited, and none of them matched this."

I was luckier than I could have expressed to have washed up here. It was all blind luck, ridiculous timing, a good decision made at a moment of crisis. My throat tightens at all that I would never have known.

And right behind it, a subtle worry crawls down my neck again—that television camera, right on my face the night of the club fire. I had been in the CBD with Nan and was headed back to the ferry when I saw the news crews. Before I registered what was going on, I stared right into it for the space of three heartbeats.

Careless, but honestly—how many news events happen on an average day? Not even a cataclysmic nightclub fire would spend much time in the spotlight.

At the top of the headland, we pause briefly, leaning on a bunker built in WWII, and catch our breath. It's one of the best views I know of anywhere—the islands and Rangitoto, the skyscrapers of the CBD, the quaint tumble of villas along the Devonport seafront.

"We are so lucky," Gweneth said.

"Yes." I bump her shoulder. "We have each other."

"Sisters," she says, flinging an arm around me. "Forever."

No one will ever be my sister except Kit, but I can't bear a life without close female friendships. "Sisters," I agree, and lean my head on her shoulder, looking east across the water to where my sister lives. For a faint, foolish moment, I wonder if she is looking toward me too, across time, across the miles, somehow sensing that I am still alive.

Chapter Nine

Kit

I ride the elevator down to the eighth floor. It's still very early on a Friday morning, so there aren't many people about—it's between the crack-of-dawn, before-work crowd and the post-school-run moms. The area is nearly empty, only one person swimming laps.

The pool is wildly inviting, full Olympic length, the water a rich turquoise, maybe three lanes wide. Windows look out to the high-rise-building forest, and I'm cheerfully anticipating a good swim as I kick off my flip-flops. The man in the pool is swimming vigorously, powerfully, and comes up for air at the far end where I'm standing.

Damn.

Of course it's Javier.

"Of all the gin joints in all the world," I say.

"Pardon?" He gives the word its Spanish intonation as he wipes water from his face. A face, I note with some despair, that is just as fabulous as it was yesterday. Maybe even better.

"Never mind," I say, and pick up my towel. "I won't bother you."

He easily hauls himself out of the water and stands there with wet skin and powerful shoulders and modest swim shorts still showing a lot. "No, no, please. I'm nearly finished. You can have the pool."

"Stay. It's plenty big enough for both of us."

"Sure?"

I feel like an idiot. "I'm sorry about last night."

A twitch of his shoulders. He gestures to the water. "A race?"

"That's not fair. You've warmed up."

"Warm up, then." He sits on the side of the pool, folds his hands.

Light trickles over his skin, and I look away, cast off my wrap, and braid my hair, knowing that he's looking at all my parts. The suit is a one-piece designed to contain my chest and modestly cover my butt, but it's not exactly a garment that leaves much to the imagination. Securing my braid, I slide into the water. "Oooh," I sigh. "Ozone." I dive under the surface of the silky pool and kick my way half the length before I come up for air, swim hard to the end, and turn back to the start.

He's still sitting on the side. His legs are covered with black hair. "Impressive."

"You can't just sit there and watch," I protest. "You have to swim."

"Let's swim, then," he agrees, and slides back into the water himself, taking off without warning.

So we swim. Laps, mostly. I'm conscious of his skin, only an arm's length away. I'm conscious of my own skin, swept by the water. And then, as always, I forget anyone else and the problems of the day and meld with the water, moving easily, rhythmically, the world forgotten. I don't even remember learning to swim, any more than I remember learning to walk.

He stops before I do, hooking his elbows backward over the wall, his hair slicked back. I keep swimming, but then I'm worried he'll leave before we have a chance to talk, which is backward from what I wanted last night. But maybe for once I'm going to go with what I actually feel instead of what I think I should.

When I lap back, I come up and pause. "Are you leaving?"

"Do you want me to?"

I shake my head.

"There is a spa pool over there," he says, and points to a door going outside. "I will wait there if you like."

"Yes, please."

He doesn't smile, and neither do I. I lean back into my stroke and do a few more laps before I give in to the lure of him and climb out, wrapping a big towel around my waist, which is ridiculous, because then I just take it off.

The spa pool is protected, but it is outside, with views of the office buildings around us. I drop my towel on the chair. "How is it?" I ask.

"Quite good."

I step into the hot, swirling water and sink down, letting it cover me to my neck. He sits on a higher ledge, and I can't help admiring his well-shaped arms, the black hair on his chest. He's ever so slightly overweight, carrying the extra right over his belt line, which makes me like him more—the sign of a man who relishes life.

Or travels a lot, I think, remembering that he said he'd been on the road too much.

He doesn't speak, only dabbles his hands over the water.

Fair enough. "Sorry I bolted last night," I say.

His dark eyes rest on my face, and he lifts an eyebrow in question.

I can't hold the eye contact and look down at my hands, floating in the blue water. I shake my head. "I don't know."

"Mm."

"Look, it was stupid, and I'm sorry. Can we start fresh?"

He turns his lips down in consideration. "Okay." Offers a hand. "My name is Javier."

I laugh. "Not all the way at the beginning."

"Did you like my song?"

"You have a beautiful voice."

"Thank you." He slides deeper into the water and lets his feet rise, the toes poking up into the air. It seems strangely revealing. "Perhaps one day you can hear more than one song."

I give him a wry smile. "Maybe so."

"How long will you be here in Auckland?"

"I'm not sure, really." I take a breath and find myself telling the truth. "I'm sort of on a mission—to find someone."

"Not a lover, I don't think." His toes disappear beneath the surface.

"No. Not at all. My sister."

"Did she run away?"

I sigh. "It's a very long story."

"This is your sister who died?"

I forgot I told him that. "Yes." I give the answer a shortness that conveys my unwillingness to add more.

He nods, his eyes fixed on my face as his hands swirl over the water, graceful, strong. Beautiful hands graced with square nails. "Will you look for her today?"

A trickle of water makes its way down his cheekbone, slides along his mouth. I want to put my open palms on his bare shoulders. "Yes. I found some leads. But I probably won't be busy with it all day."

He smiles at last, and beneath the water, his foot brushes mine. "What if I help you look, and then you come with me on a sightseeing tour?"

I think of not having to spend the day entirely by myself. "All right. I'd like that."

"Do you want to know what we will see?"

With a smile, I shrug. "Whatever it is, I've never seen it before."

His smile is generous, considering. "Nor I."

Suddenly there is a sway, a splash, and I feel off-kilter. It's not my imagination—Javier tilts toward me, a hand reaching behind me for the lip of the pool.

I lift my head, looking for things that could fall on us; then I'm clambering out of the spa and heading for open space. "Come on."

"What—?"

The sway, not terrible but unmistakable, comes again. "Earthquake," I say, and hold out my hand.

He wastes no time, and we hurry out to the open passageway that leads back to the pool. "Is it dangerous?"

"No." I rest my hands on the wide stone ledge. Sunlight floods the area. "Very minor, but you don't want to be under anything that could be shaken loose."

He looks up, but there's nothing above us, only sky. The sway is less remarkable here, out of the water, and soon it's gone. "That's that," I say.

"How did you know it was an earthquake?"

"I live in northern California. They're part of the landscape."

"Have you ever experienced a big one?"

I think of the cove, scattered with the decayed ruins of what had once been Eden and our home. "Yes, unfortunately. The Loma Prieta in '89." Then add the way everyone remembers it, "San Francisco."

"How old were you?"

"That's an odd question." He's leaning one hip on the ledge, and his hair has begun to dry in swooping waves. "Twelve. Why?"

"Such a thing will leave a mark, no? More or less, depending on your age."

It was, almost certainly, the worst day of my life, but being twelve had nothing to do with it. "Really. And what does my being twelve say?"

"That it was terrible. But your face says that."

I touch my jaw, my mouth. "Does it?"

Finally he touches me, just his fingertips against my cheek, then away. "Yes."

Things I don't think about tumble out of their boxes—the rumbling, the sound of breaking glass, my urgent dive for the door. Lying flat on the ground in the open, counting seconds.

I swallow, then take one step closer and rest my palm on his chest. He doesn't bend down to kiss me, as I had expected, but only presses his hand over mine, holds it there. "Life is capricious, no?"

I think of getting to my feet when the shaking stopped to find nothing left, the house in ruins. The absolute silence told me what I knew instantly. Still, I cried out my father's name. Called until I had no voice left. Called until darkness fell.

I nod.

He is the first to step away. "Shall we go?"

I shower the pool from my skin and tame my hair with product, drawing it away from my face in the vain hope that it will behave for a few hours. To protect my skin from the harsh sun—New Zealand has some of the highest melanoma rates in the world—I bring a broad-brimmed hat. It's too hot for long sleeves, so I'm wearing the sundress again, and I slather on heavy-duty sunscreen. Carrying a rattan bag, I head down to meet Javier in the lobby.

This time I'm the first to arrive, and I wait by a bank of windows overlooking the square. Young people, mostly students by the look of them, sit in the sunshine, reading or talking in clumps of two or three. The girls have a wide array of color in their hair—sometimes silvery with purple ends or ombre shades of watermelon or leaves. One girl has streaks in a rainbow array, and she wears oversize sunglasses and bright-red lipstick.

It seems like a long time ago that I felt that young, so dewy. If I ever did. At twenty, I was buried in textbooks, working two jobs to stay afloat. It didn't leave a lot of time for lazing around in the sun. I'm piercingly envious for a moment.

"You look lovely," Javier says nearby.

I swing the red skirt. "I only have the one."

He touches his chest. "This is one of two." It's a soft gray button-up with very thin blue stripes. Expensive. "I cannot bear to bring more than a carry-on."

"I'm not that efficient," I admit as we head toward the elevators to go down to street level. Inside, I smell his cologne, a continental touch I'm unused to.

"I have become so over the years. Two good shirts, jeans, slacks, one pair of shoes, maybe a pair of sandals."

The door slides open, and we head outdoors to the heavy day. I slide my sunglasses down my nose. "Whew. I'm not used to heat," I say. "It's not this hot in California, at least not by the ocean."

"I like California," he says. "The people are friendly."

"You've been there?"

"Many times." He's dropped his own sunglasses over his eyes, very black aviators that give him a glamorous air. "It's beautiful. Where do you live?"

"Santa Cruz."

He frowns slightly.

"Just south of San Francisco?"

"Ah. So you stayed there, even after the earthquake."

"I've never lived farther than sixty miles from the hospital where I was born. Native Californian."

"Is your family there?"

"My mother. She's staying with my cat."

"Not the cat with her?"

I laugh softly. "He's afraid to leave my house, so she came to him."

"That's very kind of her."

I look up at him, recognizing the truth. "It is."

A sign alerts me to the shopping area I'd been hoping to find. "I think this is it. How much time do we have?"

"As long as you need. There is no hurry."

"I just want to duck inside here and ask around."

"Of course."

In a bar of shade, I pause to pull out my phone and then find a still I lifted from the video of the nightclub fire. I show it to Javier.

"This is your sister?"

"Yep." I look down at it, feeling butterflies flutter around in my gut.

"You're very different."

I snort slightly, a very unladylike sound I wish I could take back. "Understatement of the year."

He cocks his head, and a swath of light undulates over the waves in his hair. "How so?"

"She was tiny. I'm tall. She loved—loves—metaphor, and I love facts." I look up at the various shops. Boutiques with seven dresses hanging in rows. It's hard to imagine Josie ever shopping for clothing like that. "She was a complete hippie. I'm a doctor." An upscale florist. Several restaurants. "She was outgoing, and I was introverted." I don't say, *She was beautiful. I am not,* but that might have been one of the more obvious things. Josie and Dylan and my mother were beautiful. I was the sturdy, sensible one.

Not that I minded, honestly, except for that small, heady stretch of time when I fell in love with James in high school. Otherwise I was relieved to be free of the demands of beauty. It didn't seem to serve any of them particularly well, after all.

A cluster of professional women passes, wearing stockings and pencil skirts. The stockings surprise me, especially on such a warm day, and I stare after them, trying to remember the last time I wore a pair of stockings for any reason. Do people even do that anymore in the US?

Again I scan the storefronts. Javier waits.

For a second, I feel anxious and resistant and overwhelmed. Why am I on this ridiculous errand? And what am I going to do if I find her? The thought makes me feel queasy.

"Do you wish to show her photo around?"

I take a breath. "I guess I do."

He takes out his phone and shoots a photo of my screen. "I will try the shops across the way, yes?"

"Sure."

He heads across the way, and I weave in and out of the boutiques and shops on my side. At the end of the row, he joins me, and together we approach the Italian restaurant I spied earlier on Google Maps. I pause, faintly nervous, to glance at the menu attached to an elegant stand, and my mouth waters a little. "Ooh, they have Sicilian-style cannoli."

"What makes them Sicilian?"

"Ricotta instead of cream inside. So good."

A tall, tidy woman with a shiny fall of copper hair stands at the open-air hostess stand, getting things ready for the day. As I approach, she gives me a bright smile. "We're not quite ready to serve, but I'd be happy to take your name."

"No, thank you. I'm looking for someone."

"Oh?" Her hands still on the napkins she's folding.

I hold up the phone with my sister's face. "Have you seen this woman?"

Her face smooths. "Yes. She's a regular, but I don't think I've seen her for a while."

A bolt of shock runs through my body, like lightning. *She's alive.* "Do you happen to know her name?" She cocks her head, and I realize too late that it's odd that I have her picture but don't know her name. "I know her as Josie, but I think her real name is something else."

"Hmm." Her face shutters slightly, and if she does know the name, she's not saying it. "I'm afraid I don't know."

"Okay." I tuck the phone in my pocket, pushing down both disappointment and relief. "Can you tell me if there was anything happening around here the night of the nightclub fire? Like an event or a concert or something?"

Her lips go pale. "Was she in the fire?"

"No, no. Sorry. I just wondered what else might have been going on."

She glances at Javier, and something I can't quite read crosses her face—admiration, recognition, startlement. Her spine straightens even more. "I can't think of anything."

"Thank you." I glance up at Javier and nod once. "Let's go sightseeing."

"Sure?" He touches the small of my back as we depart, and I see him nod at the woman.

We head for the wharf. "Was that like your father's restaurant?" he asks.

"It has some things in common. The cannoli dessert, the fresh mozzarella, pasta with squid ink, and there's something"—I look over my shoulder—"about the way it looks. I think if my sister knew about it, she would probably like it."

He nods and doesn't press me for more information. It's only a couple of blocks to the wharf, and we duck into the comparative cool-ness of the building. "What would you like to do?" Javier asks as we stand, side by side, looking up at the offerings.

I'm deeply relieved to have something besides my sister to focus on. None of the names has any meaning to me, and I half shrug. "I have no idea."

"Shall we do everything?"

Recklessly, I say, "Why not?"

He pays for the tickets, so I buy us some coffees in paper cups and a couple of pastries from a vendor. Settling on a white bench in the ferry building, I sip a flat white and nibble an apple Danish, watching Javier make a tidy diorama with a napkin spread wide on the bench, his coffee at one side, his pastry in the middle. After the morning swim and walk, I'm starving, and I watch people milling around talking to each other, the irritated kids hauled by their parents, tourists from ev-erywhere. A line of people dressed in good hiking gear are lining up to board for an island volcano. The boat bobs gently.

"I love ferries," I say.

"Why?" He's hung his sunglasses from the placket of his shirt and admires the flaky edges of his pastry. A finger of sunlight makes a shadow fan of his eyelashes across his cheekbone, exaggerating their length. He takes a lusty bite.

"I don't know," I admit, and think about it, naming the images as they pop up in my mind. "The stairs. Those tidy rows of chairs. The open air on sunny days." I sip my coffee. "It's just being on the water, really. I always like that. In my family, we always say we can't sleep if we can't hear the ocean."

"It is a soothing sound," he agrees. "I like ferries because you climb in, and the boat takes you where you're going. No bothering with maps and cars. You can read."

"I thought all men liked driving."

An expressive shrug. *Not so much,* it says, *but what can you do?* "It's a modern necessity, but it brings no pleasure most of the time."

I incline my head, trying to guess what he drives. "Huh. I would have imagined you flying down some twisty road in a convertible."

A very small grin lifts one side of his mouth. "Romantic."

"Sexy." I hold his gaze. "Like one of those sixties movies of the guy navigating the coast of Monaco."

He laughs. "I'm afraid I would disappoint you."

I lean back. "So what *do* you drive?"

"Volvo." A small translucent square of sugar falls on his thumb. "How about you? Or shall I guess?"

"You won't get it."

"Mm." He plucks the sugar from his hand and tucks it in his mouth, narrowing his eyes. "I don't know American cars so well. A Mini?"

I laugh. "No, but they are cute. I drive a Jeep."

"A Jeep? Like an SUV?"

"Not exactly. I need room to take my surfboard to the beach, so—" I scan the horizon. "It's practical."

"Ah. Surfing." He looks a bit perplexed.

"What?"

"I have to think how to say it."

I smile, knowing what the struggle is. "Take your time."

"I thought only teenagers surfed?" he says, instead of saying, *Aren't you too old for that?*

"Well done." I crumple my napkin and drop it in the paper bag they gave us, offer it to Javier. "I started surfing when I was seven years old." I think of Dylan standing behind me on a longboard, his hands in the air beside me in case he needed to catch me. He never did. "It's in my blood."

"Is it dangerous?"

"Not really. I mean, I guess it is a little, especially if you don't know what you're doing, but I do. Have you ever tried?"

"I have never had the opportunity." He leans backward against the bench, one arm along the top, the fingers of his right hand warm behind my shoulder blade. "What do you like about it?"

I cross my legs, lace my hands around my knee, and look toward the water. I think of my palms skimming the water, the taste of salt on my lips, the board shivering under my feet, Dylan offering encouragement— *there you go, that's right, you can do it.* "It's exhilarating to get a wave just right, ride it a long way. You don't think about anything. Just that."

For a moment, he's silent, his eyes resting on my face. His fingers touch my back, edge along the bone, and it sends an alert through my body, 100 percent chemistry, which flickers and brightens the longer he simply looks at me.

"What?" I say at last.

"Nothing." He smiles. "I like to look at you."

I smooth a hand over my hair, liking his regard but also slightly tongue-tied, which is unlike me. I'm often the pursuer in these things, since men can be intimidated by my profession, my height. I drop my hand to my lap and look back at him. At his brow and his powerful nose and the opening of his shirt, where I can see his throat. In the sunlight, I reassess his age upward. At first, I thought he was early forties, but now I think it's more. Midforties. Maybe even slightly older.

It doesn't matter. As I look, the light touch on my back combines with the steady, clear regard to give me a sense of expansion, as if the field of my energy is stretching out, trying to find the edge of his. It warms me, and I think of that study that says you can fall in love with someone by looking into their eyes for thirty seconds.

I don't fall in love, but I think I'll remember this moment long years from now. His hand moves, open palm against my neck, thumb light against my earlobe.

Who knows how long we stay like that, both of us captured? A voice announcing our ferry brushes against it but doesn't kill it, like a spiderweb still clinging to fingers. He takes my hand as we board, and I'm glad of the touch, grounding me, connecting me to him, him to me.

"Upstairs?" he asks.

For one moment, I think of how bad my hair will be when the wind and humidity have their way, but I nod, and we take our seats in the open air, in the bright sunshine of New Zealand. As naturally as if we've been together a hundred years, Javier picks up my hand and laces his fingers through mine. And even though it's a little sweaty and I'm not really the hand-holding type, I let him.

Chapter Ten
Mari

Rose and I have flipped six houses together. She's a sturdy, busty black-haired millennial who wears her hair very short. Her uniform is T-shirts with ironic sayings, jeans, and vintage Doc Martens. Her boyfriend wears a man bun in his curly hair and a thick beard that obscures what I am not sure is a particularly interesting face, but he's good to her, and that's really the only thing that matters.

We meet at Sapphire House midmorning, and she's squealing and oohing all the way through, much the way I did, but she's even more knocked out over the wood than I am. Her father runs a lumberyard, and she knows every variation of wood available in New Zealand and then some. With awe, she traces the inlays along the walls of the foyer and names the varieties of wood in the stairs, the banister, the framing, the doors. "My dad'll go blimmin' mad for this." Her accent is as thick as they come, peppered with Maori slang, and when she talks quickly, I have a hard time deciphering her words.

"I thought of him," I say. "I wonder if he knows anyone who does tile work."

"I reckon he does."

Our process is smooth after so many jobs. She starts work in the first room to the left of the front door and heads clockwise around the main floor with a stack of Post-its and duct tape in three colors, moving with surety through the rooms, tagging everything in a pattern we've developed over the years. She has a master's degree in furniture design, and I can trust her to know the difference between junk and antiques worth exploring; this particular era is her favorite. She makes furniture herself in a shared studio space with a handful of other artists, and they sell a lot of it in Napier, where an earthquake nearly leveled the city in 1931. When it was rebuilt, it was all done in the Art Deco style, which was very up-to-the-minute, thus the inhabitants of the town wanting furniture. Eventually I'm going to lose her to the furniture, but for now she's invaluable.

While she works on the main floor, I head upstairs with a kit of the same materials and start in the bedroom. Settling my box of tape and Post-its on the bed, I open the French doors along the balcony and then step out to admire the view—my view. The sea is dark and unfriendly this morning, waves slapping the shore almost petulantly, and I smell a storm. I am as close to the sea here as I was in our house by the cove, where the window of the bedroom I shared with Kit hung practically over the cliff. If you stuck your head out, you could see straight down the rocks below, the little cove with its stairs off to the right, the harsh rocky shore curving into infinity to the left, all the way to Big Sur and, farther still, Santa Barbara and then LA.

I used to miss that coast, my coast, but New Zealand has cured me. It wasn't part of the plan—there wasn't really much of a plan—but it sometimes feels like a hand of fate brought me here, to the green mountains and the endless coastline of an island, where I would meet a man who was unlike any other I'd ever known, and fall in love with him, and marry him, and have his children. With that man, my Simon, who bought this house because I love it, I will sleep in this room with the French doors flung open, listening to the sea.

A slight, faint aftershock rumbles through the earth, moving my body in an almost infinitesimal sway. My hands grip the railing, hard, and I wonder if the house has any protection from earthquakes.

A flashback overtakes me, a sound memory—the beeping of alarms and water rushing where it shouldn't and people making a song, soprano screaming and tenor moans of fear and deep, bass cries of pain. I smell smoke and leaking gas.

It fades relatively quickly, just a flash and gone. All these years, you'd think I'd finally get over the PTSD. But it doesn't seem to work like that. My therapist says I spent so much time drinking and drugging away my trauma that it's just going to take a long time to work through it all.

And even she knows only the tip of the iceberg. I was on a sad and terrible errand that day, awash in scalding shame mixed with grief, emotions too large for the child I was, though I thought myself so adult.

A lot had already been lost by the day of the earthquake, but the way it completed the wreckage of our lives—Kit's, my mother's, and mine—marked us all irretrievably. Sometimes I miss them most when I want to touch that reality, that day standing on the bluff, looking down at the collapsed heap of timber and concrete on the beach, all of us clustered together, howling.

Enough.

In the bedroom, I get to work. The bed is covered with a silk spread that is too fine to be original. I take a photo of it and then the bed, pulling back the spread to look at the mattress, ancient and unimaginably dusty.

From my kit, I take a notebook and scribble information as I shoot photos. The closets are a dream, enormous, as would be needed by a movie star and all her dresses. Where have they gone? I make a note on another page to look up the history of Veronica's death and the disposal of her things. Maybe the sister donated all of them or something.

In the bathroom, I make note of the light fixtures, light bulbs, colors of tile work, but there's not much that will need doing here. It's untouched, practically brand-new. Someone has cleaned it regularly, so there's no dust built up anywhere. A pair of long, multipaned windows opens toward the sea, and I crank them open, letting in the breeze.

A sharp scent of seaweed and salt triggers a visceral memory—sitting on a blanket with Kit, eating tuna sandwiches and Little Debbies our mother had packed into a basket for us the night before. We carried it down to the beach after a breakfast of cereal and milk at home, as we often did. She didn't like mornings, our mom.

The morning was cloudy, smelling of sea and rain, and chilly enough we wore hoodies and jeans. Cinder sat with us, chewing on a piece of driftwood between his paws. Kit said, "Is this Monday?"

I plucked a leaf from my sandwich. "You know it is." The restaurant was closed on Mondays. Our parents were sleeping late, and we'd learned well enough not to disturb them.

"Aren't we supposed to go to school on Mondays?"

"You don't have to go every day. Especially not in kindergarten." I was in second grade and, aside from lunch and the rows of books we were allowed to check out, didn't care a lot about it. I had taught myself to read before I even started school, and who needed all the rest of it? The other girls were snotty, and they liked dolls and dresses and all kinds of dumb stuff. I liked only books, Cinder, Kit, and the ocean.

Kit's hair was braided into one long plait, but then she'd slept on it for a couple of days, and now curls sprang up all around her face and the top of her head like she'd stuck her finger in a light socket. Freckles covered her nose and cheeks, darker with the sun all summer, and her skin was almost as dark as the wooden walls of the restaurant, deep reddish brown that made people say we couldn't even be sisters.

But she just took after my dad. His pale olive skin, his dark hair, his big, wide mouth. She was tall like him too, as tall as me, even though I was older.

Now she said, "But I *like* to go to school. We learn good stuff there."

"Ew. Like what?"

"We have a plant experiment in the window."

"Doing what?"

She took a bite of her sandwich and chewed it thoughtfully. "We planted five different seeds to see which ones grow faster."

"That's dumb."

"I like it. They have different baby leaves. Some are round, and some are pointed. It's interesting."

"Huh." I didn't want to say *BOR-ing*, but I thought it.

"School is something to do."

"We have plenty to do!"

She shrugged.

"You could tell Mom you want to be there every day."

Her lids dropped. "She'll yell at me."

I poked her foot. "I'll tell her, then. I don't care if she yells at me."

"You would?"

"I guess." I flung hair out of my face. "If you want."

She nodded, her big green-gold eyes shining like coins. "I really, really want to go to school."

In Auckland, decades later, I run a finger along the tiled sill of the window. It wasn't until Dylan came, another whole year, that she got to school every day. He made sure of it.

After making notes in the bedroom, I begin the second part of my day—scouring the house for papers, letters, diaries, anything that might help me put things together about Veronica's past. As I'd already discovered, the bedroom had been cleared out and never used again, and the study had proven to be no help at all. In Helen's suite of rooms, I find stacks of magazines, some dating back to 1960, carefully stored in plastic bins stacked to the ceiling. I mark them TRASH with a Sharpie. In a closet, I discover heaps and heaps of yarn, every color and variety and weight, which I note on my clipboard will go to the charity shops, along with most of the paperback books, mostly a very old-fashioned form of romance, and the kind of thick novels about the upper classes in England that seems to go over well with a certain set here. I'd never seen them in America, though glitz novels probably fill the same need.

I scan the books carefully, one title at a time, but after several tall stacks realize there isn't going to be anything I need to save. It's hard to turn my back on such a wealth of reading material, but I learned early in the flipping game that I'd rue carting home a lot of books. My own reading threatens to bury us, so I don't need to bring any in from somewhere else. On my clipboard, I note "used bookseller," who often pays me a sum by the yard just for the chance to find anything important.

The rest of the rooms have even less to offer. They contain the last modest possessions of a reclusive old woman. Her television is from the '90s, and the desktop computer that sits in one corner is a behemoth of yellowed plastic. I turn it on just out of curiosity, and it takes a while, but the screen finally comes up. It doesn't appear to have an internet connection and boasts very few programs—a word processor I haven't seen in use for quite some time and a few old-school games. I smile, thinking of Helen in her flowered dresses, playing FreeCell.

I click on the word processor, and while it readies itself for the enormous job of opening, I check a text that has come in on my phone from Nan.

Got your message. Meet for early dinner?

I leap at the distraction from my empty house. Yes! The usual?

5:30?

Yes.

I'll make a reservation.

Pleased at the social prospect, I tuck my phone into the back pocket of my jeans and scan the list of files on Helen's computer. It's tidily arranged, with a file for letters, one for daily tasks that I quickly discover is a list that can be printed, and one for "Other." I click on that.

Journal entries. I open a handful of them, just to see if there are instructions or anything in there. It makes me feel guilty—journals are very, very private things, and you never know, going in cold like this, what you'll find.

In this case, however, it's a simple accounting of her day. She knitted a pair of socks for a neighbor's child. Ate toast and jam for breakfast. Needed to leave an envelope for the cleaners. I close it up again, but I'm not letting the computer go. I feel protective now of Helen's privacy.

The rooms are sunny, with good light and views toward the sea. Simon will be very comfortable having his study here. Maybe we can turn one room into a little kitchen.

As is my habit, I stand quietly in the center of the big room and let it speak to me in color and style. Here, as everywhere in the house, the bones are excellent. The windows are the star—rows of squares, each framing the view in a new way. I'll leave them uncovered but maybe on each end hang some heavy drapes to pull across on rings.

No. Bare, clean. That's what Simon will like. A masculine shade of green and the carpet taken up. Bookshelves that Rose will want to decide upon. The good wood detailing stripped and restored.

As I'm heading downstairs with my notes, it occurs to me that Helen must have kept journals all along. What did she do before computers? And where did she stash them?

There must be an attic or other storage. I walk along the open upper gallery, peering at the ceiling, and at the end, there's the loop. Glancing at my watch, I realize I've been at it for hours, and if I'm going to make my dinner with Nan, I've got to get down to the CBD. If I time it right, I can capture a parking spot from a departing office drone.

Rose is cataloging the items in the pantry. "Find anything interesting?" I ask.

She nods, gesturing with her pen toward the glass-front shelves. "Somebody collected Coalport cups and saucers. They're amazing." She takes a cup out, dark blue with gold interior and a pattern of stars or dots on the outside.

"Breathtaking. Are they worth anything?"

"Some, definitely. Some maybe not. Beautiful, though." She shakes her head as she returns the cup, picks up another with a wide background and elaborate, colorful enamel work in red and pink and yellow.

She loves vintage everything, and I don't always see the appeal, but these cups are amazing. "They'll inspire you."

"Yes. Are you leaving?"

"I'm going to meet Nan in the CBD. Do you want to stay?"

"No." She makes a face, looking upward. "This one feels a little more alive than I like."

I nod. "I get it. Nearly scared myself to death the other day."

She settles the cup in its place and closes the pantry door. "I've got heaps of notes I'll type up later and send over to you, but I got a pretty good start."

"Tomorrow or the next day, I want to get into the attic. I'm looking for things like papers and anything that might have belonged to Veronica. Clothing, jewelry, notes, scripts. Any of it. Might be a museum that'll want them."

"No doubt."

"Want some feijoas?" I ask, smelling them on the breeze as we walk out. "There's a ton of them around."

"Uh, no. My mum has two trees, and I'm already ducking her."

I laugh. "See you tomorrow."

Chapter Eleven

Kit

The harbor tour allows us to disembark at any number of stops. Javier and I wander into a little village with thick shade beneath the trees and rows of Victorian-like houses. The air is hot and still, the mood very quiet along the streets. Peaceful. He points at things now and again but seems content to simply take it in. I like that he doesn't feel the need to fill every silence with words.

A bookstore draws us both in, and I lose him within two minutes when he dips down an aisle of moldering history books. I wander on by myself, looking for light reading to bring back with me, but there isn't much in that category. I content myself with leafing through a book of botanical drawings, then a history of flowers. I wind down a few more aisles, turning this way and that, until I'm somewhere in the deepest heart of the place, surrounded by the hushed whisper of the books and the faint dusty smell of them, in front of a deliciously huge collection of children's books.

I pick up a couple, open them at random to read a page. Nancy Drew and the Boxcar Children, Harry Potter in many different formats, some regional work I don't recognize and that intrigues me. I shoot a photo of their spines to look for them later.

And there, in the middle of it all, is a battered copy of *Charlie and the Chocolate Factory*. I gasp a little under my breath, as if someone dead has come back to life, and pull it out, holding the weight gingerly in my hands for a moment. It's the same edition we owned, a book Dylan brought home from a trip to San Francisco. I open the cover, flip to the first page, and fall back in time.

To a cold afternoon long ago, me and Josie with Dylan between us. I leaned into his hard ribs, smelling the soap he used to scrub his hands of garlic and onion. "I can't wait to read this to you," he said. "It's such a good story."

"I can read it myself," Josie said, and it was true that at eight, she could read anything she wanted.

"But if you read it," Dylan said, "then we don't get to sit here like this, together." He dropped a kiss to each of our heads. "Doesn't that sound better? We can read a chapter a day before you take showers."

"Why do we have to take showers every day?" I asked, falling across his lap. "Mommy doesn't make us."

He pinched my side, tickling me a little, and I giggled, shoving his hands away happily. "Because you smell like little goats after you've been out there playing in the sand all day."

"We take showers in the ocean," I yelled, and he laughed, putting a finger to his lips.

"A boy in my class told me I had disgusting ankles," Josie said, holding one skinny leg up for inspection.

"It's kind of disgusting," Dylan said, grabbing her leg. "Scrub it tonight."

"Scrub it *how*?" Josie asked. She licked her thumb and rubbed at the grime, and it started to give way.

"Quit it," Dylan said, slapping her hand. "It'll wait until your shower. You can use soap and a washcloth."

I liked lying across his legs, looking up at him. I could see under his chin where little shimmers of blond whiskers caught the light and his ponytail hung over his shoulder, bright and messy. It was safe with Dylan, warm. Although I complained about the shower, I liked having someone who knew when our clothes needed to be washed and who made us follow a system—shower, brush and braid hair, brush teeth, lay out clothes for the next day. My sense of worry had calmed a lot since he'd arrived. "I can see up your nose," I said, giggling.

Dylan laughed. "Get up, you monkey. Let's read."

I scrambled upright. Josie crossed her legs and leaned in, her long, long hair falling like straw over her skinny limbs. Dylan took a breath and turned to the first page. "These two very old people . . ."

Twenty-five years later, in the dusty bookstore with a copy of the same book in my hands, I hold very still to let the cactus spines in my lungs settle. From experience, I know it will get worse before it gets better, that I can't move, only breathe with the shallowest breaths possible, and it will still be like a hand brushing back and forth against the spines, creating waves of deep pain. Each spine is a memory—Dad, Dylan, Josie, Mom, me, them, surfing, s'mores—and all of them ache at once.

As I stand there, breathing shallowly, I can sense a person coming down the aisle, but if I move, it will take longer for the ache to disappear, so I stand there, head down, as if I don't know the person is there. Maybe they'll turn around and go back.

But they don't. *He* doesn't. Javier touches my upper arm lightly. "Are you all right?"

I nod tightly. Lift the book to show him I've been looking at it. With a sensitivity that's rare, he settles one warm palm against the very center of my back and holds out the other for the book. I let go of it.

When I can speak, I say, "Did you find anything interesting?"

He gives me a wry grin, one that lights a dimple in his cheek. "Many things, but I have learned to just carry one book, or my bag starts to weigh too much for me to lift!" He shows me a book of Pablo Neruda poetry. "This one for now."

"But you already have a book."

"No, I have finished that one. I can leave it behind for someone else."

The ache has eased enough that I can laugh a little. "I'm taking that one, but I do know what you mean."

He hands the book back to me. "You'll have to tell me about it. Shall we find lunch?"

"Absolutely."

At the counter, he sets his book down and holds his hand out for mine. I think about arguing that I have the money, but it's a small kindness, and I don't have to push it away. "Thank you."

The village is geared toward tourists—at least it is by the waterfront. I know from experience that the town itself will have normal homes and people and schools and supermarkets. It bemuses me that this tourist town is much like my own, that everywhere the land meets the ocean there is probably some variation on this idea.

We have a wealth of options, but I love the look of a sandwich-and-tea shop situated in an old building, and we're shown to a table by the window overlooking the harbor and islands and bluffs. Somewhere out there is my sister. Now that I know it for sure, I feel a renewed sense of urgency. How will I find her?

"You are troubled?"

I half nod, half shrug, trying to dislodge the emotions the book raised. "A little. I don't know how I will find her. I mean, how do you do that in such a large city?"

"You could hire a detective." He gives the word a Spanish inflection.

I've thought of this. "Maybe I will if I don't find her another way." Then I straighten. I've agreed to this day trip with Javier because I didn't want to be lonely, and I owe him my attention for the afternoon. "This is an insanely beautiful place," I say.

Javier, holding the menu lightly, admires the view along with me. "It's restful to look at it."

A note in his voice pricks my curiosity. "Do you need rest?" I ask lightly.

"I needed time to"—he gestures to include the room, the table, the view, me—"enjoy the world."

A youth with a tumble of black curls asks us for a drink order. I'm not sure yet what the local standard drinks are—what's an L&P?—so I order sparkling water.

Charmingly, Javier orders lemonade. We study the menus. "I keep seeing kumara on menus. Is it a squash or something?"

"Sweet potato," he says. "Miguel explained to me."

Eyeing the kumara soup and a whitebait fritter, as well as classic fish and chips, I decide to go for the adventure—the fritter and soup. Javier orders oysters.

As he hands the waiter his menu, he's framed against the light from a window behind him. It haloes his hair and the square solidness of his shoulders, casts his profile into relief—high brow, powerful nose, full lips. I like the elegance of his shirt. His ease in the world.

He taps the book, cradled in a paper bag. "Tell me about this."

"Oh, that." The ache of memory comes flooding back. "Did you ever see *Willy Wonka and the Chocolate Factory*?"

"I know of it."

"This is the novel it was made from."

He nods, his hands loosely clasped in front of him. "And?"

I sip water. "My parents sort of adopted a runaway who worked in the restaurant. Dylan." How long has it been since I've spoken his name? A faint ache runs along my ribs. "He lived with us for years and years. And this"—I smooth a palm over the cover—"was his favorite book. He used to read it to my sister and me."

"What is the story?"

"A poor boy in the slums of London finds a golden ticket in a chocolate bar and is given a tour of a chocolate factory run by an eccentric man."

"Why did your friend love it?"

I consider the question. There is so much I don't know. What his history was, though he'd clearly been beaten within an inch of his life, who his family was. All he ever said about his mother was that they used to go to Chinatown sometimes. Aloud, I say, "Charlie is a poor boy who finds the winning ticket. There's magic in a candy factory, right?"

"You miss him."

"Not just him." How to explain such a tangle of loves? My mother smoking in the kitchen as Dylan read aloud, the smell of coffee thick in the air, my sister chewing on the end of her hair, my dad singing somewhere as he engaged in some physical task. "All of them, really. Maybe even my little-girl self."

His big hands reach over the table to take one of mine, engulfing it completely. "Tell me about them."

Oh, I do not want to like him so much. Lust, yes. Not like. I don't know him at all, but in this gesture I feel the heart of a lion, big and inclusive and wise. It tips open the closed doors of my life.

I take a breath, think of those days, and again find myself telling him the truth. Maybe it's him, or maybe it's just time to tell someone. "We were wild children, all of us, even Dylan. He must have run away, because he showed up like a ghost one night when he was thirteen or so and just stayed. My mother took him under her wing." I shake my head. It's still a mystery that she did that, but she loved him as much as we did, right from the start. "My sister and I adored him." I look out at the water. Even my dad, who was kind of a hard man in some ways, loved him. "It was probably the best thing that ever happened to Dylan."

"Why?"

I remember his scars, some small and pale; others long, thin lines; others fat and red. "I didn't realize it then, you know, but knowing what I know now, he must have been abused physically." It makes my skin hurt to think of it, of his small gentle self, so heart-breakingly beautiful, being punched or cut or burned. His body bore the evidence of all those and more. For a moment, a wave of loss and longing threatens to swamp me, a longing for that time, for Dylan himself, for the terrible things he suffered. "He took care of us, Josie and me."

"Why didn't your parents care for you?"

The answer is so complicated and so intimate after everything else that I'm relieved when the waiter brings a basket of bread and Javier releases my hand. Offering me the basket first, holding it with courtly manners while I select a round brown roll, he selects a seeded one and lifts it to his nose. "Mm. *Alcaravea*," he says.

I gesture for it, and he offers the roll so I can look at it. "Caraway."

"Delicious."

Every gesture he makes, every expression, is as smooth and graceful as every other. Nothing is hurried or overly considered. He flows moment to moment in a way I don't remember ever noticing in a human before. I smile and butter my bread.

And as if he senses I've reached a wall, he turns the conversation. "Tell me, Kit—is it Katherine or something else? Were you like a fox kit, and your father gave you the nickname?" As he speaks, his gaze is focused intently on my face, as if whatever words drop from my mouth will be endlessly fascinating. I had a professor once who looked at me this way. She was a nun, and I knew her in my third year of undergrad. I bloomed in her presence. I'm blooming now.

"It was my father's doing," I admit. "He thought I looked like a kitten when I was born, and he nicknamed me. My mother still calls me Kitten sometimes, and Dylan used to as well. But everyone else calls me Kit. I was quite a tomboy."

"Tomboy? I do not think I know this word."

"Not very girlie. I didn't like dolls or dresses."

His hands are stacked, just the fingers, quiet. "What did you like?"

"Surfing. Swimming." Something in my spine loosens, and I lean forward, smiling as I remember. "Searching for pirate treasure and mermaids."

"Did you find them?" His voice is lower, his dark eyes very direct.

I look at his generous mouth, then back up. "Sometimes. Not very often."

He nods very faintly. It's his turn to look at my mouth. My shoulders, the square of skin showing in my dress. "So was it Katherine to start or Kitten?"

"Katherine. It was my father's mother. And I, sadly, look just like her."

"Sadly? Why do you say such a thing?"

I shrug, easing backward, away from that swirling thing growing in the air between us. "I don't mind. But I was not my sister or my mother."

He tsks. "I saw that photo of your sister. She looks small. Wispy."

"Yes. Never mind this conversation. I didn't mean—"

"I know." He grins almost mischievously.

I laugh lightly. "You're teasing me."

"Perhaps just a little."

"Now you. Tell me something. Why do you have your name?"

"The *whole* name is Javier Matias Gutierrez Velez de Santos."

"Impressive."

"I know." He inclines his head, easing the arrogance. "My father is Matias, and my mother's brother was Javier. He was killed by a jealous husband before I was born."

I narrow my eyes. "Is that true?"

He raises his hands, palm out. "Swear. But I was never the boy who would be killed that way. I had big glasses, you know, thick." His hands went to his eyes to illustrate the shape. "And I was a bit fat, and they called me *cerdito ciego*, little blind pig."

Before he even finishes the sentence, I'm laughing, the pleasure coming from somewhere in my body that I'd forgotten. "I don't know that I believe you."

"I swear, it's true. Every word." He glances over his shoulder, leans closer. "Do you want to know the secret of my transformation?"

"Yes, please," I whisper.

"I learned to play guitar."

"And sing."

He nods. "And sing. And then, it was like a magic spell. I could sing and play, and nobody called me the little blind pig anymore."

"I believe that story. Your voice is beautiful."

"Thank you." His eyes glitter. "Usually it doesn't send women running away."

"No. I'm sure."

He touches my arm. "Will you listen again sometime?"

That swirling thing expands, engulfs us, and we're enclosed in a world of our own. His thumb rests on my inner arm, and I see that his irises are not as dark as they first seemed but lit with amber. "Yes," I say quietly, sure I don't mean it.

"Good."

———— ⧼⧽ ————

We make one last departure when the ferry stops at Rangitoto. Ordinarily it would just be a pickup, but another ferry has been waylaid, and this one is going to do double duty. We have to wait for an hour for everyone to come off the mountain. "You're welcome to disembark and explore a bit, if y'like," the steward says over the loudspeaker. "Be warned we'll be leaving at sixteen hundred hours."

Rather than sit in the hot sun, we opt to explore. I'm wearing walking sandals, and Javier is in jeans and good shoes, so we don't go far, just up to the visitors' center and a small lagoon where birds hop and twitter and gather. I hear long, fluid whistles and a squished little squawk, and around us are plants I've never seen. My mother would love it, and she'd probably be able to identify many of them. I'm drawn down a path shaded by tree ferns and land ferns and a pretty flowering tree. A bird overhead seems to be engaged in a long whistling conversation, and I grin, looking up to see if I can find him, but there are only more ferns and leaves and tropical-looking things.

My heart suddenly turns over. How remarkable that I'm standing here in this place. "It's amazing!"

The rustle of wings alerts us, and Javier touches my arm, pointing to the bird who's been making so much noise, black with a thick brown saddle over its shoulder. I admire it in wonder, mouthing *Wow* to Javier, who nods.

We wander back to the main dock area, where people, dusty and sunburned as they come down from hiking, are gathering for the trip back to the city. "Do you like to hike?" I ask Javier.

His lips turn down. "I don't know. I do like walking. Do you hike?"

"I love it. Being outside like that, all day, just the trail and the birds and the trees. I live by the redwoods. They're incredible trees."

"Mm. Would you want to hike to that peak?" He points to the top of the volcano. It's not an actual invitation but a query on preference.

I look to the top, shrug. "It would be fantastic."

He nods, measures the height. "I might not care for that."

And for the first time, there is something I'm not sure I like about him. No surfing, no hiking. I'm used to more vigorous men.

Then I remember the way he swam, with sure, strong strokes, and realize he's fit enough. Perhaps people in Madrid are not as interested in climbing mountains and challenging waves as those in California.

We walk toward the pier and lean on the railing there. A gaggle of teenage boys, all part of some tour group, are jumping off tall concrete pilings to the water below, egging on the others.

"Did you see the trees across the street from the high-rise?" he asks.

"No." It's hard to look away from the boys and their dangerous game. I wonder who's in charge, but it doesn't really seem as if anyone is.

Chill, I tell my inner ER doc. *Not everything is a disaster.*

Javier, following me as I edge farther up the pier, says, "I walked there yesterday. It's a little park or something, and the trees are old and full of character. As if they might walk around when no one is watching."

I look over at him, snared by the fairy-tale image. "Really?"

Two boys are shouting, drawing our attention, and we watch as they scramble to a higher piling and leap off, yelling. I'm tapping my index finger on the railing that separates us from the water. Below us, the boys surface and laugh, and others are scrambling to the higher piling. Tourists and hikers laze against the railing, taking sips of water from bottles, smearing on sunscreen, eating.

A very tall boy with messy black hair dripping on his back gets to the top of the piling, joking and laughing with some of the others.

I see it before I see it—his foot sliding out from under him on the wet concrete, his body tilting, shifting, arms flying out—

And his head hits the edge of the concrete, visibly splitting right in front of me.

"Get out of the way!" I yell, and I'm kicking off my shoes and shedding my dress practically before the boy hits the water with an excruciating splat. I run to the end of the dock and dive toward the place he went in. The water is cold and murky, but late-afternoon sun illuminates the shape of his body. Another body is in the water with me, and we meet and yank, both of us swimming toward the surface. Blood from his head pours out in a dark cloud.

We break the surface. The other rescuer is another boy from the group, a strong swimmer. "Head for shore!" I yell, and we swim together, dragging the deadweight of the body between us toward the seawall, where others meet us and haul the injured boy upward.

"Help me up!" I cry. "I'm a doctor."

And there are hands hauling me too, and I'm beside the boy, giving him mouth-to-mouth until he chokes and expels a gutful of water, but that doesn't raise him to consciousness. His head is bleeding heavily. "Give me your shirt," I order the other boy, and he tugs it off and hands it to me. Squeezing out the excess water, I press it to the cut, holding it there as I check his vitals and his pupils, but his eyes are so black it's hard to tell. He needs a hospital, fast.

A man from the ferry appears with another guy in a uniform, maybe coast guard. "Thank you, miss," he says. "That was amazing. We've got it." Two forest-ranger types are running down the beach with a stretcher, and I see a boat with a cross on it. The crowd parts for the paramedics, because that must be what they are. I keep my hands on the cut, and one of them nods. "You're a lifeguard?"

"Once. Now I'm an ER doctor, back in the States."

"Good work. You probably saved his life." He takes over holding pressure, and they load him onto a stretcher.

I stand up and knock the sand off my knees, and a group of people starts clapping. I shake my head, wave a hand dismissively, and look for Javier, who is standing to one side with my dress and shoes in his hand. I take in a breath and blow it out, hands on my waist. It's a classic calming pose. As he reaches me, I glance down at my ordinary bra and panties. "Glad I wore the good underwear."

He smiles, offering me my dress. "Are you all right?"

"Fine." I tug the fabric over my head, my heavy wet braid knocking to one side.

"You disappeared before I—"

"Instinct. I was a lifeguard for a decade." I smooth the dress down. The panties will dry soon enough, but the underwire on the bra is going to be a misery. For a moment, I wonder if I should walk up to the ladies' room and delicately remove it, but the entire beach has seen me half-naked already. "Give me some cover, will you?"

He glances over his shoulder, still holding my sandals, and moves his body to block me from view. The seawall is behind me. I reach beneath the dress, unhook the bra, and tug it off my arms and wad it up. "Is my bag anywhere?"

"Here." He's looped it over his shoulder so it's hanging down his back, and now he slides it down to give to me.

I toss the bra inside, take one shoe and brush it off, slide a foot in, do the same on the other side, then pull out a bottle of water and take a long, lukewarm swallow.

Only then do I inhale deeply and let it out in a slow breath, looking up at Javier. I'm used to emergencies, but this came out of nowhere, and I'm a little giddy. "Are you impressed?"

He lifts his aviator glasses and licks his lower lip, reaching out to brush my cheek. "Yes."

"Good."

He takes a breath now and lets it out, throwing an arm around me. "You frightened me. Let's find a drink, hmm?"

"Great idea."

We settle on the top of the ferry again, toward the back against the rails, and Javier leaves me to go down to the snack bar. In his absence, I watch the vast sky. Clouds are gathering on the horizon, moving like they're on fast-forward, and before he returns, they've rushed over the sun, bringing a pearly gray light to the scene.

He's carrying two beers when he returns, and we clink bottles. I'm unsettled and restless and conscious of his body alongside mine. The beer is cold and delicious. Refreshing. "Thank you."

"You're a doctor."

"Yes. ER in Santa Cruz."

"ER?"

"Emergency room."

"Ah." He sips his beer and watches a family of tourists settling on a row of seats, and I watch too. The mom is hassled, directing her three kids to put their hats back on, to stop tossing a ball among them, to sit down and stop leaning over the rail. The dad is bent over his phone. "That would account for your speed." He makes a soft sound, looks at me. "One moment you were standing beside me, and the next you were in the water."

"Here's the thing—it wasn't really that sudden. I was worried about those boys, and you'll notice I was in place when one fell." I smooth a hand over my thigh, which feels restless. "I'm a surfer, and I was a lifeguard, and you see the injuries in the ER all the time . . . so while all of you were enjoying the spectacle of youth and energy, I was imagining all the things that could go wrong."

For a moment, he looks at me, his sunglasses hiding his eyes. "Will he be all right, that boy?"

"I don't know. He hit his head pretty damn hard."

"Does it make you afraid, knowing what you know? Stop you from doing things?"

I settle sideways so I can look at him more easily, leaning my back against the railing. "Not physical things."

His eyes glitter. "What things, then, hmm?"

I look away, over his shoulder, thinking of my rules about men, my lack of travel, the empty spaces in my life, and suddenly feel a welter of tears at the back of my throat, which is not me at all. I feign nonchalance with a one-shoulder shrug. "I already knew bad things could happen."

"Ah, the earthquake, yes?"

"Among other things."

"Is that what led you to the emergency room?"

"Maybe? Probably." I pick at the label of my beer. "I always wanted to study science in some way, but that was a big event."

He touches my forearm with one finger. "Were you injured?"

"Scratches and bruises. Nothing much." I feel suddenly breathless at the pressure of so many memories rising up after so long. My sister,

Dylan, the earthquake. I lift a hand. "Enough. Your turn, Señor Velez. I've been talking about myself all day."

He smiles. The wind blows his hair over his forehead. He's such a masculine man. European, so polished, but so very male. His big hands. His broad shoulders. His strong nose and intelligent brow. "I am not as interesting as you are."

"That is not true." My body is starting to relax a little after the adrenaline rush. "Tell me why you really came to New Zealand."

"Not just to visit?"

I shake my head, go with a gut feeling. "I don't think so."

"You're right." He looks out toward the horizon, back to me. "A very good friend of mine, one of my oldest friends, killed himself."

Damn. The lake of my memories ripples, threatens to spill. A flash of Dylan's dead, still self washes out of the lake, but I'm a master at ridding myself of those images. I sit up straight, taking refuge in my professional training. "Javier, I'm so sorry." In compassion, I wrap my hand around his. "I shouldn't have pushed."

He turns his palm upward, captures my hand close. "We had been friends since we were small. Very small. I felt I should have seen. Done . . . something." His face darkens as he focuses on the horizon. "I just . . ." He sighs. "After, I found it difficult to take up my work, and Miguel invited me to come here for a time." He brushes his thumb over my fingernail.

"Suicide is especially difficult for survivors," I say, and it's too much my ER voice. I force myself to be more human. Personal. "You must miss him terribly."

"I keep wishing for it to make sense."

"It doesn't, always."

"I suppose you see it often, in your work." He gives me a sideways look, still holding my hand.

I swallow back another confession. "Yes."

"Is it difficult?"

He's raw and seeking a comfort that doesn't exist, at least not a comfort I can offer. "It's unsettling when a person dies violently in any form."

He waits quietly, and I have opened the box, this heavy box I've been dragging around with me. "Drugs and alcohol. The stupid, stupid things people do." I shake my head. "So many kids. And gangs. Good God, sometimes they're so young they don't know how to kiss, and they're carrying guns."

"Mm." His thumb edges over the top of mine.

Into the quiet, I say something I have only thought, never spoken aloud. "I've been thinking about leaving the ER. It's wearing me down."

"What would you do instead?"

I focus on the shape of his fingers, the tidiness of his nails. Well-tended hands. "I have no idea."

"Something else is calling you."

"Maybe. My interest as a teen was in marine animals, but it might be too late to return to that. I don't know. Maybe it isn't even the job as much as the place. Maybe it's time to escape Santa Cruz." I feel disheartened, as if I've wasted a lot of time. "Tell me about your friend. If you want to."

He takes a breath, lets it go. "It's all a tangle still. It hasn't been very long, only a month. He had a bad time. His wife left him, and he was drinking too much, and—" He shrugs. "There are seasons of darkness, yes? Loss and sadness all around." He tightens his grip. "But if you are patient, the circle turns, and then there is happiness all around, everything good, everyone happy." He flings a hand out, palm up, as if scattering glitter. "My friend, he just forgot that happiness is part of living too."

"That's a lovely thought." I smile sadly. "But I'm going to admit something terrible"—and I know I am doing this to skirt around the other things I could be spilling—"but aside from when I was a child, I don't know that I've had those happy times."

"Never?"

I run through the years of my life mentally, trying to find a cycle that was particularly outstanding. "Not really. I mean, I was glad to get my degree and get out of school and go to work, but . . ."

A small frown wrinkles his brow. "Perhaps we are not talking about the same thing. I mean those times when your family is well and you have work you love and maybe you fall in love and feel good. Those times."

"I'm happy right now." I sip my beer, look at the water. "I'm in this beautiful place and enjoying the company of an interesting and"—I raise one brow—"quite good-looking man. I'm not dealing with work or my mother or any of my daily things. That's happiness, right?"

The ferry is beginning to move, and a gust of wind makes me close my eyes and put my hand in my hair. When I open them again, Javier has raised his glasses to look at me. "That is a little happy. Not big, not the kind that fills you up and makes you want to laugh."

"Yeah, I don't know that I've had that." It's unnerving to realize it, unnerving how much I've revealed to this man. And yet I can't stop. Something about him—his kindness or his warm voice or something I can't even name—softens the carapace I've carried around for so long.

He asks, "When you fall in love?"

I shrug. I don't want to say aloud that I don't do that, because then he might think it's a challenge, and it isn't. I just don't want all the drama.

He inclines his head, puzzling over me, then captures a lock of my hair and tucks it behind my ear. His mouth turns up on one side, activating that ridiculously charming dimple. "Now I am convinced that you have not known the right men." He settles his beer on the ground, then takes mine. "I have been thinking today about kissing you."

"I've thought of that too."

One hand runs up my arm, and he follows the motion with his gaze. "I thought of it in the bookstore, when you looked so sad, but it was not quite right." His hand moves over my shoulder, up to my neck. "And as we came out of the café, you smiled up at me, and your throat looked long and golden." His fingers alight against my throat, slide to my clavicle. All the nerves in my body rustle to life, and yet I'm enjoying the slow caress.

"When you leaped over the railing, my heart squeezed so hard I could not breathe, because what if"—now he touches my ear, my temple, my wet hair, and pulls me closer—"what if I had lost the chance?"

I lift my face, and he cradles my head as our lips join. And then I forget to keep my guard up or shield myself with cynicism, because his mouth is as lush as plums, and he shifts slightly to fit us together more perfectly. My head is in his palm and the front of my knee against his thigh, and it's like a fragrant smoke surrounds us, makes me dizzy. Behind my eyes, the world is faintly rose. I reach out a hand to brace myself, holding on to his upper arm, and as if I've asked permission, he opens his lips slightly and invites me in, and I go, I go, reach for his tongue and it reaches mine, and then I'm lost in it, a kiss so perfect it might be a poem, or a dance, or something I've dreamed.

With a little gasp I pull back, covering my mouth with my hand as I look up to his dark eyes, eyes that crinkle a little at the corners. He smooths back my hair from my forehead. "Is that happiness too?"

I let go of a soft laugh. "I don't know. Let me try again." And I pull him closer, lean back, and invite him to press into me as the ferry chugs across the water and the family nearby shrieks over raindrops that start to fall. I'm aware of a big drop that splashes on my forehead and a pair that plop on my hand, but mostly what I'm feeling is Javier's mouth kissing me; and Javier's body close to mine; and Javier's graceful tongue, which I want on me everywhere; and Javier's back, which I want naked.

And it doesn't matter when there is more rain, a slow, soft patter that falls on us all the way to the CBD. We only press closer and kiss more. I taste the salt on his lips from the sea and the rain, and we're soaked and kissing and lost.

And I don't even think for a moment to consider this might be dangerous. That I might—that I have let down all my guards.

I just kiss him. In the rain. On a ferry halfway around the world. Kiss him, and kiss him, and kiss him.

Chapter Twelve
Mari

I met Nan years ago in Raglan, a town on the central coast of the North Island known for great surfing. I was waiting tables in Hamilton and had only just begun to allow myself to surf again, fearful of running into someone I might know. Raglan was only a few miles away, and I drove out there on the weekdays, when the crowds were small and passionate, to ride the left-breaking waves.

By then it had been nearly two and a half years since I'd fled France on the passport of a dead girl, and I had since discarded that identity too, to become Mari Sanders from Tofino, British Columbia. I found a guy to make me the papers I needed and trashed the original passport, scattering it from Queenstown, where I first arrived, all the way north.

I had not had a single mind-altering substance, not so much as a mouthful of beer, in 812 days. It was the thing that made the rest worth it and the only thing I believed would save me: to be sober, I had to leave the wreck of my old life and make a new one. Never look back.

On the beach the first day, I met Nan. Tall, skinny, black-haired, she was a law student at the University of Waikato in Hamilton, and had grown up, as I had, surfing. We clicked, respectful of each other's chops. Within months, we lived together in Hamilton and surfed every time we could manage. I worked in a café and enrolled at Wintec, the equivalent of community college. I started in cookery and hospitality, thinking of my family's restaurant, but it was a hard-partying group, and I found myself struggling against the wave of their happy drunkenness.

I made friends with a woman in landscape design and construction and made the switch. Much to my surprise, it was a perfect fit. I liked working outside, loved working with my body, and once I started to understand the basics of horticulture with a range of plants I'd never seen, I fell in love.

Nan finished her law degree a year later and moved to Auckland, but I stayed in Hamilton, surfing Raglan on the weekends, making a life for myself. We kept in touch, and when Simon, an Auckland native, wooed me north, our friendship took up where it had left off. Once or twice a month now, we meet for dinner near her law offices in the CBD and catch up.

Tonight I find parking almost immediately and walk down to the Britomart and our special restaurant, an Italian one that reminds us both of childhood. Nan stands in front, sleek and skinny, her hair swept up in a French knot that suits her cheekbones. "They're having a special event," she says. "We'll have to go elsewhere."

"No worries. Any preference?"

"Mind walking a few blocks? There's a Spanish guitarist at the tapas place. Everyone is talking about him."

"Sounds great. Let's go."

She takes a few steps, then halts. "Oh, wait. The girl wanted to talk to you."

"The girl?"

"Yes. The pretty one with all the hair? She said she wanted to see you when you arrived."

"About?"

"I don't know."

We both half-heartedly peer into the busy restaurant. "I'm sure it will wait," I say. "I'm starving."

"Me too." She links arms with me energetically, and we stride up the hill, exchanging small bits of news. A case she's been working on has come to fruition at last. She knows about the house, and I tell her about the day with Rose, checking things out.

At the tapas bar, we settle outside on the bricked alleyway, away from the crowds standing three deep at the bar, mostly made up of well-dressed millennials from the local offices. "Popular," I comment.

"It's Friday night." She orders a martini for herself and sparkling water with lime for me, and we start with roasted Padrón peppers and stuffed olives with bread. Overhead, the sky among buildings is a golden spill of light, bright with distant rain. I feel myself relax. "Tell me," I say. "Do you have a theory about who killed Veronica Parker?"

"The Maori actress?"

"The one who built Sapphire House."

"Right. She was *also* Maori. It's one of the things that set her apart."

"I remember."

"She's a fascinating figure." Nan pops an olive in her mouth, eyeing a man in a very formal suit. In general, people dress well for work here, unlike the more casual United States. "I don't know why someone hasn't done a big book on her by now. New Zealand girl makes good in Hollywood, falls in love with another native New Zealander at the Olympic games. They have a mad love affair for years, and she's murdered."

"Don't forget he died too."

"Right. It was only another year or two, right?"

"Yeah." The peppers are small and mild, my favorites in all the world, and they're perfectly roasted and salted here. I nestle one into an envelope of soft bread and take a bite. "Maybe it was his wife?"

"They cleared her almost immediately. She was with her family or something. I don't remember exactly."

Gweneth is a fanatic for the history of Auckland, and the three of us have speculated before, over book club snacks and various meals. I was grateful that the two of them liked each other. My two best friends, and as close as I could get to replicating the experience of being a sister.

"Not the wife. Not Veronica's sister," I said, ticking them off. "Not George. Then who?"

Nan lifted a shoulder, skeptical. "My money is still on George. They never found any evidence, but he was notoriously jealous. In the case of a violent death at home, it's nearly always a loved one who did it."

"But he adored her."

"Yes, but he was under a lot of pressure to—"

"No. I just don't see it. There were never reports of domestic violence, no violence at all." Enjoying the discussion, I lean my elbows on the table. "My father was a jealous man, but he would never have killed my mother."

She inclines her head. "I don't know that I remember you mentioning this before."

I realize that I was speaking of my *actual* father, not the father I made up. For a moment, a chill halts me. I've never been so careless!

But Nan is looking at me expectantly. Maybe it will ease my sense of loneliness to tell the parts of my story that I can. "I don't think about it very much"—which is a lie; I compartmentalize, but they all haunt me anyway—"but he was. Traditional Italian man, of course, and my mom was not at all traditional. They had a volatile relationship. She was quite a bit younger than he was and very beautiful. Very, very, very, very beautiful. Had this voluptuous figure that my dad liked to see in expensive, fitted dresses."

"Go on."

"I think she liked him to be jealous." I take a sip of lime-flavored water, opening the door to that world ever so slightly. I'm cautious, afraid of the flood of things lurking, but a minuscule bit of tension I haven't been aware of holding gives way. "It was how she controlled him. Men were always flirting with her, coming on to her, and she encouraged it." I see her in my mind's eye in a slim red dress with a low, square neckline that showed off a lot of cleavage, laughing on the patio overlooking the ocean. My father fetched her, grabbing her by the wrist and tugging her behind him to a dark alcove beneath the wisteria that grew in thick ropes over the pergola. He pushed her against the post, into the leaves and flowers, and kissed her. I saw their tongues and the way they pressed their bodies together. My mother laughed, and my father let her go, swatting her behind as she sashayed back out to the patio and all their guests.

Enchanted by her power, I sashayed right behind her, imitating the swing of her hips and the way she tossed her hair. I wore a chiffon negligee she'd cut down for me, and the sheer black fabric flowed around my nine-year-old body in a way that was exhilarating. To feel it all the more, I spun around in a circle, sending it spinning outward, knowing my shorts and bikini top were mostly hidden. Air touched my belly, my thighs. Nearby, a woman laughed, and a man clapped lightly. "Suzanne, your daughter is a natural."

Delighted by their attention, I played it up, twirling for their pleasure, dancing the way my mother danced, swinging my hips, shimmying my shoulders, and I knew when I captured them, my audience. A circle of faces, all turned to me as if I were the sun, as if I were a queen.

A body swooped in and picked me up. Dylan, who tossed me over his shoulder. "School night, kiddo," he said. "Wave good night."

I arched my back like an ice dancer, pointing my toes and lifting my shoulders high, flinging kisses with both hands. The patrons loved me and clapped and whistled as Dylan carted me away.

"Hel-lo?" Nan says.

"Sorry. I just thought of something I hadn't remembered in a long time." I grin. "I wonder if Veronica tried to make George jealous. Maybe it didn't work, but the other person got possessive."

"It must have been a bit more than possessive. She was stabbed a dozen times or more, wasn't she?"

"Mm."

"That's passion."

Again, I see my parents in my imagination, but this time much later, my mother throwing something—an ashtray? A highball glass?—at him.

Nan adds, "I'm sure you can find society news about them. They were a very big deal in this town at the time. Glamorous, exotic, passionate."

"Did George live with her outright?"

"You'd have to ask Gweneth, but I'm pretty sure he did. His wife made their lives a misery, but they lived at Sapphire House."

I nod, narrowing my eyes to think a bit more. And there, walking past the end of the street, is a woman wearing a wrinkled red sundress with a thick braid falling down her back. A man walks with his arm over her shoulder and dips to kiss her, as if he can't resist, and there's something in the tilt of her head that electrifies me. I'm on my feet, ready to run after her, my sister.

Kit.

She disappears around the corner, and I realize I'm being ridiculous. All the thoughts of home, the longing to understand this house and its owner, have made me a little homesick, that's all.

But I wish fiercely for one long moment that it really had been her.

As I drive over the bridge, the memory of that night on the patio wafts around, still in the days before my parents started fighting so bitterly. Where was Kit that night? I search the memory and can't see her anywhere. Maybe she was reading in our room.

No. Dylan set me on my feet by a banquette away from the action, so often empty. Cinder was asleep on the floor beneath the table, and tucked into one corner was my sister, her hair wild from dancing with me earlier. She'd shucked off the blue negligee my mother gave her and slept in a pair of shorts and a dirty T-shirt. Dylan reached down and picked her up, and she fell on his shoulder, nestling in close. He loved her more than he loved me, just like my dad did, and it made me mad. I danced away in my bare feet, wading onto the dance floor. I heard him call me. "Josie, come on! It's time for bed."

My mother, in her silly voice, enfolded my hand in hers. "Never mind, Dylan. She's with me."

I stuck my tongue out at Dylan, sure that would make him come after me, but he gave me an irritated glance and shook his head, carrying Kit around the back of the restaurant. I knew the drill. He'd make sure she brushed her teeth, then tuck her in, and if she woke up, he'd tell her a story. I almost ran after them, but my mother said, "Dance with Mama, sweetie," and twirled me around.

Billy was there that night. I'd seen my mother flirting with him, even though he was super young, just a teenager or something, a young TV star who'd originally started coming with his agent; my parents loved when he showed up, bringing the promise of cachet. He had black hair and blue eyes, and everyone said he was going to be a very big star. He came over to dance with my mom and offered a hand to me, and I forgot about my baby sister getting all the attention.

The door to the past slams shut. A lifetime of secrets and lies later, I drive through the dark back to my neighborhood. Tears run down my cheeks, and I wonder who they're for. My sister, Dylan? Or maybe that little girl dancing wildly for the entertainment of drunken adults?

I don't remember if Dylan came back and made me go to bed, but I do remember drinking sips of Billy's beer and the way I giggled over him pouring it into a coffee cup so no one would know I was drinking.

It bubbled up my nose and took away my sadness and made me dance all the more, looking up at the stars, dancing with the ocean, with the night sky, with Billy, and with a lady who came over later to twirl me around. I remember tiptoeing around to the empty tables and sneaking sips of cocktails left in the dregs of glasses. I remember thinking I could do anything, be anything.

Anything.

Chapter Thirteen

Kit

We walk up the hill together quietly. Javier throws his arm around my shoulders, which has never been comfortable before, but our heights and gaits make it seem very relaxed, so I don't shimmy away as I ordinarily would. In truth, I'm crashing after the long, eventful day.

He's quiet too, humming under his breath sometimes, mostly just walking with me. I wonder if he's thinking of his friend back in Madrid. He hasn't said much about his life there, but maybe he's just glad to be away.

As I am. I try to think about my sister, how to find her, but I can't summon any urgency. I'll get back to the search tomorrow. After all, she's been missing for more than fourteen years. She's probably not going anywhere.

For once, my overactive brain is quiet. It's cooler tonight after the rain, and it's easy to see that it's Friday night. The streets are packed with students and young professionals. Music spills out of the establishments we pass.

It's getting dark. I don't have much to eat in my apartment, and my dress is a mess. I'm getting very hungry. "Should we drag a pizza back? I don't have anything but coffee and eggs in my room."

"Are you inviting me over?"

I might have run away before but not tonight. I nod.

"I have food," he says. "Would you like to come to my flat?"

"You cook?"

"I am a good cook. Are you?"

"My father would have expected nothing less." I smile up at him, and that too is a luxury. So rare that someone is taller than me. "I'm an especially good baker."

"What's your specialty?"

"Cake."

"We don't make such sweet cakes in Spain as some places. Do you know Tarta de Santiago?"

"Yes. Almond, so delicious."

"Do you know how to cook that cake?"

"I have never done it before, but I would imagine I could."

"Maybe you will one day." He winks. "For me."

"Maybe so." As if there are more than a scattering of days ahead of us.

At the hotel, we ride the elevator up, and he leans in to kiss me. "Will you let me cook for you?"

"Yes."

I get off on my floor to shower and change, and he continues on. In the hallway leading to my door, I'm alone for the first time all day, and suddenly everything feels like a dream.

I slam back into my body all at once, and it feels sad and exhausting, and all my problems are piled up, waiting for me. The question of why my sister faked her own death, where she is, the strangely clear recognition now that I'm at a distance that I'm no longer happy in the ER. I wonder how Hobo is doing without me. I wonder if I should call my mom again, but it was only this morning that we talked.

It feels like so much longer.

I climb in the luxurious shower, washing away seawater and blood and rain from my body and my hair. The shampoo smells of tangerines. I close my eyes and work up the suds, enjoying the fragrance—

I'm back on the ferry, pressed against the railing as Javier kisses me, and I'm transported, his lush mouth, his exquisite skill, his way of holding my head so gently—

I snap my eyes open. Is this a good idea? Really?

Through the glass of the shower, I see my blurry reflection in the steamy mirror. I think of my admission that I haven't had much happiness, and it suddenly seems ridiculous. What am I waiting for?

Maybe for once in my life I might like to get a glimmering of what that feels like. It seems that he might know how to access it, where to find it. If I can grasp a day or two of happiness, why not?

A soft voice of warning tries to tell me he's dangerous to my equilibrium. I shush it, eager for once to enjoy something a little reckless. It's only for a few days. Nothing too deep can take root in such a short time, surely.

So I dry my hair and leave it in loose curls and wear simple clothes that he can take off when it's time, and I go upstairs.

———— ⚬⚬ ————

He's several floors above me, on a floor with fewer apartments. I stand before his door and pause for a moment, touching my stomach. Music plays quietly, and I hear the clank of a pan or dish. A scent of browning onions fills the air.

What am I doing? He is a lot more . . . everything . . . than I ordinarily let myself get mixed up in. I don't date suitable men. Not the surgeon who pursued me for more than six months before he finally realized I really meant it. Not the fit colonel who came in with a snapped wrist and charmed me with his chocolaty eyes.

The men I sleep with—and let's be clear that I am standing in this hallway with sex on my mind—are like the surfer from last summer, or the bartender at the restaurant I like to have dinner in a few times a month, or even the robust coworker of my mother's, dark-skinned and charming and getting a bit long in the tooth for his dream of breaking into the music business.

If I compare Javier to Chris, the surfer, they're not even the same species. Javier is a grown-up, a man so comfortable with himself that he makes moving in the world look easy. Every inch of my skin wants his hands. My ears want that sonorous voice. My mouth wants his lips.

And my belly, it reminds me, wants food. I raise my hand and knock. He opens the door and, with a flourish of a tea towel, invites me in.

"I was afraid you might change your mind," he says.

I think of how long I stood in front of the door. "You promised me food. I very rarely turn that down."

He brushes my hair over my shoulder, touches the side of my neck. "Is it the food you came for?"

I look up at him. Shake my head.

A smile edges his mouth, and with one hand, he brushes my cheek. "Good. Please sit down. Let me pour you a glass of wine."

I wander more deeply into the apartment. This one is at least double the size of mine, with a separate bedroom and a proper, glitzy kitchen made all of aqua glass and stainless steel. The styles are different from what I'm used to. The taste of Aucklanders. His unit sits on the corner, and a balcony stretches from one set of glass doors in the living room around the corner to the bedroom, all overlooking the city center and the harbor beyond. "I love this building. It's so . . . extravagant, isn't it? I feel pampered."

"You can see the building on postcards and coffee cups."

"Really?"

"Yes." He brings me a generous glass of white wine. "A local vintage. See if you like it."

"Thanks." I sip gingerly, aware that I'm teetering on the shores of a lake made of exhaustion and sexual tension and jet lag, but the wine is like a breeze, sharp and clean, not too sweet. "Fantastic."

"Good." He heads back to the kitchen. He's changed clothes from earlier, and his hair is damp at the ends. He wears a pair of jeans with a Henley in heathered blue. The fabric lies easily over his skin, tastefully clinging to his torso.

"What are you cooking?"

"So simple, *tortilla española*. Do you know it?"

I shake my head.

His sleeves are tugged up on his forearms, and the cup towel is over his shoulder as he tilts a wide skillet and shakes the potatoes and onions within. The potatoes are slightly crisped on the outside, the onions translucent, and my stomach growls as he salts the mix, then scoops it into a bowl with raw whipped eggs. "This is everywhere in Madrid, like sandwiches in the States."

"Are there a lot of sandwiches? I don't know that I ever noticed."

He makes a noise. "So many sandwiches! Every place has sandwiches! Turkey sandwiches, hamburgers, grilled cheese, and submarines."

I laugh. "Just subs. The submarine would be the boat that goes underwater."

"Yes." His grin is quick, crinkles the sun lines on his face. "Subs. I like them. With ham and salami and all those vegetables."

"Me too. I like hamburgers too. Cheeseburgers, especially, the sloppier the better."

"Cheeseburgers are excellent." He scrapes the pan and adds a fresh layer of oil, adroitly turning the pan side to side to spread it evenly. He holds his hand a few inches above the burner to test the heat and then settles the pan back down, pours in the egg and potato mix. "This is where the danger is," he says with some seriousness. "We must be very patient, let the eggs cook slowly."

We both watch the eggs, watch the edges and then the middle dry slightly, and when the texture arrives at some particular level, he picks up the pan and, with a deft gesture, flips the flat omelet into the air and catches it to brown on the other side. Leaning on the counter, he gives me one raised brow and a sideways smile. "Are you impressed?"

I laugh at my words coming back to me. "Yes. I am very impressed."

When the eggs finish, we sit side by side on the couch—"There is a table, but look where it is, against the wall, so cramped"—looking out to the view of the harbor. The eggs are perfect, the potatoes and the onions and all of it blending into a homey, satisfying meal.

We both fall to eating like hungry puppies. "So good," I manage. "I need to add this to my short list of things to cook after work." I take a sip of wine. "Except that I never seem to remember to buy eggs."

His plate is empty. "Do you want some more?"

"Yes. If it isn't too piggy."

He laughs and fills my plate again, sitting with me. We watch the lights across the harbor. The music has shifted to soft Spanish guitar, a sound that almost has a color, a pale, early green that winds around the room, sprouting flowers. I think of him on the stage, bending in to sing a love song.

"Surely," he says after a moment, "there are market deliveries for a busy woman such as yourself. I myself would starve without them."

I shrug. "I just always tell myself I'm going to shop, and then I pop in and buy cat food and milk and forget everything else."

I've made short work even of the second plate, and I don't know if it's just anticipation or genuine hunger, but I dab my lips carefully. He takes my plate and sets it atop his on the coffee table and now moves closer, brushing my hair away from my neck.

"Tell me about your cat."

"His name is Hobo," I say, closing my eyes as his mouth falls on the bend between neck and shoulder.

"I like cats," he says quietly.

"He's black. A feral I rescued." I turn toward him, settling my hands on his face so that I can kiss him properly. His jaw is exquisitely smooth, much smoother than it was on the ferry. I stroke the clean skin. "You shaved."

"Yes," he murmurs, and kisses me back. As it was on the ferry, we kiss for a long time, and I marvel that only kissing can fill so much need.

Then he stands and offers his hand, and I follow him to the bedroom. I take off my shirt and help him with his, and then my bra is gone, and our skin slides together as we kiss again and again, with increasing heat, my breath hurried and ragged as he slides his hands beneath the soft waist of my pants and helps me get out of them. I reach for his jeans, but he says, "Allow me."

And then we're on the bed, naked, and I'm so hungry I almost want to bite him. So I *do* bite him, his shoulder. The size of his body excites me. His tongue excites me. His mouth, his teeth nipping me, his hands gripping me so hard. It's a very physical, almost rough joining, and I'm glad of it, glad of the slamming energy, glad of the feeling of him in me, his urgency, and my own powerful grip. I wrap my legs hard around him, and we move, and move, and move. My voice is guttural, our skin slick, and we tumble over and lie there together in the dark, panting.

"Oh my God," I whisper against his ear, sucking the lobe into my mouth.

"Mm," he agrees, and raises his head. For a long moment, he looks at me; then very gently he kisses me. "So lovely."

And then we're side by side, my body tucked up against his, which I ordinarily don't like but feels good when I am so far from home, so far out of my depth. His body is bigger than mine at every point, and it makes me feel safe and sheltered, and because I'm so tired, I fall into a deep and dreamless sleep, far, far, far away.

——— ✦ ———

Again the dream arrives.

I'm sitting on a rock in the cove, with Cinder beside me. We're staring out to the restless ocean, and in the distance, Dylan is riding his surfboard, not even wearing a wet suit, only his yellow-and-red board shorts. He's happy, really happy, and that's why I don't want to warn him that the wave is breaking up.

And then it throws him, and he disappears into the sea. Cinder barks and barks and barks, but Dylan doesn't surface. The water goes still, and there is nothing to see but silvery water all the way to the horizon.

I jerk awake, glad of the weight of Javier anchoring me. My heart is racing, and I have to take a deep breath. *Calm down. Calm down. Just a dream.*

"Are you all right?" Javier asks.

"Yes. Just a weird dream." My bladder insists on attention, so I toss back the covers and pad naked into the bathroom. My teeth are disgusting from the wine, so I squeeze a little of his toothpaste onto a finger and rub my teeth; then I swish it around in my mouth and pad back to the bedroom. Now that I'm up, I probably should really return to my apartment, but Javier tosses back the covers, and I slide in, happy for a glimpse of his bare hip, his navel. His hair is tousled and wild, and it makes me smile as I settle in next to him. One arm falls around me. I fall too into the quiet comfort of him next to me.

——— ✦ ———

It's dawn when I awaken again. Buttery light spreads across the water beyond the windows, splashes into the high-rises around us. Within, Javier is sleeping next to me, his arms flung out in front of him, his face in repose. Beneath the sheet, he is naked, and I lift it up to look. It's a gorgeous body.

"Do you like it?" he says in a soft voice.

"Quite a bit," I say. I glance at him but don't lower the sheet, instead making a show of staring. It stirs me, and I can tell it's stirring him too. I smile and drop the sheet. "Good morning."

He narrows his eyes. "Are you cheerful in the mornings?"

"Not usually. I can be downright surly. How about you?"

"I have been working nights a very long time, and in Madrid that can be very late indeed."

"You haven't told me what you do," I say.

He lifts up the sheet, looks at my body, and makes a soft *ooof* before he moves closer. He tosses the sheet away from us with irritation and goes back to his task. I let him, enjoying the tilt of his back, long and muscular as he examines me.

"Your body is a wilderness," he says softly, and brushes his fingers over my ribs, my belly, slides between my thighs, kisses my belly button, continues down my leg. His buttocks, strong and high, are in my reach, and as he explores my curves, I shape my palm around his and slide down the back of his thighs, dipping between his legs to hear his rumbling. I laugh softly, and he rises up on his knees, offering himself.

I reach for him. "Full-frontal nudity. I like it."

And now, we make love more playfully, taking time to stop and admire and ask with a glance or a sound if this or that, that or that, is the best thing. He lingers over my body, stroking and kissing, and as I imagined, his mouth is everywhere, all over me, and I return the exploration, and then we're falling into each other as the sun slides into the room through glass doors.

Lying against him in the puddles of sunshine, thoroughly and deeply sated, I realize what I never understood about grown-up men is how much more they would have learned about women's bodies on their journey.

Or perhaps it's only Javier himself, who raises his head and leans on his elbow, brushing my hair out of my face with one hand, carefully tucking it behind my ears. An ache hits my chest at that, but I don't move. Light cascades over his powerful nose and backlights his hair, and there are marks on his shoulder from my biting him. I touch one spot. "Sorry about that. I got carried away."

He blinks slowly, moves his thigh against mine. "I don't mind. It will warn the women away."

"Do they come at you in droves?" I ask with some amusement.

"Not so much as when I was a little younger, but yes, still a lot."

I give him a frown. "Are you being serious right now?"

He lifts one index finger and rolls sideways to pick up his phone, opens an app, and then shows me the screen. On it is an album cover and a photo of a man bending over his guitar. A woman in the shadows stares at him. The title of the album is in Spanish, but I can read the name, Javier Velez, and I recognize those hands. "This is the work that keeps you up late?"

He nods almost sadly.

I look around the enormous suite of rooms, recognition dawning. This is a very expensive suite. "Are you famous?"

"Not here." He leans on his hand, splendidly naked, and I wonder if anyone from the office buildings is looking in, seeing his well-shaped behind.

I grin. "Are you famous somewhere?"

"Perhaps a little. In the Latin world, they know my songs."

The idea sinks in slowly, and rather than making me nervous, it eases my worry. If he's some big star, then I'm a distraction for him just as he is a distraction for me. "I suppose I will have to listen to more than one song next time."

He dips a finger over my navel, draws a circle around it. "Will you come tonight?"

I rise up, pushing him backward and spreading my body over the top of his like icing on a cake, my hands on his arms. "I might have to shop for something nicer to wear."

He lets himself be frosted with me, his eyes shining, his lips ever so faintly tilted into a smile. "I like the red dress."

I kiss his neck. "I'll find another red dress." I crawl up to kiss him, long and slow, enjoying the plumpness of his lips, the scent of his skin. "You smell better than any man I've ever met."

"Do I?"

Burying my face into his neck, I inhale deeply. "Like the ocean and dew and . . . something." I try to figure it out, something spicy, but I can't pull it in, and then we are switched, he icing the cake of my body, his hands in my hair.

"That is very sexy," he whispers, and bends into my neck, inhales, and sucks my skin there, once, then again, and again, and again. And somehow we are making love again, slowly, tumbling one more time into each other, into pleasure.

———— ❧ ————

A little later, I'm wrapped in a sheet, and he's wearing a pair of boxer briefs. We're drinking coffee he made in a French press and eating flaky pastries he produced from somewhere, along with little green fruits I thought were limes at first. "Feijoa," he said, and sliced one open to reveal a medieval cross of seeds within a soft fruit like a kiwi. It tastes powdery and sweet, a little like a pear.

"Delicious."

He scoops the fruit out of the skin with a small spoon, nodding. With a finger, he strokes the discreet tattoo on my inner arm, mermaid scales with *little sister* written along the outside edge. Josie has a matching one. "Will you tell me about your sister?"

I look out toward the harbor, where a sailboat is a crisp white triangle gliding toward the sea. "It's hard to talk about her."

He's silent, giving me space to move forward or not. But I am soft and wide open from making love, my carapace dissolved for the moment in a tsunami of touch. I take a breath. "She was—is—two years older than me. I adored her when we were kids. My parents were not"—I sigh—"all that great at parenthood, so until Dylan arrived, Josie took care of me."

He gives me a nod.

I sip my coffee, holding the cup between my hands. "She was a happy kid, honestly. Mischievous but never bad. She didn't like school, but she didn't get in trouble that I remember. And then . . ." I shrug.

"Then?"

"She changed. It's hard to remember, exactly, but she started getting in trouble, stealing sips of drinks from customers, particularly the men, and then as we got a little older, she stole beers out of the bar and things like that."

His fingers move on my ankle. "Your parents did nothing?"

"I don't know if they even noticed." My stomach burns a little, and I rub it, straightening my back. Amazing how much it still stresses me out. "They were fighting, very passionate fights, yelling, throwing things, all that, and they just didn't pay any attention to what was going on with Josie."

"And what about you? Who took care of you?"

"Dylan," I say simply.

"The runaway. Like your brother?"

"Yes."

"And he read to you. *Charlie and the Chocolate Factory.*"

I smile. "Yes. And many others."

"He took care of you and your sister?"

"Yes. He worked as a sous chef in the restaurant, but he lived with us." I suck my lip into my mouth, thinking about how to explain Dylan. "He had some problems, but honestly I don't know how we would have gotten along without him. He was the one who got us up for school, the one who made sure we had shoes when others got too tight. He always looked at my homework right when I got home from school, even if he had a girlfriend there, which was pretty much all the time." I am filled with the ghost of the feeling I'd had on those afternoons, sitting with Dylan and Josie, who did homework only because she was forced, and whatever girl was hanging around at the time. I grin. "He was very handsome. The most handsome boy in the whole entire world."

Javier smiles. "Were you jealous?"

"Of course! He belonged to us!"

"How much older was he?"

"Six years older than Josie, eight older than me." I incline my head, aware that he's done it again—eased me into telling my story—and I give him a perplexed frown.

"What is it?"

"You seduce me into talking about myself."

"Because I want to know everything," he says, running a hand along my shin. "And if you tell me about your sister, perhaps I can help you find her."

For a moment, I wonder if he could be too much. Too emotional, too intense. But I do feel a bit adrift in trying to solve this problem. Another mind on it might help. "Maybe you can." I straighten. "Okay, let me get it all out."

He props his head on his hand. "Please."

"So, she was troubled, my sister. She refused to go to college and spent all her time partying and surfing. The last time I saw her, she stole pretty much everything I had, including my computer and all my clothes, and sold them."

"Oof. A terrible betrayal."

"Yes. I'd just finished my first residency, so I was strapped and exhausted, and I just could not believe she'd do something like that." I rub my belly again, feeling the edges of my hurt and anger when I returned to the apartment and discovered what she'd done. "I cut her off."

"Understandable."

"Yeah." I sigh. "Except that she supposedly died about six months later in a big explosion on a train in France. I never spoke to her again." I look backward in time, to that moment when I was walking back to my apartment and my mother called. A ghost of the pain from that day runs below my skin. In those howling minutes, I would have done anything to get her back.

His eyes are kind, but he doesn't speak.

"All this time I thought she was dead." I spread my hands, looking at my palms as if the story is written there. "And then I saw her on the news from the nightclub fire. She was here in the CBD when it happened."

"You believed her to be dead until you saw her on the television? All this time?"

"Yes."

He measures me for a long moment. "You must be so angry."

"That's an understatement." The slow boil of lava in my gut gurgles. "My mother urgently wanted me to come, or I might not have."

The large dark eyes hold steady on my face. "For my sake, I'm glad that you did."

I give him a half smile. "Oh, you would have found someone to warm your bed, I'm sure."

"She would not have been you."

"You don't have to charm me, Javier." To stave off any protestation he might bring, I shake my head. "Anyway, I guess I should get back to trying to find my sister. My mother will want a report."

"What have you done so far?"

"Not much. I've tried to find her by name, but that's a dead end. I do think that woman at the restaurant knew something, so I might go back there. But also—" I lift one eyebrow. "I'm looking out there at that ocean, and what I want to do is go surfing."

He inclines his head. "Not look for your sister?"

"Surfing is how I think, and maybe I'll get some ideas." A thick discomfort rolls through my lungs, making it momentarily hard to breathe, and I straighten my shoulders to create more room. "Do you want to learn to surf?"

He raises his hands. "No, no. I'm going to see Miguel today."

"All right, then." I eat the last bite of my pastry and brush my fingers off. "I'm going to get out of here and leave you to it."

He captures my hand. "You'll come to our show tonight?"

I nod, touch his head, his thick, wavy hair. "Who else will protect you from all the women?"

"It's true. I will need it." He captures my hand, kisses my palm. "See you later."

Chapter Fourteen

Mari

When I get home from my dinner with Nan, Simon has already tucked the children into bed. I tiptoe into each of their rooms and kiss their heads, then join Simon in the family room. He's sprawled in his chair, the little dog in his lap, the others fast asleep on the rug. I can tell he's exhausted. "How was your day?" I ask, running my fingers through his hair.

He leans into my hands, moving his head, and I rub harder. "Good. Sarah took first in the fifty-meter freestyle."

"No kidding! That's great. And Leo?"

"He lost to Trevor." His gaze wanders back to his stopped movie. "I think the lad might have Olympic talent."

"Trevor?"

He nods, and a yawn overtakes him. I smile and kiss his forehead. "Watch your movie. I'm going to have a bath."

"How was Nan?"

"Good." I think of the strange spill of confession I'd allowed to fall, and I feel a vague sense of worry at the back of my neck. What if she mentions it in front of Simon? Or—

The only way I can live the way I do is by compartmentalizing everything. "We had tapas."

"We're taking the kids over to the house in the morning, right?"

"I'll take them. You sleep late." I stroke his forehead, his temples. "You've been working hard all week."

"Thank you," he says as he takes my hand and plants a kiss on the palm, "but I want to be there when they see it."

"Your call. Don't stay up too late."

As I run my bath and strip down, rain is pouring outside. When I first moved to Auckland to live with Simon, we had a villa with a tin roof in another neighborhood, and the sound of the rain was sometimes deafening. This is hypnotic.

But three hours later, I'm still not asleep, and I finally slip out of bed and head downstairs to make a cup of tea. As the chamomile steeps, I open my computer and allow myself to stalk my sister. She doesn't spend much time on Facebook, but I can sometimes see photos on my mother's timeline, which is not private or closed or anything else.

She looks good, my mom. Her hair is still long. Her face is heavily lined, and I bet she still smokes. I know she doesn't drink anymore by the millions of references she makes to being sober and to AA.

But no matter how sober she is or how good she looks, I still resent her. Raising my children has given me an understanding of just how terrible my own parents were.

A girl without a mother who protects her is a girl at the mercy of the world. How could she have been so blind to the alcohol I consumed at nine years old? Twelve? Fourteen? How could she have missed seeing the abuse that occurred right under her nose? Sarah isn't allowed to walk on the beach alone, much less spend the night there alone.

At times I soften, thinking of how difficult her life was then too. My father was a hard man, born in Sicily during the war, and although he loved my mother jealously and protectively, he also took other women on a whim. He thought we were all spoiled and privileged, my mother and his daughters.

And God, how the two of them drank and partied!

The Christmas morning after Kit's tenth birthday, we tumbled down the stairs to find not the gifts "Santa" ordinarily left but a scene of devastation. The Christmas tree blinked in mute witness to overturned furniture, broken glasses, debris scattered all over the rug. Kit stood silently beside me, her big eyes taking in the disaster.

Dylan came up behind us. "Wow."

We stood there for long minutes, completely silent. My heart sank, falling from somewhere in the middle of my chest all the way through my gut and into the floor. I felt tears welling in my eyes. "Why did they do this?" I whispered. "Why did they have to do it on Christmas?"

Kit did not make a sound.

Dylan touched her shoulder, then mine. "I have an idea. Go get dressed. Both of you. Something nice."

We only looked at him. Not even Dylan could save this.

"Go on!" he said, and shoved us a little. "Get dressed, brush your teeth, brush your hair. Meet me outside in ten minutes."

Kit and I exchanged a glance. She shrugged.

We raced through our ablutions and ran downstairs and out the front door. Dylan had changed too, into a nice pair of jeans and a long-sleeve shirt with three buttons at the neck. His hair was clean and shiny, combed neatly and pulled back into a ponytail. He was waiting by my mother's Chevy and opened the door. "Kit in the front seat on the way there, Josie on the way back."

Kit's grin flashed for the barest moment as she claimed the prized spot. "Where are we going?"

"You'll see." He rubbed my head as he went by, and mollified over losing the front seat, I buckled myself in.

"Did Mom tell you that you could borrow her car?" Kit asked.

He started the car and headed north on the highway. "What do you think, Kitten?"

She shook her head.

"Right. Let's not talk about that anymore."

He drove us all the way to San Francisco, first to the pier, which was quiet except for the homeless people, and then to our true destination, Chinatown. He parked; then we got out and walked, and I was immediately enchanted by the red balls strung overhead and the multitude of shop fronts and signs. A strange smell filled the air, not completely pleasant, but I felt exhilarated by such a different world. I skipped on one side of him, and he held on to Kit's hand. "How'd you know about this place?" I asked.

"My mom used to bring me here."

"You have a mom?"

He shook his head. "She died."

Kit asked, "How old were you?"

"Eight," he said.

I peered up at him, intrigued by this new information. "Do you miss her?"

He was quiet for a long time. "That's a hard question. Sometimes she was okay, but most of the time she wasn't. I liked coming to Chinatown, though. We came at Christmas almost every year."

"Really?" I tested this, weighing the idea of Christmas dinner as prepared by my father against the lure of something so exotic. "Did you like it?"

He gave me his sideways smile, the one that made his eyes twinkle. "I did, Grasshopper."

We walked for a while, peering in crowded windows and dodging foot traffic. In the alleyways, people chattered in a language that sounded like music to me, up and down. A woman in red pajamas walked by and smiled, dipping her head at Dylan.

I was enchanted.

Dylan led us to a restaurant tucked at the edge of an alleyway. Inside, it was bright and clean, and a waiter waved us to a table by the window, where we sat down and looked out at the street. Dylan conferred with the waiter while Kit stared out the window and I tried to catalog all the things I could see by just turning my head. Chinese letters looking like houses or snowmen or little people, paintings of houses and fields on the wall. A shelf with red teapots.

Kit simply looked out the window, not even swinging her feet as she ordinarily did. Looking at her made me feel hollow, made me flash on the mess back in the living room, so I peered toward the back of the room to a window cutout that showed two heads in the kitchen.

"We're going to have dim sum," Dylan said. "And then a lot of sweets."

Kit looked at him but only nodded.

He pulled her chair close to his and put his arms around her, pulling her head into his shoulder. "It's gonna be okay, kid."

Jealousy ripped through me like a lightning bolt. Why did she always get the attention? I stared at them, seeing the mess in the living room, the broken glass, and my fingers tingled with a need to smash something. My ears burned at the tips, and a wild rage traveled through my throat, into my mouth, and I was about to open my lips and scream when Kit burst into tears.

"Our stockings!" she cried, and sobbed.

Dylan held her closer, his hand smoothing her hair, murmuring soft words. "I know; I'm sorry; it's okay; go ahead and cry, Kitten."

I slid out of my chair and rounded the table so that I could wrap my body on the other side of my little sister. She was crying so hard that her body rocked, and I bent into her, my belly against her side, and breathed into her hair. "It's okay. It's okay. I'll get you a stocking, a better one."

She cried until the waiter brought our tea, when Dylan said, "Hey, Kitten, look at this. It's chrysanthemum tea. It's made with flowers."

"Really?" She lifted her head, wiping her tears away almost angrily. I gave her a napkin, and she leaned into me for a minute, then took a breath.

Steady. Calm now.

Released, I drifted back around to my place, feeling lost and achy for no reason until Dylan reached over and squeezed my arm. "You're such a good big sister."

A little of the ache eased. "Thanks."

"I'm gonna wash my face," Kit said, tossing her wild hair out of her face.

Dylan poured tea into my tiny cup. "It's good for calming," he said.

"I'm not upset."

He nodded. "Good." He poured tea for himself, then reached into his coat pocket and brought out a package and placed it in front of me. "Merry Christmas."

"Yours is at home!" I cried, but my heart swelled anyway. "Can I open it?"

"Wait for Kit." He placed another package, a bigger one, beside her place.

I eyed the bigger box, wondering if I should be jealous, but I decided not to be. When Kit came back, we both tore them open. Hers was a Rubik's Cube, which I would never have wanted anyway.

Mine was a pair of delicate turquoise earrings for pierced ears, which mine were not. I held them up with a question on my face.

"Your mom said you can get your ears pierced over Christmas vacation."

"What? Really?"

"Yep. She might want to take you, but if she doesn't, I will."

"What about me?" Kit asked. "I want pierced ears too."

"When you're twelve," he said. "Your sister is older, and she gets privileges you don't have yet."

I sat up straighter and held the earrings to my ears. "What do you guys think?"

Kit nodded. "Beautiful."

"Just right," Dylan said, and I basked in the aquamarine focus of his gaze.

—————— ❧❧❧ ——————

The memory runs down my spine as I look at my mother now in her photographs on Facebook.

I needed her. Every girl needs a mother who protects her with a savage fury. Mine didn't even meow in my direction.

On her page, however, I find photos of Kit. Today there is nothing new, just the same ones I've seen before. Kit in her scrubs, pale green, in the ER. Kit with a black cat who sits on her shoulder.

A doctor who surfs. Who doesn't seem to have a husband or family, because my mom would have posted those pictures. It makes me sad for Kit that she's so alone, and I wonder how much blame I bear for that.

I've given up guilt over the things I did, the losses I caused. Guilt wants erasing in a big bottle of ice-cold vodka. Regret asks for amends, and I wish I could offer them. I wish Kit could see me now, healed and whole. Would she love me again? Or would she still give me that expression of resignation that became so familiar toward the end?

The rain has stopped, leaving behind a stillness that echoes. These are the times I want to drink and smoke, when all my demons come crawling out of the closets and drawers to taunt me with my past sins. There are so many of them.

So many. The chambers of my heart feel shredded as I sit in the dark, staring at my lost sister's face. I miss her so damn much.

And by the end, I'm sure she hated me for all the ways I let her down. Stole from her, because I was hungry. Stayed away too much even though I knew she was practically dying of loneliness. So was I, but the only thing I knew then was that I had to stomp down the pain. I had sex with everything that moved, drugged myself into numbness.

It was the only way. I couldn't bear to tell her everything that had happened, the things that were out of my control and the things that were not.

The things I would change if I could.

But even if you're suffering, you don't get to do whatever you want, and even if I could make amends, even if we were living side by side, how could I?

A well of pain opens in my chest and spills into my gut. Beyond the windows, the water is restless, catching flashes of light, rumbling with intent.

I close the computer. Wallowing is not just a bad idea; it's dangerous. I made my choices, and I have to live with them.

In the morning, while I'm getting dressed, Simon inclines his head. "Will you wear the turquoise I bought a few weeks ago?"

I don't think much of it. He likes dressing me, in the best possible way. The dress is a simple sleeveless cotton that makes the most of my coloring, and it's a perfectly good choice.

We load up the family and head out first thing in the morning. Leo is annoyed at first, because he'd been hoping to spend the day with a friend with a sailboat, but Simon quashes his rebellion with a sentence. "There will be other days to sail, mate," he said, "but you'll never get another chance to join the family for the big reveal."

Leo snorts and play punches his dad in the stomach. Simon play doubles over.

We make a morning of it, stopping first at a café in Mount Eden for a decadent breakfast. Sarah is animated and cheerful—but then, it's a weekend, and she won't have to go to school for two days. Leo sits next to me, talking a mile a minute about his mates and swimming and sport and mountaineering, which is his new obsession. He's been reading about Sir Edmund Hillary, a local hero and the first to climb Mount Everest.

"How long did it take you to climb the Golden Hinde, Mom?" he asks, chomping on a piece of bacon.

I'm lost in imagining the climb up Everest and the continual need people feel to do it, and I answer offhandedly. I don't honestly remember which mountain it is, only that it's on Vancouver Island, where I supposedly grew up. "I don't know. A day, I guess."

"Not the Hinde," Simon says with a frown. "Takes a couple to ascend that one, eh?"

My heart is racing, making a noise in my ears, and I'm sure that my skin has gone bright red. "Of course!" I cry, slapping my hands to my cheeks. "Oh my goodness, I'm so embarrassed."

Simon bumps me with his shoulder. "It's all good, sweetheart. We won't put you in the home yet, will we, kids?"

Sarah says, very seriously, "I'll never put you in a home, Mum. Ever."

I reach over the table and squeeze her hand. "Thank you, baby. I love you too."

"We aren't going to put Grandpa in a home, are we?"

"Oh, no! No way." I squeeze her hand more tightly. "Your grandpa is just fine."

But I happen to look up at Simon and, as wives can do, pick up the subtlest twist of his lips. I touch his thigh beneath the table. He covers my hand with his.

———— ⚬≈⚬ ————

At Sapphire House, we forget all that, and I make a dramatic moment of our entry. "You know, children, that I have loved this house ever since I came here, right? It sits so high above everything—"

"Like a palace!" Leo cries.

"Yes, like a palace. And so when your daddy found out it was up for sale, he bought it for us to live in."

"I want to see the greenhouse," Sarah says.

"In a bit, love." I give Simon a smile. "First, let's take a look at the inside of the house and the balconies and all the great things there are here." I fling open the door and say, "Ta-da!"

They both dash in and pause. "Whoa!" Leo cries, spinning a circle as he looks in every direction at once.

Sarah is more moderate. She walks in like a girl in a storybook, taking in the setting for her new chapter. She peers up the staircase, and runs her fingers over the wall, and lets the wide bank of windows in the back call her to the view over the sea. "Mummy, look! You can see the cyclone!"

She's been taking measurements and gleefully following a weather site she loves over news of the cyclone, which has been blowing our way for a couple of days. While the sky is sunny, she's right—you can see the dark storm gathering in a line along the horizon.

"Let's go out and look at it," I suggest, opening one of the French doors.

The view is utterly gorgeous, the deep aquamarine of the water, the navy-blue mountains in the distance, the emerald grass between us and the water, the bright-blue sky, and that slim, faraway line of eggplant cloud. The layers and layers and layers of blue against green against blue against green is ever dazzling, impossible to get used to. "Isn't it beautiful?" I ask, my hand on her back. "We can have a table out here. Some chairs."

She leans on me unexpectedly. "Won't cyclones hit us here?"

"I don't know, baby, but the house has been here for eighty years. I'm sure there've been some big cyclones in that time." I stroke her curly hair. "Are you afraid of cyclones?"

"No. Strong ones are rare."

"That's true. So you needn't worry."

"I don't want to move, really. I like our house. And how'll I move all my experiments?"

"I'm sure we can figure that out, sweetheart. Your grandfather will have good ideas."

I remember the old-school telephone. "I have something to show you, and then we can go upstairs and look at bedrooms."

"All right."

She follows me into the house, and we head for the alcove. "Do you know what this is?"

"Of course. It's a telephone."

I'm deflated slightly, but there's more. I pick up the earpiece, listen, and offer it to her. "Do you know what that is?"

"No. Why does it make a noise?"

"It's called a dial tone. This is a landline, which means it's connected to the wall with a wire, and the wire is what connects it to other phones. You lift up the receiver for the dial tone to make sure it works, and then you use the ring to dial the numbers." I illustrate by dialing my own phone number, and it rings in my hand.

Sarah nods. But she's turning away, heading for the stairs. "I want to see the bedrooms."

Leo is already up there. "Mom, you've gotta see this! This room has its own little bathroom, and there are tiles all over it! Can I have this room?"

"You don't get to choose before I even see!" Sarah protests, and runs past him into the bedroom.

I follow more slowly, because four of the six bedrooms have their own bathrooms, and all of them are tiled magnificently. Leo runs into the one I knew he'd love, with its row of windows like a captain's quarters in the prow of a ship. They overlook the driveway and the city.

The children dash around, pulling open drawers and doors to peer inside. Most of it is empty. I haven't spent time in the secondary bedrooms yet. This one looks weary, with a faded mural along the top of the walls and curtains of no distinction. From my bag, I take out a notebook and scribble a few notes to myself, using a fountain pen I picked up yesterday and filled with a bright-magenta ink. The reds and yellows were always my shades, while Kit loved turquoise, violet, green. Dylan liked brush calligraphy in a Chinese style, using the darkest, blackest ink he could find. I always thought Kit seemed like a person who'd want more serious ink, the heavy blacks or browns, but no. She loved vivid shades in her colors and favored a fine tip for her precise handwriting. As I make note of the curtains, the wallpaper, I'm pleased by the elegance the stubbed tip lends even my scribbled notes.

"What about me?" Sarah says. "Which room do I get?"

"Come here." I tuck pen and book back in my bag and take her across the hall to a room very similar to the others. The walls are a faded, awful shade of grimy yellow, and the bookshelves are sagging, but all that is cosmetic. The best feature is the one Sarah narrows in on immediately: a trio of porthole windows that looks to the sea. She dashes toward them, stands on her toes to look out. On either side of the portholes are two windows that open outward, and I crank one energetically to let nature in. "Listen," I say, putting a hand to my ear.

"I do like to listen to the ocean," she says, smiling. "It helps me sleep."

My heart stings. It's something we always said—the Bianci women need to be able to hear the ocean when they sleep. For a moment, I am unbearably sad that she will never know she even is a Bianci. "I know," I manage in an upbeat voice. "That's why I thought of it."

"Thanks, Mummy." She hugs my waist.

"Let's go check out the greenhouse, shall we?"

But Simon calls up, "Mari, darling, can you come down?"

I take Sarah's hand, and we head down the stairs. A woman with a video camera on her shoulder and another wearing the coiffed hair and suit jacket of a television reporter are standing in the grand hallway.

The camera blinks red, recording, as it tilts itself upward to Sarah and me, coming down the sweep of stairs. "What's going on?"

Simon, looking highly pleased with himself, introduces them. "This is Hannah Gorton and Yvonne Partridge from TVNZ. They're here to do a feature."

My heart freezes so hard I think it might shatter. "Nice to meet you," I say, walking toward them to shake hands. Then I turn back to Simon. "Can I talk to you for a minute?"

"Of course." He follows me into the pantry, out of earshot.

"What are they doing here?"

"I told them they could come."

"Why didn't you tell me? I might have wanted some better make-up, you know!"

"I knew you'd resist, and it will be good for publicity."

"Why do we need publicity?" A frantic terror of revelation bangs around in my chest. "I don't want our private lives made public!"

"It's just business. We're going to want to sell the other parcels at the best possible price, and this will generate excitement," he says with a firmness I know will not budge. He's a lovely man in a thousand and one ways, but when he decides on something, he is immovable. "And it's only a half hour."

"What other parcels?"

"I told you—to make this profitable, we'll be developing the lower levels of the land into housing."

"I don't remember you talking about that." Pressing my fingers to my temples, I try to calm down. It's true that in the land-starved suburbs, housing parcels will make a mint. "But why do we have to put our lives on television?"

He presses his palm into my shoulder. "Come on, now. It'll be right."

For one long moment, I feel the two sides of my life in direct conflict. I feel them both on either side of my heart, pounding against each other. If I let him have his way, my face will be out on the internet again, increasing the danger that someone will recognize me. But I can't argue with Simon when he makes up his mind on something. I may as well slam my head against granite. And if I'm too resistant, he'll wonder why.

Shoving my fears down, I say sharply, "Fine," and push his hand away, then stomp back into the other room. With effort, I plaster a smile over my face and laugh in a way I've learned to do, and I let them film me in the lounge and the halfway horrible kitchen. After a little while, I let go of everything but this—showing them the exquisite stairs made of kauri wood and Australian blackwood railings, the master bath entirely tiled in the Art Deco fashion, and the amazing windows with their views of the harbor, islands slumped across the horizon.

And as we do another walk-through, I find myself falling more and more in love, feeling as if Sapphire House might be the reason for everything. The children tear through the rooms, and it's all I could ever want.

I'm meant to be here. It was fated.

Looking at Simon across the room, so hearty and cheerful, I wonder what would happen if he knew everything. My terrible reputation as a teen, my reckless, reckless behavior, my—

My gigantic lie. Eyeing my beautiful husband in his crisp shirt and jeans, with one foot kicked out in front of him and his shoulder on the wall, I wonder what it would be like to confess it all. To be fully myself with the man I love more than I thought myself capable of. It's lonely to carry a secret.

But as he smiles his honest, open, loyal smile, I know the truth. I can't confess. He would hate me. He would never, ever speak to me again.

So I do the interview, putting on my cheeriest face, my not-quite-Kiwi, not-quite-US accent, and show them around Sapphire House.

I'm captured again by the story, by the tragic love story back there in the past, by the startling, thrilling fact that I can restore it.

In the end, the reporter says with a smile, "Thanks, Mari. I think that's it."

"My pleasure," I say, but the words hurt my throat, as if they have corners. When this airs, my face is going to be splattered all over TVNZ. It will be on the internet.

Anyone could see it.

Anyone.

It is the worst danger I've faced since I arrived, and it puts everything—*everything*—at stake.

Before we go, I head up to the attic to look for artifacts from Veronica's life. It's draped with cobwebs I sweep away with a broom I brought for just this reason.

Sarah has come with me, too, and I put her to work opening boxes while I make notes on the contents. The attic is mostly barren, with a few boxes of odds and ends, none of which looks particularly interesting. A few hold clothes, and we'll want to explore those more carefully, considering the era. At last, far away in the back, are two smallish boxes that prove to be the bound diaries Helen filled. I bend over and pick one out at random. The date is 1952. I dig deeper and find one from 1945. The other box contains later entries, and I'm not as interested in those. "Give me a minute, kiddo." I sit on the floor next to the box and take them all out. They're not in any order: 1949 is next to '55, but that seems to be the latest.

The earliest, frustratingly enough, is 1939. "I wonder where the rest of them are."

"There's more boxes over here," Sarah says. "And look! Baby clothes."

Frowning, I jump to my feet. The clothes are tucked into a wooden cradle, covered with a dusty sheet. The clothes are all for a newborn or just a little older and don't appear to have been used at all. Someone must have had a miscarriage. My heart aches a little, lifting up tiny sweaters and rompers.

Sarah's already lost interest in the clothes and opened a few more boxes. They contain any number of things but nothing I can really use to get the answers I need. Where are the other journals? I need the 1930s.

Maybe she hadn't started keeping them until she moved here.

I mark the two boxes of journals and a third box of scrapbooks with an *X* for Simon to bring down.

Then I remember the stacks of plastic containers holding magazines, down in Helen's room. Maybe there will be something there. "Come with me, Sarah. I have an idea."

Chapter Fifteen
Kit

When I was seven and Josie was nine, Dylan taught us to surf.

I remember the first lesson clearly, because I had Dylan to myself for once, a very rare occurrence. I woke up in the tent, and Josie was gone. Dylan was sprawled flat on his back, hands crossed on his chest, and Cinder snored beside me, but Josie's sleeping bag didn't even look touched. I crawled out to pee. The morning was thick and overcast, the ocean restless below it, and I waded into the lapping waves, letting the cold water ripple over my arches and ankles. We swam most days, Josie and I, and this was how I kept myself ready—wading in as high as I could, then dashing back out, wading in, dashing out. Cinder must have heard me, because he scrambled out of the tent too and started running in and out with me. He found a long weathered piece of driftwood and tossed it to me. I laughed and picked it up and threw it back toward the beach. He was a retriever, but he didn't love actually swimming unless he absolutely had to. Once the water reached his chest, he always ran back to the beach, barking.

This morning, he did the same. I ran into the ocean and out, and he ran in and out chasing his driftwood. After a while, Dylan emerged from the tent, blinking, wearing a pair of Hawaiian-print board shorts, all his scars on full display—the puckered pink one that ran over his biceps, the constellation of perfect circles across his belly, and one-foot-long thin marks here and there, not the ordinary kind of scars a person had. He told crazy stories about them—that he'd wrestled a pirate, danced over coals, gotten stuck in a meteor shower in outer space.

"Hey, kid," he said now, his voice raspy. "Where's your sister? Did she ever come down?"

"No, I don't think so."

He frowned, looking up the stairs toward the restaurant. He tugged his shirt on and sat down on the sand to light a half-smoked joint he took out of his pocket. The sweet smell mingled with ocean and fog to make a scent that I would always associate with him. "You hungry?"

"Not yet," I lied. My stomach was growling a little bit, but I never, ever got to have him to myself, and I planned to enjoy it as long as I could. "Are you surfing today?"

"Yep."

"Are you *ever* going to teach us?"

He glanced over at me. "You really want to learn?"

"Duh!" I flung out my hand toward the waves. "You've been telling us for ages that we could."

He inhaled, held it. His eyes were red already from all the drinking the night before, but it only made his irises pop—those abalone-shell colors blasting right out of his face. As he exhaled in a small stream, I tried to catch it, and he laughed. "You never want to do this, little girl."

"No," I said definitely. "Drugs are bad for you. Smoking is really, *really* bad for you."

"You're right."

"So why do you do drugs if you know they're bad?"

His long hair was caught back in a ponytail, and he reached up and tugged out the rubber band, working his fingers through the tangles. I touched my braid to check it, but it was still very tight and good. "I don't know, Kitten," he said. He plucked a piece of pot off his lip. "It's stupid, but I guess I like not thinking."

"But why?" I leaned in. "I love to think."

He smiled. "You're so good at it—that's why. And that's the reason you should never, never, never do any drugs—because you are so smart." He tapped my forehead. "You're the smartest one of all of us. You know that, right?"

I shrugged. "Yeah."

"Good." He pinched the end of the joint. "Pinkie promise me, okay? You will never, ever do drugs."

I reached up my pinkie, and we twisted them together. "Promise." I wished he didn't have to do drugs either, but I could feel that darkness in him getting better as he smoked his joint. It was like he carried around some mean monster that shut up only when he drank or smoked pot.

"Surfing's better," he said, and stood up. "It's going to be cold."

"Duh."

He grinned his best grin, the one that crinkled the edges of his eyes, and held out his hand. "All right, then. Let's do this thing."

He kept his board, a longboard with red and yellow detailing along the rails, on the beach. He put me on the board in front of him and paddled us out only about five feet. Waves were low and slow, and even I knew that these were bland conditions.

We just sat on the board, our feet trailing. In his deep, quiet voice, he explained how to feel the movement, the energy of the waves, and I was enchanted by the science of it, feeling the movements, the swells. We practiced first on my belly; then he showed me how to stand up from a squat, which was easy. He stood me up with him, laughing when my balance was solid—"Kit, that's great! That's really great!"— but I wasn't surprised. I was always good at physical things.

Paddle out, stand up, feel it. Paddle, stand up. He made me stand in front, one hand on my waist to steady me, and caught a wave so small it hardly made a ripple, but we rode it down the shoreline quite a way, and I could feel the difference between that and a no-wave.

That ride, that single, easy ride on a tiny wave, made me a surfer. Behind me, Dylan murmured encouragement—"There you go, steady, bend your knees"—and his approval made me ten feet tall, the princess of surfing. Overhead was the heavy sky, around us the ocean and her secrets, and my feet on the board, the water cold, my fingertips frozen.

The wave petered out on the far end of the cove. "Hungry?" Dylan asked.

I was ready to catch raw fish and shove them down my throat, but I didn't want to quit. "A little."

"Getting tired?"

"Yeah," I admitted.

"Looks like Josie's brought food down." He waved toward the cove, where I saw my sister spreading out a blanket and pinning it with a basket and whatever she'd lugged from the kitchen. She waved back and put her hands on her hips.

We paddled toward her, and I waded out. Grabbing a chunk of cheese, I started to gobble it before I even went back to the tent for my hoodie. Ducking into the relative warmth of our tent, I found the hoodie, tugged it on to stop my shivering, and scrambled back out.

Josie stood with her arms crossed hard over her chest, glaring at Dylan. "You taught her and not me?"

He settled on the blanket, taking grapes and bread and cheese from the basket she'd carried down. "You weren't here. Did you sleep in your room?"

She gave a hard, jagged shrug. "I couldn't find you guys, and it was dark, and I just went to my bed."

"Hey, hey," Dylan said, "we didn't mean to hurt your feelings." He stood on his knees to rub her back. She jerked away violently.

He backed up, hands palm out. "You okay?"

"Fine." She fell to the blanket, her body sharp, all knees and elbows. "I'm just mad. I want to learn to surf too."

He watched her for a minute. I sat close, and he wrapped an arm around me. "Eat, kiddo."

But he didn't have to tell me twice. My gut felt like an empty, yawning hole, and I chewed as fast as I could. Josie radiated prickly light, most of it directed at me, but I ignored her, feeling my blood swaying in an echo of the waves. I watched them rolling in, little, little, little, big. Little, little, big. Little, little, little, big. Big. Really big.

"It's fun, Josie," I said, and something in me was quiet. "You'll like it."

"If I'd known there was gonna be lessons, I'd've been here." She almost sounded like she was going to cry. "No one *told* me."

Then she did cry. Crumpled over herself, knees sticking out side to side, skinny arms bracing her head, all that long hair scattering over her like a blanket.

"It's okay, Grasshopper," Dylan said, patting her head. "We have all day. We'll all surf, right?"

Josie didn't raise her head, just stayed where she was, crying softly, Dylan's hand in her hair.

Decades later, I stand on the beach at Piha, New Zealand, clad in a rented short-sleeve wet suit and holding a rented board, and I think about how much he smoked weed and drank with us. We idolized him then, but as an adult, I'm appalled.

Taking my measure of the waves, I feel the ghosts of Dylan and Josie, eyeing the waves, eyeing the sky with me, all of us quieting as the sea weaves her fingers through our hair. I find myself humming "The Mermaid Song": "We there did espy a fair pretty maid, With a comb and a glass in her hand, her hand, her hand, With a comb and a glass in her hand."

It had not been an easy undertaking to get to this beach, but the more trouble I encountered, the more desperate I was to surf, which is often the only way I can think clearly.

Or maybe it's my drug.

Either way, in the end I hired a driver to drive me the forty kilometers to the west coast of the island, and I rented the board and suit right up the road. Once I got to the shop, they spoke my language, even if it was not always *exactly* my language, given the accent, and I was golden. The dude running the joint could tell I knew my stuff, and when I asked the right questions, he got me the right equipment. My driver, a chubby Maori woman, bought a hat so she could sit on the beach, happy to sit and watch for the money I paid her to stay so I wouldn't have to call anyone else when I was finished.

The guy at the shop told me there is a cyclone up north, which is whipping up better waves than would be found ordinarily at this spot at this time of day, and I'm eyeing the line with pleasure. Clusters of waves are rolling in, some up to five or six feet, and it isn't crowded. I paddle out politely and take my place, lifting my chin as a guy acknowledges me.

One by one, the surfers take their rides, and I see this is not a serious crowd. There are some decent riders in there but only one I'd call an expert, a sturdy, dark woman with hard-braided black hair and a red-striped wet suit. She rides easily, relaxed, until the wave carries her all the way home.

When it's my turn, the waves have risen to six feet and hold their shape like they're carved, the wind pushing them to shore. I catch my wave, find my center, and ride. The air is hot, the water cold, the view completely different from my Santa Cruz vistas.

The wave ripples downward, downward, and I slide home to shore, realizing that my mind is completely empty. Exactly what I wanted.

Carrying Dylan and Josie with me, I head back out to the line to meditate some more in the sunshine and the water.

After the earthquake, my mother, Josie, and I lived in Salinas. My father had been killed, the restaurant and our house had been destroyed in the earthquake, and we were flung into a small, cold world, just the three of us. My mother worked in restaurants, all she knew, and stayed out late drinking the rest of the time, leaving Josie and me to our own devices. As ever. But it was worse then. The city was known for gangs, which scared even Josie at first. I don't know why my mother took us there, honestly. I think about some of her decisions and a lot of them were insane, but Salinas? What possessed her? I would ask her, but she carries enough scars without my adding another one.

The earthquake had caused a lot of damage, so rentals were at a premium. Maybe that was the only place she could find. The only job, the only apartment. It was in a decent neighborhood on the north end of town, but in comparison to the little jewel of our house on its hill with its Spanish touches and views of the wild ocean, it was a cardboard box. Cheerless with bad light and shag carpet left over from the seventies. Josie and I had to share a bedroom, though my mom gave us the master, and I hated sharing with her. She was a slob, her clothes everywhere, her books. She hid her pot all over the room, mostly on my side, and it infuriated me.

She wasn't there much, though. My mom worked nights, and Josie cruised, riding with this boy or that. She didn't have a lot of girlfriends. She said the only girlfriend she needed was me, but I knew the real reason was that she'd sleep with a boy on a whim, girlfriend or not, and who'd want that girl around?

I missed my real sister, the one who whispered with me, the one who used to be in my corner, but I couldn't find a way to reach her. She had disappeared into another life, and I didn't know how to follow her there.

Did my mother know she was out all the time? I don't know. That first year, we were all a mess, grieving the loss of everything—everything we'd known, the people we'd loved. In a way, it was smart for my mom to move us away from all that was so familiar. Fresh start. That's what she said, a fresh start. At first she was a hostess at a high-end steakhouse, the kind that was all the rage in those days. Steak, potatoes, wine served in tiny glasses, flickering "ambient" lights. She was a great hostess, dressed in her wardrobe of sexy dresses left over from everything. She hadn't been able to save them all, but she'd found a bunch. Plenty for her to make a splash, to make a living.

Sort of. Turned out the hostess gig didn't pay as well as tending bar. She stepped down in atmosphere at the restaurant to get a bump in cash at the bar.

The one good thing was that the apartment was close to the mall, and we loved the mall. We had a swimming pool, where Josie and my mother could stop hearts by sunbathing and turning their skin mocha. It wasn't that far to the beach, though we didn't have a car, of course, so unless we could coax my mom into taking us there, we had to ride the bus. It was fine, just time consuming, and you had to be sure to get the bus back in time, which wasn't always what you wanted to do.

When we first moved there, I was alone in a way I never had been in my life. Back at Eden, there was always someone around—my sister or Dylan or my mom or dad. Failing that, there were cooks and waitresses and musicians and delivery people. I had Cinder and the cats who lived in a feral colony in the coyote brush.

Cinder had died of old age only a few months before the earthquake. Dylan, Josie, and I had held a teary, earnest funeral for him and scattered his ashes over the ocean, then cried on one another's shoulders until we had no tears left. He was sixteen, which we told ourselves was 112 in dog years, but it didn't make it feel better. I'd never known a world without his constant presence, and I mourned him deeply. Our parents had been promising we could get a new puppy, but no one had gotten around to taking us to look for one.

Just as well, as it turned out.

In Salinas, there was only me in that bland apartment. By the time I got home from school, my mom was ready to go or had already left for work. Josie had been a party girl before the earthquake, but she quadrupled that in Salinas. I had a library card and used it whenever I could find a ride, but it was hard to get my mom motivated. Josie and I hung out at the mall sometimes but not often.

So I was alone. I read. And I watched a lot of TV. I probably saw every network TV show on the air during that time. I had to have the noise. I learned to bake while the television in the living room played *The Wonder Years*, *The Fresh Prince of Bel-Air*, and my afternoon favorite, the soap opera *Santa Barbara*, which Josie also used to watch but wouldn't deign to do anymore. I didn't care. My life and family had exploded, but everything was the same in the soap, where Eden and Cruz were still living their up-and-down life. I baked. I cooked. I checked out cookbooks from the library and taught myself every technique I could find, making supper for all of us every day. Most of the time, the leftovers went in the trash after I'd had my fill, but I liked having the meals anyway.

Baking eased my loneliness in a way nothing else did, at least until I saved enough money for a modem and cheap computer, which didn't come until a little later.

We lived there nearly five years. My mom made good money at the bar. I babysat for the single moms in the complex until I was old enough for a real job. Josie always had money, but nobody looked too closely to see why. Mainly, she devoted herself to becoming the slut of Monterey County, banging pretty much every guy who took her fancy, and they all did. Especially the bad boys, the leaders on the bad side.

And if Josie decided she wanted somebody, it didn't matter if he had a girlfriend or didn't go for white girls or what. She crooked her finger, and they came, on more than one score. She was incredible, a fantasy. Long blonde hair to her tiny ass, tanned limbs, tiny waist. She didn't have much of a chest, but everything else made up for that.

Sometimes she kept a guy for a little while, a few months or maybe a couple of seasons, and then she'd move on to the next. I think that's why a lot of them liked her, to tell you the truth. You couldn't keep Josie Bianci.

I didn't have much of a social life. I'd never really needed one, and as a too-tall, gawky teen with crazy frizzy hair, I was too self-conscious to be able to reach out now. My focus was on getting the hell out of Salinas and into college, out of this world and into one where I had some influence and understanding. I wanted order, clarity, education. I wanted to talk about Big Important Things, not the bullshit all my classmates seemed to want to talk about. Clothes. Boys. TV.

I missed my dad. I missed Dylan, who listened better than anyone in the world. I cooked a lot because nobody else was going to do it. I got a little fat because I wasn't surfing much.

I was profoundly lonely.

When I finally saved enough for a computer and modem, getting online saved me. I made friends in newsgroups, found like-minded souls on Prodigy, an online service with message boards, and stumbled into a connection with a group of aspiring medical students who nurtured my growing interest and eventually helped me navigate the college application process and find the funds to make it happen.

I'm thinking about those days while I surf, only coming to shore when my driver waves at me. "The storm, she's coming in. We gotta get back."

Shaken out of my reverie, I follow the direction of her finger, and a big, ugly bank of clouds are gathering on the horizon. "Not good," I agree.

Everyone is of the same mind. By the time I get changed and get everything dropped off, the sun has been devoured by the clouds, and a hard wind is pushing onshore. We listen to the cyclone reports on the way back to the CBD, and I ask the driver, "Is this something to be worried about?"

She shrugs. "Maybe. Sounds like it might be this time. You have food and water in your hotel?"

"Not really. Can we stop somewhere on the way back?"

She nods, and a little while later, she stops at a proper grocery store, which is packed. "I'll come too," she says, and we wade into the madness together. The water is mostly gone, but I remember something about filling bathtubs, and the one at the apartment is massive. I gather everything I need to bake and to cook a few meals, feeling a strange sense of coziness overtake me.

And yet, it could be dangerous. My apartment has a wall of glass facing the harbor.

I pay the driver and get back to the apartment just as the rain starts to fall. It's only then, trying to find places for the groceries, that I realize that Josie would never in a million years have given up surfing. I should have asked at the surf shop if they knew her.

Outside the window, a roar of wind and rain slams the little balcony. I cross my arms, shivering slightly. First a shower and a cup of tea, and then I might bake some brownies, just for the pleasure of it. I wonder if Javier is at his friend's house or if he made it back here. I never thought to exchange numbers with him.

It's not like I don't know anything about doing things alone. It will be fine.

But I find myself eyeing the glass nervously, wondering if I should close the doors to the bedroom. Is this a real storm or something I'll feel foolish about later?

Where is Josie in all this? Does she have PTSD from earthquakes? Does she get frightened at times like this?

How am I going to find her?

Chapter Sixteen

Mari

I find myself pacing after we get home from Sapphire House, stirred up by the weather and the thrashing rain but also the television crew and all the things I have never said to anyone here. Anyone who loves me now, as Mari.

With the storm blowing in, everyone has gone to their corners. Simon and Leo are watching sports, while Sarah is immersed in reading a new book on—what else?—cyclones. Only Paris, the lonely shepherd, follows me down to the kitchen, where I pull out my laptop and restlessly scroll through Pinterest boards on the 1920s and '30s. A few boards have been collected for Veronica, and I find George on a board of Olympic swimmers, but none of it is new information. Instead, I click through pages and pages of Art Deco furnishings and stylings. I find examples of furniture very like the pieces in the lounge and many examples of the dishes and light fixtures.

Once we get things cleared out, the entire house will need to be rewired, and the plumbing needs to be thoroughly inspected and upgraded as well, though I hope to keep most of the fixtures. We've had good luck refurbishing only the internal parts to keep authenticity.

What am I going to do with that kitchen? I click through photos of 1930s-era kitchens, and none is particularly appealing. Cooking is one of my great pleasures, and I'm going to have the right tools. I wonder what's out there that feels period without my having to give up the pleasure of modern appliances.

My email dings, and I click over to find an email from Gweneth, who has sent a series of links. Thought you might find these interesting, she writes. Everything I could find on Veronica and George from the local media, with a few articles from the States when they first met.

Smiling, I click "Reply." Blogger's block?

She writes back with an abashed emoji. We do what we must.

Thanks, no matter the cause, I reply. I'm in need of distraction too, and I click through the links, starting with the material from the *Hollywood Reporter*, with a short paragraph and a photo of George and Veronica cozying up somewhere. Veronica wears a fur, her lips darkly painted, and George looks utterly smitten.

For a long while, I study his face, thinking about what it must have been like for him to be chosen by a movie star. To find his life turned upside down by not only the opportunity to be an Olympian but also then to fall head over heels in love with a famous woman.

I sip my lukewarm tea. He was married too. That could not have been easy. I click through the various articles, most of them gossipy in nature, more photos, more speculation about the pair.

The last link is to a story about the murder, the morning after. It's a garish, bold headline with a photo of the mansion and a grim-faced George being led away. Starlet Murder Stuns City, the headline screams, and the article that accompanies it is equally hysterical in tone. Stabbed in her own bedroom, multiple times. Paramour the main suspect.

Which makes sense. Even the details of the bedroom and the multiple stab wounds suggest a jealous lover. And common wisdom says it's always the spouse.

The computer freezes suddenly, and no amount of fiddling brings it back up. Outside, the storm is taking on fury and power, and I retreat from the doors to the kitchen, where I find myself taking out a cloth bag full of feijoas, a couple of hands of ginger, and a bowl of lemons. I've collected a number of beautiful canning jars over the years, and tonight I dig for the Kilner Vintage jars, with their long lines that reflect the light. They'll make my chutney look jeweled.

The light is mellow over my counter. Settling on a stool with a cutting board and a wickedly sharp Japanese knife, I sense my ghosts crowd around me as I slice each lemon and feijoa with precise care. My father leans on the counter, smoking, a bourbon in his hand. Dylan sits on the floor in tattered jeans, his hand in the dog's fur. Somewhere is a baby, but sometimes I see her and sometimes I don't. Maybe she found life when Sarah was born; I don't know.

My dad rattles the ice in his glass, a big, sturdy man's man with giant, capable hands and thick black hair on his arms. All his life he wore a gold watch his father had given him before he left Sicily, and he took it off when he cooked, slipping it into the pocket of his shirt. A strip of lighter skin where the watch rested never went away.

I worshipped the very ground he walked upon when I was small. To be granted time in the kitchen with him, I would sweep floors, drag food scraps to the trash, anything. For a long time, he didn't mind, propping me up on a stool or an overturned box, my body wrapped three times around with a bibbed apron, to teach me what he loved. Cooking. Olives and fresh mozzarella, which we made the old way; squid in its own ink; and simple fresh pastas.

It is because of my father that I slice with such exactitude. My chutneys and jams are perfection. I miss him. I miss Kit. I miss Dylan. Sometimes I even miss my mother.

When I fled France on a stolen passport, I knew only that I had to change my life. I didn't stop to consider that I'd be lying forever, that I would be the only person who would know my secrets.

It's so very lonely. Sarah will never know my real story or meet her aunt, never even know where I'm really from. I've told everyone I'm from British Columbia and learned to surf at Tofino, the only child of parents who died in a terrible car accident.

A splatter of rain slams into the window, and I jump a foot, the knife slashing a small cut on the top of my thumb. Sucking on it, I turn to go look for a Band-Aid, and Simon is coming into the room, his hair tousled because he never keeps his hands out of it. I smooth it down fondly with my free hand and notice he has circles under his eyes. "Are you feeling all right?"

He catches my hand, plants a kiss on my wrist, and drops it so he can open the fridge and grab a ginger beer. "Just some work troubles, love, nothing to worry yourself about."

"Maybe you should go ahead and pat me on the head while you're at the pretty-little-lady routine."

He gives me a half smile. "I'd rather pat your ass," he says, and does. Then he bends in and hooks his chin over my shoulder. "We're having trouble with some of the instructors again, and a man had a heart attack and died last week whilst cycling. And it looks like parceling out the land around Sapphire House might be a right pain in the arse."

I listen, feeling his cheek against my neck, his hair on my temple, and lift a hand to his face. "That's a lot."

"And my wife has been acting a bit weird lately."

"Weird?"

"Preoccupied. Always thinking of something else." He kisses my shoulder. "I'm afraid she's having an affair."

"What?" I whip around. "Is that what's on your mind?"

His shoulders move very slightly. Yes/no. "You've been weird a lot."

"Oh, Simon," I whisper, and lean into him. My thumb is still bleeding, and I can't go all the way to the medicine cabinet for a Band-Aid when he's just revealed himself with such vulnerability. "Wait." I swerve to the right and grab a cup towel, wrapping my thumb tightly so I can put my hands on him. Look into his eyes. With my free hand, I lightly trace the edge of that high, hard cheekbone, touch his wide, beautiful mouth. "I would never, ever cheat on you. Don't you know that?"

His gray eyes search mine. "Most of the time."

"I love you so much it's like all the other men in the world are another species. Rats or sharks or something."

He drops his head to my forehead. "Good. You're the best thing in my life."

I close my eyes and breathe in the moment, the scent of his skin and the feel of his big, solid body around me. The perfection of *now*. Feeling even more terror, more fear, a sense of impending, inescapable doom.

As if he senses it, he moves his hands gently on my sides. "Is something else the matter?"

A whirl of images moves over the screen of my eyelids—Dylan so battered after the accident, my mother dancing with a movie star on the patio, the photo of Kit on the internet with her cat on her shoulder. "Just ghosts," I say, the most truthful thing I can come up with.

And because he thinks my parents died in a car accident and I fled from the reality in my grief, he accepts it. Another lie stacked atop the others. So many of them.

"Let's make popcorn and find a movie to watch with the kids," I say.

"What about the marmalade?"

"I know where to get more feijoas."

―――― ⤔⥲⥺ ――――

But even after a movie with my family curled around me and slow, lovely sex with Simon after, I am haunted. Lying on my side in my bed, with the whole house asleep around me, I listen to the storm and let it all come back to me, all the things I ran away from, all the things that haunt me no matter how much time has passed or how much geography I put between us.

That summer I was nine, I had an admirer. Billy was the star of a family show on television. He came to Eden often, bringing one girl after another. My mother had a crush on him and loved dancing with him, but I knew early that he liked me best. He brought me presents—Chupa Chups lollipops and Nerds, a pretty pair of socks. Sometimes he brought things for both Kit and me, like two kites shaped like fish he brought back from Japan and coloring books and big boxes of crayons. Dylan hated the guy, but my parents teased him that he was jealous of the only boy prettier than himself, and he sulked silently after that.

He kept watch, however. Over Kit and me, over Billy.

Until he didn't. I don't know how long he was in Mexico.

Long enough.

Billy was so slick. One night he ordered a strawberry daiquiri and drank some of it, then offered me the rest. Everybody was dancing to some kind of hard rock band, and the mood was loud, intense, crazy. My mom was kind of out of it, laughing really loudly, and I knew she was mad at my dad.

I drank the daiquiri and started dancing. I can't remember where Kit was. I can't remember a lot about it, honestly, even when I try. For years, I thought I made parts of it up.

Where did we go? Somewhere outside of the main restaurant. Someplace dark. And then he wasn't as nice anymore. I remember being horrified that he had his penis in his hand, and then his hand was over my mouth, and he said, "If you tell anyone, I'll cut Cinder's throat."

So I did what he told me to. Let him do what he wanted, things I couldn't stand to think about afterward. Sometimes I could hear my mother laughing not far away or a conversation that was perfectly ordinary. The music was always playing, covering the sounds he made. Mine were muffled.

I never told a soul. For a whole summer, I held my breath.

And by the time it was over, it was too late to tell anyone, even Dylan. I think he might have guessed, but by then I was dirty, as dirty as a person could get. I was so ashamed and filthy that I couldn't bear to even think about it, much less confess it to anyone. Even Kit.

When I think of it now, I want to go back in time and give that child tools. I want to shake my oblivious parents, take a hammer to the man's head.

And I want that little girl to tell her sister, to confess to Kit the awful thing that had happened. Kit would have killed him. Killed him.

He's still on television sometimes, and you'd think he'd look dissipated, disgusting, but he was a beautiful young star then, and he's matured into an objectively good-looking man. Sometimes I wonder how many other girls he—

If I had stayed Josie, stayed in the US, I would accuse Billy. Take my place in the #metoo movement.

Or not.

I've never been particularly brave. Or good. Or wise.

Or forgiving.

The knot where Billy lives in my chest is cold and hard, but the surrounding tissue burns with hatred for my mother. I thought I'd overcome it, but as Sarah grows, I see so clearly how unprotected and vulnerable my mother allowed us to be, and I think, *How could she have let that happen to me?* What did she think would happen if two little girls were left to wander through the forest of adults always filling the patio of Eden? Adults who were drunk, at the bare minimum, or stoned, or coked up. My dad too, but he was in the kitchen all the time. My mother was always out, mingling.

What did she *think* would happen?

Near morning, the rain begins to taper off, turning into a gentle, soothing background. Simon snores softly, his big hand on my hip, anchoring me. Down the hall, my children are tucked safely into their beds. This is the family I wanted so desperately when I was a child, and

I created it for myself. I've also transformed myself from a lost, drunken wanderer into a woman with purpose, a successful businessperson.

I escaped. Escaped the woman I became after Billy. I took myself back, made myself over, became a woman I am proud of.

And I would do it again. A thousand times, I would do it again.

Chapter Seventeen

Kit

As the storm swirls, I make do with a bunch of apartment-size tools to make brownies. The act of stirring them, making the specific brownies I love so much, with an ancient recipe taken from the Hershey site, eases the anxious tension in my spine. Being so far from everyone and everything I've known, I feel unmoored, as if the storm could send me flying out into the atmosphere like Dorothy.

Oh, Josie, I think, *where the hell are you?* I feel anxious now that I surfed instead of looking for her, that I avoided the journey. I feel exactly torn in half—I want to find her, but that's going to mean facing a lot that I've buried for a long time.

Do I even want to find her, really? Maybe it would be better to let sleeping dogs lie.

Except that I have to admit my life is pretty sterile. Maybe finding Josie will help me make peace with everything, give me some space to—

What?

I don't know. Change things.

My brownies are ready, and I take them out of the oven, bending my head to inhale the chocolaty, sweet scent as I settle them on the counter to cool. Outside, the storm is working itself up into a fine frenzy, and inside my head, the frenzy is in my thoughts.

When a knock sounds at my door, I practically fly across the room. It's Javier, standing there with a bottle of wine and a box of food. "I was worried about you," he says. "Can I come in?"

"Yes please." I take the bottle and the box, set them on the counter, and throw my arms around his waist. Leaning into his solid body. For a moment, I can tell he's startled, and I wonder if I should pull away, but I've been feeling so lost and tortured and . . . young, that he feels like a life raft.

After the slightest hesitation, his arms circle me. "Are you frightened?"

"No," I say. "Not of the storm." I lift my head. "I didn't want to be alone in it."

"Nor did I," he murmurs, and kisses me, and then walks me backward toward my bed near the window. We fall down together and make love while the storm rages, the air smelling of chocolate and ozone.

This time it's different. I find myself slowing down, tasting him, breathing in the scent of his skin, looking at him more carefully. His stomach is slightly soft and very sensitive, and I spend time there, kissing and tasting. His thighs are sturdy, covered with the hair I tried not to look at when he wore slightly more.

And he takes his time too, hands touching what his eyes see—my breasts and the sides of my ribs, my neck, which he kisses and kisses and kisses and kisses until I'm squirming and giggling, and then he captures my mouth and slides his fingers between my legs, and I have an almost instantaneous orgasm.

Afterward, we lie sprawled and open to the night, covering nothing. It feels lush and intimate, and a ripple of warning moves through me.

But there's a built-in limit to this connection—we live on different continents and met on a third. That's enough of a safeguard that I feel comfortable simply being myself.

After a little while, we get up to make ourselves plates and pour wine into the goblets I find in a cupboard above the sink. It's a little chilly, so we carry it all back to the bed and curl up with the covers over us, propped against the pillows. Outside, the storm rages. Inside, we eat.

"Where did you get the tapas?" I ask, popping a roasted, salted pepper in my mouth.

"La Olla, where I took you."

"Were you there?"

"We rehearsed there, and when the cyclone blew in, they gave us all plates of food and sent us home." He plucks an olive from his plate. "Miguel wanted me to come home with him."

I laugh, touching his foot with mine under the covers. "What did you tell him?"

A shrug. "Only the truth. That I worried about you being alone here." With his long fingers, he plucks out a roll of ham. "I told him that you were coming to hear me sing. And that you promised not to run away this time."

"Your holiday romance."

"Is that what you are?" He cocks his head, looking at me with those dark, dark eyes. In this light, I can see the scars of long-ago acne in the hollows of his cheeks and the network of lines time has woven at the corners of his eyes. For a moment I'm captured, falling into a cool and fragrant atmosphere that fills the air around us, binds us.

But only until I straighten to shake it off. "How long are you staying in New Zealand?"

"I don't know." He sets his plate aside and takes my free hand, opening the fingers that are slightly clenched. He smooths them flat, revealing the heart of my palm, and strokes the center lightly before he presses his against mine. It is somehow a thousand times more intimate than all the things we just did to each other. A hitch catches in my throat. "I think, *mi sirenita*, that there is more here than a fling."

I keep my gaze on our hands until he touches the tender area beneath my chin. I allow it, allow myself to feel the yearning, the sense of possibility. For one minute, or maybe two, or maybe as long as the storm lasts. Seeing my acquiescence, he smiles gently.

"Tell me something you loved as a child."

"My sister," I reply without hesitation. "We had our own little world, just the two of us—it was full of magic and beautiful things."

"Mm," he says, moving his palm lightly over mine. "What magic?"

"Mountain Dew was an actual magic elixir. Do you know Mountain Dew?"

He nods.

"There were kitchen fairies and mermaids who moved things around to make the grown-ups crazy."

"Sounds happy," he says.

"That part of it," I agree.

"And your sister, what was she like?"

I take a breath. "Beautiful—not just pretty but really beautiful, with this amazing, bright light around her all the time. Everyone loved her, but none of them loved her as much as I did."

He brings the hand he smoothed up to his mouth, kisses my knuckles. "You must miss her so very much."

I nod and take my hand back on the pretext of wanting to eat. "Your turn. What did you love as a child?"

"Books," he says with a laugh. "I loved to read more than anything. My father grew angry with me—'Javier, you need to run! You need to play with the other boys. Go outside.'" He lifts a shoulder. "I only wanted to lie in the grass and think about other worlds, other places."

"What did you read?"

"Whatever I could find—" He makes a *psshting* sound, sends his hand out in a gesture of circles through the air. "Adventure and mysteries and ghost stories. Whatever."

"You still love reading, don't you?"

"You don't?"

"I like to read. I just don't like to work hard to read. I like books that take me away the same way television or the movies do."

"Like what?"

I frown and then reach for my phone, where all the books are listed in my reader. Scrolling through it, I say, "Okay, in the past few months I've read two historical romances, a mystery by a woman I like because I can trust her not to get too dark, and a cooking memoir."

"Romance? Are you seeking love, *gatita*?"

"No," I say definitively. "Passion ruined my family's lives. I make it a practice to avoid it."

"Love is not always destructive," he says quietly, and slides a finger up my shin. "Sometimes love creates."

I'm unexpectedly caught by something in his voice, a promise I can barely see, shimmering faintly on the horizon, and that scares me enough to throw out a gauntlet. "Tell me a time that love didn't destroy what it first created." He is divorced, clearly not involved with anyone. "In your own life," I add.

He nods, stretching out sideways in front of me, close enough to touch my knee. I could press my palms to his shoulder, his head, but I don't. I keep my arms crossed, one hand cradling the wine.

"When I was seventeen, a girl came to our neighborhood. She had the shiniest hair I had ever seen, and pretty ankles, and I could not find my voice to talk to her, but one day we met at the library, in the very same row. She was looking for the very same book I was."

I'm tempted to brush the hair on his temple away from his face, but I don't. "What book?"

"Stephen King, *The Shining*," he says, and smiles up at me. "You thought it would be *Don Quixote*, yes?"

I smile. "Maybe."

"We spent so much time reading and talking about reading. And soon we read each other, you know, both of us virgins."

A ping snaps my chest, bringing me a memory of myself at seventeen, the first time I made love, to a boy I worked with at Orange Julius. James. How I loved him!

Javier continues. "With her, I learned about how easy sex can be."

Something in my expression must give me away, because he says, "Who taught you that lesson?"

"It's funny. I was just thinking about him before you came. A boy at school."

"See? Love found you."

"It broke my heart, though."

"Sure." He lifts his shoulders. "Me too. But you don't die. You just . . . begin again." He settles his hand on my thigh.

I take a sip of wine, aware of the winding promise between us. It feels dangerous and rich. "How many times?"

"As many times as life offers."

A sharp, hard pain stabs my heart. I shake my head. "I don't fall in love."

His lips quirk, almost a smile. His fingers brush my knee. "You are falling a little with me."

I smile. "Nope."

"I see." His hand curves down the length of my calf, around my heel and then my instep. I wonder briefly if he thinks my ankles are pretty. "How many times have you fallen in love, Kit?"

"Only once."

"How old were you?"

I make a noise, exasperated. "That question again. Seventeen."

"Seventeen," he repeats. "Seventeen is generous and earnest."

A memory of James and me, making love over and over, laughing and eating in that empty apartment, flickers through me. His long thighs, his tongue on me, everywhere. "Yes," I whisper.

Javier reaches for the buttons on his shirt, which I am wearing over my nakedness. He unfastens the first one, and I let him. "What was his name?"

"James."

He unbuttons two more, and his hand sweeps inside, between my breasts, stroking a line. "You were badly wounded?"

I nod, forgetting it all as he opens another two buttons and slides the fabric aside to show my breasts. Immediately my skin is alive from head to toe, every centimeter of it greedy for him. "Perhaps you can let him go after so many years, hmm?"

I'm mesmerized by his heavy-lidded admiration as he moves his hand over my shoulders, down the valley between my breasts, his fingers light as he brushes the curves, the tips, my belly, then back up.

"Maybe," I whisper, and then his mouth follows his hands, and I'm gone.

―――― ⸹⸙⸞⸙⸞⸹ ――――

When the storm is at its height, we don swimsuits and head downstairs to the indoor pool. It's very late, and the pool is empty, waiting there in blue splendor for us to dive in. We frolic like dolphins, diving and splashing, and then we both fall to swimming laps, easily and simply, back and forth. I want the water on my body and slip out of my suit, and he smiles and does the same. If anyone comes, there will be ample warning.

So we swim naked with the night blurry beyond rain-spattered windows. The wind whistles and howls, but inside is warm and safe.

When we finish, we wrap up in towels and head into the dry-heat sauna. "Heaven," I say.

The heat opens my pores, my body, wafts in waves over my breasts and knees and nose. "I would love to have a pool like that, where I could swim whenever I wanted."

"Mm. In my house in Madrid, I have a sauna *and* a steam shower."

"Decadent." I open one eye. He's leaning back against the wall, his arms loose, hands resting on his thighs. His body is strong, well shaped, with that slight extra around the middle that I find so weirdly appealing. It makes me want to climb on him again. Instead, I close my eyes and say, "You must be a rich man."

"Not poor," he agrees. "But you too—you are a doctor."

"I do all right. Housing is stratospheric in California, but the rest is fine." I breathe in the hot air, coughing slightly. "I bought my mom a condo on the beach, and I have a little house. I can be at the beach in seven minutes on foot."

"Lovely."

"Is your house old?" I ask. "I think of Madrid as medieval."

"It's old, but inside, it's modern. The kitchen, the bathrooms, the windows. I like plenty of light."

"Mine is old. Mission-style."

"Spanish," he says with approval, and I smile.

"Yes. Our house when we were children was Spanish too, tiled all through in Art Deco."

"Oh," he says, "I like Art Deco."

The words in his voice are somehow lyrical, his tongue making the syllables softer. A shiver walks up my spine, and I open my eyes again.

He's looking at me. I'm aware of my shoulders, my thighs.

"Perhaps," he says, "we should return to your room, hmm?"

Chapter Eighteen

Mari

It's hot and humid the next day, and I'm cranky from too little sleep. Inside Sapphire House, the air is thick even when I open all the windows, and I make a note to look into what it would cost to add air-conditioning. I hate the idea of shutting out the ocean, but with global warming, who knows what the next thirty or forty years will bring?

I'm working on the pantry today, recording the style and variations of all the dishes on the shelves. I always do the inventory before I bring anyone else in. It's tedious work in a way, but it gives me a chance to feel the house itself, to know it intimately before I begin the heavy work of shifting walls and tearing it apart. In some strange way, I feel I owe it to the house itself, honoring it for what it was, what it gave someone else.

It's not exactly difficult psychology to know why. Our beautiful old Spanish-style house was devoured by the earthquake—not only the restaurant and house, the buildings, but everything that was inside them. My mother, Kit, and I scoured the beach for weeks afterward, trying to find things to rescue, but in the end it wasn't much. Some of our clothes, some battered things from the kitchen. What the earthquake began, the sea and weather completed.

I still carry three things from the recovery effort. One is a ring made from a teaspoon, my father's choice for Eden, simple heavy tableware designed to stand up to harsh commercial dishwashers. It has a little carving of Mount Etna on the end, which I thought unbearably beautiful when I was small. My mother had the ring made for my twelfth birthday.

The other is a chipped guitar pick that belonged to Dylan and a T-shirt that belonged to him too. The shirt is as thin and delicate now as flower petals, and I keep it wrapped up and tucked into a drawer. I wore it for years and years, and I never once put it on without thinking of a night the three of us made a big fire on the beach.

Kit and I must have been in late grade school—maybe twelve and ten—because Dylan's hair was really long. He must have been seventeen or eighteen. He'd started growing it when he arrived at Eden, and it grew longer every year. By the end, he could braid it into a tail that was halfway down his back. His freak flag, he said, a reference to a song I didn't know. No matter how my father nagged him, he refused to cut it.

So I grew my hair out too. It was already pretty long when he came to live with us, down to the middle of my back, but by the time of the earthquake when I was fifteen, I was known for my long, long blonde hair, which swept the top of my thighs. Neither of us wore it loose very often—it tangled and matted so easily, you wouldn't believe it. Mine was thicker than his, but his was laced with more colors—silvery blond, wheat, a little red, some glittery gold. Mine was just dishwater streaked with sun highlights, but there was power in it.

A lot of power. Boys liked it, and even some of the girls on the beach, who were kind of amazed at how long it was.

On that night of that summer fire, I took my hair down and started brushing it. Kit took the brush out of my hand and applied herself to my head, which had to be one of the ten best feelings on Earth. She loved brushing my hair and braiding it, and she was both gentle and no-nonsense. "Do you want it down?"

"Yeah." It felt good on my back, which was bare from my bikini. We'd all been swimming in the hot day, and the sand under my butt was still warm. Dylan was shirtless, his T-shirt in a pile on the sand. He almost never let anyone else see him with it off—he even surfed with it on—but he trusted us not to stare at his scars too much. Cinder stretched out beside him, his paws muddy, eyes glinting.

Dylan fed the fire until it was snapping and bright orange, then hauled out the bag of stuff he'd brought down from the house kitchen, lining it all up in a tidy row in front of the long, thick tree branch we used for our couch.

"We have chocolate bars, marshmallows, graham crackers," he said. "Also real food you have to eat first. Arancini, ham, and peaches."

From the bag, he also brought out Mountain Dews, our favorite, and Kit squealed. "Mama hasn't been letting me drink them."

I pinched her thigh, which was thick and solid. "She doesn't want you fat."

She slapped my hand away, hard. "I am not fat. I'm athletic."

"Dude," Dylan said in agreement, and held up his hand for a high five. "You're perfect just the way you are."

Kit met his palm with a sharp slap, tossed her head, and settled beside him. She was still skinned knees and grimy fingernails, a kid in every way, whereas I'd learned a lot about getting attention, which I loved, so I dressed for it and cleaned up for it. Nobody really paid much attention to Kit with her crazy hair and square body.

But I was jealous of the way she leaned on him. How easy they were with each other. Kit carried around a sense of quiet with her, and it spilled into Dylan in a way I could never match. You could almost see his red aura turning a soft blue the minute she came anywhere near him, as if she carried a magic spell that calmed him down.

His hair was back in a braid. "You want me to take your braid out and brush your hair?" I asked.

"Sure."

Eagerly, I picked up the brush and squished through the sand to kneel behind him. Kit scowled at me—it was her thing to brush our hair.

I ignored her. Tugging the rubber band from his braid, I loosened it with my fingers. It was cool and soft and still a little damp in places. Running the brush through it felt good, watching it ripple under the bristles and straighten. It was all the way down to the middle of his back, where a particularly bad scar twisted over his spine. I touched it with the tips of my fingers. "What's this one?"

"Right in the middle?" He sat with his arms looped around his knees. His hair skimmed his shoulder blades, fell forward in drifts toward his elbows. "That's a scar from a sword I got in a duel with Long John Silver."

I traced the wormy pink shape of it, end to end, for the first time realizing that something else had happened to him. "For real."

He turned to look me in the eye, and there was a pain there I'd never seen. It was like a window had opened into a hell I never wanted to visit. "That's as real as it gets, Grasshopper."

My heart hurt like somebody had shoved a sword through it, and I put my palm on his face. "I wish I could kill them."

"It wouldn't do any good," he rasped, but he pressed my hand into his face, and for the first time, I thought maybe there was somebody on the planet who knew what I knew, that a smiling face didn't always mean well. Somebody hurt him, just like somebody hurt me.

I also knew the exact moment he would shatter if I didn't shift the mood. I grabbed a fistful of his hair. "We're twins," I said, and tied my hair to a hank of his. We all laughed before the knot slipped out.

But something changed. He tossed me the T-shirt. "You'll get cold."

Vaguely I heard Kit say, "What about me? I'll get cold too!" as I pulled the T-shirt on over my head, smelling Dylan-ness all around me, against my skin.

That was when he broke out his guitar, and while we ate peaches and s'mores, he started to play the folk songs he'd taught us to sing. We joined in, Kit with more gusto than tone, but I fancied myself a pretty good singer, and I tried to weave my voice into the main line of Dylan's bass. His speaking voice was raspy and low, so nice to listen to, but his singing voice was deep and clear, so rich you could almost drink it out of the air like honey. We sang a bunch of camp favorites, then moved into the ballads.

I loved the moody, sad, violent ballads Dylan had taught us. He loved playing and singing them, and tonight there was something magical in the air, as if the sparks of the fire were turning to fairies who danced around us. Kit felt it too. She moved close enough to press her bare arm into mine as we sang "Mary Hamilton" and a Civil War ballad that was Kit's favorite, "The Cruel War," and one of my favorites, "Tam Lin," which I thought could have been written for Dylan himself. As we warmed up, his voice wound around the fire and through both mine and Kit's, and we sang like we were onstage somewhere. Overhead, the stars burned bright, and the waves rolled in eternally, and if we could have just stayed right there forever, everything would have been okay.

Kit said, "You should be a singer, Dylan. Nobody is better than you."

He laughed. "Thanks, Kitten, but I just like being here with you guys."

As the fire burned down, we spread out a big blanket on the sand, pulled our pillows out of the tent, and stretched out under the vast sky. Light spilled down the hill from Eden, along with music and the sound of voices. I was sleepy as Kit and I took our places next to Dylan, who flung an arm out in either direction so we could scoot up close.

The two of us girls spread an open sleeping bag over our bodies and snuggled in, one head on each shoulder.

It was our ritual and had been for years and years now. By then, he'd been with us for five or six years and was woven completely into our lives. Often, all three of us would fall asleep, only to wake up and stagger into the tent one by one.

Tonight, the Perseids were shooting their way across the galaxy. For a while, Kit pointed to one and then another and chattered about the distance the stars traveled and how many there were and all sorts of other facts. Until she trailed off and fell asleep, just like that.

Dylan and I just lay there and watched the sky. It was perfect. He shifted so that Kit was more comfortable on her pillow, but when he came back down again, he patted the spot I liked on his shoulder, and I happily slipped back to my place. He lit a joint, and the smoke made shapes against the night.

It would have been impossible to be happier than I was right there, with Dylan and my sister close by, the stars overhead, nothing to worry about. Dylan smelled of salt and perspiration and a sharp note of something that belonged just to him.

His voice, low and quiet, rolled into the night. "I'll tell you about the Long John Silver scar if you tell me something."

I tried to pretend I didn't know what he was going to ask, but my body turned into a board. "What?"

"Did something happen to you a couple of summers ago?"

"No." I said the word in a tone of voice that made it sound like he was stupid for asking. "Why would you even ask that?"

"Mm." He took another toke, blew it out, and I reached for the smoke as it wafted over the stars, cutting the sky in two pieces, just like my life—before and after. "Maybe I was wrong."

I tried to let it go, but the question brought back the acid in my stomach, the taste of his hands over my mouth, the way he hurt me. But I lied. "You were."

"Okay," Dylan said mildly, and pointed up at a trio of falling stars. I watched it. "I told you; now you have to tell me."

"It was a belt buckle."

Impossible to stop the sudden intake of my breath. "Dude."

He scratched my head in a way I liked. "Long time ago, Grasshopper."

But now I felt bad that he told me the truth and I didn't tell him. I tried to think of a way to say it that didn't sound disgusting, and I couldn't find one. *A man did stuff to me. This guy made me take off my clothes. This guy said he'd kill Cinder if I didn't do what he said.*

"You know you can tell me anything, right?"

I twitched my shoulders, moving away from him, sitting up so I could look out to the ocean. On the far horizon, light caught and made the edge glow. "I guess."

"You guess?" He sat up too, his arms hanging loosely over his legs. "I swear you can tell me. Anything."

Chewing on my lip, I looked over at him. His loose hair was getting tangled now, little loops sticking up here and there. "You have to swear, like completely and totally *swear*, that you won't tell and you won't make *me* tell."

He touched his chest, hand over his heart. "I promise."

But even then, I couldn't figure out how to say it. A wind kicked up and made me shiver, but I couldn't say it.

As I was struggling to find the words, Dylan said, "Was it one of the guests?"

I nodded, weaving my fingers together, a panicky feeling in my chest.

"Did he . . . touch you?"

Again, I nodded, but my lungs felt strange, and I suddenly felt like I couldn't breathe. I tried to suck in air, but I couldn't, and I turned to Dylan with wild eyes, my breath stuck in my chest like my throat was broken in half.

"Hey, hey." He moved closer, took a drag off the joint, and gestured me closer. "Breathe in as I breathe out."

I leaned in as he blew out the smoke, and the acrid sting of it hit the back of my throat.

"Good," he said, blowing the rest away from my face. "Hold it as long as you can."

Immediately, my breath started moving again. It was like the booze I sipped out of glasses when nobody was looking or they were going back to the dishwasher or someone thought it was cute that I should have a sip of a martini.

I let go of the smoke.

"Better?"

"Yeah. Again."

He hesitated, but I gave him my steely look, and he took a toke, a really big one, and smiled at me as he did it. I got ready for him to blow it to me, and maybe because I was already getting high, the exchange lasted a thousand years. I looked at his pursed mouth and noticed it was pink and plump, and there were sprouts of new beard coming in on his chin. The smoke left his mouth, and I sucked it in, and sucked it in, and sucked it in, deeper and deeper and deeper, and then I fell sideways holding my breath as well as I could. And only when it was completely impossible to hold it another second did I breathe out in a big gasp.

"Thatta girl," he said, his voice low and approving.

I rolled over onto my back, my hands on my rib cage, the sparkling bright stars looking twenty times larger. Dylan fell down beside me, and we just lay there, side by side, looking at the sky and letting the wind move over us, for a long, long time.

"Dude, you got me high."

"You were having a panic attack," he said mildly. "So that makes it medicine."

I giggle.

"I'm not kidding." But he laughed too, then slowed. "Now you have something to tell on me about, so you can trust me."

I turned my head, and his eyes were right there, pale and bright as moonlight, never eyes like a real person. "You have mermaid eyes."

"I wish I was a merman. That would be pretty cool." He turned his head back to the sky, and I used my finger to draw the outline of his profile in the air.

"Might get lonely, though."

"Might." He waited a long time before he said, "You're not going to tell me, are you?"

I touched each of three scars on his upper arm—all three burns. "Did somebody burn you with a cigarette?"

"Cigar," he said. "What if you don't have to say it and I just guess?"

"Why do you wanna know so bad? It was awful, but it's over. I'm good."

"You're not, though." He brushed my hair off my forehead. "You're sad all the time, and doing things that aren't really appropriate for your age."

"I don't know what you mean."

"I know. But if I tell you that it would feel good to talk to some-body, you need to believe me."

"Talk to somebody? Like a counselor?" I looked up, horrified.

"You can just tell me."

But I couldn't. I knew he would tell. No one but me could keep a secret this big.

In the big pantry at Sapphire House, the memory rips through me. I suddenly miss Dylan so much it feels like a fresh wound. Sinking to the cold linoleum, I wrap my arms around my knees and let the tears fall.

I think now of my barely pubescent self having anxiety attacks and smoking pot to quell them and wonder again what the hell. Why didn't he tell my parents, no matter how angry I would be?

But I also loved him, so very, very much. He would have said his first loyalty was to his promise to me. In his own scarred way, he was trying to protect me.

Dylan, Dylan, Dylan. So lost, so wrong, so misguided, but all three of the Bianci women tried to save him. None of us could.

In fact, I did the exact opposite. Because of me, Dylan died.

Chapter Nineteen

Kit

By ten the next morning, the cyclone has pushed through, leaving behind a glittery, humid morning. Javier doesn't linger. "I have an interview," he says, leaning over the bed to kiss me where I still sprawl. "Are you free tonight?"

His hair catches the sunlight, and for the first time, I see that it isn't black at all but a very warm brown. I brush my fingers through it and tell myself I should say no, but I can't find the discipline.

And anyway, one of the hallmarks of a great holiday romance is the immersion factor. "I'll have to check my calendar," I joke, "but I imagine I'll be here."

"Good. Someone told me there's a very good Israeli restaurant nearby. Would you like to try it?"

"Absolutely."

He straightens, tucking in his shirt. "What will you do today? More surfing?"

"I'm going to run down some ideas I had about finding my sister."

He buttons his shirtsleeves, and I find myself wondering if I've ever slept with a man who owned a long-sleeve oxford shirt with crisp lines down the arms from ironing.

"Are you sure you wish to find her?"

I tuck the covers over myself more firmly. "No. But I have to follow it through now."

"I looked for her yesterday."

I frown. "What?"

He inclines his head. "Miguel has lived here a long time now. He had good ideas."

I sit up. "You told Miguel about her?"

"Not so much. Only that you were looking for someone."

"That's my business, Javier. I only shared it with you because we were—" I struggle with why and give an exasperated sound. "That was very invasive of you."

He seems unconcerned. "The good news is, he thought he recognized her."

"I don't care. This is my business, not yours."

As if he doesn't even hear me, he picks up my phone from the side table and hands it to me. "Take my phone number, and then send yours to me."

I glare at him. "Who do you think you are?"

Finally, he inclines his head. "Are you angry, *gatita*? I only meant to help you."

For a long moment, I only look at him, feeling invaded and upset and tangled and yet still so very drawn to him. "I'm not the kind of woman who likes to be shuttled along by a man."

"I did not intend—"

"Please don't get in my business like that."

He sinks down beside me, tucks my hair behind my ear. "Don't be angry."

"I am, though." I slap his hand.

Which makes him laugh. He tries to catch it, fails. "Sorry."

"I'm not kidding. Do you understand?"

"Yes. I swear." He holds up his hand, palm out. "I will not help you again."

Relenting, I pick up my phone and punch in the numbers he gives me, then call the phone so he'll have mine. It rings on the table in the kitchen. "There you go."

He smiles at me, the expression slow and appreciative. "Tonight, then."

I turn on my side to watch him go. My body is soft from making love, a delicious laziness in my spine. When he pauses at the door, I lift a hand to wave, and he blows a kiss.

Ridiculous. And lovely. I know better than to get mixed up with a charmer, to let down my guard, and yet—it's limited by circumstances. I'm safe enough.

I roll over to look at the harbor. The water shines an opalescent deep blue. No sailboats this morning, but a sturdy-looking barge makes its way toward the open sea. Closer in, the offices are coming alive, and I watch a woman in a dark-blue pencil skirt bustle from her office into the hallway, then pop up in an office a little farther down the way. What would it be like to live her life, I wonder, a person who works in an office, at a desk, wearing fancy clothes? In Auckland.

Not my life at all. I don't miss the ER, but it has been only a few days. I haven't had much time to consider what else I might do, what kind of medicine might be calling me next. Or if anything is calling me. It's possible that what I'm doing right now is giving me a chance to recharge my batteries.

If not for Hobo, I'd volunteer with services like the Red Cross or Doctors Without Borders. Maybe the Peace Corps.

But I can't leave Hobo.

Speaking of my cat, I need to call my mother. Tossing off the covers, I pad naked into the shower, then dress and make a pot of coffee. As it brews, I text her to see if she's free to FaceTime.

She rings in on my tablet almost immediately. "Hi, sweetheart!" she says, and moves the camera to show me a little black face poking out from beneath my bed. "Look, Hobo. It's your mama!"

"Hi, baby!" I coo.

He lets go of a pitiful, squeaky meow. "Oh no. I don't know if it's good that he hears me."

"Blink at him," Suzanne orders. "That's cat language for 'I love you.'"

"I know that, but how did you know it?"

"I looked it up."

"You did?" Pierced, I realize that she's taking this very seriously. Her devotion to the task slides beneath my defenses, reveals how much my mother has changed. She carries the tablet closer to the bed, and Hobo stays where he is, making that same pitiful little *meep*.

"Hey, Hobo," I say, and give him a slow blink. "You're safe, and I love you, okay?"

He stares at the screen as if suspecting a trick, then skitters backward, hiding behind the drop of the bedspread. Suzanne's face comes back on camera. "He's okay, honey, just scared."

This is the only creature who's ever depended on me, and I'm letting him down. "Is he eating?"

"Not as much as I'd like. He must come out when I'm gone, because he's using the litter box, but he doesn't come out when I'm here. I put his food by the bed, and he eats it when I'm out, so I've been filling a plate in the morning and then going for a walk."

Poor Hobo. "Oh my God, I feel terrible!"

"Don't," my mother says firmly. "I'm taking good care of him. He's healthy and safe."

"You *promise* he's eating?"

"I swear, Kit." She raises a long-fingered hand in an oath.

I swallow, feeling a strange welling of gratitude and softness. "Thank you, Mom."

She waves a hand. "Now, tell me what's happening with you. Any leads?"

"No, but I do have some ideas."

"Good. I have to say, sweetheart, that it's doing you some good to get away. You have color in your cheeks."

I try very hard not to allow more color to seep into my face, forcing an offhand smile. "I went surfing yesterday, and it made me wonder why I haven't done more travel like that, you know? I mean, why not?"

"You should! I could get you rooms at any of the NorHall hotels anywhere in the world." She works as a concierge at the one in Santa Cruz.

"Maybe you should do some of that yourself."

Her slim shoulders twitch. "I think I feel safer with my routines." She twirls the most recent of her AA chips between her fingers, over and over.

"Mom, you've been sober a long time. But you know, I bet they even have sober tours these days."

"Yeah, we'll see," she says, but I know it's a dismissal. "Do you like it there?"

"It's amazing." I carry my tablet over to the window. "We had the edge of a cyclone go through last night, and everything is pretty quiet, but look at that view!"

"It seems like the kind of place your sister would love, don't you think?"

Something about that comment irks me, and I turn the camera back to my face. "I guess."

"What are you planning for today?"

"I'm going to call surf shops," I say. "I don't know why I didn't think of it before. No way she'd give up surfing."

"If she was still herself, I agree. But what if she had amnesia or something?"

I frown. "I guess it's possible. Not that likely."

"You see it in books and TV all the time. And why else would she leave us to grieve her like that?"

"Because she was selfish? Because she was an alcoholic and an addict?"

Thousands of miles away in my own little house, my mother sits at my table and gazes calmly, steadily through the camera at me. This is what Josie will look like in twenty-five years, the graying blonde hair, the high cheekbones, the full lips that have thinned only a little with time. "Or maybe," she offers, "she was lost. Broken."

"Poor Josie," I say with sharpness. "You know, I was thinking about the way she drank when she was only eleven or twelve, stealing sips from everyone, getting smashed. Why didn't you stop her?"

Suzanne has the grace to look away. Her rich voice rasps a bit as she says, "Honestly, Kitten, I never even noticed. By then, I was pretty much drunk all the time myself."

The frankness pokes a needle through the balloon of my self-righteousness. "I know. I'm sorry. I just keep going over things, wondering why she got so bad so young." With a visceral sense of loss, I remember how it felt as she slipped away from me, as if she had really become a mermaid and lived most of the time beneath the waves. It was the start of my great loneliness, and the memory is so painful even now that I have to shove it away. "She was so lost."

"Yes," my mother says. It's the way she listens now, acknowledging without embroidery, but it irks me a little anyway. "It was a terrible environment."

"Obviously," I snap. "But we also had Dylan. He looked out for us."

"Yeah," she says in a droll voice. "A kid himself. And an addict." Her eyes suddenly fill with a terrible sorrow. "He was always a lost boy, our Dylan. I did him no favors."

"What happened to him, Mom? Before he came to us."

"I don't know. He'd clearly been abused physically for a long time; that's all I knew. He never said." She wiggles her fingers in front of the bedspread, where a furry black paw shows. "I should have—" She shakes her head, looks at me.

My heart aches. "Yeah."

"We can't change the past."

I take a breath, shake my shoulders. "You're right. I'm going to start calling surf shops and then maybe get out and do some sightseeing. There's a bus tour that goes up north that sounds really great."

"Good. Enjoy yourself."

"Kiss my cat when you can, okay? And you might get some more straight tuna, see if he eats that better."

"He'll be okay, Kit. Promise."

"Thanks, Mom."

"Love you, sweetheart."

I nod, giving her an open wave before I hang up. Mad at myself for not returning the endearment. She's been so good for so long, but I still have trouble letting her in. What does that say about me?

———— ❦ ————

At ten, I start phoning surf shops, and on the third one, I hit pay dirt. "Hi, my name is Kit Bianci, and I'm hoping to find a friend of mine who moved here a few years back."

"Sure, love."

"She's very pretty, blonde, great surfer, but the thing you'd remember is that she has a big, distinctive scar through her eyebrow."

"Oh, sure. That's Mari Edwards. Comes here all the time. I reckon I'll lose her now she's bought Sapphire House, but she's always been too rich for our blood over here."

It takes two long seconds for the words to fully sink in, and then I'm scrambling to write the name down. "Mary, as in M-A-R-Y?"

"No, she spells it with an I, M-A-R-I."

"Don't suppose you have a phone number?"

"Can't say I do, but you'll find her right enough. Married to Simon Edwards, him who runs the Phoenix Clubs."

"Clubs, like nightclubs?"

"Ha, no, no. Mari's a teetotaler, and old Simon's known for being the fittest man in Auckland. They're health clubs. You can see his ads on the telly."

"Wow, thank you so much. I really appreciate it."

"No worries."

I hang up and type the name into Google.

Mari Edwards.

It comes back with thousands of hits. Most mention her only in relation to Simon Edwards, but there are a handful of photos of her.

My sister. Nearly always pictured with a tall, dashingly handsome man. The rare photos of the entire family show a boy and a girl, everyone hale and athletic. In one, they're all wearing wet suits, surfboards at their sides.

A rush of cold and heat bursts through my body, running under my skin, making my heart race.

She's re-created the Tofino fantasy.

When we were ten or eleven and things got so bad between our parents, Josie and I made up a family who lived in British Columbia. We'd seen a TV special on Tofino, a town on the west coast of Vancouver Island known for enormous January waves, and all three of us—Dylan included—were madly in love with the idea of going there. In our fantasy, the mom was a teacher and a swim coach, and the dad went to The Office. Every summer, they took vacations in the car, driving down the coast, singing songs and eating in diners. They had an Airstream, and everybody loved surfing, so they always surfed together, wherever they went.

That was our real family, we said. We were only staying here at Eden because our parents were spies and had to finish up one last job. They'd be back for us as soon as they were done.

Josie—Mari—and her family look just like the one we made up.

A sense of rage rockets through me. How did my loser sister, the druggie and alcoholic who stole everything I owned at a time I could barely feed myself, land on her feet like this? When I am—

What?

Alone. I am alone. With no family. No children. No husband.

I leap up from the table and whirl around aimlessly, spun in circles by fresh fury. I want to throw something, break something, scream. She let us think she was *dead*, and she's fine. More than fine.

Lava burns and gurgles in my gut, threatening to erupt.

Get a hold of yourself.

I yank open the sliding glass door to the balcony and step out, gripping the rail with tight fists. I take in a long breath, tasting sea and city, humid greenery and exhaust. I close my eyes and breathe out.

The rage eases, leaving behind the most profound urge to sob, but I observe this too and let it go. I open my eyes and focus on the view, objectively noticing the flash of car windows crossing the long Harbour Bridge and a barge passing beneath it. Foot traffic moves on the streets below my perch, miniature human figures dressed up in miniature human clothes.

Had I wished to find her in dire straits? Do I wish her ill? Why am I *mad* over her beautiful little family?

I don't know, but I am.

Slapping the tears away, I go back to the computer and slide my finger over the trackpad to bring the photo up again. She has children. My niece and nephew. My mother's grandchildren. She looks healthy. Happy.

Restlessly, I click back to the search results and see a local news video, filmed only the day before. Heart in my throat, I click on it.

And there is Josie, in the foyer of a beautiful house, giving an interview. Tears spring to my eyes and spill over my face without my permission. I turn up the sound, and there is her long-lost voice, a little raspy, edged now with a hint of an accent, not entirely New Zealand but no longer entirely American. The sound of it burns, but I watch every second of the video, captured by my sister as she leads the reporter through the house, showing off the wood and the view and the bedroom where a film star from the thirties was murdered.

She is still beautiful. Her hair is cut much shorter than I've ever seen it, to her shoulders, and it swings in that elegance of well-tended perfection. In person, age shows on her face. All those years in the full sun, in the wind and the surf, all the hard drinking, have given her skin a weathered look, a netting of crow's feet around her eyes.

A man comes up in the frame, the same man from the photos, and slides a comfortable arm around her shoulders. He's stunningly good-looking, with thick brown hair and the kind of tan only an outdoorsman sports. The look of adoration he rains down upon her makes my stomach ache.

Abruptly, I click it off.

In comparison, my life suddenly looks very thin. Thin and wan and lonely.

Chapter Twenty
Mari

I bring a boxful of the Coalport cups and saucers back to Gweneth, who will go nuts for them. I text her to make sure she's not overwhelmed with a project and stop by her house before I go home.

She answers the door in an adorable '30s-inspired romper made of black-and-white-striped linen. Her hair is pulled back into a messy bun, and there isn't a scrap of makeup on her face. "Have you been hiking Machu Picchu or something?" she asks, holding the door for me. "You look beat."

"Thanks, sweetheart. You look amazing too." I park the box on the table and kiss her cheek. "I didn't sleep much last night."

"It was quite a storm," she agrees. "Laura slept with me."

Her house is a beautifully restored Victorian with antiques and period-specific artwork on the walls. Today the overhead fan is going full speed, but it's hot. "Still against air-conditioning? I think I might put it in at Sapphire House."

"No, no!" She waves her hands like windshield wipers. "You'll ruin the lines."

"I'm sure there's a way to do it without ruining the aesthetics."

She humphs. "Air-conditioning is a scourge."

"Or one of the greatest blessings of mankind."

"Come into the kitchen; I'll make us some lemonade."

It's bright and lovely, and I seat myself at the table overlooking the harbor while Gwen drops ice into glasses. I know the lemonade will be fresh squeezed, and almost too tart, and utterly perfect. It's one of her specialties. She brings over two frosty tall glasses and sets one in front of me. "So how's the house? I'm sorry I couldn't come this weekend, but I figured you'd want some family time anyway."

"It's going well. I just brought you a few bits of china to look over. I thought you might like it."

"I saw you on TV. Great job."

My stomach flips. "It's already on? They just filmed it!"

"Well, it's not like they have to do anything but upload it. It's a good story. You told it well."

I nod, taking a big gulp of the, yes, almost painfully tart lemonade. "Maybe someone will come forward with some kind of clue about the murder."

"Doubtful, really."

"I don't know. Maybe they've been afraid of hurting someone or getting hurt themselves. Something like that."

She shrugs. "I suppose it's possible."

"Right. I found some of the sister's journals, actually."

"Ooh, can I read them?"

"Not yet."

"I dug out my old notes and remembered that there had been talk about the carpenter who did all the inlays. Gossip that he and Veronica had a thing."

"It's outrageously great work," I say, reaching into my bag to pull out the notebook I always carry, now with my fountain pen.

"Ooh, is that new?"

I grin, holding it up. "You like?" I almost say, *My sister and I had this thing for fountain pens*, but clamp my mouth closed just in time.

"What's wrong?" Gweneth asks. "You look like you swallowed a fly."

"Just thought of something I forgot at the market." Unscrewing the top of the pen, I flip to a clean page. "Okay," I say. "I'll check it out."

"You all right?"

"Just tired." I rub my aching temples. "Maybe I ought to just go home and catch a nap before the family returns."

——— ❧⸻❧ ———

The house is blissfully cool and empty when I get back. The dogs and I trot upstairs, where I draw the curtains and stretch out on the bed, my mind full of Gweneth's speculations. Paris posts herself right beside me, and I reach out to soothe her, running my fingers through the ruff under her chin, which makes her groan ever so softly.

On my laptop, I open the file I've been assembling about the murder and the history of the house. In one file is a group of photos I've captured from the internet, Veronica in the sizzling gown that launched her career, George with his medals, looking solid and powerful and very hot, like a young Jason Momoa.

I don't have a photo of Helen, and I search for one but come up with only three. With her sister and George just after the house was finished; as a girl somewhere in the bush, her hair natural and flying in the wind; and a few years before her death, at some kind of fund-raiser. By then, she was polished and stately, her hair smoothed back into a snowy French twist, her warm skin beautifully offset by an aqua dress.

Not a beauty like her sister but good-looking enough. In the one with George, he had one arm around her and one around Veronica, and he was grinning as they both leaned into him. It makes me think, unexpectedly, of Dylan and Kit and me, and I have to shove the vision away.

Helen, George, and Veronica were all Maori. Enjoying a level of wealth and celebrity that would have been rare for anyone but maybe was even more notable for Maoris at the time.

Huh. I make a note to read more about the celebrity romance. What did they say? How did they talk about George and Veronica?

But also—sisters. That could be a very fraught relationship, as I well know. Could Helen have had a thing for George or he for her? (Naughty George, if so, cheating on his wife, then cheating on his mistress.) But once a cheater, always a cheater in my book. Men who cheated kept cheating.

Like my father.

The first time I figured out that one of the hostesses was having sex with my dad, I was eight. I'd been out on the beach but cut my toe on a rock and raced up to Eden to get Band-Aids. My dad was in the empty bar, making out with Yolanda, the weekend hostess. They jumped up when I slammed into the room, and I just glared at them. "I cut my toe."

My dad made Yolanda bandage my toe, and I could tell she didn't want to. Her lipstick was all smeared, looking stupid, and she seemed like she was about to cry. "Don't tell your mom, okay?" she said. "I really need this job."

"Stop doing that, then," I said.

"I promise. I won't do it anymore."

I went through the kitchen on my way back. My dad was the only person around, and I said, "I'm going to tell Mom."

"Yeah?" he said, and the mean look came on his face. "It's none of your business, little girl. You don't know anything."

Usually just that look was enough to send us scurrying, but I glared at him, furious when tears welled up in my eyes and spilled over traitorously. "You're stupid," I said, and then I ran before he could catch me and spank me for my disrespect.

Up until then I'd adored my father, would do anything to spend time with him. Afterward I could almost always figure out who his girl of the moment was, and he always had one. She'd have big tits and big hair and big teeth, and she'd be younger than my mom by a decade—even though my mom was already a decade younger than my dad. I made the lives of the girls miserable in a million tiny ways. Salt in their diet sodas, broken ink pens left in strategic places to wreck their clothes, stealing from their purses left in the lockers in back—never money, or least not a lot. It would more be things like lipsticks or tampons or, once, birth control pills. I spilled things when they'd have to clean them up. Anything I could think of.

How much did my dad know? I don't know. He disapproved of me, anyway, even when I was only eleven and twelve. My clothes and my hair and my grades. The older I got, the more he criticized me until by the time I was thirteen, we were engaged in a full-on war. I did as many things to drive him crazy as I did the women he kept on the side, using them, one after the other, like they were nothing, like they were shoes he'd worn a hole in.

I don't know if Kit knew about any of it. Probably not. By the time she was ten, she was all the way into her studies of marine life and climate and surfing. God, how she loved surfing! And to my chagrin, she was better than I was. I looked better doing it, with my skinny arms and long hair and tiny bikinis—they called me Baby Babe—but Kit was just plain better. She read the waves and the wind as if they were the alphabet. Everyone encouraged her to try out for surf competitions, but she wasn't interested. Surfing, she said, was just for her.

Same for Dylan. Just for himself. The two of them sometimes piled their boards into the battered Jeep he drove and headed up or down the coast, looking for some mythical surf.

I never went on those trips. By then, I had my own interests, things that had nothing to do with Kit and Dylan. I stayed home to have my room to myself, to read, to write in my journal and imagine the day I could finally escape Eden and my parents and make my own life.

I had no idea how soon it would happen.

Chapter Twenty-One

Kit

After I find Mari/Josie's pictures on the internet, I wander down a rabbit hole for an hour, shaken, looking at photos of my sister's rise to prominence as Simon Edwards's beloved wife. He's local royalty, a sailor and yachtsman who runs a chain of fitness and swimming clubs. He is a fit, big man with a winning smile, and I love the way he looks at my sister. In every picture, he has his hand laced through hers or an arm draped over her shoulder, one on a child's shoulder. Their son looks exactly like him, but their daughter—

Looks like me. Almost exactly like me. Freckled and sturdy, with thick dark hair, not blonde like her mom.

Reeling, wildly emotional, I track down their address. Devonport, which is the township that I can see from my balcony, the lights that wink at me at night. When I've been staring out at her, she might have been standing at her window, looking back across the water at my hotel.

The thought gives me shivers.

I have to go to her. Filled with a stuttering, overwhelming adrenaline, I pull on the same red dress I've been wearing for two days and realize that it smells of ocean water and sunshine, and the skirt is ridiculously wrinkled. The only other things I have clean are a pair of jeans and a T-shirt that says A Woman's Place Is in Medicine. As I look at them hopelessly, I realize my hands are shaking.

Okay, breathe.

They'll have to do. I shower and leave my hair loose to dry as crazy as it wishes in whatever way it will go, slap on some lipstick and drop the tube in my bag, and carry my hat down to the ferry dock. Because we had to wait awhile before, I'm prepared for that, but the Devon shuttle runs more regularly, and by the time I make my way to the waiting area, the ferry is boarding.

This time I don't go up top but sit down inside and watch the city center recede. Businesspeople read newspapers, which bemuses me. It's such an ordinary thing to do on such a breathtakingly gorgeous ride. A gaggle of teenagers talks too loudly. Tourists from every continent on Earth crowd the seats.

All I can think is, *Josie, Josie, Josie.*

———— ∽୧୨∽ ————

I'm too riled up to do much of anything. My phone map shows me that the address I found is only a few blocks down the sea walk, but I'm buzzing with the kind of emotion that will do no good if I confront her.

To get a handle on myself, I walk up the main village street toward a path that leads to a volcano, trying to get enough oxygen into my system that I can stop hyperventilating. The walk works up a sweat, and the air is heavy and humid from the storm the day before, and within a block I'm feeling so overheated in my jeans that I have to stand still in the shade for a few minutes and let people pass me. I thought I could make the jeans work, but I'm going to faint of heat exhaustion.

Just ahead is a boutique with dresses hanging outside. Mostly they're touristy T-shirts with New Zealand and Kiwi logos emblazoned across the front, but to my vast relief there are also a number of wrap skirts in soft cottons. Mindlessly, I grab one of the longer ones and hold it up to me, and it's fine, hitting just at my knee. Taking it off the hanger, I test the wrap length, and it works too, so I gather three others in various chintzy prints and carry them into the store. "All of these, please," I say, dropping them on the counter. "And . . . I guess I need some T-shirts."

The woman behind the counter is a tiny English thing, with shoulders the width of a dragonfly, but she moves with a no-nonsense attitude. "Turn around," she says, and measures a T-shirt against my shoulders. "You'll want that rack over there."

"All right." I glance at the colors of the skirts—turquoise, red with yellow, yellow with blue, and a striped green and blue that's really quite pretty. I toss through the shirts, find some that are acceptable, and add them to the stack.

"You'll be wanting some jandals too," she says.

"Jandals?"

She points to a wall filled with flip-flops.

"Yes." I point to them. "Jandals," I repeat. "Like sandals?"

"Japanese sandals."

"Ah. Got it." I select a pair, try them on, find the fit is fine. "Great."

She rings me up. I pay with a card. "You can change over there if you like. But if I were you, I'd wear the medicine shirt. Everybody has the New Zealand ones."

I smile. "Thanks."

"Are you a doctor, then?"

"Yes. ER."

"You're not the one who saved that boy?"

For a moment, I'm so surprised I hardly know what to say. "Uh. The one who jumped off the pilings?"

"That's him. They're all talking about you, you know. Heroic to jump in and save him."

I tuck my card back in my purse. "That was the ten years of life-guard duties, not the ER," I say. "Hope he's doing all right."

"Wouldn't be your fault if he's not. Lunatic."

I head for the changing rooms. Peeling off the jeans is one of the best experiences of the day, and I tie the skirt with pleasure. The sandals are soft and squishy, the toe hold covered with synthetic velvet.

The whole normal interchange has calmed me. I take a deep breath, blow it out. In the mirror I look like someone else, with my wild hair tumbling down my back, and the high color of a lot of great sex and sunshine, and my bare legs.

Shoulders back, I wave at the woman and head out into the day, carrying a bag with the clothes in one hand and my city purse tossed crossways over my body. I'm fortified now. I can face her.

I cross the street and round a Moreton Bay fig that spreads arms out across a massive area. The trunk has many parts, making it look like a tree that would be populated by fairies. I can see my sister and me crouched on the beach, making tiny furniture for the fairies who lived around the cove, and stole sweets, and switched sugar for salt.

The thought makes my heart ache.

But there is only one reason I am here in this place at all. With the focus that saw me through twelve years of study, I shove away my emotions and look at my phone for directions. From here to my sister's house is, by Google Maps estimation, a nine-minute walk, straight down the waterfront.

The houses must be the same era as the Victorians in San Francisco, and again I'm reminded of that city. Pedestrians stroll along the side-walk, fit retirees in pastel golf shirts and white pants and mothers with children and—

I halt, sure that I'm imagining her. A woman walking toward me with my sister's distinctive, un-self-conscious amble. She never walked fast enough for me, and it drove me insane.

She's wearing a simple blue sundress and no hat even in this awful land of skin cancers, plus jandals like mine on her feet. A million memories tumble through my brain: sleeping on the beach in our little tent, that strange summer when Josie got so weird, the earthquake, the news of her death.

She's alone, lost in thought, and I think she might have walked right by me, humming under her breath, until I reach out and touch her arm. "Josie."

Josie turns, cries out, and covers her mouth, and for one long moment, we only stare at each other. Then she grabs me, hard, and hugs me, weeping. "Oh my God," she whispers, her hand hard against my ear. I don't realize until I feel her ribs moving against me that I'm hugging her just that tightly in return, tears running down my own face. She's sobbing, her body shaking from shoulder to hips. I close my eyes and clutch her close, smelling her hair, her skin, the Josie-ness of her. I don't know how long it goes on, but I can't let her go, and I can feel her grip on me like a vise.

She's alive. She's alive. She's alive.

"Oh my God, Josie."

"I fucking missed you so much," she whispers fiercely. "Like a kidney. Like my soul."

I finally pull back. "Why did you—"

Josie looks over her shoulder, grabs my hand. "Listen. Call me Mari. My family is following me. They just stopped to buy something, and I wanted to get my steps." Her grip tightens. "They don't know anything. Give me a chance to explain to you—"

"Mom!"

The little girl is running down the sidewalk toward us. In wonder, I say, "She looks exactly like me."

"Yeah. Follow my lead."

And because I really don't know what else to do, I turn with my sister, who says, "Sarah! I want you to meet someone!"

The girl doesn't give me a toothy smile, just turns her face and looks up, waiting as Josie/Mari says, "This is my friend Kit, from my childhood. We were the very best of friends."

"Like sisters," I say, offering my hand, which feels like it should be shaking, to go along with the buzz in my ears.

"Hullo," Sarah says, and I have no idea why it's such a surprise that she has a Kiwi accent. "It's nice to meet you." Her gaze catches on my T-shirt. "Are you a doctor?"

"Yeah." I touch the words. "I am. Emergency medicine. I think they call it something else here."

"I'm a scientist. I have all sorts of experiments."

My heart melts, and I drop to her level. "You do? What do you have?"

"Weather," she says, counting it on her thumb, "which is mostly a barometer and cloud recordings. And plant experiments, and some crystal things."

"That's amazing. I used to do experiments when I was your age too. I thought I was going to be a marine biologist, but I ended up in medicine."

She inclines her head. "Do you like it?"

"Yes." I pause, swallowing. She is like me, so very like me. How could Josie have kept her a secret from me all this time? How could she have been so cruel as to hide her babyhood, her toddler years, everything? A distant howl of fury and pain sounds in the distance, and it takes every scrap of self-control I have to keep my emotions in check. "Yes, most of the time I do."

The other two are joining us, and I stand up as my sister says, "Kit, this is my husband, Simon." I can hear the pinch in her voice, her fear that I will break everything, and for one moment I want to do just that. Spill everything, let the consequences fall where they may.

But my little niece, so like me as a child, stops me. "She's a doctor, Daddy!"

He's even more good-looking in person, with a genial kindness in his face that isn't evident in pictures and a charisma field as wide as the entire park we're standing in. I reach for his hand and meet his eyes, and a ripple of surprise washes over his expression for the most fleeting of moments. "Hello, Simon."

Mari says, "Simon, this is Kit Bianci. She was my very best friend." To give the words weight, she leans on me, her hands on my arm, her face against my shoulder. "We just ran into each other. Isn't it wonderful?"

I give her a brief, shocked glance.

"Is that right?" he says. His grip is firm and warm. "Good to meet you." He turns to bring his son forward. "This is Leo."

Leo. Our father's name. I force myself not to shoot a glance toward Josie. Mari. Whatever her name is. "Hi, Leo. Nice to meet you."

He's as polite as his father. "You too."

"Just like Tofino," I say to Mari.

She takes my hand. "We were lucky to grow up there."

"Mm."

"We're just going down to have supper," Simon says. "You must join us."

For a moment I consider it, consider sitting with my niece and listening to her tell me about her experiments. I think of what my mother will feel, knowing these children are in the world and that she knew nothing about them. I look into Josie's face, so familiar and yet so unfamiliar, and I can't sit here tonight and pretend.

I'm not ready. Not yet.

"I'm sorry," I say, turning to Simon. "I really do have plans."

"Oh, not really?" Mari cries. "You can't just go! We have to catch up, tell each other everything."

I hand her my phone, and now my hands are shaking with rage. She sees and grips one tightly. Her eyes are fixed on my face, and I see the faint, small shine of tears. For a long second, I'm overwhelmed with gratitude, with love, with a hunger to touch her face and hair and arms, to assure myself that she's not some robot version of herself but Josie, my own Josie. Here. Alive.

"Give me your number," I say. "We can get together as soon as you have time."

"First thing in the morning," Mari says. She punches in the number and then calls it, making her phone ring in her pocket. As if to show me the evidence, she pulls it out, still ringing. Her eyes meet mine, steady. More assured than I ever remember, and something about that softens my fury the slightest bit.

"It's good to see you so happy," I say, and bend in to hug her. So quietly only she will hear, I add, "But I am so furious with you."

She hangs on, tight, tight, tight. "I know," she whispers. "I love you, Kit."

I let her go. "Call me."

Sarah steps over. "I hope you'll come see my experiments."

"I will," I say. "I promise."

And I force myself to keep walking past them, toward the address where they live. I walk there so I won't run into them, and I see the house, which is a pretty thing with a porch and a second story looking out to the water.

None of us can sleep if we can't hear the ocean.

On the ferry to the CBD, I'm back to a whirling mental state that tosses out a thousand images, moments, emotions. I veer between extreme fury and melting sentimentality and something that feels like . . . hope. Which makes me even madder, and the whole thing starts again.

In my pocket, my phone buzzes, and I pull it out.

Finished, Javier texts. Shall I pick you up at 7?

Yes. That would be great. I hesitate and then add, It's been quite a day.

I will look forward to you telling me about it.

His face rises between the screen and me, and I know he will listen. Quietly and intensely. I can see him taking a bite of food, his hair shining under the lamps of the restaurant, then focusing on me babbling and babbling. Because that's what I'll do. If I start talking, it's all going to spill out, the bad and the good, the ugly and the beautiful.

Do I want him to know me that well?

No. I don't want anyone to know me like that.

But at the same time, I don't have any defenses left at the moment. All my tricks and tools have been deployed in this whole business of tracking down my sister.

I had not expected to be so undone by my niece. By a face that looks so much like mine and a heart that's like mine too. *I have experiments.* I want to know every single thing about her.

And Josie named her son after our father. Which is such a weird choice after how long they were at war. When we were small, they were close, but all I remember is how much they fought later. Constantly, furiously, violently.

He once lost his temper with her and slapped her so hard her lip bled. He was instantly ashamed, but she stood there staring at him like a warrior goddess, her hair a long cape around her tanned body, her eyes shimmering with the tears she refused to let fall, her lip split and bleeding. I wanted to cry for both of them, but I huddled in my corner, defending neither.

My mother snapped, "Josie, go to your room until you can speak properly."

Dylan wasn't there. Maybe he was working. Or on his motorcycle. Or with one of his many girlfriends.

I only know that he heard about it later and confronted my father, and then the two of them had a fight. An actual fistfight, which sent all three of the Bianci women into hysterics, trying to break them apart. Dylan had youth and speed on his side, and he tried to simply duck away from my father's beefy fists, but my father had blinding fury on his side, along with size and power and the treachery of age. He broke Dylan's cheekbone, a fact none of us knew until later, and ordered him out of his house.

My mother caught my father's arm and hauled him out of the room, into the kitchen of the small house, but Dylan had already grabbed his keys and flung himself out the front door. Josie and I ran after him, yelling his name. "Dylan! He didn't mean it. Come back—where will you go?"

Josie tried to jump on the bike behind him, flinging her arms around his waist, and for one second, I hated her. She had caused this mess. She always made trouble everywhere, and now I would lose them both.

But for one second, I saw how alike they were, how lost. Dylan's face bloomed with a bruise. Josie's lip was still swollen. Each of them was so beautiful, like creatures from the sea, all limbs and fair hair and shining eyes.

Dylan barked out an order. "Get. Off."

Josie started to protest. "Please, he hates me—"

"Get off the bike."

He didn't look at her. His limbs were rigid with fury. Josie slid off, and the instant her feet hit the ground, he was gone.

Gone for days.

When he returned, he was broken in a dozen pieces, that broken cheekbone the least of his injuries.

Chapter Twenty-Two

Mari

By the time I was fourteen, I stole entire bottles of vodka and tequila out of the storage closet and shared them with boys on the beach. Not the cove, our safe, isolated little place, but the actual beach, which I reached by hitchhiking down the highway.

I learned to sip, not guzzle. Learned to space out the drinks so I didn't end up heaving my guts out behind some rock or accidentally black out and have sex with someone. I never went all the way, but I would make out with just about anybody once I started sipping the vodka.

I learned so many things.

One of them was that there was a crack in the wall between Dylan's bedroom and the one I shared—ever more reluctantly—with Kit. The house was sliding down the cliff long before the earthquake hit, and everywhere the walls were cracked, the floors uneven and full of tripping hazards. It makes me feel dizzy to imagine it now, that all these things revealed the fact that the house was going to fall into the ocean at any minute, but my oblivious parents did nothing. What if it had happened when we were all sleeping?

I discovered the crack along our closet door, along the shared wall with Dylan's bedroom. It was situated above our heads, so you had to stand on the end of Kit's bed to see, and then you had to close one eye, but it was a perfect view of his bed.

Where he had a lot of sex.

The first time I spied on him, I felt guilty and giggly. I could see the girl's naked butt and her tattoo of a butterfly. The girl covered Dylan the first time, but another time I watched him lying on the bed naked while she touched him, and I was both fascinated and repulsed. It was technically some of the same stuff Billy had made me do, but it was different somehow with Dylan.

Kit would have thrown a fit if she'd found out, so I did it when she wasn't around. Everyone said he was like our brother, and I know that's how Kit thought of him, but I never felt that way. Never.

We had a special connection. Everybody commented on it. People thought we were actual siblings because we both had such blond hair, such long legs, and could ride a longboard like we were the original Hawaiians. Because we spent so much time in the sun, we were tanned as dark as varnished cedar, and if he was the most beautiful boy on the beach, I was growing into the most beautiful girl. King and queen of the ocean.

The big secret we shared was the weed. From that first time, when it calmed me down, I loved it. It soothed the shattered, angry girl who lived inside me, screaming all the time. It mellowed me out, just as it mellowed Dylan. We'd lie on the beach in the cove long after everyone else was in bed, after the restaurant was closed. We smoked. Often, we didn't even talk, just sprawled there looking at the stars.

Sometimes we did talk. One night, I asked about his life before he came to us, and he sighed the longest, saddest sigh. "You don't want to know about that."

I turned my head, and the movement sent soft, happy ripples through my body, a combination of the beers I'd stolen and the pot he'd brought. I was so very high, I was pretty sure I couldn't get up even if I tried. "Maybe I do want to know. Maybe you need to tell somebody."

"Do I?" he asked, and his voice rasped into the night, unsure.

"That's what you told me."

"I did." He touched my hand with one finger, and in his eyes were the stars that had fallen. "Will you tell me?"

"You first."

"Not this time."

I looked back up at the sky. "You know what happened. A man made me do things."

"What things?"

I shook my head, feeling myself tremble all beneath my skin. I felt the places in my body where he hurt me, and something swelled right over my throat to keep me from speaking.

"You know it isn't always going to be like that, right?"

A vision of his current girlfriend's bouncing breasts rose up behind my eyes, and I giggled. "Yes. I spy on you."

"What?" He sat up.

I had a sneaking suspicion that I wouldn't be pleased with myself later, spilling this secret. "I can see you through a crack in the wall."

"Having sex?" He didn't sound mad, just confused. "You watch me having sex? How long?"

"Ooh, long time. Since Rita."

"Huh." He fell back down. "You know you shouldn't."

"Of course." I closed my eyes, and to think about it, to see his shoulders, the kissing, the heat moves between my legs. "It makes me feel good."

He picked up the vodka bottle and took a big swig. "We shouldn't be doing this either." He fell back on the sand. "Jesus, I'm so fucked up."

I laugh. "Me too!"

"You're only fourteen," he says sadly.

"Yep."

"You shouldn't know *any* of this stuff."

"But I do," I sang, and felt like I was rising up from my body. In my imagination I took the place of his girlfriend, and it was me he was kissing and touching, and I was doing it back. "It's not your fault, though. It's Billy's."

"Billy Zondervan?"

"Who else?"

"That motherfucker. We should tell your parents, Josie. He should go to jail."

I hauled myself upright. "No! Never."

"Why? Why don't you want to punish him?"

"They won't punish him," I said fiercely. "It'll be all about me, and everyone will know, and—" I could just see the way people would look at me at school, and in my drunken state, I burst into tears. "You promised!"

"Oh, baby." He hugged me. I thought he might be crying. "I'm so sorry. I should have protected you better."

I buried my face in his shoulder, feeling relief and peace. I was so very, very tired. "It wasn't your job."

"Yeah," he said. "It was."

We lay down on the beach, and he held me. Just held me, while we looked at the stars.

After so shockingly running into Kit on the promenade in Devonport, I make it through my family's dinner by focusing on the stories everyone else has to tell. If I let myself feel even the tiniest edge of it, I will lose control, and that is the one thing I absolutely cannot afford. So I'm perfectly Mom and Mari over dinner.

The effort of pretending gives me an enormous headache, however, and when I get back to the house and settle the children, I head for the kitchen to make a pot of tea. "Do you want some chamomile?" I ask Simon.

"No, thanks," he says, typing something into the computer on his lap. Toby, the little mop dog, is perched on the arm of the chair, and the TV is on, playing the evening news. For a moment, I look at all the disasters happening around the world, and my drama seems ridiculous and small, all of my own doing.

But it's not about comparison, as my counselor used to say. My pain is my pain.

Paris pads into the room as I fill the kettle and leads me to the back door. I prepare the pot with tea and turn the kettle on, then take her out. It's a gorgeous night—soft and utterly clear, the stars overhead as bright as strings of patio lighting.

The feeling of Kit's body in my arms slams back into me. I close my eyes to feel it again. So tall and strong, so incredibly fit that I know she still surfs all the time. She smelled of herself, that undernote that is entirely Kit, grass and ocean and sky. That smell made my heart hurt, physically, as if something were pressing on it very hard.

What have I done?

As if she can read my thoughts, Paris trots over and leans on my legs, letting go of a sigh. "You miss Helen, don't you, baby?" I murmur quietly, threading an ear through my fingers. "I'm sorry about that. I would make it better if I could, but I think you've just got to be sad for a while."

She tilts her head back and licks my fingers.

Simon comes out and stands behind me, his hands on my shoulders. "Beautiful night."

"Perfect."

We stand there, all the unspoken things between us, until he says, as he did the other day, "Do you want to talk about it?"

"About?"

"Whatever is bothering you."

"I'm just surprised, that's all. I'm just thinking about old times."

He steps closer, crosses his arms over my chest. "You know you can tell me anything, right?"

I close my eyes and lean back into him. If only that were true. His body is warm and solid, and I would know his scent in a football field full of men. "Thank you, sweetheart," I say, unable to bring myself to say there's nothing to tell.

"Have her to supper tomorrow."

"Yes, good idea."

"Sarah took to her in a flash, I thought."

"She saw her T-shirt. She's a physician."

"Is she? Do you think she might have been the one to save that boy on Rangitoto?"

"What are you talking about?"

"A woman, a tourist who was a doctor, dived off the pier at Rangitoto when some boy cracked his head. It was in all the news."

"Could have been," I say, finally finding a reason to smile. "She was a lifeguard for years." *A lifesaver,* I think, though she couldn't save any of us.

"Does she surf?"

"She did, back in the day. We were quite competitive."

"Who was better?"

I grin to myself. "I refuse to answer that question."

He laughs, low and deep, the sound rumbling through my rib cage. He kisses my head. "I thought it might be that way. She's a very fit and powerful-looking woman."

I slide sideways to look up at him, teasing him. "Did you think she was hot?"

"Maybe," he says, and kisses my neck. "But not as hot as you, my one and only love."

"Pssht." I push his hands away, laughing, but he captures me again and kisses me, and then we're taking it inside, where the kettle has boiled and quit. If Kit comes to dinner tomorrow, this might be the last night I ever have with my beloved Simon. To be sure I don't forget, I kiss every inch of him, pressing the taste of each into memory—the place where his jaw meets his neck, the crook of his elbow, his navel, his knee.

As we come together, so sweetly, so perfectly, as if our bodies were carved of one piece of wood, I find myself praying.

Oh, please, I think to the universe. *Give me one more chance to set things right with everyone. One more.*

Chapter Twenty-Three
Kit

By the time I get back to the apartment from Devonport, it's too late to call my mother. And really, I'm so depleted from all the emotions that have been careening around my body all day that all I want to do is sleep for a while anyway. I toss the keys on the table, drop the bag of new clothes, take my bra off through the sleeves of my T-shirt, and fall face-first on the bed. In seconds I'm asleep, shutting out everything.

Sleep is my superpower. It proved itself over and over and over when I was a child, and when I was so lonely in Salinas, and a hundred times over when I was in med school and after.

And it doesn't fail me now. I fall deeply into the nothingness of sleep. No dreams, no sense of anything. For no reason I can name, I wake up almost exactly one hour later. It's six thirty. Not much time to shower, but that's how it goes. I dash in, wash away the humid, sweaty day, dash back out. My hair is insane from all the humidity, so big it almost makes me laugh when I look in the mirror. Leaving my skin to air-dry, I calm the crazy curls and frizz with product and water until it's something like normal-person hair.

But that's just about all I can manage. I am suddenly ravenous and nibble on a brownie as I get dressed in my last pair of clean underwear, one of the wrap skirts, and an aqua T-shirt with a fern in copper on the front. I have no taste for makeup, though I dig through my bag for a lipstick.

Javier is as continental as ever when I open the door to him, and he's freshly shaved, smelling of some spicy cologne that makes me want to lean into his neck. I'm suddenly awash in nerves. "Sorry. I'm a bit underdressed, but it was so hot this afternoon, I had to stop in a tourist shop and buy something. Come in."

He's carrying a bottle of wine he settles on the counter, and then he turns to take my hand. Just my hand, running his calloused fingertips over my skin. "Are you all right?"

"Uh, yeah." I pull away, start looking for my shoes, but I can't find them, and I stop in the middle of the room with my hands on my hips. "I bought some jandals. I can't find them."

He bends over. "These?"

"Yes, thanks." I slip them on. "Ready?"

"Wait." He touches the small of my back with one hand, somehow urging me around to face him. "What is the matter?"

"I'm so hungry, Javier, I'm going to turn into a monster any second. A real live monster with horns and everything."

"Mm." He brushes hair away from my face. "Tell me."

I'm standing so close to the door that I can feel a breeze coming through at floor level, and I'm aching to flee those dark, kind eyes, his tender gesture, his willing ear. I start shaking my head—"I'm fine"— and then, to my horror, tears are streaming out of my eyes, pouring and pouring, entirely against my will. I feel six years old, and yet I'm mute, only looking up at him.

From his pocket, he produces a handkerchief and, without a word, presses it into my hand and leads me over to the sofa. I sit down, and when he sits next to me, I lean into the space he's made for me against his shoulder and let go. It's a wordless, seemingly endless wave of emotion, and I'm helpless against it. It rolls out of me, unattached to any one thing but all the things, everything.

Javier simply holds me, one hand smoothing my hair, running down my back, the other anchoring me to the earth with its weight on my knee. Dozens of images pour through my mind—Dylan running on the beach with Cinder when he was sixteen or seventeen, happy when Cinder tackled him and licked his whole face. I ran after him and licked Cinder and licked Dylan, and Cinder licked me, and then we all ran toward the waves . . . My father teaching me how to slice tomatoes perfectly, always a sharp, sharp knife, you see . . . My parents dancing literally cheek to cheek, so in love, so beautiful . . . Josie bringing me a giant mermaid cake she and Dylan had baked for me, alight with eight candles and more candy glitter than we could possibly eat.

And more. Curling up with Dylan and Josie and Cinder in the middle of a windy night on the beach, smelling their bodies like the perfume of happiness. Sitting very still so my mom could put makeup on my face for Halloween. Sitting in my dad's lap while he pressed my hair and told someone I was the very image of his mother.

And Josie. Josie on the beach in a tiny bikini, always falling off her skinny brown body when she was little. Josie twirling around the dance floor at Eden, her long hair flying out around her. Josie appearing on my doorstep half-starved and unwell, when I swung the door open and let her in.

Finally, I am out of tears, or at least out for the moment. "I'll wash my face."

He offers me a clean towel, and I recognize the green cross-hatching of the kitchen linens. I'm mortified, but I take it and start mopping up my tears. "Sorry about that."

His lips turn downward, and he shakes his head. "No apologies." Again, that kindly hand smooths my hair, pushes a damp tendril off my forehead. "Do you want to tell me?"

I take in a long, deep breath. "I found my sister, but here's the thing: I haven't eaten all day." I can't talk to my mother yet, not until I figure out what to say. He's been a good listener. It's always easier to talk to a stranger or, in this case, a temporary lover. "Let's go to the restaurant, and I'll tell you all about it."

"All right." He gives my hand a kindly squeeze. "We're going to need a lot of wine, I think."

I snort and wipe my nose as I stand up. "Amen to that." His shirt is damp on the shoulder. "Do you want to change?"

He slaps a hand over it. "No. These are precious tears."

A lump forms in my throat. I *like* him, that's the trouble. Like his easygoing nature, his ease in his skin. "Do you have any flaws at all, dude?"

He laughs, spreads his hands in a *what can I do* gesture.

It makes me smile. "Thank you, Javier."

He winks. *"De nada."*

⸻ ❧ ⸻

The restaurant is called Ima. It's just starting to fill up, and we have seats in the back, tucked into a corner so we can sit at right angles in the booth. It smells so good, my mouth is watering. Javier asks for wine and bread, and the server brings a basket of bread with olive oil and a bottle of Pinot Noir.

Javier is engrossed in the menu, asking the server questions as she pours water for us both, and I can see that he's familiar with the kind of food on the menu, which I am not. He orders a roast chicken and an array of vegetables for dinner, then something called *brik* for an appetizer. "A treat, I promise," he says, handing the menus over. "Egg and preserved lemons and tuna in a pastry. So nice."

"My father loved preserved lemons," I say. "They're not traditional Sicilian fare, but he spent some time in Morocco as a young man, and he loved them. He used them a lot in his dishes."

"Do you remember any of them?"

I sip my wine. After several generous gulps, I'm feeling the magic on the back of my neck, down my spine. There is again space in my lungs for breath. "He made a roast chicken with olives and preserved lemons that was to die for. It was one of my very favorite things when I was a child."

"Most children like blander food."

"He didn't believe in giving children different food from adults. We learned to like things very young."

It's his turn to pause. "Were there things you did not like?"

"Not really. Josie was pickier than I was. She didn't like a lot of different kinds of fish. They used to fight about it." Again, I'm back at Eden, a child trying to hold the center of a dramatic and intense family. "She's called Mari now. With an *I*." I repeat it. "Mari with an *I*."

"Did you speak with her?"

I nod a bit stiffly and take another tiny sip of wine, suddenly aware that alcohol might not be my friend when I'm in such a state. "More than that. I found her. Saw her." The moment comes back to me, visceral and more powerful than I'd anticipated. "Briefly. She's done very well for herself—a mom, wife, entrepreneur. She just bought a big house that belonged to a famous movie star from the thirties."

He nods.

"I tracked her to her neighborhood, and then by chance I ran into her on the promenade in Devonport."

"Not by chance," he says, and nudges the bread plate toward me.

"No, you're right." The moment of our meeting rushes back through me. "She looks so good! I expected something else. I don't know what." Dutifully, I dip bread into the dish of oil. "The last time I saw her, I was in med school. She just showed up one day, and she was . . . a mess. Like she hadn't bathed, and her hair was greasy, and she looked like she'd been living on the streets, which I think she actually had. She wasn't drunk, but she was desperate, and it broke my heart to see her like that, so I let her in." I tear the bread and take a bite, remembering. "She stayed with me for a few weeks. I had an apartment, and she slept on the couch, and she made meals for me, which I appreciated so much I can't even tell you. And then one day, I came home and everything was gone. Just gone." I shake my head. "I still can't believe she did that." My throat is so dry, my voice rasps. "Stole everything."

"Was she an addict?"

I nod. "I'm pretty sure she was an alcoholic by the time she was thirteen, and she was drinking long before that." A wisp of horror crosses his face, and I wave my hand. "I'm sorry. It's a sad, terrible story. I don't know why I'm dumping it on you."

"You are not 'dumping.'" He covers my hand with his own. The weight of it eases the fluttery sensation along my nerves. "I'm here to listen."

And really, I'm too tired to dissimulate. "When I was little, she was the star of my life. I mean, the very middle of everything. My best friend, my sister, my—" I halt.

"Your . . . ?"

"My soul mate," I finish, and a welter of tears swells in my eyes. I have to swallow hard to control them. "Like we've known each other always."

"In Spanish, we say *alma gemela*. Soul twin."

The words sting the raw space of my heart. *"Alma gemela,"* I repeat.

"Good."

"The thing is, my soul mate abandoned me, over and over again." I shake my head. "After the earthquake, I was so lonely, it felt like a disease. Like something I could die of."

"Ah, *mi sirenita*." He picks up my hand, kisses my wrist, holds my palm against his heart. Quietly, he says, "People do. Die of it."

It's such a relief to spill this out, to feel the heat of his body close to mine, the solid strength of his hand. "I just don't know what to think about any of this."

"Perhaps," he says gently, "it is time to stop thinking and feel."

But the very idea makes me dizzy, because I am so very full of lava, simmering, simmering, beginning to boil. If I allow those feelings out, the spew will burn us all to pieces.

To keep it safely in place, I take a breath and sit up straight, give him a rueful little smile. "All I've done since I met you was talk about myself."

For a moment, he only looks at me. "Your quest is powerful. You needn't apologize for the space it takes." He covers the hand he's holding with his other. "That *you* take. You are important too. Not only your sister."

I swallow, looking away. Nod.

Thankfully, the server brings our appetizer just then, easing the mood at the table. It's an envelope of thin, crispy pastry wrapped around tuna and a cooked egg that spills yellow onto the plate when I cut into it. The taste is sea and heat and comfort. "Ooh, that's amazing."

He smiles, closing his eyes. "This one is very good. I thought you would like it."

I spear the fork into the egg yolk and a red paste that's quite fiery, taste the two apart from the pastry. My tongue rejoices at the mix of heat and fat. "What's the red?"

"Harissa."

"It's amazing."

"It is such a pleasure to eat with you," he says. "I think I would like your father, if it was he who gave you such passion."

I nod. "Yes. And he would have liked you too, I think."

"Is he gone?"

"Yes. He died in the earthquake."

He waits, and I realize I didn't even know I was taking a breath, bracing myself.

"The restaurant and the house were on a bluff above a cove, and when the earthquake hit, we were only a couple of miles from the epicenter. Both the house and the restaurant fell down the mountain. My dad was in the kitchen, which is where he probably most would have wanted to die."

He swears under his breath. "Were you there?"

"I was in the house, but when it started, I ran out the front door. They always tell you to get out, so I ran out to the road. It knocked me down, and I just lay on my stomach with my hands over my head, waiting for the end."

"Pobrecita." He touches my back. "You must have been out of your mind with fear."

"Yes and no. I was frightened, but I also knew"—I laugh without much humor—"because I was such a geek, that the shaking usually doesn't last more than thirty seconds or so, and I just focused on the actual experience. You know, thinking about the amazing fact that the earth was moving against itself."

His smile flashes.

"I did realize that this was a big one, and I started trying to estimate what it would be on the Richter scale—definitely a seven. Maybe even an eight, which would be super rare."

"And were your estimates close?"

"They were." The waiter approaches with our food, and I lean back to allow it to be set in front of us. "It actually only lasted fifteen seconds, officially, at six-point-nine, with seven hundred and forty-five aftershocks."

The plates give off a grounding scent—a succulent roast chicken along with a big plate of vegetables, carrots studded with feta, a tomato salad, rice with lentils, and spinach. It smells of everything whole and homey in the world, and I barely notice the waiter taking away the empty dish, refilling our glasses, disappearing again.

"Allow me," I say, reaching for the knife to cut and serve the chicken. Some for Javier, some for me. We dig into the vegetables, and then, as if we are puppets on the same string, we both put our hands in our lap and pause. Not a prayer but certainly a moment of gratitude. "It's beautiful," I breathe.

"Yes," Javier agrees.

Across the table, my father sits down and plucks a tidbit of chicken from the plate, tastes it, nods happily.

We all dig in.

"When I was a boy, I liked disasters," he says. "Pompeii, the Black Death, the Inquisition."

"Cheerful subjects." I savor a bit of carrot. "Do you remember the details?"

"Oh, sure. In seventy-nine AD, Vesuvius exploded with a force equal to a hundred thousand times the force of Nagasaki—"

"A hundred thousand?" I echo skeptically.

He holds up a hand in oath. "I swear. It sent stone and ash thirty kilometers into the air and killed two thousand people where they stood."

"Have you been there?"

"Mm. It's a strange and haunting place." He pauses, looking at the tomatoes. "Delicious. Have you tasted them yet?"

"Yes. Have you tried the rice?"

He nods, moving things on his plate with the tines of his fork, admires it all. "Miguel told me this place was wonderful, but I did not expect it to be . . . so perfect."

A wave of emotional weariness passes over me. I want to let go of all the heaviness of finding my sister, the heaviness of the past, and look forward instead. I suddenly wish that I could sit with him like this many times, over many years. I can almost see a ghostly version of us, sitting in this same place, a decade or two out. His hair will silver by then, but those long lashes will still frame his lovely dark eyes, and he will still eat like this, reverently.

Cool it, Bianci, I tell myself, and shift the conversation. "Miguel is your ex-wife's brother?"

"My brother now; it has been so long."

"Does he play with you often?"

"No." He inclines his head. "We are . . . not in the same circles."

It's my turn to smile. "You're being modest right now, aren't you?"

He lifts one shoulder. "Perhaps."

Helping myself to more of the carrots, I invite, "Tell me about your ex. Were you married a long time?"

"No, no. We were young when we met and very good together in bed, you know?"

Jealousy, green and hot, ripples down my spine. Weird. Jealousy is not usually my thing. "I'm sure all women are good in bed with you," I say, aiming for something light and realizing only as it falls out of my mouth that it's quite the opposite.

His eyes glitter. "I will take that as the compliment you have so graciously offered," he says in a low voice, "but it is unfortunately not true. The chemistry must be right with lovers, or else—" He makes a *pssht* sound, spreads his hands.

I nod, pretending that I'm not feeling the heat of my cheeks.

"We married, and it was good for a while. She liked to travel with me, liked all the crowds and celebrity, you know?"

I take another bite of succulent, exquisitely seasoned chicken. "Mm."

"In the end, I think she only wanted an ordinary life. Children and a dog and trips to the plaza to see friends on summer nights."

"A nice life."

"For some."

"Not you."

"Not then. That was a long time ago."

"And what about now?"

"Now? Do I want that life?"

I lift a shoulder. "That life. That woman."

His eyes narrow faintly. "Not the woman. Sometimes, yes, maybe the life." He picks up a slice of bread. "You do not strike me as a jealous woman."

"I'm not," I say, and admit to the rest. "Usually."

"My marriage was long ago. It's to me like a story I read once."

On the table, my phone buzzes, and I glance at it in alarm. "My mother is the only one who'd text me, and it's the middle of the night there."

"Yes, of course."

I turn the phone over. We should plan a meeting place for tomorrow.

The lava boils in my belly, and I think of Pompeii. "I forgot I gave it to my sister," I say, turning the phone back on its face.

"I won't mind if you answer."

I shake my head, covering the phone with my palm as if to keep Josie out of my life. She made me wait long enough. "She can wait."

Chapter Twenty-Four
Kit

On the ferry to Half Moon Bay the next morning, I'm as calm as a surgeon. Which, honestly, is another word for bloodless. I've known a few who had some juice, but you've got to be at least part robot to make that life work. I was a nervous wreck on my surgical rotations. Give me an emergency every time.

Anyway. I'm drinking a cup of coffee in the nearly empty commuter ferry. At least on the way out—the people pouring off when it docked at the CBD didn't seem as if they'd all fit.

This one is not geared for the tourist trade, so I sit by the window and watch the scenic spread of volcanic islands and think of what it would be like to see one erupt at 100,000 times the force of the Nagasaki bomb. It's hard to even picture it, given the serene blue water and bluer islands. Javier did not stay over, at my request, and I slept so hard my face had lines all through it.

But I admit I kind of missed his company this morning. He hasn't texted. I almost did and then thought better of it. He knows that I'm going to meet my sister, because I texted her on the way back to the hotel, and she suggested where we should get together.

Which I am anticipating and dreading in equal measure.

I haven't talked to my mom yet either, because I hardly know what to say. *Yes, she's alive. Yes, she's fine. So fine! And you have two grandchildren who are nine and seven who you've never had a chance to know.*

Maybe say it better than that, as Javier suggested.

So I'm putting it off for a little longer, until after this meeting today.

After a few minutes of the agreeable movements of the ferry, I find the water doing its usual magic. I watch a guy in a kayak avoiding the wake of a motorboat, then swirling through the wake with joy, and it makes me smile. I'm falling in love with this place. It's so *much* water, so much sky. I love the village centers that feel a little out of time with their covered walkways and shops of all sorts, and the very real way the landscape dominates everything.

Like the way the ferry carries me into a bay I hadn't seen before, hidden and surrounded by hills. A marina boasts dozens of sailboats and yachts of various sizes, and the hillside above is a tumble of houses. I disembark, and there is Josie, hair pulled back from her face, sunglasses hiding her eyes. She has a hat in her hand, and she uses it to wave to me.

I lift a hand and both admire and hate myself for my cool. It doesn't encompass the way I feel, which is nervous and shaky and on the verge of tears, which I would hate more than I can possibly say.

When I get closer, I see that tears are streaming down her face, which infuriates me, and when I'm close enough, she reaches for me. I hold up a hand to stop her, my voice icy cold. "No. It caught me off guard yesterday, but all this time you knew how I'd feel, and you let me suffer, thinking you were dead. How could you *do* that, Josie?"

"Mari," she says, and I hear her voice deflating. "My name is Mari now."

"I don't—" I want to *hit* her.

She must see it on my face, because she says, "Look, we can do all of that." She shifts her glasses to the top of her head, and I see that there are circles under her eyes. "You can yell at me, and I'll answer any question you ask as honestly as I can. But can we just . . . start . . . in a better place?" Her eyes are as dark as buttons, just like my dad's. Swimming in their depths, I'm captured.

It softens me. "Okay." I start. "You look good, Jo—Mari. Really good."

"Thanks. I've been sober fifteen years."

"Since you *died*?"

She meets my eyes, her chin up. On this, she is not ashamed. "Yes."

"Mom too, actually."

That causes a flicker. "Is that so."

"Yep."

She looks at me, really looks at me, my hair and face and body. "You've grown into a beauty, Kit."

"Thanks."

"I google you all the time. Stalk you on Mom's Facebook."

"You do?" It strikes me that she had this freedom, but I did not. While I was grieving her, searching crowds for her face, she was reading about me online. I look away, shaking my head.

She touches my arm, the inner flesh of my left arm, where my tattoo is. Quietly, she says, "You're a doctor. And you have a cute cat."

I relent. "His name is Hobo."

She smiles, and right there, in that easy gesture, I see my lost sister— Josie, who read to me and cooked up schemes with me—and it nearly doubles me over.

"Hey," she says softly, taking my arm. "Are you okay?"

"Not really. This is hard."

"I know. It is. It's hard for me, and I've known all along." She gently turns me toward the parking lot. "I packed snacks. I thought I could take you to a place I like, so we can just talk. It might be awkward in a restaurant or something."

I think of myself weeping and weeping and weeping on Javier's shoulder. "That's a good idea."

She leads us to her car, a black SUV on the smaller end but luxurious. In the back seat are things that clearly belong to kids. I start to climb in on the right side, and then I see the wheel and round the car to the left. The passenger side.

"Sorry it's a mess," she says. "I'm starting a new project and it's just—I never get everything done."

"You were never exactly tidy."

She lets go of a quick, bright burst of laughter. "That's true. I drove you crazy."

"You did."

"Where the hell did that come from? It's not like Mom was neat." She starts the engine, and it hums into quiet life. A hybrid, which gives her points in my book. "Our destination is a little bit away but not terrible. Water?"

"Sure."

She hands me a metal water bottle, very cold. "Sarah outlawed all plastic a while back." In the words, I hear the hint of a New Zealand accent, the syllables slightly shortened. "Nothing plastic in the house at all."

I'm quiet as we pull out, my emotions compressed and contained. It's very hilly. We climb a steep one, go around and down another, up again to a village center that's just as quaint as the others I've seen. "This is Howick," she says. The streets fall away to the water, houses lined up all the way down.

"Pretty. The whole place is pretty."

"It is. I love it. I feel like I can breathe here."

"We can't sleep unless we can hear the ocean."

Her breath catches audibly, and she looks at me quickly, then back to the road. "Right."

I imitate her accent. "'R-iii-ght," I sort of drawl. "You don't sound American anymore."

"Have I picked up the accent?" she says, exaggerating the pinch of the words.

"You have, a bit. Maybe you sound Australian, though I wouldn't really know."

"Have you traveled, Kit?"

"No," I say, and for the first time I let myself be myself. "I haven't, but since I got here, I've really wondered why."

"You work a lot, I guess."

"Yeah, I mean, but I have a ton of vacation time stacked up." I look out the window to the sea that sparkles on the other side of a hill. "Seriously, look at this place. Why haven't I ever seen it before?"

"So what do you do instead?"

"Surf." I pause, trying to think of anything else. "Surf and work and hang out with Hobo."

It sounds pathetic, so I'm doubly irritated when she says, "Not married, then?"

"Nope." A gurgling heat bubbles in my gut, the lava going liquid as I think of my empty house and the little girl—my niece—who stood on the promenade and told me she has experiments. "How long have you been married?"

Her hands, slim and tanned, show white at the knuckles where she's holding on. The ring on her finger is discreet but a beautiful stone—some kind of pale green. "Eleven years. We've been together thirteen. I met him surfing at Raglan."

"Wait. Raglan—*the* Raglan?" It was one of the litany of places we all recited to each other, me and Josie and Dylan.

"The very one," she answers, smiling. "It's gorgeous. Not very far away. We could drive down there and surf another day if you want to."

"Maybe." The entire conversation is surreal. But normal. I mean, what do you say to someone you haven't seen in so many years? Where do you begin? Surfing is one of our languages.

On cue, she asks, "Have you surfed since you've been here?"

"I went to Piha. Which is actually what made me think of calling surf shops, which is how I actually figured out where you were."

"Smart."

Silence settles, only the soft radio playing between us. She asks, "How did you know to look in Auckland?"

"I saw you on the news, when the nightclub fire killed those kids."

She sighs. "I figured." A pause. "Yeah, that was a terrible night. I was having dinner with a friend at the Britomart when it happened."

"At the Italian place?"

She looks at me. "Yeah. How'd you know?"

"I went there. They said that you came in, but they didn't know your name."

"Good girls."

A ripple of rage burns beneath the skin of my face at this brazen reinforcement of her long lie. "Mom saw you on the news too. She was the one who wanted me to come find you."

"Hmm." Her tone is unreadable.

"She's different, Josie."

"Mari."

"Right. Because if things are not convenient, you can just leave them behind."

She glances at me. "It wasn't like that."

I look out the window, wondering why I even bothered to come. Maybe I would have been happier never knowing she was alive. Again, tears—when I never, ever cry—threaten to well over. I mentally count backward from one hundred.

We turn off the main drag and start driving uphill under a thick canopy of local forest. Tree ferns with extravagant leaves and some kind of flowering shrub line the road, which is rutted and uneven. It ends in front of the house that was on the New Zealand television show.

"I saw this on the news. Why did you bring me here?"

She turns off the car and looks at me. "Because I need you to see the life I've built here."

Stubbornly, I stay where I am. "Are you going to tell me the truth about what happened? Or are there just going to be more lies?"

"I swear, on all that I hold holy, that I will never tell you another lie as long as I live."

I open the door and jump out. I'm not sure if I really want the entire truth. The prospect fills me with a sense of hollow anxiety. I look up toward the vivid blue sky and suddenly sense a host of half-known things lurking in gray darkness at the edges of my mind. My arms break out in gooseflesh, even though a soft breeze soughs over us as we walk toward the house. I rub my arms, trying to calm myself. "What is this place?"

"Sapphire House. It was built by a famous New Zealand actress from the thirties, Veronica Parker. She was murdered here."

"That's not creepy or anything."

My sister, whose name feels strange on my tongue, stops before we get to the door and points back the way we came. In the distance is the ocean, in between a vast spread of the city. "At night, it sparkles all the way to the coastline."

"Great. So you have a mansion and a family and nothing bad to bother you."

"I deserve every single ounce of that. But can we do this part first? Please?"

I take a breath. Nod once.

She turns to the front door and unlocks it, and I follow her inside to the cool interior, which is just like the shots I saw on TV, only more amazing because of the scale. The foyer is round, opening to several rooms and a staircase that leads upward, and everything, everything is Art Deco. "Wow."

"I know. C'mon."

I follow her into a long room that faces the sea, a green sea tossing all the way to the horizon. A wide lawn spreads between the house and what is probably a cliff, and I'm drawn outside through the glass doors to the grass. A very soft wind rustles over my skin, lifts my hair. I capture it and look up to the back of the house, where balconies line the entire upper floor.

"Holy shit," I say. "It's gorgeous."

"I've been flipping houses since 2004. I started down in Hamilton. When I met Simon, he lived in Auckland, and he convinced me to move up here with him. The market is insane here, as bad as or worse than the Bay Area, and I've done very well."

"This is a flip?"

"Not exactly." She tucks her hands in her back pockets. She's as slim as ever, and just as flat-chested, and her hair suits her. "I've kind of been in love with the house and the story of it pretty much since I got here. We used to live over there a bit, and I could see it from our living room, shining up here on the hill. When the sun rises, it washes the whole thing pink, and it looks like a . . ." She pauses, looks at me, then back to the house. "A mermaid house."

I cross my arms.

"Simon's family has been in Auckland for a long time. They came with some of the first settlers, so he knows everyone and everything that's happening, and they've been 'dabbling'"—she puts the word in air quotes— "in real estate for a century. When the owner died, Simon snapped it up."

"Because you love it."

Simply, she turns to me and says, "Yes."

I can only look at her for a moment, then look back up to the house. "I saw pictures of your family and you when I found out your name. He clearly adores you."

"We have a good life, Kit. Much better than I deserve. But it's real and true. We've built a world together. We have children, and now I'm going to make this house over for all of us."

I look toward the sea, back to the right where a tall line of tree ferns make a scallop of the sky. "But it's all built on a lie, right?"

She bows her head. Nods.

"I don't know why you think that bringing me here would change how I feel right now!" The carefully contained emotions are restless beneath my skin, deep in my abdomen, there at the base of my skull. "You landed on your feet. Great! How does that change the fact that you faked your own death? You let us believe that you were dead!"

"I know, I—"

"No, you don't know, *Josie*. We had a memorial service for you!"

"Oh, I bet that was very well attended! Did you hire homeless guys to come in and cry or something? Because the only people left when I supposedly died were you and Mom. You hated me, and I hated her, so—who exactly was there to mourn me, Kit?"

"I never hated you! You hated yourself." I refuse to let the tears fall, but they're thick in my throat. "And believe me, I mourned you!"

"Did you?" The words are skeptical. "Really? Even after I cleared out your entire apartment?"

"I was furious, but I didn't hate you."

"I tried calling you. You never picked up."

Which has haunted me more than I want to admit. "I had to keep my distance, Josie, but that didn't mean I hated you."

And for the first time, I see the lost Josie I knew then. "I'm so sorry I did that."

I shake my head. "I mourned you. I didn't want to," I admit. "But I did. We both did. For months and months after you died, I combed the internet for any possibility that you could have survived." I shake my head, winded. "For years, I'd think I saw you in a crowd and . . ."

She closes her eyes, and I see that tears are gathered on her lashes again. "I'm so sorry."

"That doesn't really help all that much."

She takes a step closer. "Don't you see, Kit, that I had to kill her? I had to start over."

We're standing face-to-face, both of us with our arms crossed. I'm so much taller than she is now. I think of the things I think I know about her, about what happened to her, this tiny woman who once loomed as large as a dragon over my life. "How did you do it?"

"Let's go inside. I'll make tea."

She shows me around as the kettle boils, and then we carry our mugs into the lounge, where she opens all the doors to the sea breeze. We face each other on a sofa, and she tucks her legs up under her. Something about the way the light comes in strikes her scar, an uneven zigzag through her eyebrow that healed poorly. "The doctor who stitched you up did a terrible job," I say. "I could have done better first year."

"I think it was because it was so long before it got attention." She touches it, the old wound. "Everybody else was so much worse off."

"Triage," I say.

"That's right. You're an ER doctor." She smiles. "By the way, did you save a kid's life on Rangitoto?"

I blink. "What? How did you know about that?"

"Simon asked me. It was in all the news. Human interest story and all that."

"It was me, but it wasn't exactly a big deal." She starts to interrupt, and I raise a hand to stall her. "Remember how kids always jumped off the cliffs? And how every year somebody would crack their head wide open? It was me standing right on the rocks where they go in and seeing that somebody knocked themselves out on the way down." I shrug. "I was in the water before he was, I think."

She laughs. "I love it. Still heroic."

"Whatever." I'm feeling a little faint or something and take a long gulp of tea. "Tell me the story."

"Okay." She takes a breath. "I was in France with some people. We'd been traveling all over, surfing. A lot of drugs." She looks down into her cup, and I see the weight of it on her shoulders. "I was . . . bad." She lifts a shoulder, meets my eyes. "You saw me. When I stole all your stuff. I'm so sorry about that."

"Later."

A nod. "So the plan was to go to Paris and then down to Nice. I didn't have much at that point. A backpack and my board. That's all most of us had. We caught the train in Le Havre. I went to find a bathroom, but the first one was filled, and I just kept going down to the next one. I was high, shockingly enough, and when I came out, I turned the wrong way, and I got all the way to the back of the train before I realized it."

My stomach aches with the tale.

"The bomb blew when I was in the back. The cars were all derailed, and I was thrown out." She's frowning toward the past, over my left shoulder. "I don't honestly know what happened right after, just that I woke up, and I was . . . okay."

She stops. Looks at me with alarm.

"What?"

"I just realized that I've never told anyone this story. Ever."

And because I loved her once, I reach out and touch her knee. "Just tell it."

She closes her eyes. "It was awful. People were dead. They were screaming. There was all this smoke and sirens and . . . noise. Smells. I just wanted to find my friends, find my backpack—like, that's all I could think about. My pack."

She stops. Looks out to the ocean. Taps her fingers against her cup. I'm quiet, letting her tell the story.

"The closer I got to where they should be, the worse it got. Like, not just dead people but . . . pieces. An arm. I saw an arm, and I threw up, but I just couldn't stop. I don't know why. I don't know what I was thinking; I was just fixated on that pack."

I nod. "Shock."

"I guess." She takes a breath. "My friend Amy had this ridiculous little-girl pack. It was pink with flowers, and she thought it was ironic, but it was just stupid.

"I found it and picked it up and kept looking for mine. But—" She stops. The silence stretches for thirty seconds, a minute. I don't interrupt it, and eventually she says, "I found Amy. Her face and her chest were fine, but something fell on the rest of her. She was dead. I could see other bodies and a surfboard, and I just—I just grabbed her pack and started walking. I walked . . . away. I walked all the way into Paris. It took hours."

Outside, a bird makes a robot noise. The sea crashes against rocks somewhere. Inside is still.

Josie looks up. "She had a New Zealand passport and three hundred dollars. I found a ride on a freighter and took off. Came here."

My heart suddenly aches. "Damn, Josie. How did you get so bad?"

She lets go of a sad, short laugh. "A day at a time."

I bow my head. "Why didn't you let us know? I mean, you took off constantly."

"When I was on the freighter, I detoxed. It was awful. I was sick as a dog for weeks, and when I was finally done, I had plenty of time to think. It takes a while for a freighter to go from Paris to New Zealand." She presses her lips together. "I had to start completely fresh."

I close my eyes. "You abandoned me."

She knows I'm not talking about when she supposedly died. "I know. I'm so sorry."

"Simon doesn't know anything about this?"

"No." Her lips pale faintly. "He would hate me." She shifts gears suddenly. "You have to come get to know the kids, Kit. You'll love Sarah. She's just like you."

My calm snaps. "What are you even *talking* about? We're just going to forget everything and start over like nothing happened, like you didn't break our hearts into a million pieces?"

"That would be my preference," Mari says, and the words are calm. Clear.

It makes me wonder if I can just let it all go. Set down the burden, drain the boil, and stop punishing everyone, including myself.

Mari says, "Come to dinner tonight, get to know my family. See who I am now."

"I don't want to add to the lie." But if I'm honest, I'm aching to spend time with my niece and nephew. I also feel uncharacteristically nervous, and my mind goes immediately to Javier. Despite my usual solitariness, I feel the need for someone in my corner. "Can I bring someone?"

"A boyfriend?"

"Not exactly."

"Of course. Come at seven." She swallows. "My life is in your hands, Kit. There is nothing I can do to stop you from telling the whole story if you so choose. Please don't."

I stand up. "We'll be there at seven. You can take me back now."

She nods, and I see that she's again weeping.

It infuriates me. "Stop it! You don't get to cry over this. You're not the one who was left behind, the one who was lied to. If anyone should be crying, it's me."

"You don't get to tell me what to feel," she says, her chin lifting.

"You're right." My voice is tired when I say, "Just take me back."

Chapter Twenty-Five

Mari

I drop Kit back at the ferry. I offered to take her into the CBD, but by then she was done with me. As I head home over the bridge, I'm captured by a traffic jam caused by an accident somewhere up ahead.

Stuck, I roll down my window and turn up the radio a jot. Lorde, the local hero, sings her song "Royals," about a bunch of blue-collar kids imagining what it would be like to be rich. In my current mood, it brings back a lot of yearnings and memories. I wonder what Kit actually knows about everything. Billy. Dylan. My addictions, which grew with the weed Dylan and I shared and multiplied after the earthquake when we went to live in Salinas. I wonder if she knows I was selling weed then to keep myself in whatever I needed—booze, weed, some pills, though I was never much of a pill popper. Too unreliable.

Traffic edges forward slightly, and I realize it's nearly three, and I've invited Kit and her plus-one over for a dinner that isn't even started. Is there anything to cook in the house? I briefly consider takeaway, but I really want to cook for her. Cook something from our childhood, something beautiful and comforting, to show that I've turned over this leaf too. She did all the cooking after we moved to Salinas, food my mother and I often ignored or took for granted—stews and soups in the winter, fresh salads and homemade pizzas in the summer.

What would she like? What would my dad have cooked for such a family reunion?

Pasta, for sure. I run through a bunch of ideas—ravioli will take too long; lasagna is too ordinary. Bucatini is lovely but also time-consuming. My mouth tastes eggplant and red peppers, some olives, some Parmesan. Yes. *Vermicelli alla siracusana* with my dad's favorite preserved lemons, which I keep on hand. And cauliflower salad. And cake. Chocolate cake. I can do all of it even if it takes an hour or more to get home. On the steering wheel, I push a button to make a phone call and tell my phone to dial Simon. He doesn't answer, but I leave a message to let him know Kit and her friend are coming for sure, and he needs to pick up wine. We rarely have any in the house.

Kit, in my house. With my children. My husband. The delicate, sturdy life I've built here.

My stomach turns over. It's the most terrifying thing I've done in my life, and a part of me wonders why I'm doing it this way, the most dangerous way. Anything could go wrong. A slip of the tongue. A full revelation from Kit.

But it feels like the *only* way, as if I have to cross a tiny, rickety bridge to the next stage of my life or remain here on the precipice, poised to fall, forever.

It occurs to me that I don't have to wait for the revelation. I could just tell Simon myself.

But I imagine his face turning to stone, and I can't. I just can't.

Traffic is immovable. My mind wanders backward.

Helplessly, I follow.

When my father and Dylan beat each other up in the kitchen of our house, we didn't see Dylan for days and days. There were no cell phones then, so we couldn't call and nag him, just wait for him to return.

Which he always had before.

Kit was furious with me for fighting with my dad, for supposedly *causing* the fight with Dylan and Dad, but it wasn't my fault, and I wasn't about to take the blame. My dad and I weren't really talking either, and neither were my mom and dad—unless they were fighting, bellowing at the top of their lungs, throwing things.

Everything was falling apart.

We found out where Dylan was when the hospital in Santa Barbara called. He'd been in a brutal motorcycle accident only days after he'd taken off, and his injuries had been so severe that they had induced a coma. "How severe?" my mother asked over the phone. The hand that held her super-skinny Virginia Slims cigarette trembled, and my stomach dropped out of my body. Kit, standing nearby, went stone-still.

The three of us drove down to see him. He was conscious again but really drugged, his face swollen, black and red, his mouth torn and stitched, his right arm broken cleanly, his collarbone broken, his skull cracked. But the worst of it was a mauled right leg, broken in four places, pinned back together precariously. He wouldn't be able to walk for six months.

The doctors showed my mom his X-rays when I was sitting there. Kit had gone to get snacks or something, and I don't know why the doctor said anything when I was there. Maybe he thought I wasn't listening, because I'd been reading *The Little Prince* to Dylan, even though he was asleep.

"Is he your son?"

"No," my mother said, without adding the usual justification that he was her nephew. "He works for us, helps take care of the girls."

"How long has he been with you?"

She was uncomfortable. I knew that he had lied and said he was sixteen, but he was really only thirteen. She went with the lie and then some. "Three years. He was seventeen."

It had been six years, and she knew it.

"Well, you see the new damage here, on his leg, his arm, his collar-bone. Cracked cheekbone seems almost healed." I watched the pointer pick out bright-white spots on the gray bones.

She nodded.

Then he moved to the other leg, a ragged gray line across the ankle, one in the wrist, several across ribs. Old injuries, the doctor said. "I'm not sure he ever had medical attention for them."

My mother covered her mouth. "Jesus wept. Who would do such a thing?"

"You'd be surprised," the doctor said.

I stood next to Dylan's bed and covered the old broken wrist with my hand, then bent down to put my head against it. I thought of all the scars, the cigars and the belt buckle, and I wanted to kill somebody.

Very slowly.

It was a brutal, powerful emotion.

When Kit found out, she cried and cried, but I never shed a single tear.

———— ⚬⚬⚬ ————

When he was able to get out of the hospital, he still faced a long recuperation, with three eager nurses to fetch and carry, bring him books and play cards and games with him. At first he was withdrawn and sad, huddled in his room refusing to come down, even when we figured out he'd be safe coming down on his butt. He spoke to none of us, just looked out the window listlessly.

But he hadn't counted on the Bianci women. My mother aired the room every morning, opening the curtains, letting in a fresh ocean breeze, changing his sheets and his dressings, forcing him to endure a sponge bath, which she administered privately until he was well enough to do it himself.

Kit brought him shells and feathers and told him about surf conditions and who'd done what out on the waves.

I read to him, sometimes for hours at a time. I went to the library at school specifically to find adventure stories and to a used bookstore in Santa Cruz for paperbacks I thought might have a good story to keep him involved. He vetoed anything violent, which left out a lot of horror and adventure, but I kind of got it. I found some books in my mom's room that were thick historical tales, not exactly the Johanna Lindsey I liked so much but more involved. *Green Darkness*, Taylor Caldwell, stories about the past. He liked those.

My dad was contrite—he knew he'd been in the wrong over both the fight with me and with Dylan—but his only concession was to let Dylan come back, with the promise that he'd have a job when he healed.

Sitting in traffic on the Harbour Bridge, barely moving, I wonder why I was reading to him instead of him reading to himself. It seems like there was some reason, but I don't remember what it was. I read to him all through the spring and into the summer as he started to heal.

Physically, anyway. Mentally, he was not okay. He didn't talk much. He took a lot of pills—back then no one had heard of an opioid crisis, and the doctors were very free with Vicodin and Percocet.

The summer was hot. We had no air-conditioning, and I tried talking him into coming downstairs, at least, where he could sit on the deck overlooking the ocean and get some sunlight. "You're as white as a ghost," I teased.

He only shrugged.

It was summer. I was surfing and hanging out with my friends on the beach down the road from our cove. I was fourteen going on fifteen and hot, hot, hot. I knew it too. My hair had grown down to my butt, and when I took it out of a braid, the blonde waves against my dark-brown skin made the boys crazy. It also made them crazy that I could out-surf most of them. Not the way Kit could—even two years younger than me, she was a better surfer. She was too tall and hippy to be considered cute, but that seemed to play into the respect the guys gave her on the waves.

I didn't care, not really, if she was better in that way. I was queen in all other ways. If I wanted a guy, I could get him, even if he was older, like eighteen. On the beach at night, smoking dope and learning to snort coke with the beach bums, I gathered a lot of tricks for pleasing guys too. Hand jobs, blow jobs. I let them take off my top, but nobody touched my bottoms. I liked kissing, a lot, feeling that pressure and the power it gave me.

I didn't go all the way, which somehow made me think it was okay. I was young. I lived on the beach. I surfed and partied and made out. What else was there to do?

Kit did things another way. Dylan's injuries, past and present, focused her attention on the body, on medicine, and she applied to some geeky camp in LA for aspiring doctors, and naturally she got in—which curtailed my partying because my parents were also going to be out of town for two weeks at some conference for restaurants, and it was in Hawaii. They were making it a second honeymoon. By my count, it was more like the fifth honeymoon or the twentieth. Over and over and over, they battled furiously, then came back together.

This time, I was left in charge of Dylan. I was pissed off about it at first. He was so boring that it was ridiculous. Even when I read the really sexy parts in books, he didn't look at me or respond or anything, just kept staring out the window.

But he'd been there for us, both Kit and me, and I couldn't leave him lying upstairs all alone for two weeks. The first couple of days, I tried again to coax him out of bed, get him downstairs, but he would only use his crutches on the upper level. He hadn't gone downstairs since he'd come home.

I carried his meals upstairs. Carried his dishes back down. Brought him clean clothes. Medicine. Helped him to the shower. "Wash your fucking hair this time," I yelled.

Three or four days in, it was close to evening, and hot, and I was sick of the whole scene. "Come on, Dylan. Get your ass out of bed, and let's get outside."

"You can go," he said. "I'll be fine."

I rolled my eyes. "This is ridiculous. What the hell is wrong with you?"

His silvery aqua eyes glowed in the twilight. "You wouldn't understand, Grasshopper."

"Oh, why, because you're the only person who ever had bad things happen to them?"

He whipped his head around. "No!" He reached for my hand, and I let him take it. "I'm just so goddamn tired."

"Of what?"

He closed his eyes, and his lashes made long shadows over his high cheekbones. His mouth, so battered, was healed now, and the soft evening washed his lips with pink light. He was like a fairy who'd stumbled into the wrong land. It made my chest ache to think that he might really actually kill himself one of these times. Acting on some wild impulse, I leaned in and kissed that beautiful mouth.

It was electric. My mouth buzzed, and it sent a shock through every nerve in my body, and for a long moment—I don't know how long—a minute, maybe, or two, he responded, almost as if it was automatic or he was high, or both, probably. It didn't matter to me why. My body blazed so hard I thought I might faint as we kissed, as his lips parted and our tongues touched.

He pushed me away. "Josie. Stop. No."

I yanked back, aware that my face was bright red. I tossed my hair over my shoulder. "Just wanted to get you moving." I dropped his hand. "Get over yourself, dude."

From the top of the dresser, I grabbed his pain pills. "I'll be downstairs."

It took two days, but he finally roared out his frustration and came down the stairs on his ass. His hair had come loose, and he wore only a pair of boxers, his leg too awkward for even split shorts. "Give me the fucking pills."

I smiled, walked over, and dropped them in his hands. "Want some water? Some food?"

He started getting better finally after that. He came down to play card games at the table, and a couple of times, his friends came bearing rum and serious weed, buds so crystallized with THC that they looked like they'd been dipped in diamonds. Even a couple of bong hits knocked me on my ass.

And maybe he hadn't noticed that I'd grown up a lot, but his friends sure did. One kissed me in the hallway when we'd all been drinking rum and smoking so much that I couldn't form a coherent sentence. I pushed him away, shaking my head. He was in his twenties, already sporting a pretty hefty spread of hair on his chest. I was pretty sure he wasn't going to let me off the hook with a blow job.

Dylan came around the corner while the dude had his hand on my ass, and he lost his shit. "What the fuck are you doing, man?" He slapped his friend's hand away. "She's a kid."

Dude laughed drunkenly, backing off with his hands in the air. "All right, all right. But, buddy, she's no kid. Have you looked at her lately?"

In my very inebriated condition, my ears buzzed, and I wanted, suddenly, for Dylan to see me that way. See me as a *girl*.

And when I looked up, I saw that he *was* looking at me. It was the two of us, drunk and high off our asses. He didn't have a shirt on, only a pair of low-riding jean shorts. He leaned on a crutch, just looking at me. I felt it. On my shoulders. My hair. My bare belly beneath the crop top I wore. I was as tan as I ever got, dark as pecans, and my hair was loose, trailing over my shoulders and arms and my braless boobs. For one second, I thought about how easy it would be to take off my top and show myself to him, to that expression that really did, to me, look like the same one I saw on other guys' faces.

"You're so pretty, Grasshopper, but you're still just a kid. You've gotta be careful around guys like that."

He turned around and left the hallway, leaving me with a crystal-clear understanding that the only guy I wanted then or ever was Dylan. It had always been that way. It would always be that way.

I also knew, in some gut-deep place, that it was the same for him.

My parents would be home in five days, so I didn't have a lot of time. I thought of a thousand ways to seduce him, and some of them I actually employed—I didn't tie my halter top quite tight enough, so that when I helped him get into bed, a lot of side boob showed. He didn't seem to notice. I wore a thin blouse without a bra under it, and when I looked in the mirror, I was pretty sure I could see actual nipples, accented by the triangle of white skin that didn't get tanned. I wore it the whole day, and he never saw me at all.

I read a Johanna Lindsey to him, but he stopped me when we got to the really juicy part, covering his ears with a laugh.

One evening, crickets were whirring and the ocean was singing on the beach. Overhead, stars gleamed like diamonds. "Let's go to the cove," I said. "You can make it with a crutch now, can't you?"

He inclined his head, passing me the bong. "Maybe. You want to grab some tequila out of the storeroom, maybe?"

"Yes!" I took a hit, gave him the bong, and said, "I'll be right back."

I gathered up a bottle of tequila, limes, and my secret weapon—a tiny cellophane packet of cocaine I'd found in my mom's nightstand—and stashed them all in my pack, along with a blanket we could sit on and four sodas to keep us from drying out completely.

"Let's go."

He gave me his half smile, and I was so happy to see him being something close to himself. "Wow, dude. It's good to see you again."

He laughed, and we made our way down the wooden steps to the cove precariously, me in front in case he stumbled. When we reached the sand, I whooped.

He threw an arm around my shoulders. "Whoo! Whoo!"

We spread out the goods—the tequila and limes and salt, the bong and a bag of weed, and then I produced the tiny envelope of cocaine and lifted an eyebrow.

"You're kidding, right?" he said.

"Nope. The real thing. Mom's cocaine."

"She'll kill you when she finds out it's gone."

I rolled my eyes. "She'll never know it was me." Ceremoniously, I gave him the packet. "You do the honors."

"Have you ever done it before?"

I lied and said, "Couple of times, but only a little."

He set up the lines, and we snorted them, and it was in ten seconds the best high I ever had. I leaped to my feet and started dancing in the sea breeze, arms over my head. "Wow!" I cried breathily. "Wow."

He grinned, watching me spin. All my inhibitions were gone. I became my little-girl self, dancing for all the customers in the bar, my hair swinging around me, my head full of songs. Music from the patio reached us, and I embroidered on it. I was wearing a blouse with swinging sleeves and hem, and I could feel the breeze swirling over my middle. It made me horny. On a wave of heat and delight, I fell on my knees, pulled my shirt over my head, and kissed Dylan, all in one movement.

He tumbled backward, driven by the force of my body, and his hands fell on my bare back, on my arms. For a time, a long time it seemed to me, he kissed me back, our bodies rubbing against each other's. I could feel that he was hard under me, which made me bolder. I sat up, my crotch against his, and pulled his hands to my breasts.

He started to resist, to protest, but I moved against him. "Show me what it's supposed to be like, Dylan. Just this one time. We never have to tell anybody, ever."

"Josie—"

I pressed my hands to his face. "Please," I whispered over his mouth. "What we have is special. Real. Please." I kissed him again.

And in the darkness of the beach, high on cocaine, he gave in.

In my fantasies before that night, we had sex like in a movie, all soft focus and music playing a romantic score. In real life, it was both better and worse. Touching him and kissing him was a million times more charged than I'd ever expected. It was like we melted together, and I slid under his scarred, wrecked skin and into the blood that still flowed in his body. He swam into my blood, into my soul, and I became something else, someone else. He showed me, gently and slowly, what it should feel like when somebody who loved you touched you in just the right way. I learned to have an orgasm for the first time, and it blew the pieces of my body out into the stars, bringing starlight back when they settled into my flesh again. I learned to please him too, and at that I'd had some practice.

But the actual sex hurt. A lot. I pretended it didn't, but it wasn't easy, and he took some time making it work. Finally it did, and I pretended to like it, but I didn't. At all. There was a lot of blood after, which I hid from him.

We fell asleep on the beach, drunk and high and also sated, wrapped up together like puppies.

One night. That one night.

The end of everything.

Chapter Twenty-Six
Kit

When I get off the ferry after meeting Mari, I stop for ice cream and sit on a bench to watch people streaming past. Ice cream is a weakness, the creamy sweetness, the cold, the depth of satisfaction. As a child, I would eat as much ice cream as my parents would let me have—giant bowls of it, triple-decker cones in three flavors. Today I've chosen vanilla bean and a local favorite called hokeypokey with chips of honeycomb toffee that is so good I find myself wishing I'd ordered both scoops in that flavor.

With adulthood comes discipline, however, so I give the ice cream my full attention, aware that I'm using food to soothe my aching heart and not caring a bit. Sugar and cream ease my nerves, and the flow of humanity passing by reminds me that my problems, however big they might seem at the moment, are dew in an ocean.

But damn, I feel unmoored.

After Josie "died," my mom got serious about getting sober. She detoxed in a thirty-day residential program, then dedicated herself to AA, going to meetings every day, sometimes twice or three times. She worked the steps, found a sponsor, and became the mother I wanted so badly when I was five and nine and sixteen—present and able to listen.

Most of all, she put me first in her life.

In the beginning, it freaked me out. I didn't know how to handle the change. How to talk to her when all she cared about was sobriety and her daughter. I didn't have time for it, honestly. It was the end of my fellowship, and I had a lot of writing to do in addition to the responsibilities of the work—and even *that* was okay. She let me know she was available if I needed her. She patiently called once a week or once every other week, and even though I nearly always let it go to voice mail, she left upbeat messages, a little story about something at work or on her long daily walks. For the first time in my entire life, she didn't have a man, and she didn't want one, and without the constant struggle of men and booze, she had a lot more time. She threw herself into houseplants, which cracked me up—it seemed such a funny thing for the least nurturing person I knew—but when I saw her orchids, I stopped laughing.

After a while, I started taking her calls. I moved back to Santa Cruz and took a position at an ER there. After a couple of years, I bought my house. A couple of years later, I realized my mom's sobriety was going to stick and I could trust this new version of her, and although I have never really been able to fully warm up, as is often true of the children of alcoholics after so many years of neglect, I did buy her a condo on the beach so she could hear the ocean at night.

Taking a small bite of ice cream, I think I should call her. It's evening there. I could get an update on Hobo.

But what will I say about Josie?

I walk back up the hill to my apartment, and it occurs to me that I can probably make arrangements to go home now. I've found my sister. I'll hang out with the kids tonight, maybe take an extra day or two to surf. Hang out once or twice more with Javier. I still haven't heard him sing again.

A pang cuts through my chest, but I brush it off. We've had a good time. Of course I'll miss him. We can stay in touch through email, and in a few weeks, we'll forget the urgency of now.

You are falling a little with me, he'd said.

I test the emotion. Am I?

Maybe. Or maybe I'm stirred up by everything that's happening. The search, the place, the fact that we've been having really, really satisfying sex. Beyond satisfying. Fantastic. Thinking about it makes me wish for his solid, naked body right now.

Not love, though. It's not an emotion I can trust.

The luxe marble hallways of the high-rise are empty this time of day, midafternoon, when all the residents are working and tourists are out sightseeing. I suddenly do not want to go up to my room and stare at the water again. Instead, I turn around and cross the street to a park that climbs a steep hill, a path weaving in long zigzags toward the top.

I pause at the foot of it and loop the strap of my purse over my body; then I climb the first part of the hill. It's a dense green landscape, dappled sunlight and shadows covering thick green grass. The lushness makes me realize how dry it's been in California.

As I follow the asphalt path upward, it's the trees that steal my attention. Giant, old trees, Moreton Bay figs with their improbable span, their very long arms stretching out over the landscape in a most human way. I slow to touch one, running my hand over the bark, and follow it toward the trunk, which is as wide as a small car and full of nooks and crannies. I step over the roots and into a hollow made by the bark, and it's big enough to live in. I'm sure people did, once upon a time.

As if the trees have cast a spell over me, I find my turmoil calming down, sliding away. I wander through the trees, admiring the shapes the roots and branches make—here is a fairy stretched out, sleeping in the grass, her hair falling all around her; there is a small child, peeking out of the branches.

Around me are students from the nearby university, walking in pairs or singly trudging up the hill with a heavy backpack. A group of young men has strung a thin strap between two tree trunks, and they are attempting to walk it, and the more advanced do tricks. One spies my fascination and invites me to try. I smile and shake my head, wander on.

At last, I come to rest on the cupped curve of a tree trunk, which has clearly been worn smooth by other bottoms over time. It cradles me perfectly, and as I lean back and stretch my legs in front of me, I feel all the sorrow and anger and dismay drain right out of me. It almost feels as if the tree is vibrating very subtly against my body, nourishing and aligning me. I take a breath, look up to the canopy of leaves, and a breeze rustles them softly, touches my face.

It's like being in the ocean, waiting for a wave. Sometimes I don't even care about the wave. It's just so quiet to be out there, in the middle of this ancient body, part of it and not part of it.

That's how I feel now. Part of the tree, the park, the city that has captured my imagination in such a short time. It gives me the space to think, *What do I want?*

What do I want from my sister? What did I think I would find?

I don't even know anymore. I don't know what I expected.

From the ground, I pick up a twig and turn it round and round, and my mind is full of images. Josie bringing me chicken soup when I had the flu and sitting with me, reading aloud from a book of mermaid stories. Josie dancing wildly on the patio overlooking the sea while adults watched approvingly . . . Josie intervening, as savage as a bobcat, when a guy at our school tried to trap me in a corner and feel me up. She slugged him so hard that he sported a bruise for weeks, and Josie herself was suspended. The guy never bothered me again.

And more—Dylan reading to us when we were small and braiding my hair and waiting at the bus stop with us, and Dylan that last summer, his addiction wearing on him, making a scarecrow of him. I think of his scars, so many of them, and the way he made up stories for each of them.

I think finally of the way the house and restaurant looked after the earthquake, spilled down the side of the cliff like a tipped-over toy box, and my mother screaming, screaming, inconsolable.

Closing my eyes, I rest against the tree. What I want is to go back in time and fix them all. Josie and Dylan and my mother.

I don't want to ruin Mari's life. I'll go tonight to dinner, enjoy the children, and then leave her to it. I don't know how to work out the business with my mother, who will want to be a grandmother desperately. I feel in my gut how much she'll want that, and clearly *I'm* never going to give it to her. My mother. She's suffered too. Why haven't I ever told her that I'm proud of her, that I know how hard it was for her to change her life? She's . . . remarkable, really. Why am I still holding myself aloof from the one person who has shown me that she'll be in my corner no matter what?

The recognition washes through me like a soft wave. She's in my corner.

The next wave brings the recognition that I don't have to sort out all my feelings right now. There's time. I'll be kind to Mari and her family and keep the secret. I'll also tell my mother the truth, and I'm going to let Mari/Josie know that too. They can work it out from there.

Eased, cradled by a mothering tree, I fall asleep in the middle of a park in the middle of a heavily populated city. At peace.

───── ☙✺☙ ─────

When I get home, I wash the red dress I've been wearing so often. With the jandals I picked up in Devonport, it's passable. I consider braiding my hair, but thinking of Sarah and her wild mane, I leave it mostly free, only weaving the front part into braids to keep it out of my face on the ferry ride over.

I'd texted Javier earlier to ask if he'd come with me, and he solemnly agreed: It would be my honor. He answers the door with a phone to his ear and waves me inside with a mouthed *Sorry* and one finger held up. A minute.

He speaks Spanish, obviously, but I haven't heard him do it before. It brings home the fact that I've known him only a couple of days. He sounds as if he's working out a problem, going back and forth rapidly with the caller, ending in questions and then an authoritative tone. *"Sí, sí,"* he says, and bobs his head back and forth as he looks at me, his hand making a chattering gesture. More Spanish. *"Gracias, adiós."* He disconnects and comes toward me, arms outstretched. "So sorry. My manager. You look beautiful."

"Thank you. It's the dress."

He grins, shakes down his sleeves, and buttons them. "I will never see you in that dress without seeing you strip it off, toss it at me, and dive into the water." He animates the entire sentence with gestures, ending with a whistle and hands pointed down toward an imaginary bay. His hair is tousled, and without thinking, I lift a hand to smooth it back from his forehead. My fingers graze the heat of his skin, and I touch the tip of his ear on the way back down.

"How are you doing?" he asks me.

I think about it for a moment. "Okay."

"You talked with your sister?"

I smooth the front of his shirt, press the crisply ironed pocket flatter. "Yes."

He inclines his head. "No more anger?"

"Oh, I'm angry." I take a breath. "But . . . there's no point. It's all water under the bridge."

"Mm."

"What? You don't believe me?"

His hands fall on my shoulders. "Maybe not easy to make it go away so fast."

I gesture behind us, toward the park. "I fell asleep in the arms of a fairy tree. She probably erased my anger."

He smiles and kisses my nose. "Maybe. Let's go meet your Lazarus sister." He takes my hand.

———— ⚬⚭⚭⚬ ————

On the way down the promenade in Devonport, in the soft New Zealand evening, he continues to hold my hand as we walk to her house. "Did you phone your mother?"

"Not yet. She was probably at work this afternoon."

"Must be difficult to think what to say."

I glance at him. "Maybe." I stop. "This is it."

The house is lit from within, making it look like a cake with its gingerbread finishes. It makes me dizzy to think how far she came to land here, in this pretty little place with her children. A dozen images of Josie rush across my imagination—her little-girl self draped in mermaid jewels; her as a fierce preadolescent standing up for me, for herself, against the fighting of our parents; her promiscuous teen years; her druggie surfer years.

She said to me, *Don't you see, Kit, that I had to kill her?*

Maybe there really had been no other way. But I am too emotionally weary to think about that right now.

A dog pops up in the window and barks an alert. The little girl appears at the screen door. Sarah. "That's my niece." I tug Javier's hand. In this, I am eager. I wave as we come up the steps, and she swings the door open. A golden retriever comes wagging out, half his body going with his tail. Another, a sober shepherd, hangs back. "Hi, Sarah. Remember me? I'm Kit."

"I'm not to call you by your first name. Is it Miss?"

"Right. Sorry. I'm Dr. Bianci."

Her eyes light up. "Dr. Bianci!" She offers her hand to shake, and it's a good solid grip for a seven-year-old girl. "Are you Mr. Bianci?"

Javier steps up solemnly. "Señor Velez, at your service."

275

She giggles. "Come in."

We follow her into a room lined with windows on two sides, casement with internal shutters I imagine must be for storms. The walls are a sunny yellow, the fabrics sophisticated patterns in primary shades. The whole is light and welcoming and cheerful, so like the childhood Josie that it nearly slays me right there.

Sarah introduces the dogs: Ty, a golden retriever; a fluffy little dog named Toby; and Paris, the solemn black shepherd. Just as she finishes, Simon comes loping into the room, drying his hands. "So sorry. Hello again!" He reaches for my hand and then kisses my cheek. "Is it Kit for everyone, or is there some other name I should call you?"

"Dad, she's a doctor. You should call her Dr. Bianci."

Our eyes meet, and I highly approve of the sparkle in his. "Do you mind if I call you Kit?"

"Kit is great."

The men introduce themselves, and then we're swept into a conservatory overlooking a spectacular garden with a greenhouse, where a table is set for six. Candles flicker in the middle, and here the colors are softer, blues and greens in the placemats, the cushions on the chairs. "This is beautiful."

My sister appears at last, wearing a simple blue summer dress with a thin white cardigan, her hair covered with a bandeau in the same blue as the tablecloth. It sets off her cheekbones and the line of her neck but also makes no attempt to hide the scar. Her cheekbones are flushed as she comes forward to greet me, and something about her tight hug annoys me all over again. "I am so happy you're here," she says, and lets go to greet Javier.

She pauses ever so slightly, and he takes her hand, kisses her cheek. "Javier Velez," he says. "Pleased to meet you."

"Oh my gosh!" She gets a little fluttery, holds his hand between both of hers. "We're honored to have you." She turns to Simon, smiling. "He's quite a famous Spanish singer."

"Is that right?"

I give Javier a quizzical glance. He shrugs a little, tips his head, as if this might be a breach of etiquette to admit to his real life. "Perhaps a little famous in some little places."

Simon chuckles. "I see."

Mari gives me a look, shaking her head slightly. "You should have told me your friend was a famous musician, Kit."

"Uh." I look up at him, feeling disadvantaged. "I forgot."

All three of them laugh, but Javier lifts my hand to his mouth and kisses it soundly. I should not like it, such a boyfriendly gesture, but it buoys me now. "Which is one thing I quite like about you, *mi sirenita*."

The boy comes down then, Leo, and he's the spitting image of his father and as relaxed in his skin. He has been playing video games but makes no fuss about stopping.

I wander back into the kitchen with Mari, and the smells envelop me like a blast of home. "Oh my God. What did you cook?"

She smiles at me proudly, and I'm pierced by the earnestness with which she displays the meal. *"Vermicelli alla siracusana."*

"With preserved lemons." I bend down to inhale the mingled scents, and they're so heady, I'm practically dizzy. "Beautiful. Like . . . my father's."

She touches my arm, the one with the tattoo. "I covered mine tonight," she says quietly, "but they will notice. Little sister."

I touch it, green and blue mermaid scales with a scrolly script that looks as if it were written with a fountain pen that says, LITTLE SISTER. "Friends," I say with a shrug.

She nods. "Of course. But you're obviously the *big* sister."

"Ha. That's the joke, right?"

"Yes." Again that accent, making her someone else. She touches my arm. "That was the first time I tried to get sober for real. After I saw you and we ate at the diner. When we got the tattoos."

"Really? I didn't know that. Why?"

She shakes her head, looks toward the purpling sky through the window. "You were so focused on your career. It was inspiring. You weren't letting"—she takes a breath, blows it out—"everything that happened hold you back."

I think of how sad I felt this afternoon that I've never told my mother how proud I am of her. "You did it, though," I say. "I'm proud of you."

She swallows and turns to the stove. "Thanks."

Sarah comes into the kitchen. "Do you want to see my experiments?"

"Sure. Do we have time before dinner?"

"Only a couple of minutes, honey," Mari says. "Don't be long."

"Sweet!" Sarah takes my hand and leads me to the back door. "Do you want to see?"

I'm so happy to have her little hand in mine. "I used to do experiments all the time."

"I have some plant experiments going," she says, pointing to the greenhouse. "My papa helps me set them up. We're growing three different seeds to see which ones grow best, and we're also growing avocado seeds in three different environments. And celery."

I'm startled by the sophistication she displays, her articulate descriptions. "Have you learned anything yet?"

"We had to throw away the fourth avocado seed because it died. They don't like salty water."

I nod and let her lead me through her barometric center and her measurements, piercingly recorded in her childish handwriting. We visit the rock crystal center and the mini greenhouse for avocado seed number three. Overhead, rain begins to patter onto the glass roof, and I hear Mari call, "Come on, you two, before you get soaked."

We both laugh and then dash for the house, our legs getting wet. At the door, she says, "You'll have to take off your shoes. Otherwise my mum will get mad."

I bend down to unbuckle my sandal, and she touches my hair. "We have hair just the same."

I grin at her. "We do. Do you like it?"

"No," she says sadly. "A girl at school makes fun of me."

"She's just jealous of your amazing brain."

"Papa says just the same thing!"

"Papa is Simon's father," Mari says, holding the door for us. "Do you want some socks?"

"No, thanks."

She touches my bare arm again, as if I am her child. It disarms me. "I'm so glad you're here, Kit. You have no idea how much I missed you."

"I think I do," I say, and slide away from her touch.

Chapter Twenty-Seven

Mari

Over dinner, I finally find a way to let go of my held breath. Kit is so tender with Sarah, and she laughs at the jokes Leo makes trying to impress her. She's dazzling, a fact I hadn't expected and should have. She has my mother's slim shoulders and robust cleavage, my father's laughter and wide smile. Together with the confidence she lacked in her younger days, it's quite a package. Both my husband and my son vie for her attention, while Sarah simply worships, rapt, at her side.

As does Javier. He looks at her as if she's the sun, as if she might command flowers to bloom and birds to sing. It's clear that he's trying to hide it, to be cool, but he's smitten with her.

It's less easy to read Kit. Over the years, she's created an urbane but kind shell that lets little of her true self leak through. I catch sight of the real Kit every now and again, when she listens to Sarah and she leans close. When Javier touches her arm or shoulder or pours her a little more water from the pitcher.

Mainly I see her when she engages with Simon. As if she wants to know and like him, which gives me hope.

But it's also Simon who is making me fret. Every so often, he looks perplexed or surprised. In his smooth, lovely way, he nourishes the conversation, asking Javier about his music, Kit about her passion for medicine. But every now and then, he gives me a glance, a little frown. Is he looking at her tattoo?

Leo notices. "Hey, you and my mom have the same tattoo!"

Kit holds up her arm. "One difference, though. Can you spot it?"

He peers at it, frowning. "Oh! Hers says *big* sister." He frowns. "But you're bigger."

She glances at me. "I wasn't always. She grew tall first, and then I did."

Javier says, and I get the feeling he does it to distract from the tattoos, "I expect you're going to be quite tall one day. Do you play sports?"

"Yes." He sits back down and dives into his pasta. "Lots of them. Lacrosse is my favorite, but my dad likes us to swim because he has the clubs."

"Hey, now. You'll give me a bad name," Simon protests, but he laughs. "You're free to give it up anytime, son." He takes a slice of garlic bread from a plate. "But that will guarantee that Trevor will take the lead this season."

Leo scowls. "I'll never beat him. You know I won't."

"You can do what you believe," Kit says calmly.

"You don't know how this kid swims. Everybody says he'll be going to the Olympics one day."

"He might," Simon said. "You may as well give up."

Leo shoots him an evil glance, and Simon chuckles. "That's what I thought."

It all goes remarkably well. Leo and Sarah clear the table while I make coffee. The other adults settle in the more comfortable lounge, and Simon cues some music from his phone, some midcentury jazz and pop that set a mellow stage. These are our habits, the dance we have created. When he comes into the kitchen, all feels completely normal until he asks quietly, "Why does this feel so stilted tonight?"

"Does it?" I look up at him guilelessly. "I hadn't noticed."

"You're as jumpy as a cat. She must know a lot of secrets about you. Where all the bodies are buried."

"Don't be silly." I wave him away. "Get back in there and entertain them."

His fingers brush the top of my back, and then he's gone. Laughter spills out in the other room. Leo asks if he can play Minecraft, and I dismiss him. Sarah isn't finished circling the sun of her new idol, and she helps me by carrying a plate of petits fours into the other room.

"Don't tell me you made these as well," Kit says.

"No way. Simon picked them up at a bakery on the way home." I pour and pass cups of coffee. "It's decaf," I say.

Sarah sits next to Kit, who says with some humor, "Your mother was the worst cook ever when we were young."

"Really?"

Kit gives me a look and settles her cup on the table. "Really. Like, couldn't even cook bacon."

"Why didn't you just put it in the microwave?"

"We didn't have one," Kit says, then recognizes her slip. "None of us did."

"You didn't?" Sarah echoes, wrinkling her nose.

And in that instant, with the faces of my sister and my daughter mirroring each other, both with the same nutmeg curls, the same tilt of eyes, the same freckles on the same nose, I recognize there is no way this secret can be kept. Sarah is Kit's mini me, down to inclinations and eye color.

At that moment, Sarah says, "Hey, we both have the same toes!"

Kit looks at Sarah's foot, held beside hers. One short leg, one long, the same second and third toes, such a specific genetic order, webbed in exactly the same way. Kit looks up at me, touches her niece's hair. "So we do. That's crazy."

My heart speeds up, and under my hair, the sweat breaks out. I look at Simon, who gives me a perplexed shake of the head. He spreads his hands. *What is this?*

He speaks to Sarah, however. "Sweetheart, it's time to go upstairs."

She lets go of a huff, and I think she's going to protest, but she only turns to Kit and says, "It's adult time. I have to go. Will you come back?"

"I'll do my best."

Sarah hugs her, hard, and I see how it shatters my sister, the way she squeezes her eyes tight and her fierce arms circle my child. "It was so nice to get to meet you."

"Bye," Sarah says in a small voice, and heads upstairs.

A vast silence fills the space beneath the music as she departs. Kit glances at Javier, and he takes her hand in a protective way, moves closer.

At last Simon says, "She couldn't look more like you."

Kit bows her head, looks at me.

And here it is, the moment I must have known was coming. I've been feeling it bearing down on me for weeks, this collision of my old life and the new one. I take a breath, meet Simon's eyes. "We're sisters."

He's bewildered. "Why wouldn't you just say that?"

I take a breath, unable to halt the tears that fill my eyes. "You said I could tell you anything, but—" I look up. "This is a really long story."

Kit stands up, her hands fluttering over her skirt. "We should go. This is between you two."

Simon waves her down. "Please don't go yet. I'd like to know the story."

She hesitates, looking first at me, then toward the stairs, then gives Simon a short nod. She tucks her skirt beneath her legs and perches at the edge of the couch, ready to flee at any moment.

A shivery fear makes my skin cold. "It would be better if we talked first, Simon. Seriously."

He shakes his head.

I've already lost him. I can see it in the set of his shoulders and the loose, apparently relaxed way he holds his hands. He hates lying. He won't tolerate it in employees or friends, and I've known that for almost as long as I've known him.

But not before I fell in love with him.

Sooner or later, you have to face things, face your life. Here is my reckoning. "Okay. Short version is: My real name is Josie Bianci. I grew up outside of Santa Cruz. My parents ran a restaurant. Kit is my younger sister. Dylan was our—" I look at Kit.

"Third," she says. "Not a brother, exactly. Not a relative. But our"—she looks at Javier—"soul mate. *Alma gemela.*"

"I don't understand." Simon blinks, as if he's trying to see through fog. "Why lie about something so ordinary?"

"Because," I say wearily, "until a few days ago, Kit and my mother thought I was dead." I swallow, meet his eyes. "Everyone did. I walked away from a terrorist attack in Paris and let everyone think I died."

He pales, the skin around his eyes going white. "Jesus! Is that how you got the scar?"

"That was the earthquake."

"That's real, then." He runs a finger over his own eyebrow, a gesture that means he's striving for control. My heart squeezes—ordinarily I would be the one to offer comfort. "Jesus."

Kit stands. "I really have to go."

Javier stands too, his hand on the small of her back.

Kit says, "Simon, I enjoyed meeting you." She turns to me, and I see that there are tears in her eyes. "You know how to find me."

All the grief and hope and terror I've been stuffing back down into my body now rush upward, and I stand and fling myself into her arms. And for the first time, I feel her wholeheartedly grip me, loving me back. If I let even one tear fall, I will be lost, so instead I am only trembling from head to toe. She holds me fiercely for a long time; then she pulls back and puts her hands on my face. "Call me tomorrow, okay?"

"Don't worry; I'll still be sober."

"I'm not worried in the slightest." She's so tall, she kisses my fore-head, and I realize in a bright, sharp moment how much time I've lost with her, how much I've deprived her of. Both of us. "Can I say good night to Sarah?"

"Yes," I say before Simon can step in, and I go to the foot of the stairs to call her.

She tumbles down so quickly that I worry she's overheard it all, but even if she has, we need to have a better talk before it all comes out. She halts three stairs from the bottom so she can look Kit in the eyes, she says, "I'm so very glad to have met you. Will you write to me when you go back?"

Kit makes a sharp, strangled little sound. "I'll do better than that." She reaches into her purse. "This is one of my favorite pens. It's a fountain pen, and right now it has my favorite ink, which is called Enchanted Ocean. I'll send you a bottle, and your mom can show you how to refill it."

"Oh, this is lovely!" She holds it in her hands, as smitten and awed as I've ever seen her. "Thank you."

"What's your favorite color?"

"Green," she says decisively.

"I'll send you some green inks too, and you can decide which ones you like best."

Sarah nods.

"May I hug you?" Kit asks.

"Yes, please," says my polite little girl.

And they do. "Please come back," Sarah says in a small voice.

It pierces me, how much my daughter has wanted an ally, a person to look up to. Someone *like* her.

Had it been that way for Kit too?

Both Kit and Javier touch my shoulder on the way out. I kiss Sarah's head and send her back upstairs.

I take a breath and go into the lounge to face Simon.

My husband is sitting on the sofa with his hands clasped in front of him. I'm trembling as I sit down in the chair nearby, not right next to him as I usually would.

For a long time, he says nothing. The music is still playing, quiet Frank Sinatra that makes me think of my father, a piece of information that I would previously have squelched. "My dad loved Frank Sinatra."

"The actual father or the one you made up? The one who was killed in a fiery crash or—"

"You have a right to be angry," I say. "But you don't have a right to be cruel." I raise my chin. "My actual father died in the Loma Prieta earthquake. It wasn't fiery, but it was violent."

He drops his head in his hands, a gesture of such anguish that I reach out to touch him before I hold it back.

"There are good reasons," I say quietly. "I don't expect you to understand that right away or to forgive me instantly, but in light of the fact that we have made a good home and a good marriage together, I would ask that you at least hear the truth before you make any judgments."

"You lied to me, Mari." He raises his head, and I see that his eyes are red and shimmering with unshed tears. "Or Josie, was it?"

"I'm still Mari. Still the woman you loved this afternoon."

"Are you, though?" He makes a little sound. "You started off lying to me and have lied to me for nearly thirteen years now. Were you ever going to tell me the truth?"

Slowly, I shake my head. "No. I killed the woman I was before for good reasons, Simon. You would not have liked her at all." It takes everything I have to keep my voice from trembling. "I hated her. Hated myself. The opportunity presented itself, and I just took it. I had to kill her or die."

"Were you really an addict, or was that a lie too?"

"Oh, no. That part is absolutely truth. It was what made me so wretched. My mother was also an addict, but Kit says she's clean now too." I look at my hands, the rings sparkling on my wedding finger. "She quit when she thought I was dead. So I guess it made two of us sober."

He doesn't respond. My chest aches at how much I've broken him, but I can't think of what else to say.

"The thing is," he says, "that we are the culmination of our experiences. You can't be Mari without being Josie too." He looks at me. "You can't be Sarah's mother without being Kit's sister."

"But I did just that."

"You made it all up!" he shouts. "None of it is true. Tofino, your dead parents. All lies. How do I even know who you are?"

I bow my head and toe a spot on the carpet where a yellow flower winds around a blue wall. "I know you're too angry to hear it right now, but I wish you would give me a chance to tell you the whole story."

His jaw shows his immovability, his struggle for control. "I don't know." His voice is utterly cold as he meets my eyes, and I know how those who've fallen out of favor with him must have felt. I've been cast from paradise into the wilderness. Banished.

And yet I see the sorrow in his eyes too, and I know how much he values self-control. He will be furious if he reveals how I've broken his heart. I make a decision. "I'm going to go stay with Nan or at a hotel or something."

"What?"

"Give you some time to"—I struggle for the right words—"sort through everything."

His jaw hardens. "I'm so disappointed in you, Mari."

A blister of anger rises through my terror. "Life is not all black or all white, Simon. Your life has been so easy." I fight the impulse to weep, to fling myself on his mercy. "You've had everything given to you from birth. You're handsome and wealthy, and your parents took really good care of you. Kit and I . . ." Emotion crowds my voice. "We only had each other until Dylan came." I can't help the tears that spill over my face, but I'm not going to be weak, not now. Not after all I've had to do to get here, to stand here. "It was not a good childhood."

"And yet there's Kit, who seems to have done all right."

It's fair. And unfair. "Yes," I say, and find a place of calm. "We protected her, me and Dylan. As much as we could. It wasn't always enough."

Maybe he hears the despair, the loss, some hint of the reality that was my life as a child. "I will listen to your story, but I can't do it right now."

He's very close to tears. I see the effort it takes for him to hold himself together. He will hate it if I witness his breakdown. "I'll give you some space. Give me a few minutes to get a bag."

One of the hardest things I've done in my entire life—or should I say my lives?—is to go into the bedroom I've shared with my beloved husband for more than a decade and take out a bag and pack it, knowing I might not ever be back here. To keep it together for my children. I can't think about that, not yet.

I tuck into each of their rooms. Sarah has put herself to bed, as she does, and she's fast asleep, fountain pen in her hand. I kiss her forehead, lightly so as not to wake her; turn off the lamp; and tiptoe out.

Leo is still playing Minecraft. He looks up guiltily. "I thought it might be all right, since you were talking with—"

I raise my eyebrows.

He turns off the game. "I'm off to bed now."

"Wait. I need to talk to you for a minute." I sit on the edge of his bed and pat the plaid duvet.

"Okay." He plops down beside me, his skinny arms brown from all the swimming he's done this summer.

"I'm going to take Kit down to Raglan to surf in the morning, so you guys are on your own for a few days. Look out for your sister."

He nods. Presses his lips together. "I heard you and Dad fighting. She's your sister, right?"

"Yeah. I'll tell you all about it when I get back. Can you wait that long?"

"Yes." In his hands, he rolls his shirt up into a tight ball. "Dad is really mad. Are you getting a divorce?"

I shake my head, kiss his hair. "He is mad. We just have to talk things out, okay? Sometimes grown-ups have conflicts too. "

"Okay."

"Love you, Leo Lion," I say. "Be good."

"Have fun surfing."

"Dude."

It makes him laugh, and I leave his room and go down the back stairs to the kitchen. The dogs are asleep on the tiles, and I want to take one of them with me, but that wouldn't be fair to them. Instead, I head out into the garage, toss my bag in my car, and climb into the driver's seat.

And there's really only one place to go.

Chapter Twenty-Eight

Kit

The imprint of my niece's hands on my shoulders stays with me as Javier and I walk to the ferry. It's a mild night, with stars twinkling above the water and the dazzling lights of Auckland thinning to each side as the landscape moves into housing. I can see the waves of hills the city is built upon, each carrying its own spray of lights. "This place is beautiful," I murmur.

"Yes," Javier says.

A cocoon of quiet muffles my feelings, my thoughts, my words. I have nothing to say as we board the ferry and sit down inside, watching the dark water move by. He never pushes. He doesn't hold my hand, which I couldn't bear right now. He only sits quietly beside me.

As we dock, I ask, "Are you singing tonight?"

"I could."

I nod. "I'd like that."

"All right." For a moment, his eyes search my face, but instead of asking if I'm okay, he simply brushes a lock of my hair back from my temple. "She is a lovely child. It makes me wish I could have known you then."

I think of myself on the beach, digging my feet deep into the sand while Dylan built a fire for all of us, and the lava in my belly gurgles.

Urgently, I push the image away. I can't bear even one more teaspoon of emotion. "Her experiments are wonderful." I touch my heart. "I was just like that. A little odd. So passionate about the things I cared about. It makes me feel protective of her."

I'm sick that my pursuit of the truth might lead to disaster for my sister. After so much time, so much effort, it seems wretchedly unfair. It's still awful that she faked her own death, but—

I don't know.

In my purse, my phone buzzes, and I yank it out urgently, worried about what transpired once we left. It's from Mari. Be ready to go surfing at 6 am. We'll be gone all day.

"Sorry," I say to Javier. "It's my sister." I type, I don't have the gear, so I need to rent.

I have access to everything. What's your board these days?

Short board, doesn't matter.

See you at six, in front of the Metropolitan.

Cool. I pause, then type, Are you ok?

No. But none of this is your fault. See you in the am.

I look at Javier. "We're going surfing in the morning."

"Good." As the ferry comes to a stop, he takes my hand and pulls me to my feet. I take comfort in his grip, which feels like it will keep me from flying away into my thoughts or falling into the bubbling power of my tangled emotions, where I might be burned to cinders.

Cinders. I smile, thinking of my old dog. "I had a dog named Cinder when I was a child," I say. "He was a black retriever, and he was with us every minute of every day. Did you have pets?"

"Yes. Many. Dogs, cats, reptiles. A snake once, for a little while, but he escaped, and I never saw him again."

"What kind of snake?"

"Ordinary. He probably lived in the garden till the end of his days."

We walk up the hill toward the Spanish restaurant where Miguel plays, and I realize I've mapped out some of the routes, from ferry to apartment, apartment to market. I'd like to expand my reach, see what lies beyond the park full of magic trees. Go to the other side of the bridge, see what the lights to the north are, but I suppose I'm out of time. "I guess I have to get back to my real life."

"So soon?"

I twitch a shoulder. "My mother is staying in my house, taking care of things. I left my job without a lot of notice. And I've done what I came to do."

He nods. His hand is still holding mine. Ordinarily it feels sweaty and claustrophobic to hold hands with someone, but his fits mine better than most. I almost pull away as I think that, but it doesn't matter. I'll be leaving.

Before we go into the restaurant, he stops and faces me. "If you stay a few more days, we could explore a bit together. You could have a true holiday, enjoy getting to know your family."

Light from the doorway cascades down the center of his nose, catches on the curves of his mouth, illuminates the column of his throat. "Maybe."

"Think about it."

"Okay."

When we go in, Miguel spies us and hurries over. He's wearing a turquoise shirt this time, the color making the most of his dark hair and warm skin. *"Hola, hermano!"* They give their man hugs, slaps on the back and then away. "You must be Kit," he says, offering me his hand.

I accept his handshake. "I'm happy to meet you." In my mind are the eyes of a little girl, haunting me, making me ache. "Javier has told me a lot about you."

He closes my hand between his own. "As he has told me about you, though he could never have fully expressed your beauty."

I laugh at the extravagant compliment. Javier tsks good-naturedly.

"Are you going to sing?" Miguel asks. "We have missed you. But of course, we do not wish for your date to run away. Was it so terrible you couldn't bear it?"

"Pay him no attention," Javier says, his hand at my back. "He thinks he's clever."

"I had pressing business last time," I say. "So rude. This time I look forward to hearing every word."

Javier swings his arm around my shoulders, kisses my temple. "It will be my pleasure to serenade you."

"Is that what it will be, a serenade?"

His eyes go sleepy. "Every word will be words of love," he murmurs close to my neck. "And they will all be for you."

Again it's extravagant, but our little idyll is nearly over, so I let it slide past my barriers and settle in my blood, warming me. I lean into him and let him kiss my forehead, and only when I am settled at the small cocktail table near the stage do I see the eyes on us, envy and curiosity and eagerness. "Everyone is staring," I murmur.

"Because they wish to know who that beautiful woman is with Señor Velez," Miguel says, giving me a wink.

Then they're taking the stage, and the crowd goes crazy, whistling and clapping as Javier picks up a guitar. He lifts a hand and settles in a chair before a microphone. The two men begin to play, the guitars weaving in and out of each other, rising and falling, and I think it must be flamenco.

A woman sits down next to me, slim and middle-aged, her perfume spicy in the beery room. She leans in, offering her hand. "You must be Kit. I'm Sylvia, Miguel's wife."

I give her a frown. "You know my name?"

She smiles. "We are his family. He talks."

"Ah." It makes me uncomfortable, but I take her hand, nod in acknowledgment. A waitress comes around, bringing beer and shots. "Right?" she asks, bending close. "Ale and tequila?"

I'm startled but lean close enough to say, "Yes, thank you."

"Anything else?"

"No, thank you."

She settles a glass of wine in front of Sylvia and a glass of water.

"It's her job to care for the musicians and their parties," Sylvia says. "And Javier is . . . well, himself."

Himself. I glance at the stage. At the people leaning toward him so eagerly.

The music shifts, and they dive into another instrumental piece. This one sounds familiar. It's exhilarating, full of thumping on the guitars and speedy transitions. I've never been a musician, but it's thrilling to watch them.

Thrilling to see Javier in his natural habitat. He and the guitar are both woven of flesh and wood and strings and notes, all coming together to create enchantment. His fingers fly over the strings, up and down, strumming, slapping, strumming some more. His hair falls on his forehead, and his foot taps on the floor, and he looks up at Miguel to see where they are, and the two dive into the next section, and—

I feel something in my gut. Wild and deep, in tune with his strumming hands, aching and pulsing. It takes on color, a rich yellow, the color of sunlight, and it begins to spread through my body, every single part of me becoming points of light that pulse in time with his strings. It makes me dizzy and makes me feel alive.

"Wow," I say aloud.

Sylvia laughs beside me. "Yes. Every time."

The music rises to a crescendo, and then they fall silent. Javier tosses his hair from his forehead and begins rolling up his sleeves. He looks toward me and raises a brow. I touch my hands to my heart, and he smiles.

And then, as last time, he pulls a microphone close, adjusts his guitar, and leans in. His voice is rich and full of layers, caressing the words one by one, the notes weaving in and out. I don't understand what he's saying, but I love the way he sings, earnestly, intently. He never looks at me, but I feel his attention, plucking those points of connection through my body, first yellow, now orange.

Next to me, Sylvia leans over. "Do you speak Spanish?"

I shake my head.

She interprets,

> "In the whisper of the waves, I hear your name
> In the caress of the sunlight, I feel your lips
> In the hands of the wind, I feel your touch
> Everywhere, in everything, there you are
> I will not forget you, sweet love."

I close my eyes because it's almost too much. His face, his hands on the guitar. But even as I shut the visuals out, his voice weaves through me, and I see him bending over me as we kissed the first time, and his hands gliding over my body, and the way he laughs at my jokes.

His song trails off, and he picks up a bottle of water to take a drink. The room erupts in clapping, cheering. Javier waves a hand, looks at me, gives me a nod.

And it's like that for all the time he sings. Beautiful love songs, songs about loss, all the music plucking my heart, piercing my soul. I allow myself to fall into the flow of it, allow it to carry me away into a world that's more bearable than the one where I've caused my sister's life to come tumbling down around her, where I might well have deprived two children of a family that was, until my arrival, perfectly whole.

When he finishes, I lean into his neck and say, "We don't have much time. Would you rather sit here or go back to my bedroom?"

He chooses my bedroom.

———— ∾☙☙∾ ————

At midnight, I'm lying on my stomach. Javier lies next to me, tracing the dip in my spine with light fingers—up, down, up, down. It's hypnotically soothing. "Tell me about your broken heart," he says, "this one broken heart that has kept you away from love for the rest of your life."

"Oh, it's not that dramatic. I haven't had a lot of time to fall in love."

"Psssht. Love does not need time."

I turn my head to look at him. My carapace of protection has disappeared, and I don't even know where it is at the moment. "His name was James. I met him when I was very lonely, after the earthquake." Easily, I trace the round of his shoulder, trail a finger down his biceps. "He had a girlfriend, but we started working together at Orange Julius." I pause, remembering. "I had the worst crush ever. I could hardly breathe when he was in the room."

"I am a little jealous."

I smile. "He broke up with his girlfriend, and for a whole summer, we were inseparable. We taught each other everything, really. No one was ever home at my house, so we just hung out there and explored each other." On my back, Javier's touch has shifted to an open palm, moving up and down. "I was so very much in love. It filled every part of me. And really, it was the first time in a really long time that I was happy."

"And?"

"And—his ex-girlfriend started threatening me. My sister heard about it, and she got into a fight with the girl. Josie broke her nose."

"Oh." There's amusement in his voice.

"It wasn't funny. She was one of the prettiest girls I'd ever seen, and—"

He chuckles, bending to kiss my shoulder.

"James was furious with my sister, and *they* got into an actual fist-fight too, and that was that. We broke up. He quit Orange Julius, and when school started, he was back together with his old girlfriend, and he never spoke to me again."

"He was a pig, that one."

"No, I think that was you, wasn't it?" I turn, teasing him.

He laughs, sliding his hand around my ribs. "But I was never so cruel."

"No," I say quietly. I suddenly and urgently wish I could stay right in this room forever. I pat his stomach. "I like your tummy."

He laughs. "In the winter, there is more of it. You wouldn't like it so much then."

"I think I would still like it."

He sighs sadly, pats it. "That fat little boy is always ready to take over. I might be a fat old man someday."

I place my hand on that belly, soft over the muscle beneath. "Still."

"You can find out how it looks in the winter if you wish."

I look away.

He touches my chin and slides down so that our faces are close. I can see the way individual lashes grow and the flecks of gold in his dark eyes. "So your heart was broken, and you cannot bear to let anyone in now."

"It wasn't just that. It was everything—the earthquake and my dad and Dylan. All of it."

"I know." He leans in to kiss me, gently, and pulls back. "I need you to listen for one minute without saying anything in return."

Something flutters in my chest.

"You think I am only flirting when I say that you are the most beautiful woman I have ever seen, but I am not. It is not extravagance. It is not a way to get you in my bed . . . though I see that it may have been a good tactic."

"I need to remind you that this is my bed, señor."

"Well, either way." He touches my mouth. "When I saw you, I recognized you, like I've been waiting, all this time, for you to show up. And there you were."

My heart aches. "We live on different continents."

"Yes." He bends and kisses me, longer this time, and I find myself kissing him back. "But I think you also have found feelings for me."

I take a breath, and for once in my life, I am honest. "Yes, I have. I might actually have been falling in love a little bit."

"Have been?"

"I'm leaving in a few days."

"Mm. That is true." He kisses my throat, and flutters move elsewhere. "Unless I convince you that you should stay longer."

Burying my hands in his hair, I pull him closer. "You can try, I suppose."

I find myself memorizing the feel of him. His shoulder blades and the tip of his ear, his voice in my ear, murmuring in Spanish, the feel of his thighs between mine, the taste of him on my mouth.

For remembering later.

Chapter Twenty-Nine
Mari

I drive to Sapphire House, which draws me like a siren. I've never been there at night yet, and the view is astonishing, even more magical than I imagined. Standing on the bluff, looking over the glittering spread of the city, I think of the day Simon brought me here for the first time.

My husband, back when he adored me and bought me a legendary house. A hole tears in my heart as I think of it.

I let myself into the dark, empty rooms. I turn on lights as I go, trying to bring in warmth, but it's just so very empty. I'm never alone at night. My family is always with me.

Is this how it will be, going forward? The possibility is agonizing. I had no idea how much I needed and wanted a family or how good I would be at it.

In the kitchen, I set the kettle to boil and lean against the counter, waiting. The light in here is green and unpleasant, and one of the things I want to install is better, warmer lighting. Did Helen not mind it? I think of her here with Paris and Toby, alone in the giant house for decades and decades and decades. Why did she stay? Why not sell the house and find some more appealing bungalow somewhere? There'd have been plenty of money. It's the first time I've thought about it, and now I wonder why it hadn't occurred to me sooner. Was she hiding something? Doing penance?

Carrying my mug of tea to the lounge, I let myself out the French doors and sit on the deck. The sound and smell of the sea ease the tension in my neck.

What a disaster. Had I really believed that I'd get away with it forever?

Yes. I mean, why not?

And yet now that it's all out in the open, I'm relieved. Everything in my life is turned upside down, but I can finally tell my real story. The people I love can know me—on both sides of the line. The people who knew Josie, and by that I guess I mean Kit, and the people who love Mari. Sipping my tea, watching the half moon skim the surface of the water, I try to imagine how Nan will take it. Gweneth.

Mom.

I've carried a torch of hatred for my mother for so long now that it's hard to even see beyond the straw woman I've made of her. With moonlight and sea wrapping me in the same light as childhood, I remember another side of her, the one who so tenderly took Dylan in, who gave that lost boy a home. It's startling to realize that she was younger than I am now when all that was happening. I was born when she was only twenty-one, so she wasn't even thirty when Dylan washed into our world. The sexy young trophy wife of a much older man.

Leaning back against the wall, I wonder what that must have been like. My father was almost fifteen years older than her, and at first totally obsessed with her.

When had he started taking lovers? When did she find out?

It makes me sad.

Out of nowhere comes a memory of when I was only four or five. My mother and I sat together on the vast patio of the restaurant and watched the ocean. She sang to me, a ballad about a mermaid who warned sailors of a shipwreck. A knot in my chest aches as the vision unspools—the waves crashing, the quiet moon, her voice and her arms around me.

Mama.

The day of the earthquake, we were in downtown Santa Cruz. She bought me ice cream, not because I liked it but because she did. I was stunned and sad, my uterus cramping after the violent cleansing it had just undergone, and she was uncharacteristically silent. "Are you okay?" she asked at last.

I shook my head, fighting tears. "I'm so sad."

She reached over and took my hand. "I know, sweetie. I am too. One day, when the time is right, you'll have babies, and I'll be a grandmother who spoils them rotten."

The pounding ache in my chest spread through my body, pulsing hard in my throat with an almost unbearable pressure. "But this one—"

"I know, sweetheart. But you're barely fifteen."

And that was when the earthquake started. It wasn't like we'd never experienced one before, but you could hear this one coming, rumbling beneath the surface of the ground, coming toward us. The first wave hit the building with a slamming bang, knocking cutlery and glassware and baked goods from the counter onto the floor. Almost at the same second, the plate glass window next to us shattered, and my mother grabbed my arm and yanked me violently out of my chair to haul me toward the door. Before we got there, the ceiling started falling down, crashing around us, and a big chunk smashed into my head, knocking me down. My mom's hand was ripped out of mine, and I screamed for her, feeling like I would faint, like my heart would stop beating.

She bent down and hauled my arm around her neck. "Hold on!" She dragged me to my feet, and we staggered outside, but even there, it was loud, and people were screaming, and things were breaking, falling, groaning all around us.

Blood spilled into my eye, and I pressed a hand to the throbbing spot on my head. It was a big cut, and blood was soon leaking down my arm. My mom was holding on to me, hard, as the world shook itself apart around us. It was violent and loud, and I was trying not to pass out. It seemed like it went on and on and on, though later they said it was only fifteen seconds.

When it finally slowed to a stop, my mom let go of holding me so tightly as she looked around.

She said, "Jesus wept," and I had to see too.

The air was filled with dust and debris, making it dark, and it looked like a bomb had hit, with the front of buildings crumbled into individual bricks on the sidewalk. One building looked like it had imploded. People were crying, and somebody howled, and I saw a man who was so dusty, he looked like he'd walked into an exploding bag of flour. Alarms were going off. I smelled gas.

My head hurt loudly, with a noise to it, and the blood dripped to the ground from my elbow. A woman hurried over and tugged off her sweater. "Sit down before you faint," she ordered, and pressed the sweater to my head. "Mom, you need to sit down too."

"Oh my God!" my mom cried, and she was literally crying, shaking so hard that when she reached for me, it made me think of the shivering of the earth, and I moaned, ducking away. She sank down beside me. "You need to go to the hospital."

"We need to call Kit!" I cried. If it was this bad here, what happened at Eden? Panic squeezed my lungs so hard that I couldn't catch my breath, and I grabbed my mom's wrist hard. "Kit!"

"I will; I will." Mom stood up, stared around her, looked at me. "You're bleeding so badly, I don't want to leave you."

The woman lifted the sweater. "Yep, you're going to need a bunch of stitches. Can you walk?"

I tried to stand up, but another wave of noise and shaking overtook us, knocking me down. Someone started screaming again, in little bursts. My mom was on her hands and knees. "The hospital is too far away. We need to call an ambulance."

"Every ambulance within a hundred miles is going to be busy."

"Let's just stay here. They'll be down here soon enough."

The woman had the air of someone who was used to getting things done. She hesitated, looking around us, then sank down beside me. "You're right."

A roar filled my head. "Kit and Dad! We need to call them!"

"Yes. Right. I need to call home," Mom said. "I'm going to try to find a phone."

I nodded, but I was feeling dizzy and sick, and only lolled against the planter. I was covered in blood, and my gut was cramping in rhythmic waves that mimicked the earthquake or maybe the ocean.

My mom came back, looking sick. "No answer."

And there was nothing to do but wait. Wait while people staggered by, while they tried to drive cars that couldn't go anywhere because the streets were broken into waves, while little kids screamed at the top of their lungs. While the smell of smoke filled the air and increased the darkness, and sirens finally wailed into the space, carrying police and EMTs who assessed the injuries of the people scattered like more litter around the area.

We leaned into each other. I wondered how we'd even get home.

It was hours before anyone could clean and stitch up my still-bleeding cut. By then I was incoherent with pain and terror, and to this day, I don't remember getting to Eden. A stranger in a Jeep helped us, our Good Samaritan.

There were no lights as we drove up, only blackness and emptiness where the buildings had once stood. After the long trauma of the day, I couldn't comprehend what I was seeing.

And then I did. My heart shattered a thousand times, over and over and over. I jumped out of the car and screamed, "Kit!"

She ran into the light of the headlights, her face a mess of tears and dirt. I hugged her so hard it made my head ache.

"Where's your father?" my mother asked.

Kit shook her head. Pointed.

On the beach of the cove were the remains of our house and the restaurant, a wreck of lumber that looked as incoherent as my mother became in seconds. She screamed and then screamed again, falling to her knees on the rocky ground.

Chapter Thirty

Kit

Mari picks me up right on the dot of six. She looks exhausted. "Hey. I brought you coffee."

"Oh my God, it smells so good."

"I didn't know how you took it, so I figured milk, and you can add sugar if you like." She points to a thick stack of sugar packets in one of the cup holders.

I laugh. "I'm not eight anymore, you know."

"Once an addict, always an addict."

"Takes one to know one." I realize too late that it sounds mean. "Sugar addict, I mean."

She glances at me, moving into traffic smoothly. "I get it. And I am the worst. Taste this."

I take a sip, and she's right—it's like a milkshake. "Too much for me."

We ride along in the quiet until I gather my nerve and ask, "How did it go after we left?"

She shakes her head. Sips her coffee. "Simon is a proud man, and he's cut of old-school cloth—men are meant to be men, manly and strong." She sighs. "I have no idea what will happen."

For the first time, I reach for her, squeeze her arm. "I'm so sorry for my part in this, Josie."

"It's not your fault. None of it."

"Still. I'm sorry."

She nods, changes lanes. "I was going to take you down to Raglan, but the surf forecast for Piha is awesome, and it's not so far."

"Crazy how you always know now, isn't it?"

"Right? Just call up the reports, and Bob's your uncle."

I laugh. "What did you just say?"

"Bob's your uncle, mate." She laughs. "Best slang in the world, right here."

"I get why you love it here. It's amazing."

"It is. I'm never leaving."

It's an overcast morning, and the traffic is heavy as she makes her way through town. The radio plays a local pop station, modern top-forty stuff. "When did you start liking pop?" I ask. She was always into the heavy-metal bands of the '80s and '90s, Guns N' Roses, Pearl Jam, Nirvana and the doomed Kurt Cobain.

She shrugs, easy in herself in a way she never was back then. "Heavy metal makes too much noise in my head," she says simply. "I start disappearing, and then I make bad choices."

I nod.

"What do you like?"

"The same things I always have, really. Easy things to listen to."

Her sideways smile is sly. "Like flamenco?"

The word gives me a flash of Javier playing last night, his body and the guitar becoming one thing, lighting every nerve center in my body. "I never knew I liked flamenco before, but yeah."

"How long have you been dating Javier?"

I laugh slightly. "'Dating' is overstating it a bit. I just met him."

"What?"

"Yeah, he sat down next to me the first night I got here, at this little Italian place in an alleyway by my apartment, and we struck up a conversation."

She's quiet for a minute. "It doesn't look like a new relationship."

"Again, 'relationship' is overstating it."

"He looks at you like you created the earth and heavens all by yourself."

It jolts me. "What are you talking about?"

"Are you kidding me? You don't see it?"

"No." I sip the coffee. "We've had a great time, but it's just a holiday romance. He lives in Madrid."

"So you're not that interested?"

I shrug. "I don't really get involved."

"That's a nonanswer."

Something in me snaps. Irritably, I say, "It's none of your business, actually."

"You're right. Sorry."

The exchange reminds me of the reality here. We can't just pick up our relationship as if nothing has ever happened. I feel myself lifting my shell, protecting myself against her long knowledge of me, her insight into things I work hard never to reveal.

Except with Javier. I frown.

We head off the highway to a smaller road. At a red light, she looks at me. "Have you had a serious relationship, Kit?"

She knows about James, and maybe she thinks that doesn't count. I sip my coffee, look out the window. "Too much drama."

"Not always." The light turns, and she pulls forward. "Not every relationship is like our parents'."

"I know." I keep my voice light, unconcerned, but on the sidewalk is a man walking with the same liquid grace that marks Javier's movements, and I'm aware on some distant plane of a low howl of yearning. *That,* it says. *Him.* Without rancor, I say, "Don't try to fix me, okay?

I'm fine. I love my job. I have a cat. I have friends and go surfing. Take a lover when I want one."

"Okay." She shrugs, but I can tell she has more to say.

I sigh. "Go ahead. Say the rest."

"When I was watching you and Javier last night, I thought about what beautiful children you would have."

And suddenly I can see them too. Sturdy little girls and plump little boys, all wearing glasses and collecting rocks and stamps. A welter of tears strikes the backs of my eyes. I have to look away, blink hard. "Stop it, Josie," I say quietly. "You have what you want, but I don't have to want the same thing you do."

"Mari," she corrects, and nods. "You're right. Sorry. I guess old habits die hard."

"I've done just fine without you, sis."

"I guess you have."

———— ∞———

"Wow," I say as we carry our boards to the beach. "Look at those waves." They're rolling home in steady, strong crests. A few riders are on the line but not as many as would have crowded the ocean in Santa Cruz. "Where is everyone?"

"Tourist season is heavy traffic," she says, yanking herself into her wet suit, a high-end version with turquoise stylings, "but the rest of the year it's pretty mellow." She points out a bunch of cottages scattered on the other side of the road and up the hill. "Those are baches, holiday places. It's amazing how many people have them here."

She's wearing a T-shirt over a bikini top, and I see her once-flat, once-tanned abdomen is networked with substantial stretch marks. Not surprising for such a small person.

"Ugly, right?" she says, but strokes them kindly. "But every time I look at them, I only think of my babies."

I meet her eyes, start laughing. "Dude, did you really just say that?"

She shrugs. "It's true."

"That's pretty cool." I zip up my suit, braid my hair tight. The scents of ocean and wind play on my nerves, and I just want to get out there. "Ready?"

We wade into the cold water and then paddle over to the line. "You first," she says.

"I'd rather just sit for a minute, watch the breaks."

"Cool."

We position ourselves a bit away from the main action, straddling our boards and watching the waves roll toward shore. Overhead, the clouds are looking meaner. "Is a storm coming?"

"I don't know."

"Maybe we'd better do this thing."

At her nod, we paddle out and wait our turn. The guy in front of me is showing off a bit, but he's solid. The waves are six feet, eight. I take my first ride, and it's exhilarating, the sky and light and board. It holds together beautifully, giving me a long, elegant ride that I take nearly to shore before coming off and heading back to the line. I pause to look for my sister, and there she is, right behind me, her goofy stance, arms steady. Her grace is better than it was, and her calm. She surfs like she's got nowhere to go, nothing to do but this.

She sees me watching and flashes a shaka, whooping.

I flash it back and paddle toward my next wave.

After an hour, we're both tiring, but rather than head in, we sit on our boards in the undulating ocean. With my eyes on the horizon, I say, "We need to call Mom."

Her hair is slicked back, messy. "I know." She turns her dark eyes on me. "I also need to tell you a couple of things."

"Do you have to? Can't we just let sleeping dogs lie?"

She lifts one side of her mouth. "None of the dogs are really sleeping, though, are they?"

I relent. Shake my head.

"Do you remember that actor who used to come to Eden, Billy Zondervan?"

"Sure. He used to bring us kites and candy and stuff. Nice guy."

"Yeah." The water moves us up, down. Something brushes my left toes. "Well, that nice guy raped me when I was nine. Repeatedly."

"What?" I paddle closer and feel the ER doctor step in, protecting me. Offering clinical distance. With fury, I push back, trying to show up as myself. "That bastard. How . . . ? I mean, we were always around."

She shakes her head. "Pretty sure I wasn't the first kid he molested. He had it down to a fine art. Presents, sips of his drinks, and then threats. He told me he would slit Cinder's throat if I told anyone."

"When was it?"

"That summer we learned to surf." She looks into the distance. "The first time was the night before I came down to the beach and Dylan was teaching you."

A punch of horror slams my gut. I think of her weeping and weeping when she found us surfing without her. "Oh my God, Josie," I whisper, and paddle close, touch her leg. "Why didn't you tell us?"

She shakes her head, and tears are sliding down her cheeks. I realize they're sliding down mine too. "I felt so ashamed."

I reach for her wrist, wrapping my hand around it hard. "I wish I could kill him. An inch at a time."

She slaps tears off her cheeks with both hands. "Oh yeah, me too."

"How long did it go on?"

"A summer. Then he tried to start something with you, and I told him if he ever touched you, even one finger, I would stand in the middle of the patio on a crowded night and tell them all exactly what he'd done to me."

A hollow opens up in my gut. "I don't remember that. I don't remember him being gross."

"No, he was slicker than that. Remember those little dolls he brought you from Europe, the ones that have dolls inside and inside?"

"Oh yeah. I do remember those. They were painted, pretty."

"Yep. That was the opening gambit."

"He stopped coming to Eden, right?"

"Yes, thank God."

"You never told anyone?"

"Not for ages. I told Dylan."

"Why the hell didn't he expose him?"

Her face has a strange expression, as if it's just dawning on her that he should have. She looks at me. "I made him promise not to." She frowns. "I mean, he tried to figure out what was wrong with me for a long time, and I wouldn't tell him. It's impossible to express how much I thought it was my fault."

My heart feels like it's filled with shards of glass. "You were nine," I whisper.

"Dylan should have told," she says quietly. "Why didn't I see that until recently?"

I shake my head. "Because we both loved him like he hung the moon."

"And all the stars."

I bow my head. "Why didn't anyone protect you?"

"Believe me, I've asked myself that a thousand times. But you know, honestly, it wasn't until I had Leo and Sarah that I realized how bad our parents were. We were sleeping on the beach, alone, when we were four and six, before Dylan came."

"Yeah, I remember."

"Think about that. A four-year-old sleeping alone with her sister on the beach."

I half grin. "Well, we did have Cinder."

She grins back. "Yes, we had Cinder. Best dog in the world."

"Best dog in the world." We high-five.

"So Billy never did anything to you?"

"No. I swear. No one did." In the distance, a seagull rides the currents, and I'm reminded of the cove, our little beach. "Dylan was even more messed up than our parents, though. Remember the time he dived off the cliff?"

She shudders. "It's a miracle he lived through that."

"I think that was the point. Just like the motorcycle accident."

She looks so sad all of a sudden that I feel bad. "Sorry, Jo—Mari. Bad memory."

"Yeah."

"The beginning of the end," I say with a sigh. "Pretty sure that was one of his suicide attempts."

She looks at me, eyes wide. "Oh, for God's sake. I'm such an idiot. Of course it was. That's why he was so pissed when we brought him back to the house."

I frown. "You seriously never realized that before?"

"No." She shakes her head, splashes water on the front of her board. "I miss him so much." She looks at the horizon. "So much."

"Me too." I imagine I can see him on his longboard, arms out. "He really was like some creature from a fairy tale, cursed and blessed in equal measures." I think of his gentle hands braiding my hair. The easy way he folded clothes. The way he stood with us at the bus stop. "I wouldn't be who I am without him."

"I know. And you did him so much good."

"Both of us."

"No." She shakes her head. "You gave him peace. I think you were the only person who ever did."

"I hope I did."

"We should go back to shore. I think the storm is coming."

By the time we wade back out of the water under an angry sky, my legs are weak and I could eat a large-size cow. Peeling out of my wet suit, I ask, "Did you bring food?"

She gives me a look. "Duh. Do you still eat the earth and all the moons of the galaxy after surfing?"

I laugh. It was something Dylan used to say. "I do. But look"—I spread my arms—"I didn't get fat."

"You have a very hot body," she says. "Look at your abs, dude."

"It's all surfing."

"I thought we might eat on the beach, but it's getting too windy."

We hustle back to her car and load up the back again with boards and wet suits. I don't have a fleece and wish I did; seeing my goose bumps, she hands me one she drags out of the back seat. It must be Simon's, and the warmth is delicious. We settle on the leeward side of the car and eat pies filled with meat and potatoes, washed down with a lemony drink. For dessert, there are slices of cake. "I love how much they love cake here," she confesses. "Such amazing cakes too."

"This is so good," I comment, immersed in mine, a chocolate and passion fruit concoction that melts in my mouth. "I could seriously eat a couple more moons."

"I'm jealous of your size."

I laugh. "That's a turnaround." Wiping my hands, I say, "We should call Mom."

For a moment, I think she's going to refuse, but then she capitulates. "Okay. Let's do it inside the car. Too windy out here."

Now I'm nervous as I dig in my purse for the phone. I check the world clock, and it's only early afternoon. Perfect. I take a breath and text. You free?

It's not five seconds before she texts me back. Yes! And then my phone bleats the FaceTime ring. I glance at Mari, and she gives a nod. I punch the button.

And there she is, sitting on the floor with Hobo on her lap. She's wearing a pair of jeans with a T-shirt, her hair in that messy bun she likes so much lately. "Look who loves me now!" she says.

Josie, because she's Josie right now, starts to cry at the sound of her voice.

"That's great, Mom. Thank you so much for doing that. Listen, I have some news."

"You do?" Something in my voice must have alerted her. She sits up straighter. "What?"

"I found her." I turn the camera to the other direction, and there is my sister, so unmistakably herself.

"Hi, Mom," she says.

My mother makes the most piercing sound, halfway between a howl and a laugh. "Josie! Oh my God."

Josie is crying too, tears streaming down her face. She reaches for the screen, touches it. "I'm so sorry, Mom."

For a long time, they only weep and look at each other, murmuring things: "You look so good." "I can't believe how little you've aged." "I just want to look at you."

Finally, Josie sits up and, for the second time this morning, wipes tears off her face. "You look amazing, Mom!"

"Thank you. So do you. You quit drinking."

Mari nods. "Quit everything."

"Me too."

I roll my eyes. "Okay, can we have the AA meeting some other time?"

They both laugh. "I have so much to tell you," Mari says.

"I want to hear every bit of it. And Kit!" She yells the last like I'm in another room. I click the camera around to my face.

"I'm right here, Mom."

She looks stricken and happy, and she wipes her face. "Thank you. I can't wait to hear about your journey too. Are you okay?"

I pause, thinking of the search and Javier and now the terrible recognition that my mother's neglect allowed my sister to be raped at the age of nine. "Yeah," I say, but it's clear that I'm not sure. "I will be, anyway."

"Okay."

"Let me talk to her again," Mari says, and I hand her the phone.

"Mom, there are two things I need to tell you today, and then we have to go because there's a storm on the way. I'm married and have two kids, so you're a grandmother."

My mother makes a noise, and I can see her in my imagination, covering her mouth.

"Their names are Leo and Sarah, and Sarah is like a mini Kit, all the way down to those webbed toes. You will love her, and you have to come see her."

"I will, sweetheart. I promise."

"Things are kind of crazy right now, though I hope they're going to work out, but no matter what, I want to see you. And, Mom, thank you for the day of the earthquake. I never said thank you."

Now I can hear a slight sob in Mom's voice, and it gives me a weird anxiety. "You're welcome."

"We have to go, Mom," I say when Mari gives me the phone back. "Kiss my kitty, and I'll let you know when I get tickets back. Very soon."

"Take your time, honey. I'm happy, and you see Hobo is fine."

I hang up the phone and hold it in my hand, aware of a faint, low trembling of reaction running beneath my skin. Josie leans her head against the window, tears running down her face, looking at something far in the distance.

Chapter Thirty-One
Mari

On the way back to the high-rise, we're quiet, Kit and I. My heart feels shredded into ten thousand pieces, and I still haven't told her the last thing. My thoughts are skittering forward to Simon, and back to the look on my mother's face when she saw me, and the way Kit sobered when I confessed the truth about Billy Zondervan.

"You should turn him in," she says as we get close to the high-rise. "He's probably still doing it."

I nod. "Obviously I couldn't do it before, but I'm thinking about it now. I just worry that it might make people feel sorry for me. It might make my kids think differently about me."

"The first thing—no. No one will feel sorry for you if you get a pedophile off the streets. On the second—maybe they don't have to know." She shakes her head. "Yeah, right. I mean, I get that part. Only you know what they can handle."

"Thanks." I pull into the small drive in front of the high-rise.

"I'm probably going home in a day or two," she says. "Get back to work."

My gut twists. "No! Not yet!"

"I know. It's fast, but we can keep in touch."

As if we are just old friends who bumped into each other. But I have to give her space. "Thanks for coming out. Thanks for talking to me. Thanks for all of it, Kit. I mean it."

She softens and leans forward to hug me. I smell her hair, feel her muscles. "We'll stay in touch."

"Javier is in love with you, Kit. I think you might want to give that relationship a chance."

"Mm," she says, and sits back in her seat. "I hope things work out with Simon."

"Yeah." I run a thumb along the seam of the leather on the steering wheel. "Are we just leaving it like this? That's it?"

"I don't know. What are we supposed to do? I'll call you when I get home."

"Okay. Sarah will love writing to you."

"And I will love writing to her."

I take a breath. Consider keeping this one last thing to myself. Rain starts to plop down hard on the windscreen. "Kit, there's something else I need to tell you. So everything is out in the open."

Wariness fills her entire body. "Maybe don't."

"We can't go forward with any more secrets."

She bows her head. Touches her fingernails. "Go ahead."

"When Mom and I went to Santa Cruz the day of the earthquake, I was having an abortion."

She raises her eyebrows. "I'm sorry that happened," she says. "But it's not exactly a big shock."

"Well, actually, I did make out with a lot of boys at that time, but I didn't have sex with anyone. I was afraid. But then I did." The burning in my chest feels like it will melt my bones. "When you were at that doctor camp and Mom and Dad went to Hawaii, I got Dylan really drunk, and I had sex with him."

Her body goes so still it's like she's turned into a photo of herself. All the color leaves her face.

"The abortion—it was his. And he was dead, so what could I do?"

She still doesn't move for the longest time. Rain patters down on the roof, obscures my view of the world. "Why didn't you tell me, Josie?" she asks quietly.

"I didn't want you to hate me. Blame me for his death."

She sighs, closes her eyes. "That's why he drowned himself," she says, and it's not a question.

My bones all melt, and I can't look at her. "He was so angry and ashamed. I should never have done it. I don't know why I did. He was so fucked up." Tears I can't halt fill my eyes. "He never spoke to me ever again."

"You kind of deserved it," she says, and then opens the door and jumps out, then turns around to face me, the rain pouring down on her head, soaking her hair, tipping her eyelashes. I love her like she's one of my own organs, my eyes or my heart. "No one ever protected you the way they should have. But *I* would have." She's crying. "I would have."

She slams the door.

Chapter Thirty-Two

Kit

Two weeks before the earthquake, when I was thirteen, I found Dylan's body.

It was a cold, misty morning, with a fog so thick I almost couldn't see coming down the steps to the cove, and I had carried down a breakfast of Pop-Tarts and a bottle of milk to get away from the endless fighting that filled our house. My mom yelled at my dad. My dad yelled at Josie. She yelled back. On and on and on. She'd done something bad this time, but I didn't know what it was, and honestly, I didn't care anymore. They called her names at school, really bad names, and after four years of steadily declining behavior, I was over trying to understand her. Her actions embarrassed me.

Dylan was lying facedown on the hard-washed sand, just about where we used to set up the tent long ago. He wore the same shirt he'd left with the day before and jeans and no shoes. His hair was loose and tangled. On his left wrist was the leather bracelet I'd made him in fourth grade, the one he never took off, with silver beads. There was no question he was dead.

I sat down beside him. Touched the bracelet. My heart in my chest was exploding, a scream I couldn't allow into the world. Once I told them that he was here, I would lose him forever.

So on the beach where we'd spent so much time, I sat beside him and wondered if his ghost was still around. If he could hear me. "I wish you hadn't done this," I said, and took a bite of Pop-Tart. "But I guess you just couldn't stand it anymore. I guess I knew you would eventually." Tears welled up in my eyes, and I let them fall down my face. "I just want you to know that you made my life better. Like, so much better, dude."

Some of my tears fell on my upper chest. I took another bite and chewed it, in no hurry. "Number one, you helped me get to school every day, and you know how much I liked that."

The fog eddied and moved, and between tufts I thought I saw Cinder, sitting with somebody. "Number two, you taught me to surf, which you know I love as much as you do." Meditatively, I took another bite and a sip of the milk. "I sorta thought surfing might save you, really. Like maybe it could have if—I don't know, maybe if people hadn't been so mean to you when you were little.

"Number three." My voice broke. His hands were flung out beside him, and I thought of those hands on books, reading to us. I thought of them on knives, flying through a zucchini. I thought of them in my hair, braiding it every day so I didn't look like a crazy girl.

"I'm so sad. I'm as sad as I've ever been in my whole life, and I really don't want to get up and go tell them that you're dead because then it will be real and I will never, ever see you again."

I bent over and tried to breathe against the pure, searing pain that washed through me, as violent as a riptide sucking me under. I didn't know how I could live with a pain like that, which made me think of how many things he'd lived through, and I sat up. Swallowed.

The fog was beginning to thin. I ate the last of my pastry, then reached over and untied the leather bracelet on his arm. It was old, and it took me a long time to get the knot undone. It bothered me that his skin was so cold, but I knew dead things couldn't feel. He wouldn't care.

When I got it free, I tucked it into my pocket. Over by the cave where I'd found the pirate booty that morning ages ago, I saw them, Dylan and Cinder.

I lifted a hand and waved.

They disappeared.

Chapter Thirty-Three
Mari

I'm in Helen's room that evening, going through the stacks of magazines she's kept, looking for clues or maybe a stashed diary. Something. It's still raining, and to keep the ghostly sounds from bugging me too much, I'm playing music on my phone. The sound is tinny, but honestly, I'll take what I can get.

The tedious work is good for me. I have to engage my brain just enough that I'm not fretting incessantly about everything, but somewhere the information is being processed in the background. This goes there, and that goes here, and eventually it will all make sense. My mother. Simon.

Kit.

God, the hatred on her face when she left me! Maybe I shouldn't have confessed everything. Maybe she didn't need to know right now. But honestly, if we're going to have a relationship at all, there can't be any more lies. I've had enough lies to last me a millennium.

Because of the phone music, I don't hear Simon until he's standing in the doorway. At the sight of him, my heart stops momentarily. I really do love him like a being created just for me. His eyes are shadowed, his shoulders slightly bowed like Atlas's, carrying the world. "Is this a good time to talk?"

I can't read his tone, but I leap to my feet. "Of course. Shall we go down and have a cup of tea?"

"Sure." He doesn't come in the room to kiss me, and he's careful not to touch me as we head downstairs.

"Are the kids okay?"

"Fine. They think you just went to be with your friend. Did you surf?"

"Yes. Piha Beach. It was great."

The conversation feels as stiff as corsets. I busy myself with the kettle and cups, while Simon sits down heavily at the small table. "This is a strange room, isn't it?"

"I know. Why did Helen do it over like this? When she had the money to do whatever she wanted. Why this grim green room?" He shakes his head, and I see the weariness in it. "Are you all right?"

"No, Mari, I'm not. I'm gutted."

I bow my head. "I'm so sorry. It was stupid, but I really thought it would never come up."

"Christ."

"Are you ready to hear the story?" I hope it will go better with him than it did with Kit.

"I reckon I am."

So I tell him. Everything, starting with Eden and Kit and Dylan on the beach. I tell him about the neglect and about the molestation. I tell him how wild I was and how early I became an alcoholic. I tell him about the abortion, and Dylan, and the strange relationship we shared, part lovers, part siblings, part mentor and mentee, entirely, completely screwed up.

And yet.

"We both loved him so much, me and Kit. He just fell into our lives and then fell out again."

"Why didn't you tell me? At some point, somewhere?"

I can't look at him. "I don't know. I guess . . . I thought if you knew everything, you wouldn't love me."

He shakes his head. "Why? What about me made you think I would love you less if you told that story?"

I'm struggling to keep myself from crying. "Nothing about you, Simon. It was all my own shame. Dylan killed himself because of me. I ripped off my sister. I faked my own death." I pause, my hands tight on my thighs. "The person I left behind was not someone I was proud of."

"Oh, Mari. How shallow you think I am." He still looks bowed. He sips his tea, then pushes it away. "I'm sorry that all happened to you, Mari. I am. No one should live like that."

I lean back in my chair, waiting.

"But I can't forgive you for lying to me for so long. You had so many opportunities to tell me the truth, and you didn't take any of them."

My heart sinks.

"I'll have my lawyer draw up an agreement. We'll split custody and figure out the best way to do that. I'll keep the Devonport house, and you can have this one."

For a long, long moment, I stare at him. "You've got to be kidding me, Simon."

"I assure you that I'm not."

"More fool you, then." I stand up, round the table, and push him upright. When there's space, I slide into his lap, face-to-face, and put my arms around him. "What we have is *great*."

"Was great." He looks surly and sad, but he's not shoving me away, and that's a good sign.

My hands are on his shoulders. I move them to his face. "I've paid for everything I did, Simon, and then some. When life gave me a chance, I figured out a way to turn it all around. And look at us, Simon! What kind of idiot takes such a hard stand on the moral road that he throws away his wife and his entire family?"

"I'm not throwing you away."

"Uh, yeah, you are. If you stay with this hard-ass stand, all of us suffer. All of us—you, me, the kids. That would be stupid."

He pulls my hands off his face. "Trust is everything, Mari. If everything you've told me is a lie, how can I believe anything you say going forward?"

I sigh, fear starting to dig its claws into my heart. But I have also become someone who can fight for the good in her life. A woman who doesn't run from things. "I didn't lie about anything in our lives from the time we met, only about the past."

He starts to shake his head again, shift me off his lap.

"No." I tighten my grip, hands and legs. "We're not going to wreck our family over this. We will not do that." My hands are in the hair over his ears, in fists. "This is not some depressing Victorian novel where a woman who makes bad choices inevitably dies a terrible death. I'm not Veronica Parker, paying for the sin of having the life she wanted. This is me and you. We fell in love the minute we met, and it's been good ever since."

Tears are gathering in his eyes again. "I'm so angry with you."

"I know. And you have every right to be. Be mad. We can work through that."

He only holds me close, and I know he's crying, trying to be manly about it. "You can come home, but this is not over."

"Okay. I'm okay with that."

"I don't know how to do this," he says raggedly.

"Me neither." I allow for the reality of everything that has happened. "Maybe, in the end, you won't be able to forgive me."

"I'm afraid that may be true."

I close my eyes. "I love you so much, Simon. More than I've ever loved anyone until our children were born. You are the sun in my world, the most normal thing that ever happened to me."

He closes his eyes, and the tears spill out below his lids. "I just love you so much," he whispers. "And it was all so perfect."

"If this is the worst thing that happens to our family, we will be lucky people indeed."

He sighs, his hands on my waist. "You're my Achilles' heel."

With my thumb, I brush away one of the tears, and I bend in to kiss each eyelid. "No. I'm your sunshine in the morning, your moonlight at night."

He lets go of a choked laugh, and then his arms are around me, so tight, and it's my turn to make a hushed, grateful sound. "I need you," he says.

"I know. And I need you." Into his neck, I whisper, "It's all a big mess, but we'll work it out over time."

We sit, exhausted, together for a long time. "I talked to my mom on FaceTime," I say quietly. "I told her to come see us."

"Will she?"

"I hope so," I say, and I mean it.

Now, if only Kit will forgive me, everything will be all right.

Chapter Thirty-Four
Kit

I head straight up the elevator to Javier's floor. My hair is wet from the rain, and I'm trembling in every inch of my body, and I'm having trouble catching my breath. I keep thinking that if I can find him, talk to him, some of this will make sense. Dylan and Josie.

Josie.

Javier is not home. I pull out my phone to call him, and then I just tuck it back into my bag, feeling airless, as if I will fly apart, dissolve into the universe. Standing in the hallway, shaking, I can't think what to do. What my next step should be.

I can't do this. Can't sort this out. I can't breathe or think or even settle on a single thought. Josie and Billy. Dylan and Josie. My poor, poor sister, carrying it all for so long. Finally killing herself off rather than deal with it anymore.

Dylan.

Images of him spill through my mind. So beautiful, so lost, so tortured.

How could he have had sex with Josie? How could he have kept a secret about her abuse like that? Knowing she needed counseling. Needed help. He saw her spiraling, drinking, drugging, and he didn't just not stop it; he encouraged it. How could I have missed all this?

Overwhelmed, I spin around and head for the elevator.

Home. I just want to go home. Lie in my own bed. Sit on my patio.

I want it so desperately, all of a sudden, that it's all I can think about. I return to my rooms and start throwing everything into my suitcase, willy-nilly, not folded. Bras and dirty underwear and new T-shirts. It feels like I've been on a very long, challenging journey, as if I have traveled around the world and taken part in a million festivals and now I'm leaving, a changed person.

The view this afternoon is moody and soft, the water roiling, turned a steely gray by the rain, and it makes me ache. I haven't known it as well as I'd like. I wanted to learn more, but it's just impossible to stay right now. I have to get back home, to my refuge, to the world I've built.

From my laptop, I make reservations on a plane for this very evening. It costs a fortune, but I don't care. I kick it up another notch and go first-class. It leaves at 11:45 p.m., and I'll be home in the morning. I'm already packed. Maybe I should just go to the airport.

A knock sounds at my door, and for a moment I consider not answering. The only person who comes here is Javier.

But it would be deeply unkind to leave without letting him know. Taking a moment to center myself, I open the door. He's wearing soft jeans and the long-sleeve heathery T-shirt that fits him perfectly. His feet are bare, which awakens that physical part of me that still wants him.

"Hey," I say, trying to sound normal. "I just knocked on your door."

"I was practicing guitar," he says, and his eyes sparkle. "Anything I can do for you?"

"Come in."

He sees the suitcase on the bed. "What is this?"

"My sister—Dylan—There is . . ." I shake my head. "I just can't do this. I need to get home."

"You're leaving? Now? Today?"

I throw another shirt into the suitcase. "Yes. It's time. I have to go."

He frowns slightly. "Did something happen?"

"Yes. Confessions of all kinds. Things I didn't know. Things I didn't want to know."

"Are you all right? You look—" He reaches for my arms, kindly, and I dodge him, unsure what will happen if he touches me. "Distraught."

"I'll be fine once I get out of here and back to everything normal." I swallow. "I'm sorry, though, about leaving so abruptly. I really have enjoyed your company."

He licks his lower lip, and there's something in his eye that I haven't seen before, something darker. "Enjoyed?" He steps closer to me, and I step around, and he follows, as if we're dancing.

"Stop it," I say. "I'm not that woman."

"What woman is that, Kit? The one who falls in love, who lets her emotions come to the surface?" He brushes the very back of my nape with light fingers, and I shudder. It freezes me, and I can't seem to move away as he closes the distance between us and kisses the place he touched, lingering and light. His hands slide around my waist, and I can feel my heartbeat in every part of my body—my palms and the soles of my feet, my thighs and breasts and throat.

He turns me in his embrace and firmly backs me into the wall behind me. I hear myself gasp as our bodies connect, and he smiles faintly. "*Enjoy* is a little thing, like olives." He runs his hands up the backs of my thighs, under the skirt I'm wearing, and hauls me closer. "This is much, much more than that, and you know it."

He bends to take my mouth in an insistent kiss, his whiskers abrading my chin. I find myself making a soft mewling noise, and my hands are on his body, pulling him into me. He kisses me, and kisses me, and kisses me, his hands roving, rousing. There are tears on my face, and I don't know why—I don't think that's ever happened before—but all I can think is that I need his body, all of it.

Our joining is nearly violent. No exploration. No ease. Just lips bruising and clothes ripped away, my shirt and my swimsuit top and panties, his jeans. Then we're rocking hard against each other on the bed I will never sleep in again. We're both lost in it, lost, lost, lost, dissolving and melting and reassembling, me in him, him in me, my molecules lost in his skin, his lost in my bones.

When it's over and we're panting, he doesn't move but cups my face in his hands. "That is not *enjoy, mi sirenita*. That is passion." We're both breathing hard. He holds my gaze, bends to sup my lower lip. "That's love."

Tears are running from my eyes onto my temples. I slide my hands into his hair and feel his skull. "How can I trust that, Javier? Insta-passion?"

"Is that what it is?"

"I don't know. I'm terrible at all this."

"Don't trust me," he whispers, running his index finger along my jaw. "Trust us. This."

For a long, long moment, I wish I were someone else, that I had some tiny bit of the heedlessness that marks my mother and sister. "I can't," I whisper. "I just can't."

He gazes down at me, touches the tears. "The ice is melting." Gently, he kisses me. "You go. But I want your email. I have been writing all day. I want to send you a song."

"Oh, don't." I close my eyes. It's weird that we're having this conversation this way, half-dressed, messy from sex. "I can't bear it."

He laughs softly. Kisses my chin. My throat. "You will like it, *gatita*. I promise."

In the end, I relent. He stays with me until it's time for me to go to the airport, but we don't talk a lot. Just sit in the quiet and look out at the rain, his hands in my hair.

I'm fine until the plane lifts off and circles, and I see the city spread out in yellow lights and carved bays below me, and it feels like my ribs are breaking, as if I grew long roots there in that place, like one of the Moreton Bay fig trees, and now I'm ripping them violently out, all at once. Why am I leaving?

What's wrong with me?

Chapter Thirty-Five

Kit

One month later

It's been a brutal night at the ER, a teenager killed when he crashed his car through a barrier wall and landed in the river; a fentanyl overdose we couldn't revive; an old woman who broke her leg in two places falling down the stairs, a hideous injury with bones protruding.

Which sets me off on some weird level. I am furious with the world in general for the rest of the night.

It's busy. All the usual things. Broken wrists and knocked-out teeth and food poisoning. The human body is a delicate, amazing creation. It takes almost nothing to completely destroy it, and yet it takes a lot. Most of us manage to stay on the planet, in our bodies, for seventy or eighty years, all of us amassing scars along the way, each one with a story. The chunk of plaster that marks your face forever, that belt buckle, those cigarette burns.

My mom texts me: Want breakfast this morning? Blueberry pancakes.

She's worried about me. I know she is. And I'm trying to be at least somewhat normal so she doesn't have to be afraid to leave and go see her grandchildren, a trip that is arranged for the middle of next month. I'm happy for her. She's done the work. She's earned it. I text back, Sure. I'm surfing. Will come after.

I haven't been able to settle into anything since I got home. Work makes me restless. I can't sit for more than five minutes with my mother. Can't read. Hobo is fine, just as my mother said, and she thinks he might want a companion.

All I do is surf, whenever I can get out there. This morning, the surf forecast is not particularly brilliant, but I don't care. I load up my board and, on a whim, head for the cove. I haven't been there since I've been home. Maybe I'm looking for answers.

To what, though? Everything that ever happened to anyone, ever? Life is sometimes just wretched; that's all. I was lucky to have the good years at Eden with Dylan, and Josie, and Cinder. All of us happy, on the beach, before everything that happened. Some people don't even get that.

One of the things I can't make peace with is Dylan. I thought I knew him and understood him, but Josie's revelations destroyed that vision of him.

Or maybe, honestly, I knew.

I saw them sometimes on the beach, late at night. Saw them bending their heads together and laughing, as if they were partners in some secret caper. It made me jealous enough that I think now, I did know. Appropriate or not, they had an intimate relationship, one that had nothing to do with me.

But what does all that mean for my relationship with him? My memories of him? All this time that was the one thing I could count on. Dylan loved me. He made my life better. He saved me, in so many ways.

It's still true. It's also true that he contributed to my sister's downfall. I don't know how to reconcile those two versions of him.

On the water, I'm fine. I don't have to think. I don't have to feel. I can just ride the waves, become part of nature. Out there, I wonder if that's what Dylan was doing, dissolving into nature. Trying, anyway.

In the end, that was exactly what he did. Drowning was the perfect death for him.

The waves are honestly not great, and I head back after only a half hour, peeling off my wet suit and donning a pair of sweats and a T-shirt, my hair tied up in a knot on top of my head. My mom won't care.

My phone dings with a personal email, and I stand against my Jeep on the bluff where Eden used to be and open it.

> Mi sirenita,
>
> The sky tonight shines with orange light, reflected in the water. I walked to Ima for dinner, where I go very often now, and ate roast chicken and thought of you.
>
> I hope you're doing well. Your sister invited me to come for supper, and I told her I would be pleased. Sarah will be sad that you are not with me, but I will bring her fountain pen ink and tell her it comes from you. Perhaps you'll truly be here soon. We are all waiting, wishing for your company.
>
> Yours,
> Javier

Every day, he writes something. A paragraph, like this one. A fragment of a poem—he's quite fond of Neruda's love poetry. It's touching and sweet, and I write him back only every third or fourth time. It seems a foolish connection, one bound to fade away. And really, we had only a few days together. It's ridiculous that I should be in a funk about it. Which my mother has carefully not commented upon.

I stand on the bluff over the empty cove and feel the ghosts around me. Dylan leans on the car, smoking a joint. My dad slaps the dust off his jeans, his watch in his shirt pocket. We never found it, and I cried for days over that one thing.

Neither of them was perfect. One was a hard man raised in a hard place. The other was warped by abuse.

Just as Josie was.

The revelation is soft, rolling through my body like a summer breeze. It eases the knots in my belly, unfurls the protective thorns over my heart. Maybe I don't have to choose between Dylan as a villain and Dylan as my beloved hero. Maybe he was both. Maybe Josie was—is—both too. Heroine and villain.

Maybe we all are.

The ocean is calm. For the first time in weeks and weeks, I feel calm too. I still haven't sorted out what to do about my job. I am tired of patching up humans who hurt themselves, and maybe I want to go back to animals. My first love was the sea, animals and fish in the water, and God knows they could use all the help they can get right now. I have plenty of money saved. I could look into arenas of study.

Maybe.

My stomach growls, and I hop in the Jeep, drive to my mom's place. The sun is starting to peek out through the clouds, and it lifts my mood slightly. Maybe I just need a long vacation in a sunny place. I climb the stairs, sorting through the possibilities—Tahiti, Bali, the Maldives.

Spain.

Even the word makes all the hairs on my body hurt. I have to stop on the stairs and breathe through it, stuffing all those things back where they belong. Did I really fall in love with Javier?

Not in less than a week. That's just ridiculous.

But then why do I miss him so much? It feels like the stars have fallen from the sky. Quite apart from everything else, I miss Javier specifically. I miss talking to him. Being myself with him.

I stomp the rest of the way up the stairs, yank open the door, and halt, uncomprehending.

"What are you doing here?"

"Surprise," says my mom.

"Surprise!" says Sarah, and she bolts across the room to fling her body at me. "We all came to see you!"

Her body feels so solid and strong. My hands fall on her back, and I'm so glad to see her, so very, very glad that I'm afraid all my emotions are going to split their seams and rush out onto the floor, so I take some deep breaths. "I'm so glad to see you."

Mari is standing with my mother, and Simon is behind them, and Leo is trying to look engaged.

And there, as if I conjured him, is Javier. He's standing in the middle of my mother's living room, looking elegant and European in a fine pale-lavender shirt with darker purple stripes, and tailored slacks, and good shoes, and he is wearing cologne and looks like everything good that ever was. *"Hola, gatita,"* he says, and smiles.

I look from one person to the next. "I don't understand. What—"

"Sweetheart," my mom says, "this is an intervention."

Sarah is still leaning on me, hard, and I clasp her back. "Intervention? But I—"

My sister says, "Mom has been worried about you. She asked us to come."

"Why? I'm fine."

Simon shakes his head. It surprises me, and I say, "I was just out surfing, that's all."

"It's a love intervention," Mari says.

"Love?" The lava of emotions that I've been safeguarding, keeping carefully in place, starts to gurgle.

"Yeah," Mari says, and comes forward, joining her daughter by putting her arms around me. The scent of her hair washes over me, making me dizzy, and then Simon joins, and my mother, and Javier. Even Leo, though I don't think he really wants to. "We wanted you to know," my sister says, "that you aren't alone anymore."

"I don't know what you mean," I say. "I'm—"

"We abandoned you," my mother says. "All of us, in one way or another. Me and Josie and Dylan and your dad."

"Not me," Sarah says, and holds me closer.

"Nor me," Javier says in his deep voice.

Simon chimes in, "You're not alone anymore. We are all your family, and you can count on us."

"And me," says Sarah.

And there's no holding back that lava flow. Like Mount Vesuvius, I blow. All the tears I've never cried, all the grief I never expressed, all the fury and the sorrow come pouring out until I'm sobbing like a very small girl, wailing while their hands stroke me and pet my head, while arms hold me solid and voices whisper, "Go ahead and cry; we've got you."

I've been so lonely for such a very long time.

We've got you.

When I'm finally finished, and poor Leo has escaped to the beach outside, and my mother has led me to have a shower and wash my hot face, we all sit down to breakfast. She has only the two chairs at the table, so we hold our pancakes on our knees as we sit on the couch. Josie/Mari sits next to me.

"This has your fingerprint all over it," I say. "You planned it, didn't you?"

"Of course." She smiles at me. "Not quite as good as the unicorn cake but not bad."

My throat gets tight. "Way better than the cake."

"Dude, there were at least two bottles of sprinkles on that cake."

I laugh. "True." I look at her. "Still. This is better."

"I'm glad."

Simon joins us. "Did Mari tell you that she solved the great mystery of the murder of Veronica Parker?"

"No! Who was it?"

She sighs deeply. "Sadly, it was George after all. He caught her having an affair with the carpenter and attacked her. He probably didn't mean to do it, but that was that."

"How did you find out?"

"Helen's journals," Simon puts in. "They were buried in about a thousand pounds of magazines, but she clearly couldn't part with them."

"She was in love with George too," Josie continues, "and she's the one who leaked the affair, maybe hoping he'd turn to her in his grief. Instead, he killed Veronica, and Helen covered for him."

"That's a very sad story."

"It explains why she only lived in that tiny corner all those decades."

I nod. Across the room, Javier is listening intently to my mother, but as if he feels my gaze, he looks up. He tilts his head toward the door, and I nod. "Excuse me."

We walk down the stairs in silence, and then he stops. "I need to remove my shoes for a proper walk on the beach."

I wait while he takes off those very expensive shoes, and his socks, and rolls up the hem of his slacks. His bare feet, white and strong, make me think of the hot tub in Auckland, of the day he came down in bare feet to my room and I was leaving.

I swallow.

We head for the edge of the waves, and he takes my hand. "Okay?"

I nod, suddenly shy. Embarrassed that I've not responded to his emails very much and that I've been such a bitch, really. "Thank you for coming," I say politely.

"Pssht," he says. "I was very nearly on a plane the next day, but it seemed you might need some time."

"We haven't known each other very long."

"That's true," he says. His hair lifts in the breeze, blowing away from his extraordinary face.

"It feels rash."

He looks down at me. "Love is rash."

"Is this love?"

"Yes, *mi sirenita*." He stops and takes my face in his hands. "It is absolutely love. For me, certainly."

I look up at him, resting in those big hands, trusting him. "I'm so afraid."

"I know. But you are not alone—I promise you that." He kisses me very gently.

"What does *mi sirenita* mean?"

"My little mermaid," he says, smiling.

"And *gatita*?"

"Kitten," he says, as if it's obvious.

The beach is empty of my ghosts, but I feel Dylan with me, laughing gently. "Those were Dylan's names for me."

"Mm. They're my names now." He kisses me, and I kiss him back, and I have a million questions, but they'll be so much easier to answer if I don't have to answer them alone.

"I missed you so much," I whisper.

"I know. Because we are twin souls, you and I."

"*Alma gemela,*" I say. "Can you have more than one?"

"Of course! My friend who killed himself, he was one of mine. Your sister is one for you, and your niece." He chuckles.

"Yeah. Sarah for sure."

He nods, tucks my hair behind my ear. "Let's walk."

So we do.

Epilogue

Kit

In the early dawn, Josie and I go to the cove and carry our surfboards down the bluff. We're wearing heavy wet suits against the cold water. It's a little blustery, the wind creating sharp waves. We don't speak, just stand on the hard-pressed sand where we once slept in a tent and made s'mores and gazed at the stars, watching the waves roll toward us, one after the other, endlessly, as they will for all time.

She looks at me. "Ready?"

I nod, and we paddle around the rocks out into the open. A lot of other surfers are there too, eager to ride, but it doesn't matter. Every surfer and every wave is a unique combination. We're all there for the same reason. For love.

My sister and I lose ourselves in the moment, in the salt on our lips, the boards under our feet, the tickle of water along our fingers. I follow her blonde head as I've always done, and then suddenly she waves for me to lead, and I do. The wave is beautiful, breaking in a powerful curl, and I leap to my feet at exactly the right moment, feeling everything in my body center and steady.

All of time condenses and coalesces, and I can feel Dylan behind me, his arms at my sides in case I fall. He laughs at my power, and I grow twenty feet tall.

I am alive. I am human. I am loved.

Behind me, my sister whoops, and I glance back, raising a shaka, and whoop myself.

Acknowledgments

If it takes a village to raise a child, it takes an army to get a book into the world. I'm wildly grateful to my whole team at Lake Union—editors Alicia Clancy and Tiffany Yates Martin, who help make my work shine so much brighter; Gabriella Dumpit and the entire marketing team, who do such fabulous work behind the scenes; and of course Danielle Marshall, whose vision guides us all. Thanks to my warrior agent, Meg Ruley, for all the things she does all the time.

Thanks to my beta readers, who helped me scout for errors— Yvonne Lindsey, native Aucklander, a great writer and kindly friend; Anne Pinder, for help with Madrid and the quirks of Spanish speakers; Jill Barnett, for her insightful read and suggestions and knowledge of California, the Loma Prieta earthquake, and surfing. Any mistakes remaining are entirely my own.

And most of all, thanks to my readers, all of you. I love each and every second of our communion.

About the Author

Photo © 2009 Blue Fox Photography

Barbara O'Neal is the author of twelve novels of women's fiction, including *The Art of Inheriting Secrets*, *How to Bake a Perfect Life*, and *The All You Can Dream Buffet*. Her award-winning books have been published in more than a dozen countries, including France, England, Poland, Australia, Turkey, Italy, Germany, and Brazil. She lives in the beautiful city of Colorado Springs with her beloved, a British endurance athlete who vows he'll never lose his accent.